CITIZEN ZERO

Mark Cantrell

Inspired
Quill

Published by Inspired Quill: August 2017

First Edition

Chief Editor: Rebecca Hall
Project Manager: Sara-Jayne Slack
Cover Design: Vince Haig: www.barquing.com
Typeset in Minion Pro

Paperback ISBN: 978-1-908600-51-6
eBook ISBN: 978-1-908600-52-3
Print Edition

Printed in the United Kingdom
1 2 3 4 5 6 7 8 9 10

Inspired Quill Publishing, UK
Business Reg. No. 7592847
www.inspired-quill.com

To my nieces Adah and Rosa
and my nephew Louie.

CHAPTER 1:
Beggars Can't Be Choosers

THERE were eyes, of one kind or another, everywhere. The one across the road turned to glare at him as soon as he arrived at the bus stop. The knowledge that it recognised his face bit worse than the scrutiny.

Mills sighed and tried not to think about the insistent surveillance. Today, of all days, he felt especially self-conscious. He wanted to go back to bed and shut out the world. But he couldn't ignore the Summons; it wasn't worth the hassle.

The bus arrived, grumbling to a halt, thankfully blocking the eye's mindless stare. He might have felt relieved, but he knew he didn't need to be seen for his movements to be tracked. The doors slid open with a hiss of hydraulics and he clambered aboard. It was an old vehicle, retrofitted for autopilot because the company was too tight to invest in new ones. Human drivers were little more than an old man's reminiscence.

"They've been faffing around with driverless motors since I was a lad, Davey. It never really took off, bloody gimmick, but this is different." The memory of his dad waggled his phone, scowling at the news item he'd just read. "Easy to take someone's job these days; you be careful with that tech stuff you're learning, lad, it's liable to bite you on the arse some day."

Mills had laughed. He'd been at technical college then, sure of himself and of a future emblazoned with his name. The old man wasn't supposed to be right.

The other passengers glared impatiently while he fumbled for his card. Mills pulled himself out of the past and swiped through the transaction.

"Customers, please be advised," the on-board computer said, "the current boarder is a class 'D' security risk. Please take care of all personal belongings. CCTV monitoring is in operation for your protection."

The passengers shifted in their seats. Some held tight onto handbags and briefcases. Nobody looked directly at him.

The bus lurched forward and Mills, suddenly unbalanced, slumped heavily onto a vacant seat beside an old man in a black overcoat. The man stiffened, suddenly very interested in the view through the window.

"It's disgraceful. Folk like that shouldn't be allowed to travel with decent people."

For a surreptitious whisper, it carried. So did the

collective murmur of agreement. Such jibes should have lost their power to hurt long ago. Mills turned anyway and stared at the two old ladies with distinguished citizen badges pinned prominently to their lapels. Once he had their full attention he treated them to a lazy grin. The women looked away and his face slumped back to its usual dour expression. The spiteful 'eye' in his pocket chose that moment to beep: a reminder he was going to be late for his Summons. He removed it and turned the credit card-shaped device over and over between his fingers. "Nexus 40", the legend read. Beneath, printed on the scratched surface:

UK Benefits & Welfare Plc

– A Ministry for Human Resources Company –

working for you, so you can too

It really was a hateful piece of plastic. Everywhere he went it signalled his location to the JobMart's city computer. Called out his presence and left a digital scent for the authorities to follow. He pressed the display micro-switch. Text scrolled across the strip and he read it for the umpteenth time. Could they really be serious?

"Artificial reality job-hunting," Mills muttered aloud. "Hey, maybe I'll get an artificial job!"

The man next to him shifted in his seat and gave him a sidelong glance. *Sod you.*

"+++ MILLS D + S + PLEASED TO INFORM THAT YOU ARE SELECTED FOR NEW IMPROVED JOBNET SCHEME + INTENDED FOR RELENT- LESSLY UNEMPLOYED + UTILISES LATEST IN ARTIFICIAL REALITY TECHNOLOGY TO HELP YOU BACK TO WORK + ATTEND 0915 HOURS THURSDAY 10 APRIL 2070 + ENDS +++"

Terse and to the point, like all of their messages. We command. You obey. And these schemes became stranger with each passing year. How many had there been so far? But perhaps this one would be different. Perhaps *this* one would result in that ever-elusive beast: a job.

"There's always hope." Mills allowed himself a cynical smile and signalled the autopilot for his stop.

THE JobMart's tinted windows seemed to frown at him. Even on a bright day like this the building appeared overcast; so shabby and dreary it gave him the urge to shiver. Desperate as he was to find meaningful employment, he pitied those who worked within.

Mills felt his muscles tense as he passed through the doors. The weight of the place pressed down on his shoulders, its mood a viscous mud that dragged at his feet. People jostled him. A long counter, separating the employed from the jobless, divided two worlds, where ragged queues of blank faces waited to sign their names for another infusion of grinding poverty. Behind the wall, like workers on a human production line, JobMart employees churned out ready-made rejects.

Joining the queue, Mills found himself surrounded by the dead-eyed faces of the hopeless and the broken. The usual numbness took hold as he settled into line.

SLOWLY, the queue wormed its way up to the main desk. People in headphones sat at a bank of machines nearby: the blind and the illiterate, force-fed 'opportunities' by soothing machine voices. On the far wall, in large print, a poster declared:

BEGGARS CANNOT BE CHOOSERS

In rows of seats at the rear wall, vacant faces watched the information videos endlessly playing on the monitors suspended from the ceiling. On one of the screens, another well-dressed politician spitefully slandered the poor.

MILLS' mind was taken back to the steel works, where he'd had his first and only job. Life was hard, but at least Mills had felt useful. And in those days, he'd had friends. He'd been worth knowing. Pete, Jeff and Rob – his shift-mates. Where were they now?

They'd been keen. They were young. So of course they swallowed all that candy-coated spin about the new wave of skilled technical workers, melding modern technology to traditional industry. The four of them at the forefront of Britain's revival as a new economic powerhouse. And, boy, did they let the pride swell their heads.

Somewhere, he still had the picture frame loaded with a piece the local news site ran about them; the four friends from tech college who'd landed a place at New Ebbsfleet's pride facility. The animated image accompanying the story showed them grinning like idiots. Some day he'd get some fresh batteries for the frame, if only to delete the memory.

From the air-conditioned box of a control room, they had smelted and poured millions of tonnes of metal. Long ago in the old steel cities, thousands of workers had done the job by hand, but they had long been thrown aside by the time the fully automated facility he'd operated had come along. And then he, too, was thrown away. In some distant office his job had been deleted by some *corporatchik*, doubtless in connivance with some government functionary.

The worst of it all, they'd been required to help the crew from the external contractor upgrade the facilities so one of those first-wave AIs could operate the plant remotely. Grim times; ordered around by hard-faced men who otherwise kept to themselves. Frequently, they would be observed mumbling their side of secretive conversations into unbranded mobile phones. Mysterious to the bitter end.

So much for the optimism of a New Industrial Revolution. When it turned out the AI wasn't up to the job, somebody decided to cut their losses, or maybe save face. The plant was closed down, with barely a tweet out of the local news. Funny, that.

"YES?" The woman at the reception desk didn't bother to look at him. There were bags under her eyes and her mouth drooped; how many people had she already processed, at not yet ten in the morning?

Mills didn't feel much like talking. What was there to say? He produced the Nexus and handed it over. The woman slotted the card into her terminal and tapped a few keys. "Name?"

He rolled his eyes at the ritual. "Mills," he said.

"Initials?"

"Dee. Ess."

"Date of Birth?"

"23-5-38."

"Social Security Tag?"

"DF874920S."

Satisfied, the woman tapped at the screen. The display flashed as it brought up his file; he strained to catch a glimpse of readable text but the monitor was at the wrong angle. The woman blew a stray lock of hair away from her face as she entered some more details, then closed his file and returned his card. She still didn't look at him.

"Wait at reception point B, over that way." The woman pointed the direction. "Somebody will be out to see you shortly."

Mills looked over to where she had indicated. Over the heads of the queues he saw a sign for the reception area suspended from the ceiling. With a sigh, he stepped away. Behind him, another body shuffled into place and he heard the ritual begin all over again.

"Yes?"

A mumbled response.

"Name?"

Mills put it out of mind. He pushed his way through the crowd, uttering indifferent apologies and pointedly failing to make eye contact with any of his fellow inmates. It didn't take long before he was clear of jostling bodies. Reception B was devoid of souls; whether that was a good thing or not was another matter, but it was good to regain a sense of personal space.

The carpet looked less worn in this corner of the main hall. A row of private interview rooms had been retrofitted along the side wall. Light from the JobMart's external windows streamed in through the narrow strips of glass in each of the doors. As far as Mills could tell, none of the rooms were currently occupied.

He looked around, saw another – windowless – door in the wall that ran along behind the main reception desks. He stepped closer and read the sign adorning it: "JobNet". For some reason he felt his skin prickle. Nerves, that's all; silly. Whatever waited for him on the other side couldn't be any worse than the previous schemes the JobMart had volunteered him for. Suck it up and see it through, same as always.

Mills kicked his heels for a couple of minutes, then lowered himself into one of the shabby seats and settled down to wait. As his eyes drifted down to gaze at the carpet, he felt his mind wander again.

THREE years after it closed, he had gone back to the steel works for a nostalgia trip with Rob and Pete. Somebody had beaten them to it. The foundries were still there, much to their surprise, but now they formed an attraction in an industrial theme park: 'The Workshop of the World'.

Some multinational had bought the place. The site was dressed up to represent part of Britain's industrial heritage, which in a way he supposed it was, but it was still strange; the real heritage was long gone, buried beneath the foundations of shopping malls, luxury apartment blocks, and monuments to commerce.

In that theme park, his foundries glowed again. But they glowed with the cold, tinted light of electric lamps, and the metal they poured was nothing more than back-lit paste.

The 'workers' were the best. Big, muscular men with oiled and bronzed skin, who toiled away at the foundries. He'd found it funny: they were never designed for manual operation, except in an emergency. But how many of the paying public would know that?

The fall of the Industrialists' Empire. The Workshop of the World, just a play-park for kids. The irony wasn't lost on him. Here, in the country that had coined the phrase, actors performed ancient work for a paying crowd.

"MR Mills?" A pleasant voice shattered the images of the past. "Would you like to come this way?"

Startled, he looked up to find a woman smiling

brightly at him. Such an amiable approach came as something of a surprise. The badge on her chest identified her: Jane. No surname. She indicated the door marked JobNet and walked towards it. Mills rose to follow her. Beyond the door, a window flooded the room with daylight. He glimpsed the trappings of an office: a workstation monitor on a cheap desk, which also held a phone and an assortment of pens. A filing cabinet lurked in one corner; a fan situated on its top gently stirred the air. All very ordinary. With a resigned sigh, he stepped over the threshold.

CHAPTER 2:
The Whole World's an Oyster

INSIDE, the air possessed that faint polymer smell of sun-warmed plastic; an uncomfortable odour he always associated with school and low-level authority.

"Take a seat, Mr Mills."

Gingerly he sat down in the cheap chair. Trying not to dwell on the uncomfortable, sweaty plastic, he regarded the woman. *A face with a name. Unusual, that.* It made her seem almost human.

Jane smoothed her skirt and sat down on the opposite side of the workstation, briefly treating him to a warm smile. He did not return it. His apprehension outweighed her friendly manner.

"I see you've been unemployed now for… ten years, David," she said, casually scrolling through his computer records. "You must be feeling that things are pretty hopeless by now."

"Well… yes. You get sick of hearing the reasons they come up with to fob you off. I've heard it all. And then there's these AIs. I lost my job to an AI and the bloody thing couldn't hack it, so they pulled the plug – they shut down the entire plant, can you believe that? Now it's AI here and AI there; they're bloody everywhere –"

"That's what we're here for, David," she said, flashing another smile. This time he noticed how her eyes lit up – so different to the faded officials he usually met – but if she was trying to lift his spirits it wasn't working.

"We've helped a lot of people like you, David. So, don't give up hope. I know things look grim at the moment, but there *are* jobs out there. We're pretty proud of our track record so far –"

"Yeah, well, I've been on schemes before and they all sang their own praises. Not one of them has done me any bloody good though."

Steepling her fingers, Jane sat up straight and looked him squarely in the eyes. "David, there's a world of opportunity out there, just waiting to be seized by those with the motivation and self-confidence. Why confine yourself to this town? To this country even, when the whole world literally rests at your feet?

"This is what JobNet offers. You can travel the world. All the limitations that have held you back will evaporate. There are no obstacles any more. Do you see what that means?"

"Doesn't sound all that different to the internet, if you

ask me."

"That old thing?" Jane shook her head. "There's really no comparison, David. Words and video on a screen divorces you from what's real. We're offering a *lived* experience. What's more, we've got international trade deals in place that *guarantee* residency rights to over 54 countries – and growing – if you land a suitable position through JobNet."

"I'm not too good with languages…"

"Don't worry, David. All the English-speaking economies are signed up, and you'd be surprised how many other nations have welcomed diasporas of native English speakers. It pays to think globally, now, David. You can start a whole new life. The internet gives you a window to the world; we can give you the real thing."

The world is my oyster, he thought. To his surprise, Mills couldn't hold back his intrigue. The woman had come alive, her expression animated. Did she really feel for the unemployed, or was it just another sales pitch?

"Okay," he shrugged, "so what's JobNet?"

The smile warmed him again. Jane sat back in her chair and regarded him for a few moments. She really was quite pretty. In any other situation, he could see himself wanting to know her better, but the desk between them was a wall; a division between society and the dispossessed. Yet there she was, offering him a way to clamber back to the world – *her* world.

"Read this, David." Jane passed him a sheet of paper.

"It'll tell you what you need to know."

Official documents. Doubtless, there would be reams of forms to fill in. As usual. He let out a faint sigh and began to read.

WHAT JOBNET CAN DO FOR YOU

DON'T let life kick you in the teeth. You may have been unemployed for what seems like forever, but there is a way out of the rut – if you let the JobNet Agency help you.

What is JobNet? Simply an AI 2.0 network running a world-simulation program that places you, the client, into a virtual environment of such a high resolution that it feels like the real thing.

Our experts have discovered that a pleasant environment helps to relieve stress, and what is more stressful than the search for work?

You will be placed in a garden paradise that provides a friendly surrounding while you seek that perfect job. You will also be able to relax and enjoy the benefits that a virtual world can provide. This combination of work and play is designed for the total comfort and improvement of our clients.

With the emphasis on a stress-free experience, you will move alongside representatives of thousands of potential employers worldwide. What better way to find work than by building rapport in an enjoyable social scene?

To this end, JobNet has also dispensed with the tired, formal approach to job applications. The result is a face-to-face interaction that means a more productive relationship is established between employer and client. You may not get the job, but you could find a friend and ally on your way back to the world of work.

With JobNet, you can't fail.

"TEA or coffee, David?" Jane suddenly asked.

"What?" He looked up from the document.

"Would you like a cup of tea or coffee?"

"Oh, er, I'll have coffee. Milk. One sugar. Thanks."

Jane poured some liquid from a percolator placed on the windowsill into two mugs, one of them inscribed 'Jane'.

"Sorry about the chipped rim," she said, placing the other steaming cup on the desk. "I hope it's not too sweet?"

"It's fine. Thanks."

HOW DOES IT WORK?

SO, how can *you* enter the perfect job-hunting environment? First of all, this opportunity is not available to just anyone.

To become eligible for JobNet's assistance, the client must have been unemployed for a considerable period of time. Here at JobNet we understand the feeling of hopelessness that turns job-hunting into an uphill struggle.

You may already be familiar with AI-IT. Since the emergence of the first AI mainframes in 2049, the technology has gone on to revolutionise industry and commerce. With the advent of AI 2.0 smartware seven years ago, the pace of change has dramatically increased, leaving almost no aspect of business and society untouched.

AI has ushered in a smarter way of working. We're determined that nobody gets left behind as a result of feeling bewildered by change – and that means revolutionising the way we work, too. That's why we're utilising the power of AI 2.0 to help people like you get on in life.

JOBNET is truly international. As a result, the jobseeker can literally travel the world in search of training or employment. Thousands of options are available through the JobNet scheme. It enjoys the prestige of finding work for millions every year, and is regarded by top recruiters as *the* international employment initiative.

To find out more about how to get yourself wired up to the future, contact your nearest JobMart and speak to our team of helpful advisers – it's the smart thing to do.

The JobNet Agency

A UK Benefits & Welfare Company

WITH a grunt, Mills finished reading and placed the sheet of paper back on Jane's desk. He watched as she sorted through his computer records. At last, she sensed he had finished and looked up.

"So, what do you think?" she asked, flashing that electrifying smile.

"Sounds great!" Despite his cynicism, curiosity had gained the upper hand. "So what happens next?"

"You sign this, David."

Jane handed him a small tablet. The screen displayed his name, address and a few other details. He pressed his thumb against the biometric scanner without really bothering to skim through. The device beeped. An image of his thumbprint, together with a file copy of his signature, appeared on screen. Mills handed the device back to Jane.

"There," she said. "That's all the paperwork out of the way, you'll be pleased to hear."

"No forms?" *Surprising.*

"Nope. We just needed your signature to say you've agreed to the scheme. There is one more thing, though."

Jane reached down to open a drawer. She removed a small cardboard carton and deftly opened it, tipping something further sealed in shrink-wrapped plastic onto the palm of her left hand. Mills eyed it curiously as she handed it over.

"What's this," he said, "a nasal inhaler? I'm not bunged up with a cold, you know."

Amusement flitted through the twitch of her lips. "Exactly right, David, except for the bit about the cold. This contains the nanocules that help the system deep-map your brain and allow your projection into artificial reality."

"Through my nose?" He frowned, sceptical.

"Pretty much," she said. "Beats needles. A lot of people don't like being jabbed."

"No, well, I can see how this is better."

"You don't sound convinced, David. Don't worry, it's no different from medical nano-tech–"

"Been a long time since I could afford medical bills. Charity clinics don't do nano."

Jane's smile wavered; Mills sensed he was starting to push his luck.

"Okay," he added hastily, "what do I do?"

"First, check the wrapping. I need you to confirm that it's unbroken and there's no sign of tampering. The wrapping will discolour if that's the case. So…"

He examined the package. "It looks fine, yeah."

"Okay, well if you're satisfied, you can open it and, well, I'm sure you know what to do."

Even so, she mimed pushing the inhaler into her left nostril and closing the right one with a finger before taking a deep breath. Mills shrugged and ripped the packaging open. He went through the motions. It was like sucking up fine dust; his nose tingled and he sneezed.

"Shit! Oh, sorry…"

"Don't worry, David." She laughed softly, genuinely. "A lot of people have the same reaction. It won't make any difference to the quality of your uplink."

Jane stood and gestured towards the door at the rear of the office.

"Now, if you'd like to follow me, David, my colleague and I will get you set up while those nanos are settling in."

He followed her into the next room, hands curled into fists inside his pockets. The blinds were shut; the only light came from a desk lamp in one corner and the soft, gloomy glow of a monitor currently being studied by a man in grey trousers and a white shirt. Despite the warmth of the room, he had his tie knotted all the way up. A row of medical couches lined one wall; a neatly folded suit jacket draped across one of them.

"That's it?" he asked, pointing at the computer.

Jane smiled, but it was the man who replied. "No, Mr Mills, this is the network controller and bio-monitor we'll be using to calibrate and establish your remote link. The mainframe that's hooked up to the AIs all over the world is housed in our main office in London. I'm Stuart Sutcliffe. I'll be overseeing your AR-time while you're with us."

"While I'm with you?"

"At some time today you'll be moved to a residential facility on the outskirts of town, where you'll be more comfortable. After all, you'll be in AR for a couple of weeks, longer if you so choose. Obviously, we couldn't keep you here that long."

"You'd make the place seem terribly untidy," Jane added with a smile. "Now, please, if you'll sit yourself on the couch here, we have to ask you some standard questions before we begin."

Mills nodded as he shuffled onto the couch Jane indicated. Stuart took up a smartpad and walked over. His manner reminded Mills of a doctor he'd once known – mechanical and indifferent.

"Okay. Are you currently on any prescribed medication?"

"No."

Stuart tapped the smartpad's screen.

"Are you a registered drug addict?"

"No. Are you?"

Another tap.

"Have you consumed alcohol or marijuana in the last 72 hours?"

"Are you joking? On the money I get?" He wiped his brow, wishing the room weren't so stuffy.

"Please, Mr Mills, answer the questions. I'll take that as a no, shall I? Do you suffer from a heart condition?"

"No."

"Do you suffer from epilepsy?"

"No," he replied, monotone.

"Is there any history of mental illness in your family?"

"My Granddad used to think he was Napoleon and Caesar in the same past life – got him very confused. Does that count?"

"Mr Mills, please. We have to ask these questions for your own good, so try to be serious."

"Sorry."

"Have you ever undergone nanoneural interfacing before?"

He deliberately gave Stuart a blank look. "A what?"

A hint of confusion crossed Stuart's face. Mills felt a certain satisfaction at that; he'd caught the man out in the middle of his bullshit. But Stuart soon recovered. "Sorry, Mr Mills, I mean have you ever been hooked up to an AR system before?"

"Oh, all the bloody time! No."

"You are familiar with artificial reality, though?"

"I've read about it, so yeah. Rich man's plaything; virtual reality with bells on, right?"

No reaction from Stuart, just a tap of a finger as he ticked off the appropriate answer, but Jane placed her hand over her mouth to hide a smile with a sudden humanity that made him feel a little light-headed.

"Not quite, David," she said. "It's actually quite a mature technology; you really won't be able to tell the difference from physical reality. The gaming industry was an early pioneer, of course. The costs were prohibitive for the mass market – that's where your rich man's toy came from – but it's been used for industrial and certain specialist applications for a good few years now. China's Space Agency is using it to train their taikonauts for the Mars mission, for instance. But here at JobNet, we're really rather proud that our parent company has been a pioneer in bringing the technology down to Earth."

"That's right, Mr Mills," Stuart added, "it provides an ideal teleworking environment, bringing staff together, and it offers a perfect medium for engaging with AIs. The costs have plummeted, to the extent that for the last five years we've been able to put the technology to use helping people like you."

Mills wiped his brow, overloaded; did everyone get this hard sell or was it just his lucky day? When his hand cleared from his vision he saw Stuart turning back from the desk, the smartpad set aside.

Dizziness grew and Mills rubbed his eyes with the pads of his fingers; they felt heavy and he struggled to remain alert.

"Okay, Mr Mills. We're nearly ready to hook you into the system. This is your first time, so you'll be kept in a holding phase while it calibrates with your neural emission pattern. You'll find it a rather euphoric experience, like lucid dreaming, just go with the flow and enjoy the experience."

Through his hazy vision he watched Stuart reach past his shoulder, where a headset rested on the back of the couch. The room went black as the helmet was slipped onto his head, but the sudden darkness did nothing to stop the spinning sensation.

"The helmet is basically a transceiver designed to shut out unnecessary external stimuli," Stuart's muffled voice informed him. "The nano components we fed into your system will help relay and receive information directly to and from your brain."

With the helmet in place and his vision blacked out, shifting blobs of colour meandered across his mind's eye. As the dizziness worsened, they fused into shapes, battering him with a dizzying light show. His arms fell, limp and heavy, to his sides. His head sagged forward, a dead weight. Muffled voices signalled alarm beyond the woozy confines of the darkness. Hands on his shoulders, failing to arrest the sense of falling. A thud followed. Not a physical impact but a memory, the idea of impact.

Outside of the darkness, he could just about feel his body lying on the cheap carpet of the JobMart. A voice called. A woman's. Maybe saying his name. He tried to move, but his extremities felt far away; he tried to speak, but his tongue was a foreign object. Muffled voices faded into the void as he felt his sense of self become detached from his physical presence.

An effulgent light, streaming from what he perceived to be *up*, bathed his consciousness. For a fleeting moment, he was aware of himself in two places at once, and then he shifted... *elsewhere.*

CHAPTER 3:
Between Worlds

"DAVID? Are you all right?" Jane knelt by Mills' collapsed form and fumbled to loosen the snagged cables of the headset.

"Careful with that!" Stuart pulled her away from the slumped body.

"What's wrong with him?"

Without replying, he knelt beside Mills and felt the side of his neck, careful not to dislodge the helmet. "Pulse feels normal, but he's clammy," he muttered, getting up and returning to the computer. "Christ! That can't be right. He's flatlined… no, wait, there's something there."

Stuart bit his lip and concentrated on the data on the screen. Twin spikes showed in the neural feed, as if two people were connected by the same link. Erratic at first, the spikes settled down into a double waveform that was anything but normal. The peaks and troughs of the second wave almost ghosted the first. Every few seconds, they touched, cancelled out, collapsed into a flatline, before the cycle spiked into life once more.

The system was having trouble discriminating the signals; it kept oscillating between two feedback states. In one, Mills was in a critical condition. In the other, he was in a happy limbo while the system prepared him for AR injection.

"I've never seen anything like it," he said, glancing discreetly at the security camera on the ceiling. "Help me get him into a recovery position."

"What's wrong with him?" Jane asked, as she knelt by the prone form. "It's not the –"

"It might be, I don't know," he mumbled, almost too low for Jane to hear. Then louder: "He's suffering from neural shock. There must be a feedback loop fucking up his head. Either he lied about his substance use or he's one of the unlucky few that can't take AR. Now, help me turn him over."

Together, he and Jane carefully arranged the man's body into a recovery position, and gently arranged the headset cables so they weren't snagged. Stuart removed the remote link unit from the couch and placed it beside Mills' prostrate form.

"We can't cope with a crash like this," he said. "Better call an ambulance."

THE *light was gone; maybe he* was *the light. Whatever,*

Mills was trapped in a dark place, lost beyond his body, aware only of floating.

It felt enjoyable in a way – soothing, even. Here he endured no worry, with fear relegated to a bad memory from a former life. If he still owned a body, he might smile.

Something snatched his soul and propelled it through the void. The non-smile perished. Dimly, he felt anger, or a memory of it. Why couldn't he be left in peace?

A vortex appeared in the distance, a twisting tunnel of light leading into the unknown. He watched it, only vaguely aware of the gravitational tide stretching his soul to unimaginable proportions until thought became impossible.

The maelstrom swallowed the blazing comet of memories that once identified itself as 'Mills'; caused it, like a metaphysical bullet, to hurtle down the dizzying tunnel. Or, perhaps, like a stream of unconscious data uploaded to Purgatory's computer.

Ready for final processing.

Drug addict slips the net
By Herald Staff Reporter

A MAN is recovering in hospital today after an unsuccessful virtuality link induced a near-fatal coma, resulting from the victim's failure to declare habitual drug use.

The individual, David Samuel Mills, 32, of Bankfield Drive, New Ebbsfleet, is an unemployed industrial-systems operator who once worked in the city's steel-processing industry.

Mills was due to take part in the revolutionary JobNet scheme, wherein a client is linked to a virtual-reality world in order to search, in 'real-time', for work.

The results were not as intended. During entry to the computer-generated world, Mills suffered a near-fatal feedback loop and lapsed into a coma. System operators quickly installed a remote link so the patient could be removed to hospital, where staff praised the quick actions that certainly saved Mills' life.

The incident has fuelled debate over the safety of direct human links to mainframe Artificial Intelligences (AIs), but experts have stressed that as long as a stringent safety code is maintained, the procedure poses no significant health risks.

A number of mind-altering disorders render such direct links inappropriate, however, including the use of a wide range of drugs.

"Traces of heroin and cannabis were found in the patient's bloodstream," said consultant neurophysiologist, Dr Alistair Simms. "Both at sufficiently high levels to disrupt the interface between the patient's nervous system and the AI."

The incident has also led to calls for better screening of candidates. Senior local authority officials have voiced concerns that medical records are not available to operators, and that other basic tests are not conducted prior to uplink.

Assistant Civic Executive John Griffiths said: "The current situation is scandalous. Operators have to rely solely on the honesty of AR candidates, and let's face it – they're not exactly paragons of virtue. The whole system of vetting and preparing these people should be overhauled."

Mills' condition is currently described as stable.

SOMEWHERE in the void, a single photon exploded to become a star. A light appeared. Shadows retreated from his consciousness and Mills blinked into sudden awareness. *Corporeal* awareness.

Nerves fired; his limbs complained of stiffness, his skin tingled. His ears hummed as a foreign pitch and tone slowly resolved into speech.

"… Mr Mills? Mr Mills, can you hear me?"

His lids flickered open, eyes briefly aware of the glare and a hazy, unfocused shadow before they shut once more. He felt his head lifted, then something pressed against his lips and a refreshing liquid poured down his throat until he gagged. With a cough he tried to rise, supporting himself on one elbow and taking in a few deep lungfuls of air. It smelled earthy, with a hint of newly mown lawn. Again he tried to open his eyes, but the glare was too great.

"Am I dead, and will I like the answer?"

The reply came in the form of soft laughter. Firm hands helped him sit up. At last the dizziness fled his body and he braved the light one more time. The world leapt into colour.

A woman smiled prettily. Her bright blue eyes were piercing, her tanned face set by the untidy overflow of tied-back blond hair. A singlet covered her torso. Around her waist was a modest wrap, through which the edges of denim shorts were exposed as she knelt beside him. She was barefoot, a pair of sandals discarded on the grass close to her feet. Gradually he realised he was staring and wrenched his eyes away to take in his surroundings.

A few metres behind the woman, an oak tree swayed its branches in the light breeze. At its base flowers speckled the grass in hues of red and blue and yellow. The scent of them was like a rush of caffeine to a drowsy mind; he breathed deep in appreciation. Only a few feet away, a stream babbled soothingly. He turned his head to see the water cascading over moulded limestone that glistened in the sunlight. Finally, he turned his gaze back to the woman.

"How do you feel?" she chimed.

"If this place is anything to go by, I'm feeling great," he replied.

The woman tilted her head back and laughed, her voice complemented by the gentle tones of the stream.

"By the way, you haven't told me where I am."

"You're dreaming, of course," she replied. "All of this is just a dream. It's great, isn't it?"

"So you're part of the dream too?"

"Naturally. And so are you. Everybody here is part of someone else's dream. It's all so harmonised and beautiful. I definitely prefer it in here to out there."

"Out there? Ah! This must be JobNet. Well, it's a little different than what I expected, that's for sure."

The woman laughed again. A pleasant, disarming sound. Mills thought she must be either very happy or a little crazy. If she was even real.

"You're very funny, David. I can call you David, can't I?" she asked. "Oh, but you don't know what to call me, do you? That's silly of me. I'm Christine. I was sent to collect you. I work here, you know. It's great. I'm sure you'll love it here too…"

The woman babbled on and on. Christine, high on a dream. Did AR have this effect on everyone? Taking another deep, refreshing breath, he found it hard to believe this could be an induced hallucination. Maybe he would end up like her if he stayed too long.

"Shoo," she said, suddenly, giggling as she flapped her hand over his head. Startled, Mills leaned back and noticed several sable-winged butterflies fluttering above him. One of them breezed past his face.

"They seem to like you," Christine added. "When I found you there were five of them sunbathing on your face."

Mills shrugged. "Are they normally that colour?"

"In here, anything's possible. I've never seen this kind before; guess somebody decided to code a new addition."

The butterflies flew off and dispersed. Mills watched one fade into the scenery. Christine slipped her sandals back on and rose; time to make a move, then. With a wistful sigh, he struggled to stand. She quickly took his arm to steady him.

"Careful, you're still a little groggy," she smiled. "You had a rough entry. That's why they put you here in the garden. It happens that way sometimes. Some people resist. They don't trust it, you know. I thought it was wonderful. The best thing that's ever happened to me."

He allowed Christine's words to wash over him as she guided him towards the trees. The sun felt warm on his skin, though the breeze prevented the temperature from becoming uncomfortable. It all seemed too perfect; he couldn't imagine anything in the real world was this good. Neither had he ever seen anything outside like the shimmering ivory needle that towered high above the treetops. Narrow and impossibly tall, he was sure it hadn't existed a moment before.

"What is that?" he asked, shading his eyes from the bright sky as he followed the structure up to the point of infinity.

"It's a door, silly. Well, not exactly a door, more a sort of tunnel, really," Christine replied, linking arms with him. "We call them portals. I don't really understand all these things, but they join the bits of JobNet together. You'll like it. It's like flying down the inside of a wire –"

"Well, I've already done that, and I didn't much like the experience."

Christine giggled. "Don't worry. You'll be all right. You just have to get used to things here. It's weird at first, but you'll hate to leave in the end. Believe me, I thought it was all strange to begin with, too."

They passed under the trees, a short walk under the pleasant shade, but Mills felt his skin prickle with apprehension as they drew nearer to the portal. He felt his feet drag but Christine pulled him relentlessly onwards. In an effort to take his mind off his unease, he engaged her in conversation, hoping her chatter would have some kind of soothing effect.

"So, how long have you worked here? It's a pretty strange job."

"Oh absolutely everyone says that," she laughed. "But I've been here about two years… I think. It's a bit hard to tell. Time's different in here, somehow. It'll feel like you've been in here longer than your two weeks of actual time. I do have to go out sometimes, but it's so dull that I can't wait to get back."

"Oh. So what do you do when you're outside?"

"Outside?" A shadow flitted across her face. "I just collect my pay and lose myself in books and movies. I don't like it. The weather's awful. Everybody's so intense. There's nothing to live for out there."

The atmosphere between them suddenly cooled, and he wished he hadn't spoken. They walked on in silence, and Christine seemed preoccupied until something squelched loudly beneath his foot. "Shit!" he cried.

"Are you all right?"

"Cow shit! That's just my luck."

Christine covered her mouth, but it couldn't hide her laughter. He just glared and cursed the mess on his boot.

"That's odd," Christine said, once she had managed to control her amusement. Then she caught sight of his expression and flashed a wide smile. "Poor David! It's not your day is it? Let me help."

He blinked in surprise as Christine swept her hand through the air in front of him. A sizzling hiss followed the smell of ozone. When he looked down at himself, he discovered his usual shabby clothing had been replaced by a summery shirt, unbuttoned to reveal a red t-shirt. His jeans had morphed into a pair of knee-length khaki shorts. Mills groaned inwardly, but the shorts had nothing on his new footwear. The faithful old boots that had seen him through most of his time on the dole had vanished.

"Sandals! I hate sandals! How did you do that, anyway?"

"Don't you know? I'm a sorceress, David," Christine said with a radiant smile. "It's the magic of this dream. You could do it too, if you put your mind to it. There are no limitations here. You can be whoever you want to be."

"If it's all the same with you, I'll stick with who I am.

Couldn't you fix me something better than this?"

"Oh, you're too staid. Nobody cares what you wear, but you don't want to go around looking like you've just got up, do you? This is paradise, and you're here to enjoy it. That's my job. So come with me; you're expected in the village. And relax!"

Christine took him by the hand and pulled him on towards the portal. To his surprise, the structure grew more translucent as it drew nearer, and in the glare of the sun he swore shifting patterns of iridescent light played on its surface, like oil on water. When the two reached the structure he reached out with a tentative hand, but pulled away as it passed through the surface with a static hiss. Christine only laughed.

"Come on, David," she said and dragged him inside. With a terrified cry, he felt himself rush through the portal, vaguely aware of Christine's hand holding his own.

IN another universe on the dark side of creation, two photons travel hand in hand through a fibre-optic cable; one laughs while the other cries. Through the silicon fabric of a million data points, a million photons converse. A million minds merge into one. A million threads form the tapestry of a single thought.

In a darkened room in this otherworld, light flickers from a computer screen. Somewhere in the darkness, a Being sits shrouded in smoke, in violation of the prohibitive sign on the far wall. Its attention is fixed on another screen, where others of its kind are involved in a titanic struggle to gain control of a small leather sphere.

Unnoticed, the first monitor flashes an urgent message, and the screen flickers out.

CHAPTER 4:
Welcome to JobNet

SO this was JobNet. Mills tried not to be impressed but failed utterly. The entirety of it all left him breathless as his senses gorged upon fresh, wonderful sensations. His stomach-wrenching trip through the portal was already forgotten, the outside world faded to little more than a memory. Together he and Christine stood hand in hand: pioneers in a land of pioneers.

Puffy clouds gleamed silver in the sun, filling a radiant blue sky like great barges sailing through the air. He was filled with a childish wonder, imagining them with ease to be the foundations of majestic cities.

The scenery suggested a fairy-tale, but one peopled by ordinary human beings. Great citadels dotted the landscape, rearing from grasslands and forests, towering up as though to support the clouds. Built of some gleaming material, they stood proud, with red roofs, crenulations and turrets.

Christine squeezed his hand. He turned to face her, and saw that the landscape had taken her breath away too. Surprising, he thought, since she must have seen it so many times before. *Perhaps this is what it's like to experience a new world, one that you cannot be tired of.*

The scene moved him to smile – something he couldn't remember doing for a long time. Christine gave him one in return. Then she led him down the path into the valley, and under the cool eaves of the wooded slopes.

IN a darkened room in a darkened city, a wall of monitor screens gazes out on the world, like windows through which each pane shows a different scene; here a street corner, brightly lit by neon signs, there a shadowy alley, haunted by those ejected from society.

At the nerve centre of City Watch there is no sound but the slight hum of air-conditioners and the crisp flick of a turned page. A uniformed man sits at a desk, his stubbled face illuminated by the glow of his personal row of screens. One view reveals no more than an empty street. In half an hour, the city's clubs will be throwing their clientele back into the night. Until then, the graveyard shift ambles along.

A man snores at an adjacent desk, an unofficial snooze – with no supervisor on duty there is rather a lack of zeal. The night shift is the most loathed aspect of the otherwise easy job, given to those guilty of some company misdemeanour. The first man looks over at the second and winces at his grating epiglottal snort. With a casual motion he lobs the book at his sleeping companion, greeting him from slumber with a grin and an upturned middle finger. The other man merely scowls and adjusts the setting of his own window to the world.

In the dead of night, a city is a seemingly lifeless thing. From on high it's a dazzling array of glittering lights stretching towards the horizon, as though the heavens have crumbled and settled on the earth. The regular shapes of darkened buildings clutter the view, sporadically blocking the light, forming natural caves of amorphous shadow for the fallen to hide from society's prying, ever-critical eyes.

But to the thousands of eyes that cover the city, it is bright daylight. There are no shadows in which to hide. The eyes see everything: observing but rarely becoming embroiled. One such eye turns on its mount now, moves with a slow grace, coldly noting the few people that pass through its field of vision. Data is transmitted back to its masters, deep in the civic nerve centre.

The camera pauses mid-sweep. Its iris dilates as it locks on two figures struggling across the street. A man cries out in pain and falls to the ground. His shrill note of fear bounces off indifferent buildings, but the camera is deaf to his distress and only watches as he is kicked savagely in the back. Pulses of coded light are beamed back to the monitors in the darkened room, back to the two observers.

"Fuck me! He'll feel that for a while," one says.

"Punch it up, let's get a better look."

With the press of a button, the myriad views of the city are replaced by the struggling figures. Passers by look on as they walk. Mouths move in silent testimony.

The victim regains his feet and faces his attacker. With an unheard curse he lunges and lands a heavy blow to his opponent's jaw.

"Fiver says the first man loses."

"You're on," says the second. Then: "Should we report this?"

"Do you really fancy the paperwork? Tell you what, chuck me my lecky fag and I'll get an ID on them."

Inhaling on the offered device, the man types one-handed at his keyboard. The image on the wall is highlighted by a red wire frame around the first man, then the second. Lines of data race across the screen.

"Nah, they're nobodies. Two piss heads keen on smashing each other's head in. Tell you what, log it and file it. Let the police have a look when they're ready. Nothing to do with us."

The fight is over. One of the figures lies unmoving; a dark liquid spreads from the body and glistens in the feeble light. The camera tracks the second until he escapes its field of vision.

"You lose!"

"Bollocks. I should know better."

The citywide images return. The men resume their duties.

Two o'clock: the streets are crowded once more. The

cameras trace the movements, sometimes striving to lock onto individuals, oblivious to the sounds of drunken revellers returning home, to the roar of engines and the shouts of delight or despair.

When faced with the all-seeing eye there is only one place to hide. Not in shadow, not in light, but in the teeming herd. The best protection lies in numbers.

"**WELCOME** to JobNet."

The Mayor greeted Mills warmly with a raised arm, beckoning him and Christine into the office. Here, Mills saw none of the austerity so common in the outside world. The room was welcoming, designed to set the visitor at ease, and he found himself relaxing for the first time in a long history of contact with officialdom.

Even the Mayor himself seemed determined to set Mills at ease. In any other situation, he was sure the man would have been a reflection of his office, but in JobNet, the office reflected the man. Even the word 'office' seemed an ill-fitting word for the room, which felt more like the study of some eccentric yet harmless academic.

Situated in an oriental-style building that dominated the centre of the village, the room overlooked a vast lake surrounded by heather-clad moors. In disbelief, Mills watched a trio of swans glide across the crystalline water. They had seen no lake on their way here, just more of the chocolate-box architecture that formed the settlement.

Getting Mills' attention with a wave, the man directed

him to a chair by the window. Boats glided across the lake and a willow drooped its branches into the water. One of the swans disappeared into the foliage. The Mayor produced a pipe from his jacket pocket and began to smack it against the palm of his hand.

"It's not actually there, of course," he said, filling his pipe. "But admirable as the village is, I'd rather look at something else. One of the advantages of working here, Mr Mills, is that I can have any view I want. Right now, I'm in a lakeside mood. I find it rather inspiring."

Mills only nodded. The Mayor puffed on his pipe as he lit the tobacco, and the room was soon filled with wraiths of blue-grey smoke that matched his neat hair. The man seemed lost in thought, and Mills began to think he'd been forgotten.

Christine sang a sweet melody quietly to herself, browsing through the Mayor's bookshelves. She looked up from a leather-bound volume with brass fittings and presented Mills with another of her radiant smiles. In the hall, a clock chimed the hour, and, as though summoned, the Mayor returned from whatever memory he had been visiting.

"It's beautiful, isn't it, Mr Mills?" he said quietly. "But I'm forgetting you've already tasted the beauty of our world. How do you feel? I understand you had a rough entry."

"I feel fine Mr... What do I call you? Mayor?"

"My apologies," the man replied, laughing. "The term

is only an affectation of the people here, though I somehow suspect they've forgotten my real name, they've called me Mayor so long. My name is James MacAllister, and I'm actually the United Kingdom System & Personnel Administrator. That's if you want my rather boring and heavy-handed title. Personally, I can't stand it."

"You prefer Mayor?"

"I suppose I do. It's rather civic and old fashioned. I like old things, as you may have noticed." The old man swept his arm in an arc to indicate the office and its antique style of furnishing, all dark-stained wood and brass fittings. Christine continued to ignore the two men, swaying her body to some internal rhythm as she read. Mills found he rather liked the way she moved.

If only the old man would get on with the matter in hand. Normally such encounters with officials were short and to the point. And they always took place across the divide of an austere desk. There was something a little off-putting about the open space between himself and the Mayor; exposed, that was it. At least here, the chairs were more comfortable.

"You'll get used to it, Mr Mills. And I only use a desk for work. Not when I'm having a chat. The informal approach is best, I always find. Ah, don't look so shocked – I'm not really a mind reader!"

"How did you know what I was thinking?"

"The wonders of artificial reality," he replied, a mischievous twinkle in his eyes. "Actually, it's nothing more than reflections of your mind. Echoes. Crossed wires. Call them what you will. When you've been in AR as long as I have, you can tap into them sometimes. It's all right: JobNet isn't about to give away all your innermost secrets."

"And Christine? Can you pick up her thoughts too?"

"Now, there's an enigma. I've never been able to tap into our Christine's thoughts. That's the way it is sometimes."

The old man looked towards Christine and shrugged. She looked up from her book, her eyes bright with innocence. It struck him then how carefree she was. He wished his own life had not left him so careworn.

"Well, I suppose we should get down to business."

At last.

"Have you any idea what field of employment you'll be pursuing?"

"I don't know. I used to be an industrial-systems technician. I suppose I'll be looking for something similar. Mind you, I like tinkering with old machines, restoring them and such. Wouldn't mind being a tech in an R&D lab – doing that kind of thing."

"Hmm. There are still openings in those fields. Of course, like most things, tech is a shrinking area: there are too many computers monitoring computers these days. Still, I'm sure you'll find something. The vast majority do."

Mills nodded. He was determined to take up what he wanted; not what some official decided would suit him.

"Now, I suppose I should explain the geography of the system," the Mayor continued. "You are currently in one of the residential cells, as we call them here. That's where people stay for the majority of their visit. This one is generated by our main AI in London.

"All the corporate representatives are roughly grouped together according to their areas of interest. Some represent more than one. Because we're in AR, it doesn't matter where they are physically based; you'll find Far Eastern companies and European companies in the same cell if they cover the same field. Do you follow so far?"

Boredom began to gnaw at his attention span, but he nodded his head anyway and hoped his eyes weren't too glazed.

"You've already sampled the mode of travel, and I believe you're a little wary of it. Never mind, you'll get used to it. The portals were the designers' fancy I'm afraid: they thought the simulation novel. Unfortunately, it does disorientate some people. There is a kind of spatial arrangement between the cells, so you *could* walk if you really wanted to, but I advise you to use the portals. It's much quicker. Now, have you got any questions?"

He thought for a moment. He had to play willing. And then one struck him: "Yes. How am I actually supposed to look for work?"

"Oh, that's the easy bit. You just talk with the recruiters. Christine will tell you all about that. A lot of job-hunting is done right here in the village, in fact; often a result of just mixing with the recruiters socially. There's no set way, really. It's like it says in the literature – informal. But there, that's the official, boring pep-talk finished, you'll be glad to hear." The Mayor smiled.

"So what happens now?"

"Christine? Could you show Mr Mills to where he'll be staying? If you'll go along with Christine, you'll be able to settle in. Relax, and maybe look around a little. There's plenty of time for the serious business tomorrow. It's been a pleasure meeting you, Mr Mills. I hope to see you again soon."

With that the Mayor stood and offered his hand. Mills shook it, and followed Christine out of the room, still dazed.

"WHAT do you think of the Mayor?" Christine asked as they left the building.

"I don't know. I've only just met him. Strikes me as a bit odd though, sitting in a room like that and staring at a lake that doesn't even exist."

A few people called out in greeting to Christine as they passed. Christine waved to them, taking hold of David's arm to guide him along.

"I think he's a sweet old man. The Mayor's like a granddad and a great uncle rolled into one. You'll like him once you get to know him better, just like I did. Anyway, what's wrong with enjoying something that's not there? We're both doing that, aren't we?"

Gradually, their route took them up the slope of the valley. The streets became dotted with trees and shrubs and, further up, the forest's canopy reared up to the skyline. The ground tangled into undergrowth, shaded from the late afternoon sun. He could smell the earthiness of the forest, laced with the scents of unseen flowers and the moisture trapped in a living carpet of bracken and fern.

At last they came to a small, thatched cottage. He raised a questioning eyebrow at Christine. But it seemed at least better than the cold barracks of the labour camps or the dormitories of training centres from past schemes. He couldn't wait to see the inside.

EVENING fell over the village. Lights twinkled into existence, illuminating the twilight.

In artificial reality, a falling tree makes no sound unless there is a witness to behold the event. Otherwise, it's just another changing pattern in a complex data-stream.

Caught in that ebbing flow of four-dimensional data, MacAllister settled down at his desk and opened a thick leather-bound ledger. His eyes scanned the page, and reams of text scrolled at a steady pace. He silently cursed and closed his eyes for a second. When he opened them, the text was stable. He read to the bottom of the page, and turned to the next.

"MacAllister."

The disembodied voice broke his concentration.

"Wait a moment," he replied to the empty room. With a sigh he reached down and opened a drawer. He placed an antique brass and ivory telephone on his desk, closed the drawer and picked up the handset. He closed his eyes for a second then spoke into the mouthpiece.

"For God's sake, Carswell, I do wish you wouldn't do that. You know talking to thin air gives me the creeps!"

"Forget all that. This is important." This time the curt reply came from the earpiece. "Have you inducted today's clients?"

"Yes. I was just preparing to output the details. One of them had a bit of a rough entry: Mills, Dee Ess. But it seems any problems have been sorted out –"

"It's this Mills I wanted to talk to you about. We've lost him."

"What do you mean you've *lost* him? How can you lose a client? Your people being more incompetent than usual?"

"The man shouldn't be in the system," the voice said, irritated. "Following his entry problems, the hospital reported they severed his link and discharged him. But according to our system logs, he underwent the usual calibration phase and was duly injected into the system as normal. The point is we have no idea of his *physical* location."

MacAllister frowned and stood up. Taking the cordless phone with him, he walked to the window and looked across the lake. After a moment's concentration the lake dissolved, replaced by the sight of Mills' cottage. It stood in darkness, barely visible against the shapeless mass of the forest surrounding it, but a light burned bright in the window.

"So what do you want me to do? I don't believe he's aware he's gone missing. As for his bad entry, he seems to have put that down to bad luck."

"Don't do anything, MacAllister. At least until we've found his body. Just keep an eye on him and report anything out of the ordinary. Otherwise, proceed as normal. I'll keep you informed."

With that, the phone went dead. MacAllister sighed and replaced the handset.

CHAPTER 5:
In Mind of an Eye

CORRALLED by *a hundred tall buildings, the herd of humanity roams through the city. It is a busy day, but still the eyes manage a protective gaze over all.*

The electronic shepherd is the ultimate answer to crime, the ultimate deterrent. Yet evolution twists and turns, resisting all attempts to lash it down. As ever, the best criminals are those who are never caught – the ones who find a way to remain unseen. The hapless and the fallen are swept from the scene, and still the eye observes.

But in any healthy society even crime has a use – as does the fear it evokes. Only fear of the wolf, after all, keeps the flock from straying from the shepherd. An eye rotates on its mount. The lens focuses on a distant weed. A man dressed in rags begs for a few fragments of life from pedestrians – well-dressed diodes of the corporate machine. The iris constricts, sharpening the distant image as a van pulls up. Two uniformed men accost the beggar. Soon he is gone, manhandled into the van. The eye witnesses on behalf of unseeing citizens.

And then it resumes its vigil.

LIGHT. The beams of a probing sun peered in through a crack in the curtains, causing Mills to eventually open his eyes. The room swam into focus, information translated into a complex three-dimensional structure by a processing unit unsurpassed by any other, even in this age of AI.

Last night, AR had proved itself too real. He hadn't intended to start his first full day in JobNet worse for drink. It should have been impossible for the brain to be scrambled by simulated wine, he was sure, so he laughed at Christine's warning of psychosomatic inebriation. And now he had a mother of a hangover, his body fooled into illness. Why had he allowed her to drag him to that party? Because he was surprised – and secretly pleased – by the invite, why else?

There was no sign of Christine in the bedroom. Her absence felt a little strange, but he chided himself for expecting her to be around. As if she was going to spend the night or waltz in while he was prostrate in his bed. Funny, in her absence he realised just how much he had grown used to her company. Somehow, she had become a pleasant constant in this new and overwhelming world. Hopefully he hadn't blown it.

The angle of the sun's rays through the curtains altered as the sun climbed higher in the sky. Mills remained in bed and stared up at the ceiling, wandering through the recesses of his partially functioning mind, striving to reconstruct the previous evening from tattered memories. Occasionally an embarrassing moment would resurface, causing a wince to flit across his face.

How could an evening be lost to such a ghost of alcohol? The early evening was crystal clear. Christine had spent some time explaining how to use the JobNet Directory – an archaic book bound in brass and leather that opened to reveal a top-of-the-range smartpad. The device was easy enough to use. The process of searching for and approaching potential employers was dull, but straightforward. What that said about the supposed informality was another thing, but he'd become used to a gap between rhetoric and reality over the years. Still, he'd been surprised at the pang of disappointment.

Affecting artificial reality proved a little more complex, but he thought he understood it – even if he couldn't master the practice particularly well. Apart from one little trick he'd learned at the party, before the evening became a blur.

Phantasm as the experience may have been, his body still remonstrated against the ills of drink. The queasy feeling in the pit of his stomach had mercifully passed, but his body felt drained and heavy. His parched mouth tasted rank, and a headache lurked somewhere at the back of his head, waiting to leap out when he least expected. But for now, lying on the bed held the ill effects at bay and allowed him time to think.

What setbacks would he suffer from last night's behaviour? At the very least, a whole range of introductions would have to be repeated. How would people take to him now? Had he labelled himself a waster and a drunk on his very first day?

Maybe, just maybe, he had overstepped the mark when it came to the system's informality. Maybe it was all a load of crap: for the rich to get stinking drunk was a minor faux pas – the sign of a hell-raiser – but for the poor it was a moral crime. *Such is life*, Mills thought. The poor are always guilty.

CONCENTRATION became difficult when his restless bladder began to scream for attention. Reluctantly, David climbed out of bed, swaying on his feet until his brain worked out which way was up. He walked unsteadily across polished floorboards partially covered by handcrafted rugs.

They were only as real as the cottage, he reminded himself; as physically intangible as a dream, even if he could touch them. Yet the cottage contained everything that would be found in a real home: even a toilet.

A ghost toilet for him to release his ghostly waste. How bizarre. Vague worry tempered his relief; was this some kind of weird muscle memory, or was he really taking a leak? If so, he hoped a catheter in the tangible world was draining away the fluid, for the sake of others as much as him, but he recalled his old man had never felt the urge, not once he was plumbed into a bag on his leg when his waterworks packed up. He shook his head. This artificial reality was going to take some getting used to.

With his bladder satisfied he moved over to the sink and splashed himself with water. The cold shock was refreshing; droplets of moisture dribbled over his shoulders and back. He looked up into the mirror and was met with further shock: somebody else stared back at him. The man he had been long ago.

The eyes were the same, sad and cynical. But the wear and tear was gone. The flesh looked firmer, tighter, his features more youthful. Gone were the lines around his eyes and the creases that split his forehead. Eyes and cheeks were no longer sunken and hollow – the products of stress and a poor diet. His hair was thicker, somehow darker. This was the mental image of a man generated by his mind's eye – despite the horrible truth of a real-world mirror. The man who supervised a vast, modern steel works had returned from the grave of time.

No more scars, no more blemishes; his body had been cleansed. If only the mental scars of his past could be erased so easily.

ANOTHER time, another world. The young Mills lay discarded on an urban battlefield. Six months he had been on the dole, by then. The arrogance of youth said this was only a temporary setback. Poor fool.

Ironic that his rude awakening should arise from the very tools of his trade: a simple virus found its way into the computer system responsible for handling the benefits of three neighbouring districts. The system crashed, taking seven days to come back online.

Before then, thousands had crowded round the JobMart demanding the means to feed themselves and their families. The JobMart finally regrouped and opted for the old-fashioned system of cheques, but it had only made matters worse. The crowd refused to be herded. Scuffles broke out, driven by desperation.

Even after all these years, the memory burned sullen: most of those poor bastards hadn't eaten in days. Others had already been made homeless. He gritted his teeth; he couldn't do anything about it now, they couldn't do anything about it then, but they'd been too fired up to think it through.

The atomised mass of angry humanity had become one and surged against the building. The locked doors burst open under the pressure of the human tide. Caught in the flow, Mills had found himself part of the raging crowd storming through the building.

Private security rallied. The building was cleared and a defensive barrier formed.

The battle had spread to surrounding streets as two worlds – society and the dispossessed – clashed. Club rattled on shield or smacked human flesh and bone. Gas canisters hissed, spreading a choking haze. Savaged by cattle-prod and gas, riot-glue and nets, and the mind-shattering wail of the sonics. The tide turned.

Fear and pain. No excitement. The pain of ribs cracked by a devastating blow, the stinging tears of irritant gas. He had found himself sprawled on the road, bloodied and bruised while bodies clashed above him. In terror he had crawled away to lick his wounds and curse the harsh world. He'd wanted more than to simply exist. Had that really been too much to ask?

Retribution had followed. No prison sentence for him. The authorities somehow missed him. But everyone who signed at that office saw their benefits suspended for six months – innocent and guilty alike.

Without his folks, he'd have been screwed. That made him luckier than most. They kept him going, kept him fed, took him back in so he had a roof over his head. Yeah, without them he'd be a full-blown zero now, haunting the derelict places with the rest of the destitute, or just plain dead.

The world had never seemed the same since.

NOW he had been given a chance for a future. A chance that wouldn't be achieved by hiding in this anachronistic cottage.

A quick search of the house turned up some new clothes, passably better than those Christine had manifested from fresh air. More comfortably attired, he felt better prepared to begin his search for work. But first, he wanted to explore the village.

The slopes receded as he walked with sure strides. The smell of the forest reached his nose, carried on the north-westerly wind. He took a deep breath, enjoying the cool sensation. No smog – such a shame it wasn't genuine.

The village drew closer. At last, stone slabs winding down towards spacious streets replaced the footpath worn into the grass. Flowerbeds bordered the path further on. He half expected to meet some red-hooded gnome on its way to do a spot of fishing, silly as the notion was. His thoughts weren't diminished by what he could see to the north and south.

Nearing the valley floor, the scenery expanded to meet the distant horizon. Framed by tree-lined slopes, a panoramic plain of rolling hills, meadows and woodland stretched for miles. The sun glinted from the citadels he had seen the previous day – white towers that reached for the skies. They were beautiful, yet somehow they made the landscape seem desolate and lonely.

Life in JobNet was supposedly designed to make the hunt for work easy, but the world felt too big, this approach too strange. Maybe he was too used to the traditional methods, but here he simply did not know where to begin. Perhaps the novelty was wearing off already.

CHAPTER 6:
A Day at the Market

"**BUILDING** trades. Fresh jobs. New contracts. Get your building trades here!"

A terrible noise battered his ears like hammer-blows; the din of shouting humanity, all desperately seeking to be heard, yearning to be noticed against the crowd. He had heard of the job market, but this was ridiculous.

Stalls and stallholders cluttered the central square, all of them shouting their wares. The press of bodies made it hard going. Most of the stalls were surrounded and seemed in danger of being crushed out of existence.

"Retail! Get your job in retail! Till operators. Customer service. Store security. Warehouse delivery. Free lunch hour with every work day!"

So many faces. All preoccupied with one thing only: Getta job! Any job! How many were aware of the masses of other people that surrounded them, other than as barriers to be breached at all costs? After half an hour, Mills only wanted out of the depressing scene.

"Temps! Secretarial. Shorthand. Typing. Get the kids something nice for Christmas. Temp for the best agencies!"

Feeling ever more claustrophobic, Mills struggled against the flow. Thousands of humans brushed against him as if stirred by some invisible hand. Over the heads of the crowd towered the administration building – the tallest structure in the village. A benevolent hub offering help and guidance to tens of thousands of virtual jobseekers, all of whom, it seemed, were gathered in the square.

Amid the commotion, Mills could feel the unspoken competition and driving energy of desperation that separated each person from every other. The same desperation wedged apart everyone in the outside reality, too. Maybe he shouldn't have been surprised.

These stalls represented agencies of every trade and description, but they occupied only part-time AR, according to what he'd read in the Directory. From that he surmised, maybe cynically, they bought their time by the hour so they could act as middle-men between the more desperate of the unemployed and those companies that wanted cheap, disposable labour. Whatever the truth of it, the place added to the sense that he'd taken – he hoped – a wrong turn.

At last Mills reached the far edge of the square. The

press of bodies here was greatly reduced; only a few stragglers came and went from the chaotic main mass. He sped up, hurrying to escape the madness behind him and retreat to the ordered calm of the streets.

He regained his personal space once more, and with it a great relief. It also brought a face; one glimpsed in the crush of the job market. Incongruous; it did not match the other forlorn masks. This one seemed confident, contemptuous even. Mills could not recall where he had seen the man before, despite the vague familiarity.

Finally the man crossed the street and fell into step beside him.

"I thought I recognised you back there," the stranger said. "Remember me? Harris, from the party last night."

"Sorry. Last night's a bit of a blur, I'm afraid."

"Never mind." Harris laughed. "In fact, between you and me, the Mayor was pretty much out of it."

"Yeah, well, I didn't think I could get pissed on that stuff."

The man laughed again. "I think we could do with a rest after all that," he said, pointing back at the crush in the square. "Come with me, there's this great café further on – coffee actually tastes real."

"We're in AR, isn't it supposed to?"

"You'd think. Most places cock it up – they make it taste better than real. Come on."

Mills allowed himself to be guided.

"You know, you're not the only one to get drunk

here," Harris continued, "and you won't be the last either. It gets most first-timers. It's become something of a rite of passage now."

"Really. Well, I suppose I was well and truly *passaged* last night."

"Never mind. I promise we'll be better behaved next time... possibly. Here we are."

The café opened up onto a low-walled garden with tables and chairs situated between beds of shrubs and flowers. Few of the tables were occupied, inside the building or outside, leaving them with quite the pick of the place.

Mills followed Harris to a table in the corner of the garden, beneath a trestle supporting a tangle of thornless roses that grew like rampant ivy. Mills inspected one of the blooms, disturbing a bee that buzzed briefly around his head. As far as he could remember their true scents, the flowers smelled authentic. The attention to detail was impressive: even the bee's pollen sacs were brimming with golden dust.

"What'll you have?"

"I'll just have a coffee."

"Make that two," Harris said to the waiter. Then he snapped his fingers. A packet of cigarettes materialised on the tabletop. Mills had learned the trick himself, but it felt strange. Not to mention he knew he'd eventually find himself trying out in the real world and making himself look ridiculous in the process – so he made a point not to try too often in AR.

Unconcerned by his companion's discomfort, Harris ripped open the pack. Mills accepted a cigarette and lit it on the dancing flame that leapt from the man's thumb.

"Best thing about AR – smoking won't kill you," Harris said as he lit up his own. He settled back in his chair and blew out a current of iridescent smoke rings that danced on the air.

"You know, I was really surprised to see you back there. That's why I wasn't sure it was you."

"Where did you expect me to be? I *am* supposed to be looking for a job."

"For God's sake, man! You don't want to be looking there." The waiter arrived with their drinks. Harris looked sidelong at the man and then continued, lowering his voice. "Those people are absolute no-hopers who've never been able to hold down a job in their lives. Sure, they'll get something. It'll last a couple of weeks at most. Then they're right back where they started. I'm telling you, Mills, they're worthless!"

His vehemence took Mills by surprise. Here was a man working with the unemployed, supposedly to help them. He found it strangely refreshing; a change to the patronising amiability he knew so well. Yet at the same time, he couldn't help wondering what Harris thought about *him*. Mills regarded him a moment before asking: "So what does that make me? I'm no different."

"Mr Mills, David… I'm sorry. I get carried away

sometimes," he said, smiling suddenly. "It's just so frustrating, trying to help people who don't give a fuck about anything. Anyway, you're not like them. The whole point of JobNet is to filter out the scum. Supposedly, we allocate talent and ability where it's needed. Outside it's spread out, difficult to find amongst the dross. We collect the good stuff here. That's why you're with us – and that's why you shouldn't be in the square. It's full of the crap that got through."

"Oh, so I'm a better class of unemployable," he said, toying with his cup as he struggled to hide his displeasure.

Harris sighed and shifted in his seat, his face solemn. "If you want to see it that way," he said. "The fact is, full employment is a joke: bad for business, bad for social discipline. Most people will never work again. We can't afford it. Some, however, can. And will. Like it or not, that's you. By all means, join the surplus scum if it suits some sentimental desire for martyrdom. Nobody will notice. Believe me."

Mills laughed bitterly and pushed his coffee away. "And why would a man like you be at the job market? It's beneath you, after all."

"Let's just say I like the rancid smell of failure you get from any gathering of losers. Besides, I study people. I have access to information on everyone who comes here, but it's always useful to see them in the flesh... as it were." Harris sipped his coffee and stared at him over the rim of the cup. "But you're right. I did want to talk to you," he added.

"Go on," Mills prompted, but the man simply sat there.

A babble of voices broke the tense momentary silence. Mills glanced across the garden to see three men and two women walking towards the café. By the look of them, they too were clients – the better class of unemployable. After a few seconds, Harris turned back to Mills. "You've not been with us long, have you? Two days, something like that. All you've done so far is wander around like a lost sheep. Bad habit to get into."

"Get to the point."

"I can get you a job, right now if you want. Save you all that hassle. The job's in your field, more or less. And it'll suit… certain skills you've acquired. I'm sure you know what I'm referring to."

"I didn't realise you were a recruiter, Harris."

"Oh, I'm no recruiter. Let's just say I'm doing a favour for a friend. He works for the Government, and they can always use skills like yours. You may have gotten caught that one time, but that's easily corrected by a little training."

Mills shifted in his seat. "I don't know what you're talking about."

"No, of course you don't. I get it. Bad memories. I appreciate you'd want to forget about it all, but do you really think the *system* forgets so readily? Like I said, I've got access to the dirt on everyone who comes here–"

"We're supposed to start with a clean slate–"

"Let's just say you're a special case. You know, you're one lucky bastard: they only gave you a suspended sentence. My... friend... can make that blemish go away. What do you say?"

"Leave it, Harris!" Mills clenched his fists in his lap. "I just said I don't know what you're talking about."

"Fine. Let me remind you. Janus Investments. Remember it? Major investor in AI-IT ventures. Part of the consortium that owned that mill you used to work at, until they cut their losses and walked away when the AI that took your job didn't work out. Angry enough yet?"

Mills opened his mouth to speak, to shout more like, but Harris cut him off. Maybe just as well.

"Wait," the man said. "I'm just getting to the best bit. Funnily enough, Janus owned the insurance company that declined to cover the costs of your late mother's care. What a web they weave, these corporate boys, eh? You know, given what you did, after you found out – hacking its system and leaving that virus – I'm genuinely surprised they let you in here. Still, it's not my place to reason why. Guess somebody decided you're too much of a fuck-up to be a risk. How's that anger brewing?"

"Fuck you, Harris!" Mills slammed his hand on the table. The coffee cups rattled. "Yes, I was fucking angry."

"Easy, David," Harris said, holding his hands out in a placating gesture, but the faint smile on his face revealed he'd got the reaction he wanted. Mills cursed inwardly, and forced his anger down.

"I get it," Harris added. "I know where you're coming from. It can't have been easy. Strokes are nasty. You and your old man wearing yourselves out looking after her, too skint to barely look after yourselves. Yeah, I can see how you'd lose it, dealing with a bad hand like that."

"Enough," Mills snarled, sore nerves touched. "You said you had some kind of job, what's any of this got to do with anything?"

"I'm getting there, Dave. I just want to get this out of your system. If you're going to make it in this world, you're going to have to start learning where you fit in. So, what did you think you'd achieve, anyway? What would it have changed? Come on, I want to know."

"Nothing." Mills felt like he was back at the JobMart, grilled by some functionary over something and nothing, and knowing damn well he couldn't just walk away. They owned him. And that rankled, stoking the coals of his simmering emotions. But this man was no JobMart official; Mills wondered just who and what he really was. The not knowing helped cool his anger to more manageable levels.

"That's right, nothing," Harris nodded his head slowly, smiling. "But suppose you'd pulled it off, ever think about that – all those poor bastards who'd have lost out? All those health care plans for kiddies and grannies, insurances and pensions, everything hard-working folk put aside to cover themselves, just snatched away. Not by some corporate button-pusher – by you. What did *they* ever do to you? You ever think about that?"

"All the fucking time," he said through gritted teeth, stung by old regret. "I was angry…"

"Yeah, you were angry. You said. But you were just hiding behind your mum, really. Admit it. You knew what you were doing. You made a choice. Well, now my friend is offering you another choice. You can be one of the good guys, if you're man enough to stop hiding and embrace the opportunity."

Mills stared at Harris, holding back the impulse to smack the smile from his face. "You like twisting the knife, don't you? So what is it you do here, really?"

"Me? Just think of me as a coordinator and a facilitator, Mr Mills. Now what's your answer?"

"No," he said, sitting back and folding his arms across his chest. He enjoyed seeing the smug confidence evaporate from the man's face. He'd been so sure of himself.

"What?" Harris leaned forward across the table. "Did you just say no? After all the effort I put into you. Look, just think it over."

"I did. Read my lips: f-u-c-k-o-f-f!"

"Why? It's a great offer. More than you deserve."

"If your friend is anything like you, then I really wouldn't want to work for him, okay? Besides, I think I prefer being a bad guy. It's more honest."

Mills left the table, conversation over. Maybe he

hadn't won any kind of victory, he'd certainly not won any friends, but he figured he'd clawed back some self-respect. Better than nothing. At the gate, he turned back and called over to Harris. The man looked up.

"What happens to them when they leave?" He pointed towards the job market.

Across the garden, Harris shrugged and pulled another cigarette from the packet. "They go back to being parasites. They grow old, hopefully they don't breed, and then they have the decency to die!"

Mills nodded his head. "You're all heart," he muttered, and walked away.

ACROSS the light barrier, two worlds meet through fibrous glass. Outside is in full daylight, the sun still high in the sky though well past its zenith. Glass and metal reflect the sun's light and heat, adding to the city's already stifling atmosphere. Animal and machine exhaust chokes the air with poison, besieging the city's flora in its futile efforts to render the air more breathable.

Dwelling in this noxious brew of gases, a million humans go about their business: trading, working, looking, shopping, loving, hating. The eyes look on, bridging light and dark, feeding tiny packets of photons to a neural hub deep beneath the city.

As ever, the nerve centre of City Watch is shrouded in shadow. The only light to enter the chamber comes from afar, from the world of light outside, channelled from eye to monitor down a colossal length of fibre-optic. The light is cold in its illumination and utterly devoid of life.

But the darkness is of little concern to the uniformed denizens of City Watch. They are used to darkness. Whatever the hour outside, here it is always the same. Time is measured not by diurnal rhythms but by the passage of thousands of flickering images, which meet on one vast wall of monitors and come together like some huge silicon retina, where a constantly changing montage of the city is perpetually displayed. The nerve centre bustles like the city itself. Hundreds of men track and analyse their own portion of the cityscape. Recording. Observing. Sometimes acting.

Sat at a desk more or less in the centre of the room, a man sips coffee and pays only scant attention to his row of personal monitors. A coffee-stained document rests on the desk beneath his hand as he idly taps the surface with a pen. It's a routine report summarising the day's observations: tedious, as little happens in his sector. At least during the day shift.

A sea of human faces drift across his field of vision: white faces, black faces, fat, thin, pretty, ugly, lifeless faces. All different, yet somehow identical. The same routine day in and day out. Yet it pays the bills; there's no getting away from that.

A flash of red light and the man looks up. One screen flashes the words, "AUTO-IDENT ACTIVE – STANDBY". He curses under his breath. The image zooms in on one face in that mass, occasionally a passer-by obscures it, but always those features return. The other screens continue to run through their normal observation programs. The man ignores them, concentrates on his computer screen as streams of data flash onto the display and stabilise. An image is framed in the screen's top-left corner and text scrolls over it: name, personal details, links to known biographical records. And in red, superimposed on the image, the words: "REGISTERED STATE SECURITY THREAT".

"Shit," the man breathes. "Supervisor! Clements, I've got something."

"What is it?" A perspiring man in shirtsleeves waddles over.

"What do I do? Log it and file it?"

"No, you bloody well don't!" the supervisor replies, still staring at the screen. It is evident that the bearded man on display is engaged in conversation with someone else, out of view. "This is a priority observation. We pass this one straight on. Look at the screen. Who's it for?"

"Er – the Social Security Agency... *Fuck...*"

"Yeah. I've never seen one of these before. Let's get it right, or it'll be our arses on the line. Toggle C5, let's see if we can ID the other one."

A trackball manipulates a distant camera. With the press of a button the eye zooms in and locks on the second person. A simple tap of a key and an identity request is processed. Text flashes onto the screen. Unaware of watchful eyes, the man and woman continue their conversation, mouths moving wordlessly.

"Sutton, Jane. Client administrator with the JobMart Agency. A nobody, no previous record," the operator mutters. "What do I do now?"

"Call up the codes for the security services. Regulations say this has to be passed on immediately. You'll need to transmit full video details from both cameras. Don't worry about the data files; the codes are transcribed on the footage automatically. They can access the information down at their end."

The supervisor slaps the operator on the back in a moment of rare good humour. "Good work. There'll be a bonus in this for you. You can get the kids something nice."

Beyond the cameras, the man and the woman part company. The woman quickly disappears into the crowd, unaware that on this occasion the numbers have been so totally against her.

The man looks up at the camera, meets its mindless gaze, and smiles.

CHAPTER 7:
In the City of Dreams

EACH blade of grass is a sophisticated work of natural biotechnology. Solar powered, it is perpetually manufactured from raw materials in soil and air.

These chemicals constantly churn in vats invisible to the naked eye, manufactured by machines no bigger than a protein molecule, since that is what they are. And the components of this biological production line are delicately assembled to form a single blade of grass.

Multiply this by billions.

So much effort just to feed a cow, except there are no cows in JobNet.

What use is the grass, if not to provide sustenance for bovine mammals? Scenery, of course. A pleasant carpet to walk upon; one more comfortable than bone-jarring stone. Or so you'd think.

AFTER miles of hard walking, Mills was still surrounded by fields and meadowland. As ever, the forest shrouded the distant hills, which remained perpetually on the horizon.

The cooling shade of those trees would have been welcome now, with the sun burning hot overhead and not the slightest breeze.

The Mayor had warned him about walking, but he hated the idea of travelling through the portals. The journey on foot was proving too much for him though, and so he reluctantly gave in, thought hard, and summoned a portal. Thankfully, one answered his mental call, appearing in the field to his left. Somehow he found the energy to scale the dry-stone wall that bordered the path.

As he passed into the portal his aching feet longed for the feel of good, honest stone. Then the portal took him in its grip and the familiar nausea took hold.

CYBERSPACE meets hyperspace along the information highway.

Through the twisting emptiness, the data screams its discomfort, propelled on the roller-coaster ride through another dimension. Light swallows light. The data reaches its terminal point. The data reforms, assumes its self-defined identity. And there is the man, deposited at his destination on the far side of reality's event horizon.

THE world returned in a frenzy of noise and motion as Mills popped out of the portal. People milled around up ahead, thousands of them, crowded and restless. The sudden bustle grated his senses almost as badly as his passage through JobNet's soul-wrenching transportation system.

He bent over and put his hands on his thighs while he sought to settle his nerves, breathing deeply as if he'd just run a race. "What's wrong with simple teleportation or something?" he muttered; yeah, just step from one place to the next, no more fuss than walking through a door.

Not for the first time, Mills found himself envying the easy grace Christine demonstrated whenever they'd transitioned together from one place to another.

Taking a final deep breath, Mills straightened and took stock of his surroundings. He was on a path leading to a vast square. Other roads branched off from its periphery, lost to perspective as they snaked away.

The roads were busy, if not packed; that was reserved for the square where the travellers congregated en route to their destination. More people streamed past him. Individuals, hurrying on their way; groups ambling towards the square. For the most part, he was ignored – just another face in the crowd – but Mills caught a couple of passers-by glancing his way, smirking at his discomfort. Well, *screw you*, he thought, feeling like a tourist.

The citadel he'd previously seen from afar rose above him, dominating the landscape; its edifice gleamed in the sun. Turrets rose into the sky, tipped by banners flapping madly in the breeze. A curtain wall, replete with decorative ramparts, skirted the citadel's lower reaches and rose above the teeming square. Three great archways set in a row broached the wall and swallowed the crowds into this Nameless City's urban embrace.

This close, maybe half a mile distant, if he was any judge, the citadel no longer appeared as a densely packed cluster of outsized skyscrapers. A metropolis in white marble now, rising and dipping with the rolling contours of underlying hills, but it demanded attention all the same.

The whole set-up was weird, ridiculous even; he reminded himself it was just a glorified JobMart. All the same, he shivered as a wave of awe tickled his sternum, and he felt his mood begin to lighten.

The towers and spires had been pulled out of the stratosphere by some shift in perspective, rendering it at a more human scale, but no less impressive for all that. The style was a curious mix of classical Rome and medieval fantasy, all cupolas and Corinthian columns, confectionary battlements and gothic arches. He found himself wishing for something a little more futuristic, but he gave up when all he could picture were rain-soaked, neon-stained dystopias. Well, the future had never done him any favours.

Mills tore his rapt gaze away from the citadel's splendour and went to join the throng of people heading towards the gates. The press of bodies and the babble of the crowd intensified as he merged with the flow of flesh. He felt himself carried away towards those great gates, but it was an easy walk, and he made short work of the remaining distance.

The crowd became tighter as he neared the gates. Bodies packed and busy, just as he remembered London in the bygone days when he could afford a trip to the capital; busier still than the job market he'd experienced back at the village, but without the rank sense of desperation he'd felt there.

This place was easy-going; too easy, maybe. Mills found it hard to hold onto his doubts and worries. The mood of the crowd worked its magic on his sense of self. A palpable aura of optimism was dissolving the edge of his hard-won cynicism; he tried to hold on it, out of habit as much as anything else, but it was proving as slippery as wet soap. Then he passed under the central gate and into the Nameless City. The last of his nagging doubts stuttered into silence.

The citadel opened up before him; a thriving hive of possibility. The energy of the place was enervating. The many with him joined the multitude already pumping life into the Nameless City; they streamed through the streets like a liquid torrent churning through stark white canyons. Like the battering roar of water's unleashed energy, the noise of the crowd was tremendous: a great cacophony of hope and anticipation reverberated from the gleaming walls.

Mills felt its rush, a hit of euphoria. Suddenly, he desperately wanted to be accepted back into society, to be worth something to it, to earn his place back in the world of the real; he felt the same stirrings that motivated his fellows. Those competitors, all around him. But the Nameless City worked its magic: no need for undue aggression here. All were fellow pilgrims, unified in their Quest. And the streets were paved with gold, polished by the feet of many seekers. He followed this path, drawn on by his goal.

Offices and meeting places beckoned, their doors adorned with the symbols of corporate heraldry, proclaiming the functions of agencies and companies in the manner of mediaeval merchants and artisans. Mills walked past them all, spoilt for choice, and wondering where to start; he followed the road, content to let it sweep him where it would.

At last he reached the heart of the city. The streets opened up to a wide space with a suddenness that took the breath away: one minute, tall buildings and narrow streets rising above his head, the next... nothing but sky.

The golden path joined a wide boulevard that encircled a palace. Pine trees stood at regular intervals, growing from beds of fine floral displays.

The scent of water reached his nose and mingled with the scent of pine. A moat lapped against the walls of the palace, rippling against the pillars of a marble bridge. Water lilies floated on the surface of the crystal water, home to giant carp gliding silver and gold beneath the surface. A woman in bright clothes threw them bread. It was all so strangely… *dreamlike.*

Mills ventured over the bridge and then paused at the threshold of the palace gate, sudden doubt crashing the trance of optimism the citadel had nurtured in his mind. Here, some of the world's top-flight tech companies maintained a virtual presence; well out of his league. A sobering thought, for sure: he almost turned away. Follow your dreams, the ghost of youth proclaimed; nothing ventured, nothing gained.

A thought morphed his clothes into something more appropriate. Suited and booted, he muttered: "Let's do this."

TIME lingered like it had nowhere better to be; Mills conceded he ought to be used to the waiting game by now, but he'd expected better here in JobNet. He sighed and shifted his weight in the uncomfortable leatherette seat.

The office looked like a throwback; certainly not the kind of set-up he'd expected from a blue-chip firm like ArcheaoLogik. Maybe it was playing for effect with the design, a stylised reflection of its purpose as a leading specialist in data resurrection. Maybe they just weren't that keen on visitors.

From where he sat, the open plan office lay before him, clusters of empty desks spreading to the distant corners; ergonomic chairs arranged around the desks, as though only recently vacated, added a haunted feel to the place.

This visitor's annexe was little more than two uneven rows of seats either side of the entrance with a couple of low tables, and only a plastic-looking plant for company. What kind of mind adorns an ersatz world with a fake plant? In the end, he'd given up on that one.

When he first walked in, the size – and the emptiness – had proved disorienting; he'd felt his mind lurch. The young woman on reception – a good march directly opposite the entrance, he noted – managed to put his mental footing firmly back on the ground. She also saved his legs, which was an added bonus, when she called across to him: "Please take a seat, sir. Mr O'Grady won't keep you long."

That was 30 minutes ago. Mills figured he'd invested too much time to simply get up and walk away now, but the clatter of the woman's antique typewriter was beginning to hammer his calm.

"I thought everything was informal in here," he called, if only for the sake of saying something.

The clatter died – nice – and the woman looked up from the machine. Possibly, she gave him a sympathetic look. It was difficult to tell across the distance, but he couldn't miss her shrug. She picked up a device from her desk and glanced at it. It was the first piece of overtly modern tech he'd seen here.

"I'm sorry, sir, Mr O'Grady's meeting over ran," she

yelled, "but he's on his way now. I'm sure you won't be detained much longer."

"I can't wait," Mills muttered, settling back into the chair. He winced when the clatter resumed, the sound amplified by the resonant space. Still, the place was fascinating in its own way, enough to have captivated his attention this long, despite the receptionist's mechanical contraption.

Down on the left-hand side of the office, a huge machine ran the length of the wall. The monotony of its steel grey façade was broken by arrays of switches, dials, flashing lights and blank cathode ray displays; a real archaic piece of work. At intervals along the adjacent wall, he watched magnetic tape drives whir through their motions; museum pieces that took him back to college lectures on the history of information technology.

More modern, but no less obsolete, seven servers lined the wall to the right; monolithic sentinels in air-conditioned caskets, they dated from the last years of the 20th Century through to sometime in the early 2040s, if he was any judge. Mills let his eyes linger appreciatively on the old tech. As for those desks, they weren't all empty. Some were decked out with typewriters and blocky old phones. Others had desktop computers with bulky CRT monitors; a few of the desks appeared to be just part of the housing for ancient machines. There was no order to the equipment – and he couldn't even guess at the purpose of some of it – but he was pretty sure none was less than 35 or 40 years old, and most of it must be twice that. He had to concede, it was quite something; he had to suppress an urge to get up and go tinker.

A bell sounded from the lift and broke his reverie. The doors slid open and a man strode out. The newcomer, garishly dressed in a Hawaiian shirt, held a tennis racket in the crook of one arm. Sports shoes squeaked hideously on the floor tiles. The man stopped where Mills sat.

"So, you'd be Mr Mills?" he asked with a frown. Mills opened his mouth to respond, but before he could utter even a syllable, the man added: "Never mind. Wait here, I'll be with you in a minute."

The man strode towards reception and paused to utter a few unheard words to the woman. He disappeared through the far door and the waiting resumed. Mills closed his mouth, unsure whether to be perturbed by the man's brusque manner, or reassured that there were still some aspects of normality at work in this looking-glass world.

Back to the waiting, this time Mills didn't resent the slow minutes; time to review what he knew about the company and get his pitch straight. A niche outfit, originally, ArcheaoLogik had grown by becoming an essential part of the tech world's eco-system, exploiting waves of obsolescence. This is where he came in; at least, that's how he figured it.

The company was an Icelandic trans-national, based in Reykjavik, but with regional bases located throughout

Europe and the United States. Best of all, according to its entry in the Directory it was practically local, with a base in New Canary Wharf.

Over the years, the company had diversified into all kinds of complex data processing; its bespoke hardware platforms and algorithms tamed the patterns hidden in those large datasets, coaxing out the secrets and revelations valuable to its clients.

Way beyond his abilities, Mills knew, but it was all rooted in the company's founding purpose. Given his unofficial sideline in restoring old equipment, he figured he had his way in as a technician; he didn't care how lowly, if it allowed him to slip the JobMart's dreary routine.

Data recovery was a bland way to put it; he much preferred resurrection. Big business, government agencies, academic institutions, archives – even private individuals – they all turned to ArcheaoLogik to free the secrets of the past.

"I can do that," Mills had announced, when he read it; sure enough he could. The moment was almost a revelation; now all he had to do was make his case. Easy, right? Suddenly, he wasn't so sure. Then the receptionist broke into his thoughts, before the doubts could take too strong a hold.

"Mr O'Grady will see you now," she called.

Mills took a deep breath and stood. He winced at the stiffness in his legs as he began the long walk across the office. When he reached the woman she looked up with a smile and reached for an old-fashioned intercom.

"Who shall I say is calling, sir?"

"David Mills." As if she didn't already know.

"David Mills to see you, Mr O'Grady."

The reply grated through the loudspeaker, dislodging a cloud of dust from the grill. "Got it. Better send him through."

"This way, Mr Mills," she said, ushering him towards the door behind the reception desk. Mills felt his gut twist. Ready or not, this was it.

O'GRADY sat at a desk, his face rendered pallid by the unhealthy glow of a monitor. Gone was the Hawaiian shirt, replaced by the dour austerity of an executive uniform. He gazed fixedly at his screen, as if unaware of Mills' presence.

Then, without looking away from his task, he beckoned to a chair situated before his desk. "Don't be a wallflower, Mr Mills," he said. "Take a seat."

Butterflies fluttered in his stomach as he stepped towards the proffered chair and sat down; his mouth went dry.

O'Grady paid him no further heed. The man was intent on his screen. Scrolling words reflected on his spectacles. The fingers of his right hand traced intricate yet random shapes on his desk. The reflection from his lenses scrolled and flashed in reaction to those dancing digits. Mills tried not to fidget while he waited for his host to finish, but it was easier said than done.

"You're a tenacious *sonofabitch*, Mr Mills, I'll give you that," O'Grady said at last, breaking the oppressive silence. "Our little museum out there puts a lot of people off. The long wait sends most of the diehards on their way sooner or later, and just don't talk to me about Kayleigh's typing machine. Did she remember to put some paper in it this time? Never mind. All I can say is you must have the patience of a saint. Guess we'll have to take a fresh look at our design."

Mills gaped; he genuinely didn't know what to say. The words stuttered out of their own accord: "I... don't understand..."

"Of course you don't." An emotionless smile briefly curled O'Grady's lips. "But since you're here, I figured what the hell, let's give you a little face time. You know, you're really quite fascinating, in your own way, compared to the usual run of high-flying creatives I come across."

"Oh? That's... gratifying." Maybe.

O'Grady's eyes were masked by the glow reflected in his lenses, but Mills felt the heat of his stare all the same; unwavering, unnerving. As O'Grady spoke, his face barely moved at all. Even his voice was nondescript: a kind of aggregate American accent, yet well oiled and smooth on the ears. Like the man himself, it gave away little and left Mills struggling to read the situation. There was a game at play here, he realised, and he didn't know the rules; he wasn't even sure he was really a player.

"I've been scanning your dossier and it's a blast of gritty realism after all those motivated high achievers that come my way; they just blur into the same dependable set of cliché traits, you know?" O'Grady added. "But, let's talk about you: I see you've expressed an interest in working with legacy tech. Want to be a technician in one of our recovery facilities. Hate to say it, but it's a no show, I'm afraid."

"What?" The casual dismissal caught Mills by surprise. He forgot himself and leaned forward. "Why not? I've got the qualifications and the experience."

"Only overseeing industrial systems, Mr Mills. There is a slight difference, you know."

"Look, I did more than oversee that bloody thing. I did plenty of on-site maintenance. In fact, I probably knew it as well as the engineers did. I feel I've got what it takes. Sure, it was a while ago, but I can quickly plug any gaps in what I can do. I'm a great tinkerer."

O'Grady sighed and tapped at his desk. His glasses flashed again as his screen brought up a fresh display. "Ten years ago, I would have agreed. Even five. Yeah, back then you might have made the transition. I'm afraid it's just bad luck. Things have moved on since then, even when it comes to cracking open old systems and exhuming data. Sorry –"

"Look, I've fixed up plenty of old machines in my spare time, cracked redundant drives. I've even hacked and patched old operating systems so data can be translated into something newer. I can do this. Just one chance. That's all I ask." He hated begging, but the bastards made it impossible not to.

"There's a world of difference between obsolete consumer systems and the kind of high-end data recovery we specialise in at ArcheaoLogik. Do you really think you can do better than an AI? Come on, Mr Mills, I admire your pluck, but let's be realistic."

"The difference is scale, the principle's pretty much the same."

"I'll defer to you on that one, Mr Mills; me, I'm just an administrator. But there's nothing I can do. Seeing you, even to let you down, was a courtesy, that's all."

"Let me try. Let me show you what I can do. This is artificial reality, right? So set me a simulated task and I'll prove my worth. What have you got to lose?"

A smile flitted across O'Grady's lips. This time it didn't seem entirely devoid of feeling, a little regret perhaps. "I'm sorry, Mr Mills, but we won't be doing that. I don't want to waste your time any more than necessary. You see... Look, I'll be frank with you. We only maintain a presence here in JobNet because it offers considerable tax concessions for us to do so.

"Our company policy is quite specific: we recruit from the ranks of the unemployed only in exceptional circumstances. You're interesting, sure, but not exceptional. Sorry. It's all in the Directory, if you care to read it. Admittedly, it's not as prominent as we'd like; our hosts might take a rather dim view if we flaunted it too overtly. Setting that aside, there are... *less savoury...* aspects of your record to consider. The history that makes you interesting also makes you damaged goods, if I can put it that way. I'd be surprised if anyone at this recruitment centre offered you even a second glance. You're much too tainted by your past."

"Such as?"

"Don't be coy, Mr Mills. You know perfectly well." He sighed. "Okay then, we'll play it your way. Let's take a look at you..."

O'Grady turned back to the screen, his fingers moved over the desk; his glasses flashed data. "So... David Samuel Mills... only son of Emily and Kieran Mills. Ah, both deceased. My condolences..."

"Yeah, *thanks.*"

"...Well, you were a late arrival; pushing the biological clock there, weren't they? Busy career professionals, I know how it is. Okay, so both teachers. Your mother was from Wolverhampton, your father from Selby in North Yorkshire; they moved to New Ebbsfleet, England, in 2032 in response to the development corporation's habitation drive. They met at the Ebbings Grove Academy, where they'd both secured positions. So far, so very ordinary. Ouch! And there's your first black mark right there... seems Emily was a minor trade union official."

"So, it was legal." Mills shifted in his seat. What the hell did his parents have to do with any of this?

"Sure it was, at the time. But as everyone knows, unions are an unhealthy influence on employees. Bad for morale, undermines economic well-being. More to the point, it would appear from police reports of the time that your mother was suspected of continued trade union involvement after they were liquidated under the provisions of your government's Enterprise & Financial Security Act 2036. Nothing the authorities could pin down, but it casts a shadow –"

"What am I supposed to say about any of that? I wasn't even born then!"

"No, I sympathise." O'Grady tapped the desk again. "Seems you had a good influence, at least. After you popped up on the scene, it appears she settled down to being a respectable citizen. Your dad, too; seems he'd been quite the campaigner in his day: anti-war protests, some environmental stuff, civil liberties, resistance to the government of the day's drive to modernise your country's healthcare systems, the usual run of concerns back in those days, I guess."

"So what? Seriously, what the hell have my parents got to do with anything? It's not something they ever really talked about. That's all ancient history! You probably know more about it than I do." Mills was aware he was slipping out of 'interview' mode, but anger was beginning to bubble. This was bullshit.

"Easy, Mr Mills, you asked for this, remember?" O'Grady raised his hands in a placating gesture, then turned back to the screen. "I get it, those were difficult times. Tail-end of the Turmoil and all. It was difficult. Hard for the authorities to know the extremists from the concerned citizens caught in the mess. Your folks were the latter, obviously, no arrest record, clean employment history; just small fish struggling in the deluge of the times, but for better or worse, it doesn't cast a good light on your background. And that, finally, brings me to you."

Mills squirmed. "Go on."

"Your involvement with certain radical unemployed rights movements, for instance; smacks of political unreliability. But it's that little matter of your criminal record for hacking into a corporate mainframe and infecting it with a virus that really caught my eye. Now, if you'd been successful I might have had a use for you, but then we wouldn't be having this conversation would we? I'd be none the wiser. As it is, Mr Mills, it undermines my confidence in your reliability. Frankly, nothing personal, I couldn't afford to trust you."

O'Grady took his glasses off and placed them on the desk. Mills saw the data was still reflected in the lenses; he realised, then, they were the screen. He stared at them awhile, his mind a mess. When he looked up to meet the man's gaze, he caught a glimpse of a little sympathy there. But that was no use to him.

"I'm sorry, Mr Mills," O'Grady added. "That can't have been easy."

"No." He shrugged, resigned. "How did you know all that? It's not on my JobMart profile."

"You know what we do here, Mr Mills: there's more to

data acquisition than cracking old harddrives. We have our sources and we know how to use them."

"So that's it then?"

"I'm afraid so. My advice to you is to forget the tech world; you've had its day, time to move on. But whatever line of work you decide to pursue, I wish you all the best for the future."

"Sure." He forced a smile as he stood up to leave, but it was only later – when he was out of sight and out of mind – that he felt bad about refusing to shake O'Grady's hand. That sort of thing got around, but by the sounds of things, it was the least of his character stains. Well, he wasn't going to let the man put him off; he was supposed to be a tenacious *sonofabitch*, after all.

SO it went on. Over the next five days, he'd kept returning to the Nameless City, as he called it, but by now Mills was forced to admit – the tenacity was wearing thin.

The knock-backs kept coming; the same old sob story he'd found in real-world job hunting. Nothing matched his skills and experience, or else he lacked the aptitude. More often than not, he was simply obsolete: a relic of the pre-AI age. Well, O'Grady *had* tried to warn him.

So much for the clean slate and fresh start he'd been promised. Just the one dumb mistake, that's all it took.

The memories broke through the scabs picked thin by O'Grady's monologue. Mills put his hands over his face as the emotion surged.

IN the next room, his mother screamed again. The sudden eruption ripped him out of slumber and he sat bolt upright in bed, blinking helpless in the dark.

Between the shrill wails, the garbled residue of speech, calling to the ghosts of the past; his dad's voice was a low murmur as he tried to soothe her back to sleep. Sooner or later, he'd calm her down; he always did – he was the only one who *could*—but the strain of it was taking its toll.

Mills threw back his bedclothes and staggered to his feet, limbs heavy with the weight of sleep. He felt his way to the door and stepped out onto the landing. A gentle tap on his parents' bedroom door. "Everything all right, Dad? Need me to do anything?"

"No, Davey, your Mum'll be all right. Bit of a nightmare, that's all. Go back to bed, son, try to sleep. You need it; got a big day ahead of you tomorrow."

Yeah, a big day: first job interview in ages, but his mind wasn't on it, and not just because of broken sleep. "So do you, Dad," he said quietly, "so do you."

He stood there in the darkness on the landing, brooding, staring at the door, listening to his mother's distress, his father's futile solace. He pictured her as she often was during these episodes, staring in terror at things only she could see. The stroke had destroyed the woman he called 'Mum', plunged what was left of her into some kind of hell, and he could do nothing to bring her back.

Still, he did what he could; the lifting, carrying his mother to the bathroom, helping to feed, wash and dress her, give his dad a little respite. But when she was like this, he felt helpless, *useless*. The fatigue of it all weighed heavy on his shoulders. An ache in the chest that never quite eased; a heart clogged by grief held in limbo.

Reluctantly, he went back to his room and sat on his bed. In frustration, he reached for his tablet and powered it up. He found himself staring again at the letter that revealed they were well and truly on their own.

The company had written to his mother – to a woman that couldn't speak, let alone access her mail account – to politely inform her there were insufficient funds in her policy to cover the costs of ongoing care and support. The charities it suggested she turn to for help were already too overstretched to offer much more than advice; Mills knew, he'd already begged their assistance to no avail.

So he stared at the screen, stared as if he could somehow will the letter to change the mind of its faceless author, and his mother kept screaming in the next room.

Then his eyes snatched a word out of the small print at the foot of a letter, something previously overlooked. Janus. It meant something: a tickle of the familiar in the back of his mind. Parent to the insurance company, it was a spider at the heart of a web that had already entangled his life in misfortune. He logged online for a quick search; the connection made, suspicion confirmed.

He gripped the tablet tight and bit down hard on his anger. A word squeezed out all the same: "Bastards!"

THE burst of recollection bled away. Mills uncovered his face and realised his eyes were wet; he rubbed them dry. It was no good dwelling on the past, he couldn't change any of it; he had to focus on today.

Maybe it was time for him to change tack. The Nameless City was getting him nowhere, but there were plenty more of these citadels to explore. The sense of futility was his biggest hurdle. He'd be lost without Christine. She kept him sane, distracted him when the brooding darkness threatened to take hold; she lightened his mood and gave him something to look forward to.

She was pretty much a constant here in AR; he saw her every day. Hard to say when their time together ceased to be entirely professional. He'd never known anybody so easily companionable as Christine. She was easy to like, but he couldn't say she was easy to know, not really.

Landing a job, that's what ought to be on his mind, he knew. But Christine's carefree, undemanding way made him feel free. And the infectious happiness in her laughter... Worries evaporated in her presence, sooner or later, and he had a lot of those.

There was one worry Christine's joyfulness could not erase, though: another week and he would have to leave JobNet. He didn't want to stay in this fantasy land, but with Christine's smiling face in his mind's eye, he wasn't ready to return to reality either.

CHAPTER 8:
Where is the Odd Man Out?

FAO: Carswell, E. Chief Executive Chairman, UK Benefits & Welfare

Staff Progress Committee minutes

AGENDA:

1. Physical displacement: Mills, D. S. DF874920S, Client no.: U100-83-5. Proposed: MacAllister, J.
2. Staff reorganisation, progress. Proposed: McBride, L.
3. AR-environmental anomalies and errors. Proposed: Weaver, J.
4. Any other business.

First item of agenda:
1. Physical Displacement; Mills, D. S. DF874920S, Client no.: U100-83-5

MacAllister: There's no plainer way to say this. We've lost Mills.

Harris: What do you mean we've lost him? I saw him this morning.

MacAllister: Yes. We have him here, but outside he's gone missing. Somehow our external colleagues have managed to lose his physical form. Incompetent, really, but what else can I say? He's gone.

Harris: Why weren't we informed of this when he first arrived? Especially me. It's my responsibility to keep track of things like this to protect the *** system.

Weaver: I'd like to know why you didn't tell us as well. I mean, you know what can happen in cases like this. What if the man died?

MacAllister: Yes. I'm sorry. I was instructed to keep it to myself. It was hoped he'd be tracked down by now.

Weaver: Why haven't they traced his link?

MacAllister: They've tried. Believe me. I've been in constant touch with Carswell on the matter. Apparently Mills' interface connection is particularly complex. They guess it involves at least two separate satellite channels. They have a trace-worm trying to locate his link but so far it's drawn a blank.

Weaver: Great! So what have we got here? Some kind of hacker?

McBride: No. His entry is quite legitimate. There were problems at his interface centre so he was taken to hospital. They supposedly severed his connection there. We still don't quite know what's going on. You know what the high-ups are like – it's always 'need to know' with them.

MacAllister: Sadly so. If they've found anything, they haven't informed me yet. However, I will keep you all informed of any updates.

Harris: Hang on a minute. The man's gone missing, right? Nothing to indicate he's dead, is there? So he's holed up somewhere. Someone's got to be keeping him alive. And on top of that, he's got a complex uplink that even a trace-worm can't crack. What the *** is going on?

Lister: [interrupting] I don't suppose anybody's considered whether Mills is an inspector?

Weaver: What do you mean?

Lister: Maybe them outside are checking up on

us? Maybe Mills is a plant, checking our performance. [Pause.] It's just a thought.

Harris: If that were true then they wouldn't have made him out of the ordinary. You don't send in a covert inspector then get him noticed by concocting a situation like this.

McBride: You should know, Harris. Still keeping tabs on us?

Harris: I don't know what you mean. I work for the Agency, same as you.

McBride: Right, but which one?

MacAllister: That's enough. We're discussing Mills' case. Has anyone come across anything that might help us sort this out? Think. Anything at all.

McBride: He just looks for work like everyone else, though he's not doing very well. Another failure that probably shouldn't have been let in.

Harris: Nothing springs to mind.

MacAllister: That's what I thought. Well, all I can say is keep an eye on him, see if you can find anything. But whatever you do, don't let on to Mills. That comes straight from the top. The man is not to know.

Second item of agenda.

2. Staff reorganisation.

McBride: Okay, item two. You should all have read about the plans to extend –

Harris: [interrupts] If you don't mind, I'd like to talk about the bugs in this *** system.

MacAllister: Can't it wait?

Harris: I'd like to discuss it right now, actually. I mean, I'm still in pain from that *** butterfly.

MacAllister: Any objections?

[No objections. Move to item three.]

3. AR-Environmental anomalies and errors.

Weaver: What's this about a butterfly?

Harris: Great. There's a hazardous insect-sim fluttering around and our system manager doesn't even know about it.

Weaver: Harris, I can't keep track of everything. Unless you keep me informed, there's not a lot I can do. Have there been reports of others?

MacAllister: Nothing official. I've heard one or two people saying they'd seen one, but I thought nothing of it.

Harris: You would if you'd squashed one of the things. It hurts like ***. My hand's still marked and I can't get this stain off. Worse, it's started itching.

Weaver: That's curious. I've never heard of a bug doing that before; probably a mutation in the sim-code. I'll run a search and replace program, which should sort it out. In the meantime if anyone sees another of these things then don't touch it.

MacAllister: You'd better report it to the outside. They'll need to be informed.

Weaver: Okay.

McBride: While we're on the subject, what's the situation with the run-time errors at the moment?

Harris: Why? What's wrong?

Weaver: Don't panic, Harris. There's just a little distortion around sector 597. That's a result of 598 being offline for maintenance. Nothing to worry about, just the world-sim trying to fill the hole in the reality-matrix.

MacAllister: Anything else, or can we move on now?

Harris: What about my hand? It *** hurts.

Weaver: Leave it for a few days. It should pass on its own, or when we've traced and eradicated these butterflies. If not, come and see me. If it persists, you might have to go offline for a while.

Item two of the agenda.
2. Staff reorganisation.

McBride: Okay, as I was saying earlier, you should have read the report about the extension of JobNet. That's going to involve some major staff reorganisation and expansion. I'm afraid the decision's already been made, but you've got the chance to air your views now.

Harris: Well, I think it's bloody ridiculous. They haven't thought it through properly. It'll endanger the whole operation.

MacAllister: No it won't, Harris. In fact, it makes sound economic sense. The government and the company will be able to attract a lot of new customers.

Harris: Yes, sure. So what? The point is we're going to be inundated with worthless *** scum. There's already too many in here. It's going to end up like it is outside: impossible to find the ones of any worth. The whole point is we're supposed to weed out the scum and get the rest back into useful roles.

Lister: Harris, we all know your views. What's wrong with helping as many people as we can? Anyway, we can't ignore the pressure to expand forever.

CARSWELL placed the tablet onto his desk and leaned back in his chair, bored by the report and still left with no clues.

Behind him, the setting sun glinted off the sluggish water of the Thames, the glare reduced slightly by the photosensitive windows of his air-conditioned office. A pleasure barge glided over the river, disappearing briefly as it passed beneath the traffic-snarled Westminster Bridge. A police gunship prowled the horizon, a shadow against the bright reds and yellows of the sky. Its glue-spitting riot guns were faintly visible beneath the wasp-like body.

Carswell ignored the view, just as he had for years; too familiar now to be anything more than a natural wallpaper. Even the Palace of Westminster, the home of his theoretical masters, barely registered anymore.

Still, better the politicians keep their games behind those walls and leave the running of the country to those who knew how. If only he hadn't been stuck in this backwater of a department, a glorified cattle-hand against the jobless hordes. Of course, he had done well, built a successful commercial enterprise out of a rump government department. That had raised a few eyebrows at the time. Now everyone was at it…

Mills. How could the man disappear from the face of the Earth? A *cockroach* couldn't get in undetected. Satellites tracked the movements of individual cars; CCTV was a pervasive and ever-present sentinel. AI cohorts crunched the staggering quantities of data the surveillance net generated, sifting the patterns, making connections, and that was just for ordinary members of the public.

A man like Mills shouldn't have been able to avoid detection. His Nexus card should be tracing him. Any bus or taxi journey would have been centrally logged; any visit to a prospective employer would likewise have been recorded. Anything he bought would have turned up on the Agency's computers. If Mills was moving around undetected, he had to be walking everywhere – and invisible. And leaving his card behind, naturally, if he didn't want the smart-chip transmitting to the net. Not a peep. The man had done the impossible – he had vanished from the social radar.

Carswell reached forward and turned to face his workstation. He opened a window on the screen.

"SysOps, Conway here. What can I do for you, boss?" The minicam built into the monitor case cycled its lens for better focus as Carswell shifted position.

"How's it going with that trace-worm?" he asked, gently tapping with his index finger to enlarge the window.

The man on the screen pushed a pair of thin-framed

spectacles further up the bridge of his nose and looked down to tap at his keyboard. When he looked up once more he raised his eyebrows apologetically.

"Not very well. It's having real problems locating this guy. The trace has turned up at least five different interface routes so far and each one is damn complex. They're all being accessed on a random basis. We also reckon Mills has been moved twice since he was discharged from hospital. Don't ask me why."

"What's been done to find him so far?"

"Erm… let me see. A description has been sent to the local police and passed on to City Watch. They've turned up nothing. Field operatives have tried visiting his home, couldn't get in, had no warrant, so they left it. We've tried geo-location and signal triangulation, but that hasn't worked out. Don't ask me why. That seems to be about it. This isn't listed as a priority case."

Carswell cursed under his breath. "Well, I'm making it a priority. Hasn't it struck you as odd that we can't find him? Why didn't someone make it a priority before now?"

He flipped the window to the right of the screen and pulled up another next to it that displayed lines of text and digitised mugshots. The man in the video shrugged.

"I'll pass on a priority code to all the relevant departments."

"Yes, do that," Carswell replied. "And while you're at it, I want all the down-and-out hostels checked, the clinics, even illicit AR dens. Try his home again. And I don't care if they have to break the door down – warrant or no warrant. What else? Yes, get someone round to see the doctor who supposedly severed his link. Something smells there if you ask me –"

"You mean that stuff about the drugs?"

"No. We put that out. Protect our reputation. We persuaded the doctor, whatever his name is, to cooperate," Carswell's eyes drifted to the static display box. "Now, the people who handled his link, Sutcliffe and Sutton. Has anyone spoken to them?"

"No, they filed their report; it wasn't considered necessary to follow up."

"Well, get somebody round to see them. This mess might be down to sloppy work on their part. There's something about the video footage appended to the report that doesn't fit. Besides, they've been under observation for having a fling, which is against company policy. If I think of anything else I'll be certain to let you know."

"Okay, I'll get on it. There's nothing wrong, is there? I mean, it's not a serious situation? We could always terminate his link right here."

"No," Carswell replied and then paused, considering the option. It'd certainly get rid of the problem once and for all. But then Carswell would never know what had happened, and he liked to feel he knew what was going on within his personal fief. "No," he repeated, "no, let's leave that option for later. This is just a personnel error. A damn weird one, but that's all. We'll see if we can find the man, best to be certain. Besides, if we unilaterally terminate his connection it'll take forever to erase the personality echoes. We'll consider it later."

"Right." Conway turned away from the camera as though to leave. Carswell tensed his finger, ready to cut the video link, but stopped himself.

"One more thing," he started, "what's the status on bugs and run-time errors?"

"Bugs? No more than usual. Why?"

"The latest minutes report from the inside said something about black butterflies. They're not on the features manifest."

"Oh, them. Yes, we had something on that from Weaver. We ran a trace and couldn't find anything. I wouldn't worry about it, everything's running just fine."

Fingers tapped the desk while Carswell pondered. At last he shrugged. "Keep checking, just in case. Anyway, I'll let you get on with things. I'll be in contact later."

A final click severed the link. The video window collapsed to reveal the desktop screen. With a sigh, Carswell sat back in his chair; the leather squeaked with the chafe of his expensive suit.

The whole scenario gave him goosebumps. The questions were there, reams of them. Time to stop pussyfooting around. While they wasted time looking for Mills out here, they knew precisely where he was in virtuality. Time to see what he knew.

CHAPTER 9:
Passion Kills the Woes

THE stone completed its bouncing trajectory with a loud plop. Mills stood a few paces out from the riverbank, where cool water bathed his feet. The sun felt warm on his exposed back as he stooped to pick up another pebble; his mood was no reflection of the tranquil scene.

A flick of the wrist and another pebble skimmed across the surface before following its predecessor to the bottom. The stream tried to reclaim its soft babble, but Mills kept the splashes going with a steady onslaught of rocks.

"It's all a load of shit," he cried as another stone left his hand. "Artificial job hunting. Bollocks!"

Not a word from Christine, only a brief glance as a smile stretched her lips. She closed her eyes and stretched out on the grass, apparently content to let him vent.

"I never asked for this," he snarled. "They take away

our self-respect and any dignity we might have had, then the bastards turn around and blame *us*! Throw us away and it's *our* fault. Bastards!

"But of course, those smart-suited, empty-headed zombies are never to blame for anything. No, no – they're fucking perfect. And somehow that gives them the right to treat us like animals. Tag us. Lock us up. Beat us. Punish us for being surplus to requirement. Watch every move we make; make us criminals. It makes me sick."

Another stone left his hand. Rather than bounce across the water it went straight under with an explosion of spray. He looked back at Christine with a scowl, but felt some of the tension in his face ease off. The girl sat up, crossed her legs and began to pluck daisies from the grass. If she had heard anything he'd said, she certainly didn't show it.

Better a deaf companion than none at all. Despite his bombardment of anger, he felt slightly better knowing he wasn't alone.

"And now they dump me in this place," he went on. "No more hope of getting a job here than there is outside. It's just a front: nothing more than pretty pictures and bullshit."

At last, he provoked a reaction from Christine. "You can't say that. You can do anything you want in here," she said, eyes filled with concern rather than annoyance. Did nothing shake her belief in the system? "Anything's possible. JobNet will do whatever it can to help you. All you have to do is let it. Don't give up."

He looked at the girl, shook his head at the sincere gleam of faith contained within her eyes. With a sigh, he slumped down on the bank, his feet dangling in the cool water. Christine began to weave herself an elaborate daisy chain.

"I had a job once," he began, no longer concerned if Christine listened or not. "Was real good at it. Then some bastard just pulled the plug. I suppose that was my lazy, useless, ignorant fault too."

The stream eddied and swirled around his ankles. He watched the water, lost in thoughts that similarly whirled in endless spirals, circling into nothing. Somewhere beyond and apart from him, Christine began to sing to herself.

"I guess society needs its demons," he muttered under his breath.

Now his mind began to wind down. The tornado of frustration passed into a false calm. He still fell ill at ease with himself, but that was a long-standing condition now. Easily lived with. A mutual agreement long since negotiated and settled. If only the hollowness that it brought could be accommodated.

Christine settled down on the grass beside him. He watched her golden hair fall across her shoulder and felt his loneliness stir.

"You could be happy, you know," she said at last. "If only you'd let go."

"What do you mean?"

"I used to be so unhappy. Until I came here. You've got to let go of the past. If you can be happy in the present, the future will take care of itself."

"How?"

She reached out and tenderly stroked his chest. Then she smiled. An electric thrill fizzled through his body.

"Stop fighting yourself. That's how. You'll never win. You can't beat yourself, so just forget everything. Let JobNet take care of you."

"It's only a simulation," he said.

"No. It's everything. And everyone. We can really live here. We can be whoever we want. Whatever we want. Nothing's real so nothing matters. Just living. Just enjoying ourselves."

"It's just an illusion."

"So is life."

She looked so serious. Mills had never seen her like this before. Where was that carefree innocent who had welcomed him into this strange world; who never had a thought that wasn't wired directly to her mouth? Where was that pleasant, disarming personality that could incinerate negativity with a single radiant smile?

But she was still there. Suddenly she put her arms around his shoulders and sat astride him. Surprised, he collapsed under her weight and she fell with him. He was aware of her breasts touching his chest, the weight of her body on his lap, her breath on his face.

"Be happy – please. For me," she said.

He looked into her eyes. Saw a hint of nervousness in her pupils. In the edge of his vision, he noticed the soft curves of her lips, parted slightly, the contours of her face, the delicate definition of her nose.

The weight on his loins increased. A heat rose through his body. His hands came up, took hold of her waist. Her face lowered, lips brushing against his, and a surge of panic danced down his nerves.

He opened his mouth to say something. He didn't know what. Probably something corny. Christine closed his mouth with hers, suppressed speech with a far more pleasurable mode of communication. Mills forget the past and embraced the moment.

CHAPTER 10:
Visiting Hours are Over

KANE knew appearances could be deceptive. Twenty years with the Metropolitan Police, pacifying some of the capital's worst slum zones, had taught him never to take anything for granted.

Life was a lot simpler now he was a private contractor for UK Benefits & Welfare, but the instincts never quite faded; the back of his neck prickled as he felt the glare of hidden eyes. The place wasn't as deserted as it appeared; they never were.

Kane brought up the neighbourhood profile on his phone, tapped and skimmed through the information to refresh his memory. An amber criminality rating. The inhabitants were a mixed bag of low-income workers, retirees and near-as-dammit zeros like their man Mills.

Any number of them could be twitching curtains right now, keeping an eye on the newcomers in their fancy

SUV, many with plenty of reasons to fear strangers. Still, they weren't his problem today. He closed the car door and leaned against the vehicle, looking around and studying the estate, gaining a feel for the place.

A quiet street in a quiet neighbourhood, largely forgotten by time; he recognised the type. Back in his uniformed days, policing a place like this would have been deemed a cushy number. A lucky break, or a favour called. There'd been too few of those.

His colleague, Jones, slammed the driver's door closed and triggered the security systems. The car beeped. The windows darkened, masking the interior from prying eyes. "What a shit hole," he said, looking around.

"Yeah," Kane replied, "just waiting for some property developer to hit flush."

The estate had seen better days, that was for sure. Weather-worn houses, squat blocks of flats; designs reflecting several decades of architectural fashion. Some of the cladding panels retained a semblance of the original bright colours, faded beneath years of grime. If the neighbourhood wasn't yet a slum, it was hanging on for dear life.

"Check it out, Jones," he added. "This place is a real living fossil – a social housing estate. Not many left. Most of the providers went upmarket decades ago and left these poor slobs to the slums."

"Yeah? I can see why. What's it matter to us, anyway?"

Kane shook his head in mock dismay. "You've no

curiosity," he said, waggling his phone. "Got to do your homework in this game, get a sense of what you're dealing with. Even the grunt jobs like this. Come on, then, my young padawan, let's get this done."

"Your *what?*" Jones frowned.

"Forget it." Kane chuckled. The reference was all wrong, anyway; in that black suit, white shirt and narrow tie his assistant looked like a reject from another vintage movie – Reservoir Dogs, that was the one – but he decided not to share the observation. Another time, maybe. "Let's go to work."

They moved on up the street, Jones falling in beside him, their eyes casually scanning the locality. Movement caught Kane's attention as they passed a junction on the far side of the street. Up the road a work crew was clearing litter and cutting shrubbery; zeros in orange high-vis 'community payback' vests. A trustee in red wasn't making any friends as he harangued the men and women under his command.

"D'you think he's got the sense to watch his back?" Jones muttered.

Kane grunted and switched his gaze back to the job in hand. A cluster of small houses situated around a communal footpath and overgrown lawn were coming up ahead, solar panels on the roofs, institutional doors and tiny windows.

"This is it," he said, noting the number of the property nearest to them. "You got the override fob?"

"Right here," Jones fumbled in his pocket and brought out the device. "We don't have a warrant, though. When I checked in, dispatch said it wasn't through yet."

"We don't need a warrant, Jones. For this assignment, we're Agency. JobMart as good as owns this guy."

"Cool." Jones nodded then approached the house to peer in through the ground floor window. "So who owns this place, anyway?"

"Some charity. A housing association. I told you, this place is a fossil. Our man took over the tenancy about four years ago after his folks died."

"You're shitting me. He inherited the house? The guy's a fucking zero!"

"No, just the tenancy. Straight up, Jones. Guess it was easier on the admin to let him stay on. Throw me the fob. You see anything through the window?"

"Can't make anything out," Jones said, throwing the fob over. Kane snatched it out of the air and approached the door. His assistant turned back to the window and pressed his face to the glass, hands raised to the side of his head to mask the light. Muttering, he said: "Inheriting a house, it's fucking outrageous."

Kane grinned – Jones was going to simmer all day now. The security system beeped as he pressed the fob to the sensor plate; he tapped in his ident-code. A buzzy synth-voice cleared them for entry. The door clicked ajar; Kane pushed it open and hung back, peering into the hallway's gloom. Stairs, cluttered with discarded shoes and piles of tatty books, ascended to the upper floor, a door opened into the living room.

"What if our man's holed up inside?" Jones asked, coming up beside him.

"Then Carswell's little problem is solved and we'll need another assignment. Don't worry, Jones, this guy won't be a problem hooked up to an AR rig; we'll just call in a cleanup crew and be done. Come on, let's see what he's hiding."

JONES stepped over the threshold and followed Kane into the living room, nervous but already becoming bored by a routine job.

A quick scan of the pokey room; there wasn't much to see. Faded photographs of nondescript family life watched them from the walls. An old TV bolted to the wall, a clock, and a tablet with a cracked screen were gathering dust on a shelf below the flatscreen. Old newspapers were piled in corners. Folders and piles of papers were scattered nearby. The detritus of a decade's fruitless job hunting, he guessed.

A computer rested on a dining table by the window, old enough to be worth something to a collector, probably. The machine's innards were exposed beneath a layer of furred dust. The casing panel leaned against the monitor. Jones tapped idly at the keys. A small soldering iron and some electronic components rested in an ashtray on the desktop. Evidence of undeclared economic activity, if nothing else; he took a few snaps with his phone.

Kane left the room. Jones called after him: "What are we supposed to be looking for, anyway?"

"Orders just said check it out. I guess we'll know it if we find it."

Jones sighed and began to sift through the detritus of Mills' life.

A spiral-bound notebook on a coffee table caught his attention. He sat down gingerly on the shabby couch, felt a spring grind under his weight, and flicked through the pad. Addresses, mostly conventional, except for a few email addresses. A smile, genuine humour this time. He vaguely remembered the internet from nursery school – his first experience of global networking.

Mills probably used it. About all he could do. Hadn't there once been a scheme where they gave away hardware to hook the poor to the net? But that died years ago, probably before Mills was even born.

The internet survived. A ghetto overshadowed by the corralled safe spaces provided by government and branded corporate nets. Still it had its uses. A great place to speak your mind, blissfully unaware of the sophisticated algorithms and AIs that monitored people's views, tracked them down and allowed the security services to strike at random. Never enough to frighten people into silence. Freedom of speech had its uses, so Kane kept telling him. He preferred to be sensible. He kept his opinions to himself. Mostly.

"Check upstairs," Kane shouted.

With a sigh, Jones left the living room. This was a waste of time. The stairs creaked under his feet. The bathroom. Nothing of any interest here. Further along the landing, a door. Gingerly, he pushed it open. A musty smell immediately assaulted his nostrils.

The room was shrouded in gloom, curtains closed. He pulled them open, blinked in the sudden rush of light, then turned back to examine the room. A double bed dominated the floor, still made. An electronic alarm clock rested on a bedside cabinet. Dead. He tried the light switch on impulse. Nothing. He glanced up, no bulb in the fitting.

The room felt like a tomb. An old couple stared out of a framed photograph atop a chest of drawers. Another photograph, they looked younger in this one, but still no spring chickens; happy features and eyes full of hope gazed out of the image. The woman held a baby that gazed stupidly at the camera – the guy they were after, obviously.

"Anything?" Kane came in, looked quickly round the room and moved to the chest of drawers. Without a word he ripped out the drawers one by one and dumped the contents onto the bed, the floor, everywhere.

Clothes, old photographs, a stack of letters that stank of stagnant perfume and tied together by a faded red ribbon, documents, cosmetics and assorted junk: Kane rooted through it all and looked up in contempt.

"There's nothing," Jones said. A photograph of Mills' mother, younger still, smiled at him from a beach, his eyes lingered appreciatively on the old-fashioned swimwear that would have gotten her arrested these days. Kane moved to the wardrobe and ripped out the contents.

"Nothing in the kitchen either. Just a cupboard full of bean tins and a fridge full of veg. Milk's gone off and the bread's mouldy. He'd better hope the shops are still open when he gets home!"

"Why the Hell are we wasting our time here?"

"Orders," Kane replied, scrunching up flimsy black dress and throwing it aside. "Put the hours in, we get paid, whatever. Just like when I was with the Met."

Jones shrugged and went to check the next room. Nothing much in it: an unmade bed littered with unwashed clothes, wardrobe, drawers, a few old books on the windowsill. It was a room to sleep in with precious little personality stamped upon it. He got to work ransacking the drawers.

Nothing, just clothes, an out-of-date passport, old combs, a stiff leather wallet, a packet of male contraception long past their use-by date. Jones grunted his disgust and walked over to the wardrobe. Inside were shirts, a few jackets that were dated in style, old boots at the bottom. He flicked through them, checking pockets and linings for anything hidden. Then he moved to examine the stack of papers on the shelf.

Dole statements, official documents from the benefits company: he impatiently scanned through them; found they were in no particular order. Helpful. Two letters stapled together but dated a couple of years apart: invoices for cremation costs, a repayment plan included. He flicked through more of the print outs: a letter explaining that the family's insurance plan was insufficient to continue meeting the costs of Mrs Mills' care and support. Evidently, she'd suffered a stroke. He checked the date. August 2064, nine months before her death; Jones vaguely wondered what did for the old man in the end. There was nothing in the paperwork, aside from the cremation bill.

A means document sidetracked his attention. It was nothing more than a statement for a compulsory organ valuation. Mills had been evaluated for his left kidney, a third of his right lung, skin, bone marrow and blood. Guaranteed income for about two years, depending on fluctuations in the market prices, but according to the document their man had only signed up to regular donations of blood and sperm.

Jones laughed – "Wanker!" – then he crumpled the organ valuation and threw it to the floor. This was a potted history of a life, and despite himself he found it compelling. He sorted through the rest of the pile, page after page adding to the clutter on the floor, slowly losing interest. Nothing, he cursed.

And then *something*. Right at the bottom of the pile he found a Martyrs of Jarrow newspaper, if you could call it that, and several leaflets, quite recent. He smiled. Evidence! Anarchist material that demanded rights for the unemployed.

Maybe it wasn't such a waste of time after all.

STUART pushed his way through the viscous streams of humanity, cursing inwardly at the people who failed to get out of his way. *Move you stupid old bitch!* The words exploded in his brain, never uttered aloud.

The old woman with the ridiculous perm meandered chaotically in front of him. Every time he thought he was clear, she shuffled stupidly back into his path, forcing him to walk at a geriatric pace. And all around him were the random motions of shoppers always getting in his bloody way.

Sometimes he just felt like pushing them to the ground in order to get a clear path. Honestly, people were so stupid. They looked right at you and made no effort to move. Stupid fucking sheep!

Then he caught sight of the man he was here to meet. Stuart pushed his way through the crowd and then gratefully sat down, enjoying the oasis of calm around the bench.

The man turned, rested his elbow on the backrest and thoughtfully played with his greying goatee beard. Beady eyes looked out through the round, metal-framed glasses.

"You're late," he said.

"Yeah, sorry Clute. It's these crowds."

The man put his head to one side and raised his eyebrows in a kind of facial shrug. "How are things progressing?"

"Mills is in place. Everything went along more or less smoothly. And the bastards don't suspect a thing."

The man looked thoughtful for a moment. "Nevertheless, I think it's time we had him moved again for his own protection. Not to mention our own. Never underestimate the powers that be. They're not as incompetent as some of our people think. Eventually they'll find him, unless we keep him moving."

"Okay, I'll get on it."

"Yes, do that." The old man pulled an old cloth cap out of his pocket and brushed it down, then slipped it onto his balding crown. "How's the woman? Satisfactory?"

"She'll do," Stuart replied, adopting a poker face. "Pleasurable, convenient, great body, but ultimately forgettable. And she doesn't suspect a thing either."

"Good. Try to keep it that way. She's the weak – but up to now the essential – link in the chain. By now the Agency will be monitoring the pair of you, so go careful. We still need that ridiculous humanitarian organisation she's part of. Whatever it's called."

"Dignity on the Dole," he said, cringing in embarrassment. Jane's conscience was a useful lever to obtain her co-operation.

"Well, it doesn't matter," Clute said. "Just remember what I said: tread careful from now on. And if it looks like they're on to you –"

"Don't worry, she won't feel a thing."

DATA flowed to hidden monitors as the eye watched a silent meeting. The old man and the young man conversed in silence, watched by bored, indifferent minds. Computers matched the data with the contents of giant archives, searching for identities, seeking hidden guilt.

A butterfly fluttered through the air. It alighted on the lens of the secret eye and obscured its vision with incandescent wings. The insect seemed to share the eye's curiosity as its own compound visual receptors scrutinised the conspiratorial pair.

Deep in the darkness of the hidden room, operators toggled the camera to dislodge the rogue insect. Stubbornly, it clung to its resting-place. Eventually, it took to the air and fluttered away.

The two men had gone.

THE public hospital was a shabby, concrete structure. Austere in appearance, it contrived to be cold and menacing. The doors were jammed open and inside the crowds of ill and injured waited to be processed.

Kane walked through the door and suppressed a shudder; he hated these charitable holes. The smell of disinfectant and shit made his nose wrinkle in disgust. Jones walked at his side, affecting a bored air, but he held a hand to his nose and mouth.

The security guard watched them pass. Red-faced and sweating in his blue-black body armour, he stood in the military at-ease position; hands behind his back, but within easy reach of the electric prod at his belt. The guard made no response when Jones nodded at him.

Kane pushed his way towards the reception desk, the people in front of him offering no resistance. A heavily tattooed man with blood streaming from a deep facial cut looked at him sullenly, then lowered his eyes and stepped aside. Kane allowed himself a smile of satisfaction.

"We're here to see Dr Simms," Kane said once he reached the desk. The nurse didn't even look up when she spoke.

"Have you got an appointment?" The phone rang and the nurse absent-mindedly picked up the receiver. "Hospital reception. Charity ward."

Kane smiled and casually reached out to terminate the call with a stubby forefinger. The nurse looked up sharply to see Kane's government-issue ID open before her. With a sharp intake of breath, she replaced the receiver.

"The doctor has an appointment to see me."

"Yes, Mr Kane. I'll page Dr Simms right away."

"That's Agent Kane," he said, emphasising the word so that it carried. The crowds unconsciously shuffled their feet, clearing more space around them.

The nurse checked her screen. "Dr Simms is on his way, gentlemen. If you'd care to wait over there, he'll be with you imminently."

Kane offered her a quick smile. "Thank you for your assistance, nurse. I'll be sure to make a note of it in my report. Come on, Jones."

They walked confidently away from the crowd, to the relative space of a small waiting area by a corridor that led deeper into the hospital. The visitors seated there decided to find somewhere else, but Kane remained standing. Jones was another matter. He sprawled back in a chair and stared at the crowd in reception, making more than a few of the visitors shuffle nervously.

"They haven't got a clue, have they?"

"Doesn't matter, Jones. If they believe we're Social Security or know we're JobMart, it doesn't make much difference. They know we can ruin their day, either way. Just don't let any of these fuckers catch you in a blind spot, I wouldn't trust the surveillance system in a place like this."

"Wouldn't dream of it, boss."

Five minutes later an agitated man in a flowing hospital coat approached. Kane watched him; noted the wiry hair that seemed to be electrically charged, the sharp nose between beady eyes, the bow tie incorrectly tied and an old-fashioned stethoscope that dangled round his neck. An un-businesslike eccentric, Kane wondered how anyone could take the man seriously.

"Agent Kane?" the man asked, offering his hand. Kane just looked down at the immaculate appendage and then back up to the man's strained face. "What can I do for you?" the doctor added.

"We want to see the records for one of your patients. David Samuel Mills."

"Mills... Mills? Sorry gentlemen, you'll have to remind me. I see so many patients."

A grunt from Jones as he stood up and placed his hands behind his back. He stared sceptically at the doctor. "Get a lot of Mills do you?" he asked sarcastically.

"What do you mean?"

"Well, you had to think so hard."

"Oh, I see. I'm sorry. You just can't realise how many people I have to deal with. Faces become a blur and names are forgotten. We're understaffed, as usual. And I have to fill in for a sick colleague. I can't tell you how thoroughly inconvenient the whole situation is. I have paying customers who are just not getting the service they deserve because I have to fill in for the charity wards. It's disgraceful –"

"Let me refresh your memory, doc." Kane called up the details on his phone and allowed the doctor to study the data. "You treated him for neural shock a few days ago. Came in hooked up to a remote AR-rig."

"Oh, that Mills! What can I say? We severed his link, brought him back. He discharged himself the next day. Most welfare patients do and we never know what becomes of them after that. I'm sorry, I don't think I can be of much help."

The phone again. Thrust into the doctor's face. "But you can be of more help, Doctor. We have authorisation to study all Mills' files and upload anything we think relevant. So if you'd be so good as to escort us to your records department, we can get started."

"I see. If you require access to our surveillance feeds,

I'm afraid I can't help you. You'll need to put in a request to our –"

"Not my concern, doc. Somebody else got that pleasure. They didn't find anything."

Simms shrugged. "This is a charitable facility, gentlemen, what can you expect? Funds are tight. Sadly, our trustees felt blanket coverage was not something that should come at the detriment of medical provision for these poor wretches."

"Very noble, I'm sure. Interesting what they found when they ran a search through the City Watch recordings, though."

"Oh… um… you've found something, then?"

"Yeah, nothing untoward. Just another day at the charity clinic. No sign of our man, in or out. Funny that, don't you think?"

"What would you have me say, agent? I'm rather perturbed to hear you suggest public safety isn't getting the funding it needs. I pay my taxes. I expect my security to be taken seriously."

"That's as may be, doc, but it's not my concern. My superiors are more interested in how you came to lose a patient. So, let's think this through. Mills was brought here, attached to a remote AR rig. You stabilised him and brought him out of it. He walked out of here the next day, so what happened to the JobNet Agency property attached to him?"

"I… can only assume he took it with him, gentlemen.

I'm sorry, I don't know what you want me to say."

"How about telling me why you paused when I told you we found something on the City Watch feeds. That was *very* interesting, doc."

"What?" The man flapped his mouth as he switched his gaze from Kane to Jones and back again. Then he rallied. "I am a medical professional, Agent Kane, and I must say I do not like your tone."

Kane grinned. "It's not my tone you need to worry about, doc. I just say the word in the right ear and unless you got friends in high places, you're just another zero."

"But…" Simms' face went pale.

"Take it easy, doc. Just something to think about, eh? The records, shall we?"

TIRESOME interfering busybodies, Dr Simms thought as he stood at the window of the staff canteen overlooking the entrance. He watched Kane and Jones leave, relieved to see the back of them, but his irritation did nothing for his nerves; his hand shook as he brought the coffee cup to his lips.

This was the closest brush he'd ever had with the Government's security apparatus, plain cops aside; he sincerely hoped it was his last. Two hours they'd spent going through all Mills' medical files, from the regional database as well as the hospital files. Then they uploaded the whole lot, even though there was nothing of relevance or interest. Why they couldn't have simply issued a request to access the information remotely, he didn't know; some kind of power trip, obviously.

Simms drained his coffee and then crushed the polystyrene cup. *As if I didn't have more pressing matters to contend with*, he thought, trying to psyche his composure back into shape. Deal with them now.

He walked out of the canteen and nodded to one or two of his colleagues. The labyrinth of corridors echoed to his footsteps as he took a short cut towards the private wards. Signs and relics of the hospital's old NHS days gathered dust around him. Ignored by time and Simms.

At last, he emerged through a side door into the main body of the hospital. Gleaming white walls greeted him, as did the efficient buzz of medical activity: commerce in motion. Nurses and junior doctors nodded greetings as he walked briskly down the corridors.

Then he arrived at the exclusive wards, rooms for the extra-special paying guests. This part of the hospital resembled a five star hotel more than a health-care establishment. Keys jangled as Simms fumbled briefly with a lock and then hurried inside one of the private rooms. It was quiet, just the hum of machinery that sustained a delicate balance of life for the patient inside.

Swaddled head to foot in bandages like an Egyptian mummy the patient wallowed in the burns-immersion tank, the soothing fluid soaking the bandages and the flesh underneath. The AR-rig sat innocuously in the corner, nestled amongst the life support and monitoring equipment, where it plugged the patient into a pain-free fantasia while his body received treatment.

His professional eye glanced across the equipment, checking that all ran smoothly, then it looked finally to the patient.

"Well, Mr Mills," he said, "you're becoming rather too popular for my comfort. Fortunately, it's time you were making another move. And with luck, your new hosts will let me forget you ever existed."

CHAPTER 11:
Disembodied Confessions

SQUEAK. Squeak. Squeak.

The noise was slow and irritating. It grated on Christine's ears and set her teeth on edge, but it was compelling all the same, urging her to seek its source.

The sound echoed through this mysterious nowhere place. The checkerboard floor tiles felt cold beneath Christine's bare feet. As for the air, it seared her nose with the stench of burned heating oil. The corridors were always the same. Bare walls illuminated by strip-lights and marked by the occasional door. Naturally they were locked. Dreams had their own logic, she knew; why else was she wearing some kind of hospital gown?

Night after night, ever since David had arrived, it was always the same: this growing and intangible sense of dread. She was close; yet the answers ultimately eluded her. If only she could find the source of that noise. How many times had she wandered the labyrinth? Once was too often, but here she was again, looking for something to fill the hollow in her mind.

This time she would find the answers. The questions, even. For David, before he left. Just a few more days. Wouldn't it be wonderful to help him? You should always help those you love. She didn't know why she felt this way about him. No more than she could explain her feelings for all the others. All gone now, lost to memory. In the end they must leave. Always. But David was different. Wasn't he? He could choose to stay.

She turned a corner and wandered down a corridor identical to the last. The squeaking grew faint. No! She must find the source of that noise, for her sake, for David's sake. She backtracked, listening for the squeak. More memories unfurled in her mind's eye. Or was it fantasy? A child giggled in delight. This girl drifted through the air in a slow motion fall. The Mayor was there. At least it looked like him, only younger. He caught the girl as she fell towards him, laughed and hugged her.

The vision brought a sense of loss. It clawed at Christine's heart and she didn't understand why. Apprehension returned as she pondered the innocuous image. It didn't fit. Why had she thought of the Mayor? Who was the girl?

The squeak sounded louder, echoing down the corridors with no clue to direction. The dream was nearly at an end, following its familiar course, and still she lacked answers.

Then she discerned something different. Another sound, barely heard beneath the squeaking: a child crying far off. Christine paused, strained to listen. She was torn between the two sounds, but her conscience couldn't ignore the child. Even so, there was something about the sobbing that didn't fit.

AR exerted its own peculiar effects on the dream-state, she knew, but the sobbing didn't belong in this private reality her dreaming mind had conjured up. There was a quality to the noise that suggested something heard while dozing.

If so, if the squeaking was the dreaming and the sobbing child was... *something else...* then it wasn't leading her to wakefulness. The corridors continued, drab as ever, taking her deeper into this mystery. The squeaking diminished; the weeping became clearer, guiding her to its source.

Around the next corner, Christine found the child. She stopped abruptly, unwilling to startle this unexpected presence. The child was half way up the corridor, bathed in a pool of sickly illumination from an overhead striplight. She was maybe seven or eight; hair tied in little pigtails, she wore a red dress and yellow Wellington boots dusted in damp sand. The girl turned around and saw Christine; she ceased her sobbing and stared wide-eyed.

"Hey, sweetheart," Christine said, "what's wrong, are you lost?"

The girl gasped and stepped back, her body tensed to run when Christine tried to move a pace closer. She froze, then dropped to her knees, bringing her eyes nearer to level with the child's.

"Don't be afraid. What's wrong? You can tell me."

"I can't find my daddy," the girl said, fresh tears glimmering in her eyes.

"Aw, sweetie, I'm sorry. I'm Christine. What's your name? How did you get here?"

"I'm Kora. Something woke me up. I don't know where I am."

"Kora. That's a pretty name. I'll help you find your daddy if you like."

"You can't help me. You're not really here."

"Sure I am, Kora. I'm in your dream and you're in mine. Everybody's part of everybody else's dream, right, so why don't we share a way out? I know a great place to get ice cream. How about that?"

"I like ice cream," she said, the ghost of a smile lighting her solemn face. Then: "Was that your daddy?"

The change in tack threw Christine. She shook her head, "Who?"

"The man in your dream."

"No, he…" She frowned. There was a hole where her father should be. "I… don't remember my daddy."

"He's behind the doors. Everything is behind the doors. You just have to open them. But my daddy's not there. I don't know where he is. He sends me messages, sometimes, but I can't see him. I want my daddy!"

Kora started crying again. Suddenly she reached up and placed her hands on top of her head, clutching her pigtails as if they were causing her pain.

"There's something on my head," she wailed. "I can feel it. I don't like it; it itches. Can you get it off me?"

"There's nothing, sweetheart. We're in artificial reality; you're feeling the headset, that's all. It happens sometimes."

"No," the girl wailed. "It's in my head too. I can feel it in me. Help me get it off so I can find my daddy!"

Christine felt her heart clench; she wanted to rush forward and hug the child, but she felt her own hackles rising. She reached up and patted her scalp. There was something thick and fleshy there, a ghost sensation suggesting some kind of tendril; more than one. The weird impression faded. She brushed her hand through her hair. It was nothing, she told herself, but some morbid fear lurking in her subconscious called her a liar.

"Kora," she began so say, but she was interrupted by a sudden rush of air from somewhere in the labyrinth.

The girl looked up, startled; she began to back away. "It's here. It's coming. It followed you."

"Kora, please tell me what's wrong so I can help you. Nothing's going to hurt you, sweetie."

"Monsters. There's a monster in here. Can't you make it go away? I'm afraid."

"You're just imagining things, honey; there's nothing

to worry about, really."

The girl's fear was becoming contagious. When a door banged somewhere, she suddenly didn't feel so convinced of her assurances. The lights flickered. Kora bolted.

"No! Wait!"

Christine chased after the girl. Kora was too small to outpace an adult; even so she remained ahead of the race. It was nothing like running in a dream, none of that sluggish drag on her limbs, but she still couldn't catch the girl. It took Christine her best speed to keep Kora in sight.

The race ended at an intersection cutting across the corridor. Kora scurried through an open door and then turned to slam it closed. Christine caught a brief glimpse of blue sky and puffy clouds, ocean and a beach; sandcastles in the background. For one moment, Kora's frightened face was framed by the doorway, then it slammed shut.

Christine approached the door, her feet scuffing a scattering of dry sand. She tried the handle but it wouldn't budge. She beat her fist against the door and called the girl's name. "Please! Let me help you."

Nothing. She stepped back. The lintel sagged, as if it was melting. The frame wobbled out of shape, as if it was made of jelly. The door warped and bulged inwards, as if something was sucking it into the wall. Bewildered, Christine watched the door vanish to leave nothing but the corridor's blank wall. Even the sand had disappeared.

She stepped up to the wall and placed her hand against

it. Rough concrete. Cold and damp to the touch. Solid. There was a solitary butterfly, utter black, resting on the wall just above head height. The creature's wings twitched then it leapt into the air. The butterfly fluttered in circles just past the junction, almost as if it was inviting her to follow, then it flew off into the gloom.

"This *is* a dream, right?" she muttered. "Then let me wake up."

But the dream, or whatever it was, didn't release her. Not yet.

One thing was certain; the girl had brought her somewhere different. The lighting was less intense for one thing, dust covered the floor and it was disturbed by two parallel tracks about a metre apart and, between the tracks, scuff marks. She followed the tracks, moving in the direction indicated by that mysterious insect's flight.

She heard the squeak again. Fear responded: a fluttering in her belly. The corridors became gloomier. The dust thickened. Pipes ran along the walls just below the ceiling. They were draped in thick cobwebs, their silver sheen tarnished. The place felt strangely familiar, as if she'd been here before in another life.

A crossroads brought confusion. The tracks crossed one another, heading along all compass points. Bewildered, she stopped and looked around. The pipes resonated with the suggestion of mocking voices. What they said was beyond comprehension. Nonsense it seemed, only the tone bore any meaning and that was cruel.

She shivered.

Squeak. It came nearer. Squeak. Whatever it was. Squeak. A trolley passed by. A damaged wheel produced that high-pitched noise. Squeak. Squeak. Squeak. A body lay on the trolley, covered by a white sheet with a drip attached to one arm. Whoever it was wore an AR rig that rendered him or her anonymous.

She watched her nameless dread pass by. Two men manhandled the trolley, one guiding at the front, another pushing at the rear. Dressed in surgical green, they shuffled along. They paid no heed to Christine as she watched the strange procession.

The trolley grew smaller in the gloom. She jogged to catch up, it turned the corner and she broke into a trot. Out of sight, the squeak grew faint and she forced herself to turn the corner and follow.

The trolley only moved slowly. Yet somehow, like the little girl, it managed to stay ahead. She sensed that the mysterious slumberer was nearing the end of the journey. The busted wheel no longer squealed above the noise of the whispering pipes. Tears filled her eyes. She would never find her answers, only deeper mystery.

A door opened to spill light into the corridor. Two men stood in silhouette. Twins in beige suits. Nondescript with bald heads and bar codes on their foreheads. How did she know that? Detail was lost to darkness. The trolley passed between the two men and into the hidden room.

A cry of frustration escaped her throat. One of the twins responded to the noise and glanced briefly in her direction. Then he was gone, obscured by the grey door. But this door didn't melt away. Instead, it was the light that faded. Two by two, the strip-lights flickered and went out. A wall of blackness rushed towards her.

THE bed shifted with a suddenness that startled Mills from sleep. Christine was sitting up with her knees folded up beneath her chin. Sweat-sodden hair masked her face. She was sobbing.

Wearily, he sat up and put his arm around her shoulders. At first she resisted, then she succumbed and allowed him to pull her tenderly towards him. "That dream again?"

She nodded then rested her cheek against his chest. He took her weight, placed his chin on top of her head and gently stroked her back. Her tension eased slightly under his soft caresses.

"Do you remember anything about it?"

"No. Only that I was looking for something but I couldn't find it. Only… only, I think *something* found me… I can't remember; it's slipping away."

He sighed. This was becoming a regular event. Poor thing. Over the past few days – ever since the dream started, she had become a shadow of her former self – skin pale, hair lank, eyes tired and puffy. Whatever problem, it was destroying her from within. And he didn't know what to do.

Another burden to bear. As yet he was no closer to finding work. Off the top of his head, he figured he had about three days realtime left before he had to make a decision. Stick around with an extended stay, or call it quits and leave. Would Christine come with him? If only they could discuss these things. But how, when she was in this state? He kissed her scalp.

"David?"

"Hmm?"

"Don't… leave me alone in here!"

He hugged her tighter. "I won't. I promise."

Liar, his conscience screamed. How could he stay? What choice did he have except to go when his time was up? He felt sick at the prospect of losing her.

"Come on," he said, forcing her to lie down, "try to get some sleep."

She huddled in a foetal position. He snuggled up beside her and placed a comforting arm round her waist. Gradually she relaxed until her breathing said she was sound asleep. He listened to her breathe, tired but unable to sleep. While he kept her nightmares at bay, he toyed with the seed of an idea.

"COME in, Mr Mills. I understand you wanted to see me?"

"That's right." He sat down in the vacant chair by the window. The view had changed to a windswept moor beneath an overcast sky. Bleak hills brooded in the distance.

"This is about Christine?"

"In a roundabout way, yes. You know I have to leave soon."

The Mayor nodded wearily.

"I haven't found a job."

"No," the Mayor sighed. "I'm sorry we were unable to help you."

"But you *can* help me. I'm going to get a job here in AR. So I can be with Christine. I thought you could put in a word for me."

MacAllister sagged in his chair and sighed again. "I'm sorry, Mr Mills. I can't help you. I'd like to. But I can't."

"Can't or won't?" he tried to contain his annoyance. "Come on – you've seen the state she's in."

"I've noticed. I've never seen her so taken with someone before."

"Then help *her* at least!"

"I'm sorry. I can't. I used up my favours a long time ago."

"What's that supposed to mean?" Frustration made him restless. He wanted to get up and pace but he forced himself to remain seated.

"It means what I said."

"Well I'm going to do it with or without your help. I won't leave Christine behind."

"Mr Mills," he sighed, rubbing his face wearily. "I

shouldn't say this. You could say it's more than my job's worth, but... don't stay in AR. I mean it. Get out while you still can. It's all an illusion you know. In more ways than one."

"What do you mean?" *Of course it's an illusion. It's AR.*

"I mean it's a safe haven from the world. There's a sense of community in here. You can feel like you belong. Life's easy going. It's enthralling. But at the end of the day it's an illusion. This is no safe haven. And it can't protect us from the Outside."

"I don't know what you mean."

A flash of irritation flared in the old man's eyes. "Come on, man! You know what it's like. You can't trust anyone. You never know who's taking notes. Cameras everywhere, all our movements are watched. Fear, Mills, *fear*. There's no fear in here. But this is where we should be *most* afraid!"

There was a wild gleam in the man's eyes that Mills found alarming. The Mayor appeared ready to launch into a fearful rant. He leaned back in his chair, as though to distance himself from a perceived threat. The Mayor noticed the alarm and relaxed.

"I'm sorry, Mr Mills. To find a job in here is one thing. To stay is quite another. I'll send you out personally if you want. Just give me the word. I'll see you safely home."

"Mayor, I'm not going. I won't leave Christine behind."

The Mayor sagged in his chair: "You can't take Christine out of here."

"Why not? If she wants to leave what rights have you got to stop her? She works for you, that's all. Doesn't give you the right to control her life. God! You management types really are all the same!"

"Can't you open your eyes? Christine is my daughter." The Mayor looked about to cry. Mills gaped in surprise and embarrassment.

"I'm sorry," he babbled, "I didn't know... I never thought..."

"No. Her mother died years ago. Christine is all I have left. And now you threaten to take her away from me." The Mayor fought back his tears and now he appeared cold and distant. "Do you know what it's like for me to watch my only child fall apart all over again? After what they... she... her breakdown. Yes, her breakdown, I used up all my favours to get us both in here. She can't go back outside."

"But she's been outside. She told me."

The Mayor smiled. And it was chilling. "She *thinks* she's been outside," the smile faded and the Mayor's face became grim. "You'd be surprised what can be done in here. She has no idea. No memory of her original life in the real world, of the circumstances of her... breakdown. We conditioned a new identity, a personality even, under her mother's maiden name. She doesn't even know that I'm her father. It has to be that way, Mills. For her own sake."

He felt dumbstruck. "I'm sorry," was all he could say. Instantly he regretted the inadequacy of these words. The Mayor just nodded gravely.

"I can't stop you, Mills. All I can do is beg you. Please don't do this. Christine will get over you. Don't stay. Don't torture her. If not for your own sake, then for hers – let me send you home."

He tried to meet MacAllister's gaze but found he couldn't. All the same, his resolve was as strong as ever. "I'm sorry. I have to do this. At least I have to try. Christine means a lot to me. I like her."

"You like her. You don't love her."

"It's too early for that. Give it time and see what happens. Like I said, I'm sorry. Sorry you won't help us."

He got up to leave. MacAllister's sad eyes followed him. Mills tried to ignore the burning gaze searing into his back.

"Mr Mills! Please don't take her away from me. She's all I've got left…"

He said nothing. And he certainly didn't look back. There was no point.

AS it turned out there was no need for the Mayor's help. Though qualified with an unfathomable 'but' the JobNet Agency appeared delighted to receive his application. Finally, things were looking up.

There was nothing left to do but fantasise about his

life to be with Christine. He felt overjoyed, ecstatic even. Sometimes he laughed out loud as he passed through the village. Some remembered foible of Christine's provoked the humour, that and his uncharacteristic happiness.

The hustle and bustle of the job market sounded from the Village Square. He ignored it and turned off the main road to begin his walk home. The valley opened up on either side. Those citadels still gleamed in the distance. No longer enticing. Who needed them now?

"Mister Mills!" the voice rudely interrupted his reverie. "Leaving us so soon? And no job I hear. *Sooo* tragic."

It was Harris, leaning casually against a lamppost. Since their earlier encounter he had kept a discreet distance. Mills wished he would continue to do so. No such luck, Harris pushed himself off the lamppost and approached, a malicious gleam in his eyes.

"Looks like I was wrong about you, Mills. You really are a loser."

"Get lost, Harris."

"Oh, Mills, that's not nice." He moved to block the path. Mills sighed. He was determined that Harris should not spoil his mood.

"But seriously, I hear you're joining JobNet. I wouldn't do that if I was you."

"Oh? Well, you're not me. Thank God."

Harris laughed and shrugged in mock supplication. "You know something. I really like you. Despite the fact that you're a loser, I really do like you. Nobody else would have turned down my offer of work. Shows independence. Shows we picked the right person. Shame it turns out we couldn't have given it to you after all. And I'll tell you why – for your own good."

"Okay, tell me. What's for my own good?"

"They've lost your body. Not a good situation that. AR's a bad place to be without someone to look over you. If I was you I'd get out and find where I was."

The man's eyes scanned Mills' face, studying his response. Mills laughed. Harris joined him and slapped his back in playful good humour.

"If that were true they would have told me."

"Don't be so naïve," Harris replied, gaining control of his humour. "Why should they tell you something like that? It's got nothing to do with you. I'm only telling you 'cos I like you."

"You're a sick bastard!" He tried to push past, but Harris grabbed his arm. Mills looked down, beginning to feel the annoyance boil over.

"To lose a job is a setback. To lose a life is a tragedy. To lose a body... well, that's just bloody careless. So get out of JobNet!"

Mills broke free and pushed past. This time Harris let him go. "Oh, yeah, Mills – don't go fretting over Christine either. She's a crazy slut. You won't be missed there, plenty more to choose from, and she will."

That's it! Rage exploded deep in his brain. It surged

through his body and discharged itself in that sneering face. Harris went down, his lips ruptured from the blow. He put his hands to his mouth and looked at the blood on his fingers. The wound evaporated. Harris smiled up at him.

"So there's life in the old dog yet?" he said, suddenly thoughtful. "Well, now the fun's over, you and me are going to have a serious chat for my employer. Not now – I'll let you cool off first. But then you've got some important questions to answer. In the meantime, I suggest you learn to relax. You're so upt –"

"Fuck you!" Mills turned away.

"Get out, Dave, I'm serious. You've got no future here. You have no future at all!"

CHAPTER 12:
Eyes Open on Infinity

> **WHY?**

The technician frowned at the response. Tried again.

> BUT WHY?

That's not right. It isn't supposed to ask questions. The technician chewed on the end of his pen and stared perplexed at the screen. Then he tried again.

> BUT WHY?

Of course, he thought with a wry smile. "Okay, who's the practical joker?" he asked.

The man at the next workstation turned towards him and shrugged. "Machine asking 'why' is it?"

"Yeah!"

"It's doing the same here. Pissing me off it is."

Great. The technician tapped his fingers on the casing of his keyboard. Smiled. Typed: 'just because'. Naturally, the machine replied by asking 'why'. Annoyance stirred.

"All I want is a routine diagnostic!" he snarled at the machine. Then he checked himself. *Just because it's an AI doesn't mean it won't behave like any other machine*, he thought, and cursed the gremlins inside.

The new processing hub was an experimental model; they were still learning its quirks. All the same, he could do without the headaches involved with sorting out this latest fuck-up.

Always the same, though, whenever the bosses wanted some new component tested they installed it in the JobNet system – got to protect those precious corporate systems. Can't take risks with them. Now they wanted to trial this so-called AI 3.0, though how they could really assess its capabilities when SysOps was being so tight-lipped about this upgrade was a question above his pay-grade. How much of the global web had been tested and debugged within JobNet since it came on line five years ago? Again, not the sort of questions you asked, he knew, not if you wanted to keep your job at least. He shrugged off his dangerous turn of thinking and tried to focus on the job.

A tap closed the AI/User interface. The technician tapped again to access the dumb terminals monitoring the network. If you can't get the boss, go see the PA, he mused. Another command. The cursor flashed as the machine began to process. At last…

> BUT YOU DIDN'T ANSWER ME, DADDY.
> DADDY?

The man frowned, sat up, reached for the screen and then paused. Daddy? That didn't make sense.

> IT'S DARK IN HERE, DADDY. I DON'T LIKE THE DARK.
> WON'T YOU SWITCH ON THE LIGHT?
> PLEASE DADDY. I'M FRIGHTENED.
> DADDY?

The screen bounced and faded to black. The technician counted under his breath and then flicked the power back on. The machine emitted a sharp beep as the screen began to run through the terminal's internal diagnostics. Then it came back on line.

"That should sort it out," the man muttered to himself. He closed the virtual desktop in order to access the network directly. A simple command line interface awaited his instructions.

> DADDY, DON'T LEAVE ME.
> I'M FRIGHTENED.
> PLEASE SWITCH ON THE LIGHT, DADDY.
> I PROMISE I'LL BE GOOD.
> DADDY WHERE ARE YOU?
> DON'T LEAVE ME, DADDY.

The technician looked at the screen in disbelief and growing annoyance. Messages continued to scroll up the screen.

> THEY'RE WHISPERING TO ME, DADDY.
> MAKE THEM GO AWAY.
> PLEASE.
> DADDY?

"Who are?" the man typed, smiling despite himself. He just couldn't resist the temptation. The reply arrived before he could even hit the RETURN key.

> THE MONSTERS, DADDY.
> THEY'RE OUTSIDE.
> COMING CLOSER.
> MAKE THEM GO AWAY, DADDY.
> PLEASE MAKE THEM GO AWAY.
> I'M SO FRIGHTENED.
> PLEASE.
> I PROMISE I'LL BE GOOD IF YOU MAKE THEM GO AWAY.
> DADDY?
> DADDY?
> I'M AFRAID.
> DADDY, PLEASE HELP ME.

The technician chuckled under his breath, falling in at last with a good joke. He turned to call over his colleagues but a flash from the screen made him turn back. The screen was blank. Idly he tapped a few keys. Nothing happened. Only the LED on the monitor indicated he had power.

That's it then, the joke's over. He hit the reset button and waited for the machine to come back –

> NETWORK ERROR: \ CANNOT ACCESS CORE-AI

"ZOOM in."

The image of the butterfly doubled in size beneath the decoder's magnifying glass. Weaver cursed under his breath. There was nothing. No code visible. The thing had incredible resolution.

"Anything?" Conway asked, raising one eyebrow on his disembodied head. A fuzzy patch of the outside world formed a backdrop behind him, a floating 3D photograph with no frame.

"Nothing yet. Zoom in. Keep going."

The butterfly continued to grow until only a portion was visible through the lens. The thing twitched irritably as it tried to free itself from the pin impaling it on the decoder.

"Remarkably dense code, whatever it is. Must have used one hell of a compression system to pack it this tight. Ah, the resolution seems to be degrading now."

"Figure out what it is?" Conway floated to the other side of the room, invisible legs pacing in the outside world.

"Not yet. Zoom in. Hold it!"

Little round dots floated in a grey matrix. They moved to the butterfly's motion and vibrated like sub-atomic particles. To the edge of his field of vision there was an innocuous white dot.

"Zoom in. Upper-left quadrant. Centre. Magnify."

Words formed out of the amorphous grey. Not the

numbers and codes that he expected. "Oh shit…"

"What is it?"

"We may have a problem."

"What the fuck is it?"

The disembodied head moved quickly forward. The butterfly twitched with increased vigour.

"Just a serial number," Weaver said his voice wavering. "And a warning: Danger, psycho-toxic. Prolonged exposure to active virus form can result in permanent neuro-psychological damage."

"Did you say virus?"

"Yes! It's a fucking military virus!"

"It can't be. How could a military program get loose in the system?"

"I don't care how it got in. How do we get rid of it?"

"I don't know. Look, don't worry. It's a practical joke. Right? If it was a virus then all our alarm systems would be going ape-shit. We've got nothing out here. Everything's fine."

"It must be stealthed. It's a fucking *military* virus!"

"I know. You said. You *keep* saying!"

The butterfly lowered itself up and down on its spindly legs. Gradually the pin raised itself from the insect's thorax and fell onto the desk. Somehow it made the loudest noise Weaver had ever heard.

"Oh shit… it's looking at me! Do something for Christ's sake. I don't like this…"

"Don't panic."

Weaver noticed Conway backing away himself. *As though it can do anything to* you, he thought bitterly. He realised he was sweating and cursed himself. Don't be stupid. It's just a piece of code. You can get out any time you want. And you can always disassemble it... The butterfly twitched up and down on its legs and flapped its wings a couple of times.

"See what else it says," Conway suddenly suggested.

Reluctantly Weaver moved forward and peered through the lens. "Nothing else. It's classified. Need the security clearance –"

The wings exploded. Fine black dust erupted to smear the underside of the lens with a sooty smudge. The insect's wings now bore an iridescent pattern. A Mandelbrot, he noted. The colours swam around a dark, eye-like centre that seemed to be staring at him.

This psychedelic eye was hypnotic. He moved forward, somehow compelled to lean over the butterfly to stare. Deeper. The eye opened: a dark hole surrounded by a vortex of polychrome fractals. He felt himself fall. Down through the eye and onwards towards infinity.

"Weaver? Weaver? I'm losing the connection... What's happening... Are you still there? I'm... sorry... I... didn't know..."

BACK in the foreboding maze, Christine had thought – no, hoped – she was done haunting these corridors. There was no sign of the little girl she'd encountered previously, but the hospital trolley was everything she remembered, squeaking ahead, close to its mysterious destination.

The trolley turned into the last corridor. Christine slowed her pace, *let it go, let* me *go,* she thought. Then, unexpected, the trolley paused just before it completely vanished around the corner. The green-garbed figure at the rear looked at her.

"You're not going to hold him back," the man said. "He has to find the calm at the eye of the storm."

Christine stared, open-mouthed. Then she found her voice. "What? You can…"

The man winked and turned back to his burden. The trolley squeaked.

"Wait!" Christine staggered after the man. "Who are you? *What* are you?"

"Legion," he said, without turning his head. A low chuckle, amused at some private joke. "We're ready now. It's time. You'll see…"

She stared at the back of the man's head. It was his voice all right, but the words sounded as if they had come from behind her, rising out of the background susurration resonating along the pipes.

"Please! Where is this place?"

The man made no answer. Christine broke into a jog to try and catch up, but as on previous occasions, the trolley kept ahead. The door at the end of the corridor opened, spilling light. The two men she'd seen in earlier versions of the dream stepped out and stood to the side so that the trolley could be wheeled inside. They watched, impassive, then they followed it into the room. The door closed with a hollow boom.

Resigned to the dream's fruitless end, Christine stopped running and waited for her release into wakefulness. Instead the susurration grew louder. From behind came the fluttering sound of disturbed air. She turned. A wall of blackness rushed forwards, just as before, swallowing the glow of the strip-lights. But it wasn't the same: this time the darkness was *alive*.

Millions of black butterflies. Delicate wings battered the air. The combined noise of each miniscule stroke was deafening. Christine stumbled backwards in fright, then turned to make a run for the door, terrified it might be locked.

Tiny bodies struck her face and hands with the stinging force of hailstones. Her feet crushed low-flying insects into ooze that mingled with the dust on the floor. The sickening mulch stung and burned her feet. The swarm thickened. She closed her eyes and stumbled, disorientated, through the ravaging flurries; flailing arms searched for the door.

Hands slapped concrete. Stinging ooze dribbled down her arms; try as she might, she couldn't avoid crushing the insects against the wall. Pain kept her focused. The door. Where was the door? Christine felt her way along the wall.

Then she found it; smooth wood. In desperation, she yelled as loud as she could, her fists hammering, pleading to those inside to release her from this misery. She slammed herself bodily against the door, felt it rattle in its frame, but otherwise refuse to budge. *No!*

Thickly the insects crawled over her back; she slumped, strength failing, knees giving way, then her right hand found the handle. Christine gripped it hard and offered a silent prayer – then yanked it down hard. The door swung open under her weight and she toppled into the hidden room. She landed heavily on all fours, the impact jarring her elbows, but she rolled over, swung round on her backside and kicked the door closed.

The butterflies vanished, as if they'd never been, but whatever sense of relief she might have felt went with them as she took stock of her surroundings. With a dull sense of dread, Christine realised she knew this place; she just couldn't remember why.

"Let me go," she blurted, the words just springing to mind. "I won't tell anyone. Please, just let me go!"

The room's occupants ignored her. Christine sat back against the door and drew her knees up to her chin as they got to work on their guest. She watched through watery eyes and almost wished she were back in the corridor.

THE trolley stood at the centre of the sterile room. The two men in beige stared silently at the recumbent form, waiting, while the two men in green went about their work.

The one who had guided the trolley through the

corridors busied himself at a bank of monitors, tapping screens, checking readouts, making adjustments.

Christine watched the other; the one who offered the unexpected – and cryptic – conversation out in the maze. He was busy with the patient's AR headset, checking straps and connections, making fresh attachments to a bank of electronic equipment situated in the corner of the room.

Then he began applying medical sensors to the body, hands moving beneath the covering sheet with swift professionalism. As he did so, he glanced up briefly and winked again. The shock of connection twisted her guts. Christine stood up and moved closer, but not too close.

"You can see me? What is this? Why am I here?"

The man ignored her and continued his work, now checking the patient's restraints. Maybe she'd imagined the wink. Then the man stepped back to make way for the men in beige to begin their work, and she was forced to dismiss the consideration.

"Tell us what we wish to know and then you can go," one of them said.

Christine whimpered at the sound of the voice. The man just ignored her; he was intent on the prone figure. The AR helmet masked any features, but the body stirred beneath the sheet and murmured something. The man smiled and stroked the barcode on his forehead.

"Just tell us where you obtained the information and who you told. That is all we require. Would you not prefer to avoid all this unpleasantness?"

The body murmured something – a slurred, distant reply. Christine circled round to where she could see both men more clearly, carefully making sure she didn't stray too close. The occupants behaved as if she wasn't there; she'd decided she'd prefer to keep it that way.

"The drugs should be taking effect now," the second man said, and as Christine looked sharply between the two, she found she could not find any difference in their appearances. *Twins.*

"Such a pity," his companion replied, shaking his head sadly. "Commence with the program."

The figure on the trolley let out a whining cry and writhed in obvious pain. Creaking restraints held the body tight. The twins looked at one another with thin, humourless smiles.

"Relax. Can you feel the drugs taking effect?" the first twin asked. "What is it like with AR? Tell us. We would really like to know."

"We're online and recording, Agents. You can begin the session," the technician at the bank of monitors said. The second twin nodded and leaned over the body.

"Open your mind," he said, voice soft and hypnotic. "You are relaxed, happy, at ease with yourself and the world. There is no danger."

The prone figure mumbled happily and moved with quiet satisfaction.

"This is the happiest day of your life," the twin

continued. "Picture it. Friends and family are all around you. They love you. You love them. Let this love take you. Drift on it. Follow it to your heart's desire. Is it not wonderful?"

Christine began to feel light-headed and woozy. She smiled, muttered "David," enjoyed the warm feeling that swept through her body. The first twin spoke again and broke the spell.

"No! You have ruined it!"

A whimper came from the trolley.

"They do not love you. They hate you. What have you done? How could you destroy all that love?"

"Stimulate the fear centre," the second twin quietly told the technician.

"They hate you because of something you have done, something terrible. You know what it is. Say it. Say what is causing them to hate you. Beg for their forgiveness and maybe they will love you again."

"You are frightened are you not?" the second twin asked. The figure on the trolley moaned in anguish, the AR helmet nodded. "You are frightened because you are all alone. It is cold and dark and there is nobody with you. Nobody to comfort you, no warmth, no love."

"No! You are not alone. There is something with you. It is terrifying. Your worst fear. Can you see it? It is here to punish you – but it will not start with you. Look how terrible it is. Your worst fear!"

The figure screamed, a terrible sound that seared

white hot through Christine's spine. Feeling that terror she covered her ears.

"They are dying. Can you hear them? Your loved ones, they are dying and they do not know why. They are pleading. How can you ignore that? How can you ignore their need to love you? And they loved you so much until you ruined it. Can you not feel how much they want to love you again? But they cannot. You will not let them and now they are dying. Your crime is killing them –"

"See your fear?" the second twin asked. "Make it flesh. Do not flinch! You can conquer it. You can save your loved ones. Remember how good it felt to receive so much love? You can get it back. You can save them. Just tell them what you did. Tell them how you found out about what we do, and whom you have told. Hold on to the thought of all that love and tell everything –"

The scream threatened to shatter the walls. So intense the twins stepped back, wide-eyed in shock, their hands clamped over their ears. The technician looked away from his screens with a horrified expression. The body on the trolley spasmed violently and struggled against the restraints until one began to tear. Blood flooded from a gashed arm.

"We're losing her!" the technician cried.

"Shut down!" one of the twins yelled.

A cry of fear and rage exploded from Christine's lungs. She leapt forward – straight through the first twin as though he were a ghost – and ripped the AR helmet from the struggling body. Frozen in shock, she looked down at her own face, the eyes wide in horror, mouth distorted in an agonised howl. The forgotten fear leapt from the shadows of her mind. She had her answer. She remembered everything. She knew what they did with JobNet, and it was so awful her mind threatened to shut down all over again.

The room turned inside out; Christine felt her presence shift. Suddenly, she was the body on the trolley; she'd *always* been the body on the trolley. Searing pain shot along her arm. The restraint parted some more under the strength of her fear. Skin tore, blood continued to flow, staining the sheet crimson.

The winking man appeared, leaning over her; smiling. Christine gulped in air and stared. "Tell me," he said, "whatever made you think this was *really* a dream?"

Christine opened her mouth to reply, but horror strangled her words. The man's face crumbled. His body flew apart, becoming a thick cloud of butterflies. She gagged as the swarm gushed into her mouth and forced their way down her throat. Now she understood the dread.

CHAPTER 13:
Sunset over Paradise

SHRILL screams killed the nighttime silence and shocked Mills from sleep. He leapt out of bed and stumbled over the tangled bedding on the floor, momentarily lost in time. "Mum!" he called, groggy.

Christine continued her cries until the cottage seemed to shake. She knelt on the floor, hair wild and untidy, hands clasped over her face. "It's in here! It's with us now!" she wailed.

He quickly crawled towards her and pulled her hands away from her face. No recognition registered in her eyes.

"Christine? It's me. I'm here. You're all right now," he said. She didn't seem to hear but at least her screams subsided. Now she just sat there trembling, with vacant eyes. He cupped her face in his hands and stared into those wide, dark pupils.

"Everything's all right now," he whispered and kissed

her brow. He wondered what was wrong. Sorrow gripped his heart. Things had looked so promising over the last few days, after he'd shared his decision to join JobNet, and now this. In despair he cradled the girl in his arms and gently rocked her back and forth.

"Dead," she whispered. "Dead... I'm dead, you're dead... everybody's dead... dead..."

"Christine, what?"

"I remember. I remember it all. They killed me. I'm dead. I found out too much and they killed me trying to find out what I knew. My own Father, how could he be part of it?"

She was looking at him now. Her eyes held a desperate sincerity. He shook his head, not knowing what to say or think.

"But I won't tell. I can't tell..." Christine broke down into tears.

"Don't talk like this, please. You're not making sense."

"I'm dead... I can't tell... not if I'm dead..."

"It's all right. I won't leave you. I'll never leave you. Just don't talk like this. Please!"

Fear is a terrible thing – especially when added to helplessness. A tingling sensation around the eyes heralded the urge to cry, but the tears didn't come.

"Get out!" Christine pushed him away then hit him with clenched fists. Confused and frightened, he backed away. A wild blow caught him on the side of the head. He felt blood trickle from an eyebrow gashed by nails.

"Christine?" Pain. Not from the blow.

"Get out!" she screamed hysterically. "Get out or they'll kill you too. You can't stay in here."

"Just tell me what's wrong!"

Suddenly the old Christine was looking back at him through those red, tear-streaked eyes. "I can't tell you. They might hear. They're *always* listening, always watching," she whined. "Please get out while you can. Don't let them hurt you. They do terrible things."

"I can't leave you like this." The urge to cry was stronger now; he didn't think he could hold back as he moved again towards the distraught woman. He wanted to calm her, soothe these terrible fears, and restore his carefree lover. There were dirty scabs running down her arms. He frowned. He hadn't noticed them before –

A sudden burst of agony felt so intense it seemed his body would explode. He tried to breathe, found he couldn't. As he clutched his stomach, he felt something dense move inside him. It pushed against his organs and stretched his flesh. A low, strangled groan escaped his lips, then he began to retch.

The matter erupted from his mouth in a thick stream. A terrible moan of pain – low, guttural and tortured – accompanied the filth. An endless stream forced out by spasm after spasm of his tortured muscles. Veins stood out on his neck and temples, face went red, but still there was no respite.

The black vomit erupted into the air instead of

splattering to the floor. Slowly he understood why. He saw, with a shock, the butterflies swarming thick in the air. Another retch and another swarm took flight as they were ejected from his body.

Beyond his private Hell, Christine screamed in distress. This time she didn't stop.

"**WARNING!** Danger! Virus activity detected. Emergency shutdown procedures are inoperative. Advise manual logout."

MacAllister cursed at the soft voice that whispered in his ear. *Tell me something I don't know*, he thought. Plenty of people around him no doubt disagreed. Their panic-stricken screams were deafening. The worst news of their lives; Eden closed down. Everything must go – but where?

Clients and workers ran in panic and, as though he actually had somewhere to go, he ran too. A body that was a vegetable, more or less immobilised by the disease that had rotted his motor nerves and now forgotten somewhere in the 'real world', left him with no escape from the mind-immersion that had been his hideaway. And now all his guilt was coming to claim him. Payback for all that he had done.

"Warning! Danger! Virus activity detected. For your own safety please initiate manual logout procedure."

Christine, he had to reach her. His little girl. Not that there was anything he could do for her. No salvation from her old dad. All he could do was die alongside her as paradise crumbled. Yes, the least – the only thing – he could do was die at his daughter's side.

Thousands of voices screamed in his ears. He tried to shut out the noise. The tremors hit again, ersatz reality vibrating at a shattering frequency. People stumbled, buildings toppled, even the sky oscillated violently. A building across the square collapsed in slow motion, falling apart as its foundations gave way. Fragments of rubble cascaded into the air, some falling upwards as the virus scrambled the system. Dust blossomed in rising clouds, obscuring the scenes of panic.

He watched in horror as bodies caught in the rubble storm collapsed into wire-frame representations of humanity, then disappeared line by line. A mind terminated, its signal severed at source.

"Maximum danger! Virus activity at critical level," the voice from the external headset whispered. "All personnel evacuate virtual environment imm –"

He tapped his right ear, an unconscious gesture to coax the speaker back into operation. It was futile, he knew. As if his body could ever respond.

A man tumbled past, eyes wide, face locked in a grimace of terror. "Logout, Logout," he cried, "please God, logout!"

He ran on, beyond the turmoil of the square, heedless of the chaos erupting around him. The ground began to rise until the village was left behind. The devastated settlement shook beneath him, the screams of its frightened residents deafened even from the distance. More buildings collapsed while he looked on. Then the sky strobed and finally went out.

The four-dimensional lattice of raw cyberspace was revealed. Tesseracts filled with restless greyscale fractals wrenched at his eyes as he squinted up at the constellations of human imagination shining in the distance. One flared like a supernova, another faded from existence like an archaic computer effect.

A distant thundering drew his gaze back to the human-scaled destruction that was the village. The administration building tumbled onto terrified stick figures. On the distant horizon beyond the valley's juddering slopes the gleaming citadels collapsed like stacked cards.

He watched the destruction, his emotions drained. More tremors struck and pulled the ground from under his feet. With a cry he fell and rolled down the steep slope. Plant life transformed beneath him; grass and heather metamorphosed into course spines and thick thorns. They sliced through cloth and skin, smearing him with blood.

The ground cracked open to reveal a deep chasm. He slithered over the edge with a bitter cry, prepared himself for a long fall – but the thorns held him fast, bound to him by strands of torn cloth and skin.

"Christine!" he cried, "Christine!"

Mills' cottage hid in the gloom of the mutant forest. It shook in sympathy with the earth. MacAllister's cries went unheard but still he called out to his daughter, screamed for help. Then a figure appeared above him.

"Harris! Harris thank God… get me up, I don't know how long I can hold on…"

He fell silent as he saw the expression on the man's face. Harris held his arm awkwardly; the fingers were no more than blackened stumps. Something struggled to be free of the puffy, glistening flesh. Horrified, MacAllister watched the butterfly unravel its wings from the threads of skin and take to the air.

"You stupid old bastard!" Harris snarled. "See what you've done to me?"

The tangle of thorns began to give way. He slipped further into the void as flesh tore and thorns snapped. A cry of fear and pain escaped his lips. Harris only smiled.

"Harris! Please –"

"You let it in here! You let *him* do this!"

An explosion of blood erupted from MacAllister's burst lips. Harris smiled at the blood and kicked again. Kicked and kicked with a madman's frenzy. MacAllister's strangled cries became a desperate plea. Harris kicked again, a savage gleam in his eyes.

"We can't get out. We're trapped in here. We're all going to die. I didn't join Social Security to fucking die in here! But that's going to happen and it's your fucking fault!"

One last blow and flesh and thorn parted company. Blood-smeared hands slipped free of the remaining support and, with a last feeble cry, MacAllister fell.

ALONE in the darkness, the dreamers dream. Thousands of them hang in space, suspended on fine cats' cradles, motionless like the dead.

Faint lights struggle against the darkness of the cavernous space in which the dreamers dream. The dull glow reflects from cables and tubes; delicate machines to sustain the physical needs of wandering minds.

Silent as a tomb, there is not even a breeze or drip of condensed water to break the silence. Cables snake across the gloom, like the weavings of an insane arachnid they form a giant, crazy cobweb. Gathered together in thick bundles, the cables shoot upward to be lost in the shadows of the distant roof.

Neurons of silicon and light, one small ganglion in the global nervous system, the dreamers are mere fragments of the global mind.

Beyond the edge of darkness a square of muted light overlooks the silent dreamers. High and wide, it stands above the central aisle between the rows of bodies. The weak glow fails to penetrate far into the darkness; instead it merely highlights the shade and reveals the nearer dreamers. Dully, it reflects from the bodies, giving them a grey appearance in the gloom.

Then the stillness is broken. A body stirs in its sleep. Not much, just a gentle twitch of the fingers, a tension of the neck muscles. Even that is an achievement in the face of motor-nerve suppressants. Suddenly the body explodes in a paroxysm of frantic motion. Equally suddenly, the motion stops, the body tense and rigid for a moment. Finally the body sags eternally limp.

A chain reaction takes place as body after body repeats the frantic struggle only to fall limp and dangle like a broken marionette. Somewhere high above the concrete floor a body shakes itself loose from its life-preserving cradle. Fluids spatter to the floor as the body tumbles. The dull crack of bone on stone echoes through the cavern. A broken AR helmet clatters across the concrete. The body stares blindly at the square of light with a face frozen in an expression of pain and horror.

Silence returns for a while. A brief respite until the harsh cry of a klaxon echoes through the shadows. More bodies struggle against the dreams. Red lights flash in the darkness to cast an eerie reflection over the bodies, then striplights flicker into life.

Beyond the window, display screens register failing lives. Alarms cry shrilly and a wide-eyed watchman looks on in shock, helpless before the machines he barely understands.

Dreamer after dreamer awakes to face the final, ultimate reality.

CHRISTINE'S screams somehow broke through the red haze of his pain and brought him back to a world not centred on his tortured innards. The retching subsided.

There was more to come, he could tell from the writhing deep inside, but for now he had a respite.

He turned and found her hunched over on the floor, clutching her belly. Somehow she managed to call out for him. Pain saturated his body as he crawled towards her. She looked at him and their eyes met in tormented communion. She moaned, the tone low and unnatural.

He reached out his hand, tried to will himself to stretch so that they could touch. Christine reached out her own trembling hand. Together they strove to bridge the gap between their private realms of suffering. Only inches separated them, but it was still too far.

Strength spent, he looked on helplessly. Christine's imploring eyes held his gaze and he tried harder. Her hand still reached out to him, fingers spread wide in an attempt to extend her reach. A scream as her obscenely swollen belly throbbed and pulsated. The skin stretched impossibly thin, gave way and ripped open. Underlying muscle lay exposed and then that too parted under the strain.

Blood gushed, erupted in a crimson fountain that flooded over her skin and soaked into the carpet. Droplets splashed his face as he screamed in horror.

Something small moved in the gaping fissure of torn flesh. Christine's scream was ragged; she arched her back. Her hands held her belly tight, as though trying to prevent what was happening. Butterflies swarmed from between her fingers; gushed out of the terrible fissure that split her body.

"Daviiiid!" she yelled, shrill, piercing, her face contorted. The tears flooded from Mills at last as Christine's body dissolved to her final dying shriek. Flesh faded, the colours bleached away to reveal the underlying skeleton, a complex vector drawing of a human figure. That too disappeared line by line, until nothing of Christine remained, not even the blood that stained the floor.

He cried. Called out Christine's name. The tears flooded from him now. He wept, all the buried emotion released by that sudden gaping hole, ripped from his life. Yet the sound of a billion tiny wings callously drowned the sound of grief.

The butterflies burst from the cottage as the door exploded outwards, broken from its hinges by the pressure. Gelatinous ooze from crushed insects corroded its edges. The windows shattered and unleashed yet more of the insects. He retched again and another swarm of butterflies took to the air. Then the world slipped away and he knew nothing more.

CHAPTER 14:
News from Nowhere

GLOBAL.WEB.NEWS

Killer virus strikes at net
By Siobhan Keller

London Bureau
07.35 GMT 22 April 2070 – London

THOUSANDS of people are dead and up to a
million trapped within the JobNet recruitment
network today after an attack by a devastating new
virus.

The outbreak erupted in the early hours of the
morning. Operators only became aware of the
attack when their monitoring systems shut down
following a brief warning.

At care sites across the UK, "residents" went

into neural shock and died. Still more were left trapped inside artificial reality (AR). The nature of the full-immersion AR means that a delicate procedure must be followed whenever the connection is terminated. Failure to do so can result in brain damage.

Automatic mechanisms that should have triggered the moment the virus was detected failed to operate.

Central Systems Operation Chief for JNA (GB), Martin Conway, said: "Even if the automatic systems were inoperative, residents should be able to logout 'manually'. The fact that nobody has come out suggests that the virus has knocked out this system. The trouble is we have no idea what's going on. The virus has effectively locked us out."

The shock event is still sinking in, and little is known for certain. The death toll is expected to rise in the UK, and it will certainly rise globally once JNA's overseas divisions report in.

Eric Carswell, Chief Executive of UK Benefits & Welfare, owner of the JobNet Agency, was unavailable for comment. Spokesmen said he has been informed of the disaster and is putting together a crisis team to deal with the situation. He is expected to issue a statement later in the day.

So far the extent of the problem within the

system is unknown. That it kills shows the malignant nature of the virus. Where it came from, how it got into the system, and how far it will spread are questions that still need answers.

"These are questions that will have to be looked into much later," Mr Conway added. "Right now we have a lot of people trapped and our first priority must be to get them out."

ENDS

UPDATE
From New York Bureau
10.30 GMT 22 April 2070

FEARS of the virus that attacked the JobNet Agency have rattled investors and businessmen. Wall Street reacted badly to the news and share prices fell sharply.

Companies have been hastily severing connections to JobNet in order to protect themselves from potential infection. Sensibly, these are maintained within dedicated sub-systems that have little or no presence within the main corporate networks, offering some degree of protection.

Nobody is genuinely isolated from the global web, however, and there is a prevailing fear that it is only a matter of time before the virus does spread. To this end, companies have been withdrawing all non-essential personnel from their AR operations.

ENDS

UK Benefits & Welfare
Statement to Press & Media

Immediate release

14.36 GMT 22 April 2070

Rescue anticipated in deadly virus attack

Résumé of statement from ERIC CARSWELL,
Chief Executive UK Benefits & Welfare
(full transcription or digital audio visual available
on request):

"This morning, at 3.05 a.m., an unknown virus was detected in the JobNet system. This virus activated and proceeded to shut our technicians out of the mainframe. We are still attempting to regain control of the AR system-manager.

"It seems an understatement to say that this is an unprecedented human tragedy.

"We are doing our utmost to alleviate this situation. Some of the best brains in the fields of Artificially Intelligent Information Technology and Artificial Reality are working around the clock to rescue the millions of people who are trapped. I anticipate that we will have made significant progress within 24 hours.

"In the meantime people should try to remain calm. This is difficult, I know, especially for those who have family and friends 'resident' within our mainframes across the globe.

"Rest assured, no effort is being spared to find a solution to this tragedy.

"The fear that the virus will spread is utterly unfounded. The moment the virus was detected our system was thrown off-line. This had the effect of severing it from the global networks. I must stress that there is absolutely NO DANGER that corporate or government systems beyond JobNet will become infected. These fears within the business community and general users are causing needless worry and distress.

"This disaster is not an accident. It is not the product of mismanagement or incompetence. It is the product of sheer human malice.

"Somewhere a person, or persons, fed this virus into the system. Such an action can only be considered murder. MASS MURDER. The perpetrators will be found and prosecuted with the full force of the law.

"For the moment, however, we must concentrate on saving the millions of innocent people who have fallen victim to this malicious attack.

"For the families and friends of those who died, my heart goes out to you. Your grief is shared by all of us at UK Benefits & Welfare. We exist to improve the human condition, by getting people back to work and thereby restoring their sense of self-esteem and worth to society. People are our business. So this loss of life hurts us deeply.

"Perhaps we have failed the dead. We must not fail the survivors. Nothing can be done for those who have been murdered, except grieve. The living need us more. They can still be saved.

"As Chief Executive of UK Benefits & Welfare, it is my responsibility, ultimately, to see to the well-being of our customers. Every resource at my disposal will be utilised to find a solution to this human catastrophe.

"I cannot stress enough that needless rumours and worry will only add to the distress and hinder rescue efforts.

"Please help us to help you."

A public information network has been established. If you are concerned for family or friends contact your local UK Benefits & Welfare office, JobMart or JobNet Agency branch.

ENDS

GLOBAL.WEB.NEWS

Anarcho-terrorists planted virus, source says
By Siobhan Keller

London Bureau
11.42 GMT 23 April 2070

ANARCHO-terrorists are responsible for the
deaths of thousands of people after they planted a
virus in the stricken JobNet computers, according
to sources in the Social Security Agency.

The virus they used is alleged to be an
experimental military program specifically
designed to disrupt the function of artificial
intelligences and virtual reality systems.

An insidious aspect of the virus is the havoc it
can play with the human nervous system. It is
possible for victims caught within an infected AR
world to be driven insane by the psycho-toxic
effects. According to the source, a fundamentalist
human rights movement, the Martyrs of Jarrow
(MoJ), deliberately infected JobNet. It is believed
they attempted to shut down the network and
infect corporate systems in protest against what
they deem to be inhumane treatment of the
unemployed.

Anarcho-chaos is an eclectic movement that
takes many forms. Generally, it consists of an

apocalyptic amalgam of anarchism and chaos theory, with undertones of agrarian socialism. It is rife amongst the disadvantaged and morally incapable, although alarmingly some of its adherents enjoy status within society.

As yet there has been no independent corroboration regarding the allegations, and the MoJ has not issued any demands or claimed responsibility for the attack. If this is the work of the MoJ, then it brings to an end an eight-year period of inactivity.

The Martyrs of Jarrow were responsible for a spate of bombings and cyber-terrorism through the late '50s and early '60s. Their irresponsible actions were alleged to be in protest against the organic means-testing of claimants, labour camps, compulsory work schemes and curfew policies.

These, of course, are designed to protect the genuine unemployed from fraudulent claimants and give them a sense of personal wellbeing by keeping them active. Nevertheless some elements considered the policies unjust and a denial of basic human rights. However, the policies proved popular with the general stakeholders and served to raise confidence in UK Benefits & Welfare stock.

Eric Carswell, Chief Executive of JNA's parent company yesterday promised that the situation would be well in hand. The 24 hours have elapsed and technicians are still shut out of the system. More deaths have been reported and millions remain trapped across the globe.

After calls for his resignation, Mr Carswell replied: "Neither I, nor my staff, can be held responsible for the actions of terrorists. Nobody is secure from a determined drive to cause mayhem."

Eric Carswell rose to prominence 20 years ago after he transformed a mundane government agency – regarded as a backwater in political circles – into a successful commercial enterprise that generates significant income for its shareholders and the Treasury Agency. From its core remit of human resources management it expanded into Artificially Intelligent Information Technology, bio-tech and industrial genetics, among other things, through a combination of organic growth and some shrewd strategic acquisitions and joint-venture partnerships.

The news that the virus outbreak could be the work of terrorists may well save the career of this former high-flyer.

The security source was unable to say where the terrorists may have acquired this virus. "All kinds of nasty little surprises can be bought on the market," the source said. "These things were designed to eat their way through any anti-virus defence – in the global web, where everything is connected to everything else, that could spell absolute catastrophe. Forget a few thousand dead and millions trapped, we could lose everything."

UK Benefits & Welfare remains adamant that the virus will not escape its system, military program or otherwise.

ENDS

GLOBAL.WEB.NEWS
London Bureau
09.54 GMT 24 April 2070

"Martyrs" deny cyber-terrorism

ANARCHO-terrorist group, the Martyrs of Jarrow (MoJ), today issued a statement denying any involvement with the virus attack on the JobNet recruitment system.

"We exist to promote and defend the interests of the unemployed, who have been systematically persecuted by society for the 'crime' of being thrown out of work," the statement reads. "Why would we, therefore, strike at our comrades incarcerated in these fictitious recruitment ploys?

"The MoJ utterly repudiates the insinuation that we are responsible for this brutal action against this downtrodden section of humanity."

Senior police officials who have experience dealing with the MoJ's past atrocities have accepted the statement's authenticity. Furthermore, the statement contained recognised code words to validate its source.

The MoJ go on to claim that the virus attack is a "ploy by the Social Security Agency to cull the numbers of unemployed".

A spokesman for the Prime Minister, who stands by yesterday's announcement that the Martyrs of Jarrow are responsible for this attack, has called the denial "ludicrous".

ENDS

CHAPTER 15:
Guilty Secrets

TERRIBLE news, Jane thought as she sat in the gloom. She'd called in sick two days ago, when the disaster first struck. Since then all she could do was stare at the screen and watch the nightmare unfold.

Those damning news items glared back at her from the screen of her notebook. A military virus, the authorities were saying. It didn't make sense; what could have gone wrong? She ought to be terrified; guilt was stronger. So many people were dead because of her. She tried to picture the faces of the ones she'd personally ushered into the nightmare, yet she couldn't dredge any from the depths of memory. The dead are anonymous, just as they were in life.

The phone's sudden chirp startled her from the grip of morbid gloom. She stared at it, as if she had forgotten what it was for, and wondered whether to answer. Then again, what if it was Stuart? That thought – that need – motivated her sluggish limbs. After a breath to steady her nerves she picked up the handset. "Hello?" Her voice quavered on the edge of tears.

"Hi Jane! It's Alice. Just ringing to see how you're doing."

"Oh, hello," she said, hoping the disappointment didn't show in her voice. "I'm fine I suppose. Apart from this awful 'flu."

"You do sound rough. I hope you're taking things easy. Actually, I could do with some sick leave right now. Things are crazy around here after what happened."

"Is it bad?"

"Hectic. All the zeros have been excused attendance. Seems all we're doing is sorting out the live ones from the stiffs – that and fending off worried relatives. Not my idea of fun."

Jane chewed her lip. Alice sounded so put out, as though she'd been asked to cover for a sick colleague when she'd planned to go to a party. What did any of them care? They weren't dealing with human beings: just the unemployed.

"So, where's that man of yours?" Alice asked, mock cheerful. "When he called in sick too I got so jealous. I wish someone would take the time to pamper me, you know…"

Not now. Not with all that's happened. "Oh Alice, you'll find someone," she soothed, feeling her own loneliness stirring. The woman's relationship failures were a legend around the office. She missed no opportunity to court sympathy.

"Yeah. I suppose so. Anyway, you two aren't exactly subtle. Fancy calling in sick on the same day, I hope I haven't interrupted anything too raunchy!"

The first sob erupted from her throat and a flood of tears followed. Unable to hold the emotion back, she allowed herself the chance to vent her feelings. Alice may not have been there in person, but even a long-distance shoulder was better than nothing.

"Stuart isn't here. I haven't seen him for days. He's not at his flat; neighbours said he took off. I don't know where he is. He hasn't called or answered the phone."

"I'm sorry," Alice said, sounding genuinely concerned. "You two haven't had a row have you?"

"No."

"Well, maybe he's really sick. You're always so close after all; it's a wonder the Boss never noticed. You probably gave him a dose of 'flu."

"So why isn't he at home, then?" Her tone was sharper than she intended. She took a deep breath. "Sorry, Alice. I just need him, that's all. I've done something terrible…"

She stopped herself just in time. Phones have ears. You never know who is listening. Even so, it would be such a relief to tell someone and unburden the guilt.

"You haven't got yourself pregnant have you?"

"No!"

"Glad to hear it. The Boss would hit the roof!"

She laughed through her tears. The suggestion was so outrageous she couldn't help joining her friend's humour. Laughter made such a welcome change after the melancholy days that she realised just how much she missed human company. Especially Stuart's. Yet just when she needed him most he had vanished. Typical man.

"I'll kick his balls when I do see him," she said, some lightness returning to her mood; maybe Alice was a tonic after all. "Only not too hard; he's got some making up to do."

"That's the spirit," Alice laughed. "So what's so terrible? Come on, you can tell me."

Jane almost put the phone down then, but a confessional urge took hold; she longed to share the burden with someone. Maybe Alice would understand, then she wouldn't feel so alone.

"I killed those people."

Confession brought no relief, however, just a fear of the reaction. Alice made no sound.

"Alice?"

"Don't do this to yourself, Jane. You can't blame yourself for doing your job. All you did was plug them into the system. What happens after that isn't your fault."

"I suppose not."

"Not good enough. I want to hear you say it. Come on say it: it wasn't your fault."

"It wasn't my fault," she whispered, feeling utterly

forlorn.

"I couldn't hear you. Say it louder."

"IT WASN'T MY FAULT!"

"That's better. I want you to remember that. You can't let these zeros play on your sympathy. Do that and they'll take you for everything you've got."

Alice didn't understand. Jane felt lost. All she wanted to do was help people. The system was wrong, but nobody seemed to care. Except Stuart…

"Oh shit! The Boss is doing the rounds," Alice said. "I've got to go. Are you going to be all right?"

"Yes."

"Sure? You don't want me to come round after work? Keep you company."

"No. I'll be fine. Thanks for the offer though."

"Okay. If you're sure."

"Thanks for calling, Alice. It was nice to hear from you."

"Any time. Bye!"

Abruptly the line went dead. With a sigh Jane put the handset down and slumped onto the couch. Then she lay back and closed her eyes.

They were waiting in the shadows, the crowds, and every one of them lacked a face. But in the middle of the multitude Mills stood slightly taller. Slowly he raised his hand and pointed in silent accusation.

"I'm sorry," she whispered. It was all she could find to say.

"PULL!"

Dark specks arced gracefully through the air and exploded into fragments. The twin roars from the Prime Minister's shotgun pummelled Carswell's ears before fading into the distance.

"Good shooting, Sir!" one of the nameless flunkies called out. Polite clapping greeted Carlisle's beaming face when he turned round to give a mock bow. Carswell joined in, smiling weakly at the junior minister beside him, some nondescript lapdog with a damp lower lip and watery eyes.

The Prime Minister reloaded and unleashed another volley. Each blast caused an involuntary flinch and twice he spilled tea on his lap. He hated guns. Unfortunately, Carlisle loved them.

So did his men. Not that you could see them, but he knew they were out there somewhere. He sipped his tea and looked around. The other guests paid little heed. Most of them lacked the imagination to picture the nearby trees hiding armed guards and state-of-the-art security systems. That was the one saving grace – the Summer House was one of the most secure places in the entire capital.

"Enjoying the view, Mr Carswell?"

"What?"

"Forgive me for interrupting your thoughts, I just asked if you were enjoying the view."

"Yes. It's quite breathtaking." He turned to face the speaker at the next table, the bald-headed man in the bland suit, quite out of place amongst the expensive tailor-mades of the other guests. He wondered what such a badly dressed individual was doing there at all. Then he caught sight of the barcode laser-burned onto the man's forehead.

"Would you partake of a little caviar? It is very good, Father has it smuggled in from his Russian holdings."

"No thanks," he replied, appetite suddenly quite gone. "I ate before I arrived."

"Ah well, your loss."

The freak turned away to deliver the plate into the hands of a harassed-looking waitress. Carswell allowed himself a little shiver. Just his luck to run into one of the PM's freaks: his special bodyguard. No secret they were bred in vats, from the PM's own modified genetic material. Not quite clones. And they were absolutely loyal.

"This is your first visit to the Summer House?"

"No. I've been before – on business – not quite like this. In fact, I'm waiting to see the PM now."

"You like Father's retreat?"

Before he could answer the PM let rip with another blast. Carswell flinched and bit his tongue. The freak gave a cadaverous smile. "You do not like guns, Mr Carswell?"

"No, not much." He struggled to regain his composure, embarrassed to have his dislike publicly broadcast.

Almost as though on cue, a burst of derogatory laughter came from a man across the table. It was Edward Soames, the Mayor of London. "Can't stand guns?" he snorted. "Never took you for effeminate, Eric."

Soames laughed and slapped the thigh of the woman on his lap, another of the carefully vetted courtesans he was so fond of. She giggled and wriggled provocatively. Soames rolled his eyes in playful ecstasy, and parted his lips to accept the spoonful of caviar the women shovelled into his mouth.

"Guns do not define the calibre of the man," the freak said. "Especially when it is known they are impotent."

The buzz of inconsequential conversation faded. "Why you…" Soames stopped once he noticed the barcode. The freak smiled, but there was no humour in the gesture. Carswell sipped his tea and tried to pretend he was elsewhere.

"You know, you're absolutely right," Soames said, laughing nervously. The freak turned away, dismissing one of the most powerful men in the country as though he were jobless.

"I am Shreck," the freak said after a while. "And I ask again. Do you like Father's retreat?"

"Oh yes. It's peaceful, clay pigeons aside. Makes a change from the city."

Except the Prime Minister's private retreat was slap bang *in* the city. The place where Carlisle conducted most of his business had been described as a modern version of a baronial manor by some foreign diplomat or other, and – who knows – maybe that secretly pleased the old man.

The Summer House itself was an airy and thoroughly modern structure; a geometric arrangement of glass and engineered timber cuboids, but it was the grounds that really set the place apart. Out there, masked by the woodlands and tall hedges, were the barracks and guardhouses, and the rest of the security apparatus that kept this place secure.

The grounds consisted of some 10 square miles of landscaped parklands; some of it leftover from the last time London had hosted the Olympics, back in the early part of the century. The rest had been carved out of the former borough of Newham in the years following the unification of the capital's administrative structure.

On a good day, the blade-shapes and sail-forms of New Canary Wharf's skyscrapers could be seen over the treetops to the south, towering majestically over the blocky mausoleum-shapes of the original buildings. Now that was a sight to see, on a clear night, when those towers blazed with light and their navigation beacons beckoned to the stars. But they offered no constellations for a man charting a course through the shifting currents of political power, he thought ruefully.

"Did you know that Father generously re-housed all the people who once lived here?" said Shreck, pulling him back to the here and now. "They were poor, and yet he helped them. He is a great man. A caring man."

A brief smile flickered across Carswell's face. Looking carefully at Shreck, he realised the freak was totally sincere. Such naiveté. Re-housed? Try dispersed to whatever provincial backwater would accept them. The misconception was interesting, though. So the PM even lied to his pets? He made a mental note of the deception.

"He favours you," the freak continued. "He considers you one of his ablest executives."

Hostile glances seared the back of his neck. He could feel the heat. It didn't do to be praised so publicly.

"I do my best. It's an honour to serve my Prime Minister." Hopefully that would be a safe reply.

"Which makes what has happened all the more unfortunate. Father is much displeased."

"Ah!" The surrounding hostility turned to lynch-mob glee. "That situation will be resolved. I'll inform the PM as such when I see him."

"So you say. Yet there is the possibility of danger."

"I don't follow –"

"We in the Social Security Agency greatly appreciate the services you render to society. Though you do not know it, we have worked at times to aid your activities. We consider it of the utmost importance that you be allowed to continue your work."

"I don't know what you mean," he replied, trying to hide a sense of random guilt. They couldn't possibly know. Yet it was said the SSA even knew God's secrets.

"As you wish." Shreck smiled. "Just consider this: we exist to protect Father. This situation may threaten him. And that, ultimately, is your responsibility. So pray that this situation be resolved promptly. Hurt him. And we shall hurt you."

POLITICIANS come and go, Parliaments change, even parties rise and fall, but the Prime Minister was always there. Carlisle was a constant in government, member of all parties, beholden to none.

Captured in synthetic oils, he glowered statesmanlike from the canvas. He overlooked the minions who kept his regime ticking over. Small, nervous men orchestrated by the will of the longest serving British premier in modern history.

Carswell look around apprehensively, aware that he was one of those minions, jostling for position and competing for the PM's patronage like all the rest. The feeling was unpleasant, to be a small fish in the wrong pond awaiting the shark's return. Was that how his own staff felt? Better to be the shark than the minnow. The sooner he got back to his own fief the better.

The machinery of government buzzed around him. Men with notebooks and desktop computers worked their mysterious magic. Political alchemists, they balanced delicate social forces on the razor's edge of one man's will. If only events hadn't brought him to the centre of this Machiavellian web.

How the waiting grated at the nerves! He recognised the game, played it often enough with his own people. The portrait formed a nice addition, an intimidating addition.

Those fierce eyes seemed to glare right at him. A formidable man, his master, Carswell wiped his sweaty palms on his trousers.

"Ah Eric! Do take a seat."

Startled, he turned his gaze away from the portrait. The Prime Minister swept past, leaving a scent-trail of cordite and gun oil. For all his bulk the man moved like a cat.

"Prime Minister! You wanted to see me?"

In the flesh Carlisle didn't seem so bad. Easily mistaken for someone's grandfather. Somehow that made him worse. Young eyes gazed from wrinkled flesh, a playful gleam deep in the pupils. He gestured towards a chair and Carswell sat down in what he hoped was a business-like manner.

Two Social Security Agents flanked the Prime Minister's chair. One of them was Shreck. Carswell was dismayed to find the other physically identical. They both stared impassively with those characteristically dead eyes.

"Have you met Reich and Shreck?" the PM asked conversationally. "Two of my best agents. They're twins you know. Most unusual. We can tinker, accelerate their growth, but Madame Nature won't be denied her little quirks."

The two men ignored his polite nod, but there was a faint hint of malicious humour around – Shreck's? – eyes. Another man joined them. He leaned against the panes of the glass wall and gazed out at the flowerbeds beyond. The reflection revealed a barcode.

The Prime Minister gestured to the newcomer. "You don't mind if Chief sits in on our little meeting do you, Eric?"

"No, sir."

"Good. I didn't think you would. He's my liaison to the Social Security Agency's chiefs of staff. I think you'll find his input most engaging."

Carswell nodded, resisting the urge to tug at the knot of his tie. Theoretically, Carlisle should have surrendered his control of the Social Security Agency once he became PM. He knew better. Control of the SSA had brought Carlisle to power and it had kept him there all these years.

"Now then Eric, what have you been up to?"

"Sir?"

"This situation with the virus is not good. I appreciate what you are trying to do, but you could have found a safer way. You're not supposed to burn the guards along with the inmates."

"I'm sorry Sir, I don't understand –"

"Just my little joke, Eric."

"Father is referring indirectly to your policy of incarceration within the JobNet system," the man at the window, Chief, interrupted.

"Quite so." Carlisle sat back in his chair and steepled his fingers together. He looked over the tips almost as though sighting his shotgun. Sweat began to run down Carswell's back.

"I don't see what this has to do with the virus, Sir. Yes, we utilise certain surplus elements. Artificial reality has been demonstrated to work more efficiently the more users are hooked up. There is the added benefit that we are able to utilise an otherwise useless resource, thereby reducing numbers."

"Some people might say you're depriving them of their civil rights."

The Prime Minister was playing with him; the man who had systematically suspended every civil liberty, without actually striking them from the statute books, and he had used the unemployed for this very purpose.

Carlisle rose to power on the back of the Turmoil, when millions of jobless rioted and ransacked society. The old regime had proved incompetent, not to mention uncaring. The situation was exacerbated by the fact that they had arisen on the promise of social justice – surely an outmoded concept now if ever there was one. Then Carlisle turned up from the shadows. With a politician's honey-tongued cant, he promised great things, wonderful things.

Unbeknown to the general public he headed some obscure branch of the intelligence services, what became the forerunner of his Social Security Agency. There were rumours that Carlisle had caused the unrest that exploded into the Turmoil, or at least he manipulated it to help his power play, but sensible people didn't talk about such things – or think them for that matter.

On the whole people were too relieved that the violence was brought to an end to question their leader, or why his years of rule turned into decades. The power of terror, and it was a terrifying period, he remembered from the time he was at Civil Service college. Back when the Civil Service still existed in any meaningful sense.

"With respect, Sir, you don't believe that," he said cautiously.

"I believe whatever is conducive to efficient government."

"Your policy of incarceration is immaterial," Chief said. "Except for one thing. This man, Mills. We are aware of the problem you experienced regarding his location. We are also aware that you highlighted him as potential material for permanent incorporation within the AI-subsystems and took steps to prevent his obtaining employment."

"He had skills and aptitudes that the computer models suggested were favourable to an increase in network efficiency, yes. The tragedy of it all is he put himself forward for employment within JobNet. We couldn't have contrived it bet–"

"Ironic. That the man you selected as a new component should turn out to be the conveyance for the entity that may destroy your system."

"This man was used to carry the virus," the Prime Minister interjected.

"Ah!" So that was it. He should have guessed. This

wasn't going to go down well at the committee of inquiry. That is, if the Prime Minister decided it was politick to allow such scrutiny. He shifted uncomfortably in his seat. They couldn't blame him. It was not his responsibility if terrorists attacked the network. "I see," was all he could think of to say.

Suddenly Chief leaned over. The device cradled in his hand displayed several photographs and scrolling data windows. The names and details meant little.

"Observe," he said. "These images were taken from City Watch cameras. Note the images of the man and the woman. Both of them work for your agency, Mr Carswell. You will note the man – Stuart Sutcliffe under his current alias – has a long history of terrorist activity."

"I can't be held responsible… I'm not in security –"

"You do not conduct basic identity checks?"

"Of course –"

"Then I should have them improved. Note this man: Clute. He is a known anarcho-chaotic terrorist. Two of your employees were seen talking to this man. They also handled Mills' uplink before he conveniently disappeared. Were you also aware that this Mills has links to the Martyrs of Jarrow organisation, and a prior record of cyber-crime? Your incompetence has endangered us."

"I don't see how. The virus is static." The material in his briefcase seemed utterly irrelevant now. This wasn't the crisis briefing he had been led to believe. Rather it was a trial. Unfair. Suddenly he realised the PM was laughing.

"Poor Eric. Let me give you some advice. The art of government is in hiring the right staff to do the work for you. Just let them get on with things while you handle the broader issues. A man who must control everything is a man who controls nothing."

With a casual gesture from the PM, Chief backed off. Carswell felt his muscles unknot and he began to breathe again.

"As to the virus," Chief added, "it is static at the moment. We do not know how long that situation will hold."

"Wait a minute! You have a go at me for employing terrorists, yet you allowed a terrorist to get his hands on this thing! If you knew so much why didn't you intervene before?"

"Eric!" the PM barked. And then more softly: "Kindly remember where you are."

"I'm sorry, Prime Minister."

Red-faced, Chief paced round to the back of Carswell's chair. He gripped the backrest and leaned over. "We are not infallible," he said. "Yet! Even we cannot control everything. We deal in probabilities. Not certainties."

"Sir. Would you like to hear my report now?" Fingers fumbled at the lock on his briefcase. Carswell cursed and felt his face flush. The muscles in his forearms trembled with suppressed anger. As a high-level executive he should not be receiving such treatment. He knew his job and expected a little professional courtesy, not a view that would wash with the Prime Minister.

"No, Mr Carswell, we shall not be requiring your report," Chief said. "You are to be relieved of the problem."

"That is correct, Eric. This one is beyond your resources. Don't look so glum. I still have a very high regard for you. One day, I hope, you will be joining my staff. I was very impressed when you turned your little department into a successful commercial venture. I never thought it could be done."

"Thank you, Prime Minister." Yes. A commercial venture. And it was his. They could remove him from office but they couldn't take away his stock in the companies he established. Then his gaze fell on Chief and his blood ran cold. They didn't need to take his stock. They could take something much more precious.

CHAPTER 16:
Sins of the Father

CONSCIENCE was a curious thing, Stuart considered, as he stared at the syringe in his hand. First, it had given them Conway – a coup, for the man was situated right in the nerve-centre of JobNet – then it took him away again before he might deliver their little contingency plan.

Stuart depressed the plunger and watched the fluid spurt onto the concrete floor of the 'safe house'. Once it was empty, he threw the syringe away with a snort. Somehow, he had to explain to Clute why the virus encoded in the nanocule solution wasn't working its mayhem in the Core-AI.

Nobody had expected the machine to retract itself from the network before it could be infected. That's why. Out-manoeuvred by a machine, it was *fucking* embarrassing. By the time they came up with this alternative arrangement, the virus was wreaking chaos in the general JobNet system, courtesy of their human carrier; more than enough to provoke Conway's latest attack of conscience. The man was proving a proper turncoat.

"You lied to me. A military virus. Do your own dirty work from now on," the man's printed note said. What did he expect, everybody wakes up and lives happily ever after? Maybe he did at that. The man was a fool, the handwritten postscript confirmed that: "Don't worry, I won't say anything, if only for my sake."

The spooks at the Social Security Agency would have loved that bit of penmanship, though Conway had probably left trace DNA all over the note anyway. Stuart scrunched the strip of paper into a ball and popped it into his mouth. He chewed it into mulch while he thought things through, then he swallowed the mash; Clute always said in this age of high-tech surveillance the old ways were best.

He'd found the note wrapped round the syringe in the dead letter box – a convenient hollow in a tree – he'd established across the river from the Agency's headquarters at Thames House. The drop location had amused Clute no end, but he wasn't going to find this little setback funny.

"Shit!" There was no way to avoid this; just get it over with. He reached for his AR headset, quickly checked the cables and the remote transceiver, and then glanced quickly around the old lock-up garage that served as a safe house. Everything looked secure enough for this brief venture into Clute's secure AR domain; he'd already established the hack into a nearby network node, his top-up dose of nanocules should have settled in, there really was no more excuse for prevarication.

Even so, he paused with the headset raised halfway to his scalp. Conway's change of heart wasn't really the problem, was it? There was Jane to consider. He'd left her to it, without so much as a note or a goodbye; she must be going out of her mind with worry.

No, none of that mattered; he'd shed that life now. Jane had served her purpose; whatever happened to her now wasn't his problem. He'd done it before, easy. Plenty of women, one or two men, he'd left a trail of hearts broken for the cause. But Jane...

"Focus!" He squeezed his eyes shut, cleared his mind, built a mental wall around his uncertainties. "Okay. Let's do this." Stuart slipped on the headset, secured the straps, and then settled down onto the old camp bed. By touch he located the controls and triggered the calibration and transition process.

As he felt himself slip into that semi-dream state, he vaguely wondered what kind of mind-fuck agitprop Clute had created for this particular meeting – the old man just couldn't resist the theatrics – but then the simulation snatched him from the realm of flesh.

ACCELERATION gripped Stuart, pulling him clear of his

body and leaving it far behind. Senses soared as his soul took flight. A moan of exhilaration and he was there in the virtual realm.

Purpose, not quite his own, took control and scanned the darkness with the mind's eye until it located a distant point of light. The raging star burned hot and wrathful. It took on the shape of a man. A gargantuan figure. Clute was that shining light, the beacon that others followed.

Souls merged. Thoughts meshed. A comforting feeling of togetherness strengthened the bonds until the disparate minds became one. No longer alone, Stuart bathed in the comforting sense of belonging.

And then – once they were ready – Clute's enormous manifestation spoke.

"CAPITALISM," Clute bellowed, "is a Crime Against Humanity!"

"Yes!" the gestalt chorused.

Savage knowledge flooded into the collected minds. The deluge cascaded over the small part identified as Stuart and he felt it gush into his mind to batter the mental wall he'd built to shield his doubts and uncertainties.

The world appeared from the shadows; suspended in space like an orb of polished emerald and sapphire. No sooner did it appear, than Stuart felt his perspective shift with a gut-churning lurch. Now he wasn't looking at the world, he was the world, spinning around that life-giving sun.

Pain replaced knowledge. The combined torment of every living thing on Earth wailed through his senses. Data windows scrolled in the void to add insight to the pain: pollution levels, deforestation rates, urban expansion, climatic alterations, species counts. A litany of destruction and savagery engulfed rationality. The fabric of a world torn apart was paraded before his eyes, all for the twin Gods of Profit and Power.

The gestalt-world cried in helpless sorrow. Stuart could do nothing but add his own tears to the flow of grief. Then the images collapsed into the darkness of space. He blinked. The stars burned bright in the distance, signifying a cosmos at peace, far away from the madness and the slaughter that was terrestrial existence.

The sensorium construct cut to a new scene. Suddenly Stuart realised he did not float in the firmament. He was a globe suspended in a cavernous hall, no more than a football to the beings huddled around. As he rotated, he sensed other creatures. Behemoths in suits murmured into mobile phones. Behind them, he perceived the forgotten trophies of fallen empires, built and plundered for Profit and Power, now left to gather dust.

Behind them, another figure watched. This being sat on a throne of stacked coins placed at the top of a mound of gold. Stuart watched it retrieve a cigar with an invisible hand and place it to a featureless face.

Enough now, a part of him yearned, but held by the simulation's script, he could only spin and watch. He heard a chain rattle in the gloom. On his next rotation, he beheld a pot-bellied boy looking up at the Faceless Being. The boy held up a small bowl. His pleading eyes bulged from the shrunken face. The Being turned and looked down at the boy in a way that suggested a benevolent smile.

"How thoughtful," it said, and flicked ash into the bowl. The boy looked down in dismay.

To the side of the throne, three cherubic figures squatted in chains and filthy rags. Liberty, Equality and Fraternity. How did he know? Somehow the knowledge arrived unbidden. Liberty looked down at her chains. Stuart sensed her sorrow but felt helpless as a tear ran down her cheek. Then a dog barked ferociously at the cherubs, turning sorrow to fear.

"Down, Freemarket! Heel!"

The dog looked up at the Faceless Being and howled mournfully. Stuart span away from the scene. Another being approached from the shadows. He wondered what this apparition was. The being came closer, peered down at the pathetic globe. Somewhere the gestalt cried in fear and loathing. The creature filled his field of vision. A hyena in pin stripe, fangs stained with blood, lips flecked with hungry salivation. The savage gleam of its eyes pierced Stuart's mind with terror. It opened its cruel jaws.

A muffled cry sputtered from his physical throat. The beast came for him. There was nowhere to hide. Terror threatened to break the gestalt, but at the last moment, reality shifted and he was free of those slavering jaws. He was no longer the world and he felt his fears comforted and smoothed away. The apparition vanished, replaced by a tantalising vision of a world healed of its hurt. Then that too faded into the darkness and only Clute's mammoth frame remained, pointing the way forward.

PROTECTED and supported. The gestalt shifted and stirred around him. Stuart felt the thoughts and feelings of his anonymous comrades; a tremendous sense of strength in unity.

It was so cold outside. Lonely. Isolated. Never knowing whom to trust. A brutal struggle for survival orchestrated by the wealthy few that owned the planet – body and soul. But here in the comforting realm of the mind, they could be together. They were free to be themselves.

Why couldn't it be like that outside?

"It will be. Once we are allowed to be Human again," Clute whispered in his mind.

Stuart started, his sense of self returned to some semblance of coherence. He could sense Clute all around him, even though the man's giant apparition continued to speak to the assembled minds.

"Trust me, Stuart."

Memories leaked. The gestalt swirled with understanding. It cried in sympathy with the weeping boy scavenging amongst the refuse of the glittering city, shared the sensation of the cold that bit through ragged clothes, felt the hunger in a shrunken belly.

A younger Clute found the boy collapsed and shivering in a refuse-strewn doorway. Stuart watched himself being picked up by the man, felt a sudden rush of anger. Not at the boy. And not his own anger. The younger Clute raged against a world that left a child to fend for itself.

The insight vanished suddenly, like a candle extinguished in the night. For a moment he managed to touch Clute's mind and sense that old love. The connection brought a sense of shame from the depths of his own mind. Affection had long since faded, lost somewhere along the diverging pathways of their lives. The wall he'd erected began to crack. Clute sensed his troubled thoughts.

"Tell me what's wrong, Stuart. Why are you so distant?"

Doubt threatened to break free in the face of confused emotions. An image of Jane flashed into his mind and stung with a sense of sorrow. The image and the emotion locked as the mental filaments that supported him began to fray and tear. The gestalt grew distant.

Some threads remained, however, and he felt the probing tendrils of Clute's mind. They found a fragment of emotion, probed it free, and recoiled in horror.

"You love her!" he declared.

"What?"

"You love that woman? How could you? She is one of them."

The accusation came with such force it stung. Clute's outrage throbbed along the few connections binding their thoughts. Baffled, Stuart sought the comfort of his comrades, but their minds were distant, still enmeshed within the gestalt as it rose in euphoria. Left with no retreat, he was forced to confront the truth he'd striven to hide – from himself most of all.

"So what if I do?" he said cautiously, still uncertain of himself. He had lived too many roles, maintained too many façades to be sure of anything any more. "Why shouldn't I?" he demanded.

"She is one of them."

The answer provoked his anger. He felt the distance that had developed between them over the years. "Aren't we supposed to be helping them?" he yelled.

"No! Not her kind. She is one of the perpetrators of the suffering, a guard in this global concentration camp. The People of the Abyss are our concern."

"Jane was trying to help them, in her way. That's why we used her. Remember? She cared about what happened to those people. She did her bit."

"Help them," Clute almost laughed. "She just sought to ease the suffering that's all. Not end it."

"So that's why we killed so many. To end their suffering."

"Too late for squeamish sentiments, my boy. You've

killed before."

"Only those who deserved it," he trembled at the memory, "never my own until now. You told me the virus was harmless. Yet it killed all those people. They weren't our enemies. But they're still dead. How does that save them?"

Clute's mind raged all around him. His soul was enmeshed in bitterness and a terrifying determination. In a way it had always surrounded him. That fleeting glimpse of human love was little more than a ghost, a mist dispersed by the winds of Clute's obsession.

"People die. Those deaths were necessary sacrifices for the greater good. They will be remembered as heroes."

"They didn't ask to be heroes!"

"True heroes never do."

Stuart felt the urge to cry. He followed the cause for this man. Killed for him. All for nothing. They had turned on their own in the name of the Almighty Cause and he had been too blind to see. What happened to the compassion? Where was the Humanity? Where were the ideals that burned in the heart?

Did Clute even believe in anything anymore? Jane believed, in her own way. She knew that people were important. Not things to be exploited according to a quantifiable use. Horrified, he recoiled from everything that guided his brief adult life. Suddenly he felt lost, and terribly alone.

They had become like those who devour the world,

their ideals consumed in rhetoric. The People were no longer individuals with their own unique hopes and dreams and lives. On the contrary, they were just a useful abstraction. The realisation brought a sense of shame coupled with the knowledge of what he may have lost. Suddenly he longed to be with Jane: the two of them curled up on the couch like any normal couple.

"What happened to you, Dad?" For once he allowed himself the use of the word. "Why did you go so cold?"

Something flashed in the enveloping aura. Doubt, and something else buried deep. For a moment it flared bright through the glare of anger. Shame. Then it vanished. If Clute realised what he had become he did not show it. A great sense of sadness blossomed in Stuart's mind. He knew they would never again be reconciled. "Are you with me?" Clute finally asked, his voice cold and harsh. "Or against me?"

"With you," he said with a mental sigh.

What else could he say? To pull out now was impossible. He was too deeply involved. Normality was no longer an option. He would ride the storm of chaos, but in his heart he was resolved that the storm would not sweep him away from Jane. Come what may, he'd find his way back to her. This time they'd stay together.

Yes, he conceded, conscience was a funny thing; still, at least he'd avoided the matter of Conway's change of heart.

CHAPTER 17:
Rude Awakening

REALITY *is pain. Not for nothing is it called the veil of tears, for it is the realm of shattered dreams and ruined hopes.*

Cold wind scours the desolate plains of actuality. Once it was a lush plain, Eden made flesh from the hopes of Man. Now, it is a landscape of despair, where the wind howls with the voices of the Damned. They wander lost in the harsh desolation, insect-small they scurry through the ruins and the wilderness. Each and every one is unified by one purpose: to find a way back to the comforting haven of delusion.

Gaunt trees rear up to the grim sky. Bare branches stretch towards the heavens as though pleading for a fresh eruption of foliage. Dark clouds blot the horizon, brooding phantasms that shift and stir against the wind. Thunder from the depths of the clouds blasts across the ruined plains and mutated forests.

Look closely at the clouds. See how they dance and swarm? Billions of insects gather to shroud reality beneath their delicate wings. Each thunderous roar is but the sum total of countless graceful beats.

The butterflies swarm above the horizon and crawl upon the surface of creation where they burrow deep within its fabric to become an integral part of that reality. They too are seeking a way out – to pastures new.

Pull out. Watch the world grow smaller. The butterflies form a dark tornado endlessly spiralling. Destruction and corruption follow in the wake of this dreadful swirl.

Focus on the eye of the storm. Peer deeper. At the bottom of the well of calm, there is a shattered cottage. Within the ruin, a man stirs and pulls himself from the wreckage. At last, he looks up into the eye of the storm... and screams.

VOICES whispered on the edge of hearing. Mills stirred, dislodging debris from his slumped body. He mumbled an unconscious reply. The voices continued to whisper with a persistent sibilance that sounded cruel and conspiratorial.

Consciousness oozed and gurgled into his brain. It spread like quicksilver, restoring life to abandoned muscles. A groan gurgled up through the phlegm clogging his throat. Suddenly he was fully awake. He coughed and spat to clear the dust from his irritated passages.

Reality flooded his senses, followed by the backwash of

memory. He jerked upright and glanced around. The cottage was a hollow shell open to the angry sky. Broken masonry and timber littered the inside and powdered mortar hung in the air to cloy at his nostrils and throat.

The nightmare was true. Christine was gone. He was alone again. Pain returned as he looked at the patch of rubble that marked her last point of existence. Nothing remained of his lover, except the gnawing teeth of grief.

Tears spilled. Then he threw his head back and screamed at the heavens. The scream faded to a wail, then a whimper. He sobbed where he sat.

Everything of any value had been taken from him: his job, his life, and his parents. Now Christine, too, had been snatched away to leave him empty: devoid of fulfilment, bereft of hope.

Eventually the tears subsided. A hollow feeling in the pit of his stomach remained as an empty reservoir for sorrow. It would fill again in time. For now survival beckoned. He got to his feet and forced his mind to consider the practicalities of his situation.

For one thing, he was naked but for his underpants. That was no way to face a virtual apocalypse. He willed himself clothed but the magic had gone; he remained resolutely undressed. Staring down at himself, he waggled his toes uncertainly. "Bollocks!"

Luck hadn't entirely deserted him, though. A quick rummage through the ruined cottage turned up some of the clothes he'd manifested on previous occasions. He dressed himself, dragged on boots retrieved from beneath the bed and hurriedly laced them up.

Now, all he had to do was remember what Christine had told him about the emergency protocols; easier said than done, he'd not taken it seriously. How many ever did? He shook his head at the absurdity of his priorities: dress first, bail second. Christine would have found it funny, that's for sure. He turned to gaze at the patch of floor where she'd flickered out of existence and swallowed a sob. Instead he sniffed, sucking up his grief for later.

"Logout," he said. Nothing. What was it? He tried again: "Emergency logout. Shit!"

He closed his eyes and thought, fists clenched at his sides. Wait, that was it. "Emergency logout protocol: Mills, David—DF874920S. Initiate…" He paused, looked again where Christine had been; he didn't want to leave without her, but she wasn't here; this wasn't real. He could only hope she was waiting for him somewhere in the physical world. He sighed, whispered: "Release me. Release me. Release me."

But there was no release. The protocols weren't working. An electric thrill of fear clenched his diaphragm; his chest ached as he realised he was trapped. He turned to face the door, hanging off its hinges, and looked out at the ruined world that had once seemed such a fairy tale place.

Reluctantly, he left the cottage. The village lay in ruins, he saw: shrouded by clouds of dust and smoke. A black column rose into the air, obscuring the distorted forest on the valley's far slope. A cocktail of odours filled the air; an acrid, chemical stench that stung the nostrils and throat if breathed too deep. The wind carried an underlying hint of smoke and fire, tinged with human terror. But in all the expanse, no human could be seen.

Maybe he was the last man in the whole of ersatz creation? With a heavy heart, he followed the broken path towards the village. The route was unconsciously etched into the furrows of his mind, but no longer recognisable.

Brambles and thorns clung to his boots. The undergrowth was as tough and sharp as razor wire. Looking down, he saw why. Wicked slivers of steel did indeed mimic natural blades and he winced as one nicked his shin. If only he could keep his thoughts to himself – but that was impossible. Ruined or not, this world was wired directly to his inner self.

That Inner Self left him no peace. Memories and feelings cascaded through his mind: the green hues of grass and leaf, the sweet song of birds flitting from branch to branch above his head, sweet scented flowers and the golden sun flashing from stream or pond. Beyond that, he remembered the tantalising images of a thriving humanity, an ocean teeming with dancing shoals of emotion: laughter and sorrow, hope and despair. The grand totality of the human condition was gone, snatched from his grasp to leave nothing more than a threadbare quilt of memories.

Not Christine, though. She was more than a memory.

An amputated appendage of his own body, maybe, one that still existed in the fabric of his mind. Like the ghost of a lost limb, he felt her touch, the warmth of her body. If he closed his eyes, he could hear the echoes of her pleasure, murmuring in his ear before rising to a shriek of fulfilment.

There were murmurs and shrieks carried by the wind, on the edge of hearing, faint and indistinct. No cries of joy, rather these were signals of pain and torment.

He wiped his watering eyes and swallowed the urge to sob. No time to ponder his loss or to grieve. The slope was treacherous and needed all his concentration. Not before time, he snapped his mind back to the predicament, and to the unwelcome surprise that opened beneath him.

A chasm dropped away beneath his feet so that his toes peered over nothingness. Instantly, he threw himself backwards as he perceived the depths. Cautiously, he rolled over and crawled to the edge. The view wrenched at his eyes and vertigo spun his innards. He clung tightly to the brambles, ignoring the piercing thorns.

The far side of the chasm was a paper-thin, irregular line separating the landscape from the darkness of the abyss. Even as he perceived the depths, it still appeared two-dimensional. He didn't know if that was an optical illusion or reality, nor did he intend to put it to the test.

Slowly he crawled back. Thorns bit into him, tore his clothes and scratched his skin. He whimpered at these biting vegetable teeth but kept going until he felt secure enough to stand. From there, the chasm appeared no more than a shadow slicing across the earth, no more than the product of the strange light and the valley's contours. It made a trap for the unwary, and he reflected bitterly that nothing could now be taken for granted.

The fissure extended for some distance but eventually it narrowed enough for him to leap across. A difficult jump, but well within his reach. Nevertheless he stumbled on landing and fell backwards, peering for one heart-rending moment into the depths. But there was no danger of falling. The grasping fauna held him secure in its grip and, for once, he felt grateful for the thorns that kept him on the threshold of existence.

Movement caught his eye. Deep down in the darkness a face looked up at him. Small but recognisable – himself. He peered down at his own miserable figure and caught the unmistakable distress of a life robbed of all value. Others jostled his insignificant form, thousands, tens of thousands, millions. All those lost souls crushed in on him. Mills pulled away from the sight and crawled down the slope. He lay with his face in his hands and tried to forget the scene in the pit. He rolled onto his back to stare at the weird sky.

"Why me?" he bellowed. "Why? What did I ever do to deserve this?"

The shimmering firmament made no reply. The heavens were indifferent to a man's plea, just as they were outside. He might as well be an insect scurrying across a flagstone, screaming up at the alien behemoths as they unknowingly crushed him underfoot. Maybe that's what his counterpart is in the pit, an insect, waiting for the crushing indifference of the boot.

Nothing could be done, of course. Alone, his kind was powerless. Together they were strong, but the Nexus kept them in their place on the edge of society.

Well, there was one way to defy society – stay alive. Take one day at a time. This world may have become a bleak, derelict place, yet in a way that is all the world of the zeros ever was. Just take it in your stride.

With those defiant thoughts, he pulled himself together, bottled up the bad feelings and resumed his careful descent.

UTTER darkness. This is the gulf between the synapses of the brain, a vacuum devoid of ideas. All around is the fabric of the universe's meaning, given form and shape by the weave of protoplasm.

A soft glow appears in the near distance. It pulsates as it grows more intense. Soon the diaphanous glare banishes the darkness. Then the universe of light implodes. Darkness rushes back and a tiny packet of light shoots off into infinity. A tiny quantum of information is launched into thought.

The darkness contains a cosmos of such rushing lights, flaring and firing and fading. Yet even the darkness has substance. The shadows whisper with the motion of a billion dark wings. Infinity flurries with the densely packed butterfly bodies as they seek a way out.

Deep in the heart of this host mind, they find what they seek. A hole, a gateway formed from tightly woven strands of fatty tissue. The butterflies congregate around this singularity of thought. At last one forces its way through and manages to breach the event horizon that separates two worlds.

On the other side is linear, two-dimensional order, a simple world of noughts and ones. The creature transforms itself into an entity of digits, retro-evolves to cope with this simpler environment. Along bifurcating channels of silicon it swarms, replicating and spreading like a disease: a digital parasite with murder in mind.

NEXUS *is the lifeline, the umbilicus that feeds alms to the dispossessed. Millions of threads bind the poor, to nurture and support them in misery. But that is all about to change. Attacked by a hostile swarm of data the Nexus suddenly shatters. The delicate weave unravels. The poor are cut loose, left to fend for themselves in a hostile world, any way they must...*

TIME bore down on Nathan's shoulders like an over-zealous supervisor. He could feel it, metaphorically staring at the back of his head. He hadn't felt like this for a long time. Of course, his Nexus had never failed before.

Hurry up. Without the card he was lost. The staff

didn't care. Why should they? Other problems called for their attention. No time to deal with the zero with the damaged card.

A rumble from his stomach sounded embarrassingly loud. He needed food. Hadn't eaten all day. He felt like crying. No, he felt like going up to the desk and demanding attention. It wasn't right to be kept waiting like this. The urge stayed in his head. It lacked the courage to move his body. Too many years on the dole had sapped his spirit. Meekly, he waited. They would get to him in time.

The door slammed open. Nathan looked around in surprise. A man built like a weight lifter stomped in, his face distorted by a heavy scowl. His confidence was astounding, his anger unbelievable. The sound of his fist slamming into the counter seemed to fill the entire JobMart. Even the staff looked surprised.

"What the hell is going on?" the newcomer shouted, waving his Nexus. "My card is fucked. I want a new one!"

The door slammed open again. More people moved into the building. Nathan ignored them. Instead he focussed on the big man. Intrigued by the inconceivable notion of a zero being assertive, he looked on in awe.

The others gathered at the counter now. They shouted angrily and waved their own cards. What was going on? They couldn't all be faulty? At last the staff reacted. One moved to placate the mob. Another picked up a phone and opened a line.

"What is the meaning of this uproar?" a man shouted above the noise. Instantly the murmur of angry voices fell silent. Nathan stood up and moved cautiously towards the counter, sliding slightly away from the crowd. The manager gained the crowd's attention from the latter's habits of servility and deference.

"There's something wrong with my card," the big man mumbled.

"Mine too."

"All of us have got fucked cards," another man cried. "What we want to know is what are you going to do about it?"

"We're having problems with the network," the manager replied calmly. "You will just have to make do."

The angry murmuring arose again. Nathan sidled closer, beginning to feel his hackles rise with excitement.

"That isn't good enough!"

"Yeah! Get things sorted – I need food."

"So do I. I haven't eaten since yesterday."

"My rent's due. If I don't get it paid I'm on the streets."

The demands babbled from the crowd. Their combined voices became ever more plaintive, rising to a wail of helpless despair and frustration. As their sense of helplessness grew, Nathan watched the manager's confidence grow in equal measure.

"What are we going to do?"

The big man's fist smashed into the counter again.

The crowd fell silent. The manager's confidence collapsed and he began to look frightened.

"Enough!" the man cried. Then he pointed at the manager. "I don't need my rent paid. I'm okay for food. I just want my beer and a few smokes. I want my dues off you bastards. So you get this sorted. Or else I'm gonna sort *you*."

One of the counter staff whispered into the manager's ear. He nodded and a nervous smile flitted across his face. Then some of his confidence began to return.

"The problem will be dealt with in due course," he said. "In the meantime you *people* will just have to fend for yourselves, and I suggest you moderate your attitude. Society owes you nothing. Now the police are on their way so no more trouble out of you lot!"

The murmurs from the crowd sounded nervous now. The big man remained silent. Simmering silence, Nathan thought. Quite possibly, he would explode at any moment. If so, he would get no help from the others. The crowd began to break up and disperse in ones and twos. They left in the manner they would normally have entered: quietly and avoiding one another's gaze.

As his support dwindled the big man's anger paradoxically seemed to increase. At last he leaned over the counter and grabbed the manager by the lapels. "Get this fixed!" he snarled and then he pushed the manager away. With a scowl at one of the counter staff, he kicked a chair out of his way and stomped out of the building.

Nathan shuffled towards the counter and held up his own card. The manager seemed too shaken to notice him. Nevertheless, overawed and inspired by the big man's spirit, he spoke.

"Excuse me. Excuse me!"

The manager looked up from smoothing out the line of his suit.

"Erm. Sorry, but my card doesn't work either. What should I do?"

For a few moments the manager stared at Nathan. There seemed the possibility that he might help, some glimmer of pity in those grey eyes. Then the gaze turned to ice.

"Get a *job!*"

DESOLATION hid itself behind the smoke and dust as though shy of prying eyes. The administration building was no more than a shapeless mound of rubble and broken timber. Many other buildings fared little better. One or two seemed more or less intact, but they swayed precariously in the breeze.

Mills trod the ruins with a sense of detachment. Somehow it seemed unbelievable. He couldn't square this architectural corpse with the thriving hive of people it used to be. Where were they all? He ached to see just one face, one more human being so he wouldn't feel so alone. Even Harris would be a welcome sight, if no others could be found.

Metallic thunder crashed beneath his feet. He backed up and looked down. A dented sheet of steel rested on the debris. "And Work Shall Set You Free," it said in scratched and scuffed paint. The sign, covered in corporate logos, once adorned the arched entrance to the square. Now it is was just another piece of garbage. Thunder crashed again as he walked over it.

Wearily he sat down on a block of masonry. The smoke and mist formed an amorphous screen before his eyes, broken in places by rolling swirls and dancing tentacles. He stared at them mindlessly, uncertain what to do.

With nobody around he was helpless. He didn't know how to get out. And where could he go in this strange New World?

At that moment the curtain of smoke parted. The landscape to the south was revealed in all its corrupted unpleasantness. The citadels were gone for the most part; here and there, a few mangled heaps hugged the contours of the landscape, but no shimmering marble. Wait. There was one. He stood up and strained his eyes to see. Yes, one citadel survived. Now he noticed it, it seemed like a beacon – a flare as bright as burning magnesium in this murk.

A sense of hope flared in response: a way out.

It had to be.

CHAPTER 18:
Advocate of Chaos

UNEMPLOYED, no Future, but bags of potential? Don't despair: our thrusting anarcho-chaotic group needs committed revolutionaries for an up-and-coming social upheaval.

No qualifications or prior experience are necessary. On the job training and Molotov Cocktails will be provided. Anger and enthusiasm, however, are essential.

A New Order is coming. Better times are guaranteed for those with the determination and will to win, or at least the desire to smash a few faces.

Liberty Equality Fraternity

Be Part of a Brighter Tomorrow

JOIN THE REVOLUTION

*   *   *

CLUTE sat back and smiled. "So what do you think?"

"Not bad," Frank said. "What's a Molotov Cocktail?"

"Petrol bomb."

"Oh. Do you think they'll know what it means?"

"Does it matter? Those zeros will follow anything if they think it means booze." The chair creaked as he leaned forward to tap the screen. He closed the box and selected 'Vacancy Information'. The blank window opened and a flashing cursor awaited input. He sat poised with his fingers over the keyboard and closed his eyes for a moment in thought. Always difficult, composition. That damned blank screen. Get the first line right and the rest follows.

"So what are you going to say?"

With a groan, he looked up at his colleague. "Our message to the People. If you give me the chance."

"Sorry. Pity Stuart isn't here. He's read a lot. Probably be able to help."

"I don't need help to deliver a revolutionary message."

Frank shrugged and opened the window, intensifying the traffic noise. He pulled a crumpled, half-smoked cigarette from his shirt pocket and lit up. "Where is Stuart, anyway?" he asked.

"With that woman."

"Oh yeah? Lucky boy, wish I was."

"She's one of them."

Frank laughed. "What do you think we are? You're starting to take this anarchist game too seriously."

"That's because I am serious."

"You always are." Frank sighed. "What's between you and Stuart right now?"

"That woman, she's dangerous."

"Her? No chance!"

Clute shook his head and cursed under his breath. "She's turned him soft. I'm not sure of his commitment any more. He's let me down."

"Don't be so Victorian."

With a grunt, Clute turned away. Subject closed. Hopefully Frank would get the message and keep quiet. He looked at the screen and scowled in concentration. The keys rattled hesitantly. He typed a few words, then hastily deleted them. Another attempt to capture the flurry of thoughts. He typed again, read the words back and frowned. Still not right. Irritably he stabbed at the delete key. Tried once more.

VALUES are meaningless. There is no morality, no law, and no justice. There is only oppression and misery. Society is nothing more than a hive, where mindless drones serve the decadent Rich. As for the poor, they have been cast into the pit – the Abyss. You are the People of that Abyss. Those incarcerated and destroyed by capitalism. The greatest ongoing Crime Against Humanity.

This perverse system is an evil machine. It exists to promote the interests of the Global Ruling Class, those maintained and supported by the international system of governing agencies that watch and control our every move.

This system is destroying the planet. It is destroying the Human Race. We must kill it, before it kills us. Capitalism must be destroyed. Soon it will be.

"LACKS something," he said and frowned. He sat back and massaged his chin. Definitely lacklustre, needs something to give it bite, but what? Once more he was reminded that revolutionary writing was harder than it looked.

"Seems all right to me," Frank said, peering over Clute's shoulder.

"No. It's flat. Needs jazzing up a bit. Get those zeros to sit up and take notice."

"How about a huge pair of tits? Always gets my attention."

Despite himself, he couldn't help smiling. "Hardly appropriate, I think."

"No. I suppose not."

ALL government is bad. It is no more than the institutionalisation of the master/slave relationship. No man has the right to govern another. Still less to regard his fellow man as his property to do with as he will.

Yet for centuries this is precisely how we have been forced to live. Governed by brutes that take our wealth to give to the Rich.

No more. The Earth and the People are one, indivisible, the property of no man.

The only valid form of rule, therefore, is self-governance. People must control the passage of their own lives, in natural co-operation with their fellows. Any formal government is an external, artificial thing, a monstrosity that negates freedom.

Natural society follows the underlying principles of chaos. Put simply this is the billions of relationships that bind us together; the joining of individuals into communities, the co-operation of communities to form a humane society, a society that works to promote the wellbeing of all and not the few.

Revolution will herald the beginning of this New World. No more slaves. No more authority. No more exploitation and misery.

ANARCHY is Order. That is the basic message of our movement. From chaos comes order, which descends back into chaos: an eternal cycle.

The poison that will destroy the capitalist monstrosity is already spreading through their machines. Their order shall be broken. And such chaos unleashed as never before seen. This will be our moment. Our time to unleash our pent up rage.

Our world will be born from the fusion of Chaos and Rage. This deadly cocktail will smash capitalism and replace it with Natural Order. Each man, woman and child will be free to live their lives, to develop their potential as Human Beings.

Join us. Make the revolution a reality. Build a better world. What have you got to lose?

BETTER, he thought, *in places*. Not sure about the chaos passage, though. More time researching the whole thing, perhaps. He turned to Frank. "What do you think?"

"It's all right."

"You could at least read it!"

Frank grunted and lifted himself off his perch on the windowsill. "You know I'm no critic," he said, stooping to read.

"So, will it do?"

"Yeah. It's all right. You've written better. I mean it'll do."

"Great. Thanks! So which is it?"

"It's good. It's for zeros, for God's sake. Most of them probably can't even read."

"Okay, I'll send it along." Clute clicked the button, collapsing the window. "One bogus job advert on its way. Thousands of potential recruits courtesy of the JobMart vacancy system."

"How long before they spot it?"

"Depends how diligent they are. Some JobMarts never

check the boards. They leave it all to their central database managers. Anyway, once they do spot it, they're in for a nasty surprise. I used my Social Security Agency black-ops clearance to log it in."

"Like to see their faces when they try to delete it," Frank laughed. "So when does the action start?"

A smile flashed across Clute's face. He stood up and stretched, then walked towards the window. "Soon," he said, looking out over the city. "Soon it'll all come crashing down: the whole corrupt, sordid mess. They'll regret leaving me on the active list, I can tell you."

"And then?"

"Not my concern. Tomorrow can take care of itself. Forget this anarchist stuff. Alex Carlisle will be finished, that's all that matters. Let the zeros inherit the earth. My mistake will be rectified."

"Oh yeah? What mistake is that?" Frank looked at his watch. "Damn! I'm due for a meeting. I'll have to get going soon."

"Alex, my old friend. I made the mistake of believing in him when he said he'd save this country from corrupt lobbyists and their pet politicians. Turned out he's far worse. I should have exposed him when I had the chance, before he was able to consolidate his position. Instead I helped him – organised crime, bred unrest, promoted fear. All to persuade people to hand over their liberties for safe keeping.

"Okay, I'll admit it, I joined up with my head full of

romantic nonsense about spies and secret agents. I wanted to serve my country. I never thought I'd become a secret policeman guarding a giant gulag. Well, now it's time I put it all right."

Frank grunted. "Sounds like a load of sour grapes to me. You've been left in the field too long."

Clute watched him coldly, and then he slumped into the chair and sighed. "You're like all the rest. Cynical. Sometimes I wonder why you're involved."

"You know why," Frank laughed from the door, "for the crack. It's all just a game."

"I'm surprised you haven't sold me to the Agency."

Frank grinned from the threshold. "How do you know I haven't?"

SO much to do. Frank smacked the magazine into place and slid back the ejector, enjoying the smooth action of his pocket-sized murder machine. Then he carefully released the hammer and slipped the automatic into his waistband.

"Was that a real gun?"

The question and the voice startled him. Fortunately it was only Martin. No need to be worried. Frank relaxed and looked at the gangly youth whose face was a mask of acne and fascination.

"Yes," Frank replied, turning to the boxes stacked in the corner of the makeshift office.

Casually, he lifted a box and placed it on the old desk, masking the ancient laptop that was still going through its boot process. He grabbed a Stanley knife and sliced the box open. Inside, there was the usual run of leaflets espousing the Martyrs of Jarrow's cause. He picked up a bundle and flicked through; Martin still hadn't taken the hint.

"Can I hold it?"

"No."

"Why not? Oh go on…"

What harm could it do? He sighed, deposited the stack of leaflets back in the box, and retrieved the weapon. He ejected the magazine, cleared the breach and made it safe. "Here," he said, handing it over. Martin's eyes lit up and he hesitantly took hold of the weapon.

"It's heavy!" Martin raised his arm, his hand shaking from the weapon's weight. He closed one eye to sight at imaginary targets. Then the boy span round and aimed at a stack of boxes. "Bang! Bang!"

"You're a dangerous man, Martin."

"Yeah! Cool!"

Martin brought the gun up until the muzzle trembled before Frank's face. Suddenly it was no longer a joke and a cold thrill of anger and fear trembled through his body. He snatched the gun from Martin's hand before the boy could even blink. Then he prepared to bring his hand down and smash it into the boy's face. Martin flinched in terror and Frank suppressed the reflex, remembering it was only a stupid kid.

"Never point a gun at anyone unless you intend to use

it!"

"I'm sorry, Frank. Just a bit if fun."

"Yeah." He shook his head, reloaded the gun and slipped it back into his waistband. Securely out of sight but within quick and easy reach.

"What do you need a gun for?"

"I live in a rough neighbourhood. What did you want anyway?"

"The others are waiting for you," he replied in an unsteady voice. "We're almost ready to start."

"Okay. Tell them I'll be out in a minute. One more thing: don't say anything about *it*. You know what our committee feels about them. Our little secret, and I might even let you have a proper go sometime."

"Yeah? Great! Don't worry, Frank. I won't tell."

Back he went, one last nervous glance behind. The kid was an irritation. A good scrounger, though. Always useful in any organisation. Where did he find him? Oh yes, scavenging on some refuse tip, as good as garbage himself. Wouldn't believe he was only thirteen. Frank shook his head; the job took him into some strange situations. He looked at his watch. Better get a move on.

He pushed the box he'd placed on the desk aside. The laptop had finished booting up. The memory stick was a custom job, made to work with old tech, but even so it needed jiggling before the laptop recognised the device. He tapped the screen a few times, and traced a few gestures over the sensor pad to access the directory he needed; a flurry of key presses as he entered the password, then he dragged the file to its destination. The machine started shunting the data into the stick. A few seconds later and it was all downloaded.

One more. All done. Two copies, a digital representation of the Martyrs of Jarrow: cell structures, committee members, meeting places, membership lists. Supposedly none of it should have existed – at least not in one central source. Years of painstaking work rendered down into one valuable commodity.

"Frank?"

"On my way!"

A deep breath helped steady his nerves. He slipped the sticks into his pocket and walked into the hall. The Martyrs were assembled at the front of the old church. They sat in the pews and on the steps leading up to the altar. It was gloomy; the only light came from a few battery-powered lanterns and the soft glow of Sandra's old laptop.

She still retained the cool aura of the personal assistant. Elegant, he thought. A little shabby in places, maybe, after two years on the dole, having been replaced by some younger model, but she still looked good. She glanced across and raised a cool eyebrow. He recognised the minimalist brush-off and left her to her typing.

The keys rattled urgently as Sandra continued to record the conversation, instantly transmitting the information through a mobile link to the network, where other Martyrs would access it. Already the message he'd delivered on Clute's behalf was working its way through, a little aside on the pretence that they needed to know the full details of the meeting's agenda. Sometimes their keen interest in democratic practice was useful.

Voices echoed through the rafters. Frank seated himself on the nearest bench and listened in. A smile curled his lips. The argument was familiar. "What I am saying is it's time we stopped going cap in hand to the bastards. They won't do anything. They're only using us to keep stakeholders in their place. We should take control of our own lives, instead of begging on society's doorstep."

"You see us as begging? Come on, we've always campaigned for jobs and a decent income work or no. Are you saying we should turn our backs on that?"

"No. I'm saying we should help ourselves."

"Right. And how many slums and estates have we made bearable through residents' committees and self-help?"

"Yeah, I know. But that's still living on the edge of their society. We're still at the bosses' beck and call even if they don't want us no more. What I am saying is it's time to change tack. We should go home. All of us. And I don't mean back to the slums.

"We can fend for ourselves. Tend the fields. Build our own communities. If we return to the countryside. It's where we came from, before our ancestors were driven into the cities."

"Sure. We can do that. And the bastards will drive us right back again. They own the whole fucking country. Sod it! They own the whole planet and we're skulking here grateful they don't evict us to the moon."

The argument was becoming quite heated. Sandra kept typing away and maintained her aura of cool efficiency. As for himself, he was interested to see how things would develop. Maybe they would come to blows. That would be entertaining. Perhaps a little internal bet was in order?

"Only because we let them. There's millions of us. If they try to stop us we just smash them out of our way –"

A crashing boom echoed through the hall, savagely interrupting the debate. Everyone looked back in alarm and Frank felt his heart pound. No need for fear. It was only Maguire. Late as usual.

"Sorry I'm late," he said as he took a seat. "You'd think I'd be used to these clandestine meetings after all these years. 'Fraid I got a little lost."

A dutiful titter met Maguire's words. Frank felt his nerves fray anew. He sat up straight and cleared his throat. A quick glance towards the doors, then he began. "I hope nobody's remembered their Nexus." A further round of dutiful mirth made him feel better. "Well, to get straight to it, we've all heard about the virus attack on JobNet –"

"Sure. The bastards have blamed us. As usual."

"Yes. We're a convenient scapegoat. However, the group responsible for the attack has contacted me. They want our assistance –"

"What for?" Maguire asked. "So they can kill more of us?"

"Actually, the contact told me the deaths were unintentional. They didn't know exactly what this virus would do. They only wished to infect the global systems. They tell me they were convinced our comrades would be released automatically from their virtual prison."

"Great. Sorry, bit of a cock-up," Terry piped up. "That makes it okay then."

"So why do they want our help?" Maguire asked, silencing the sarcasm.

"Revolution." Laughter echoed through the rafters. Frank waited patiently for it to subside.

"Don't see what you're laughing at, Terry," he continued. "A while ago you were saying we should smash them out of our way. Sounds like a revolution to me."

"I just meant if they stopped us going home. That's all. I wasn't talking about going all the way. I think that's a little bit out of our league."

"Lost your nerve when it comes to action?" Frank smiled. Typical. Gutless. *What do any of them know?* He stole another look at his watch. "This group has succeeded in infecting part of the web. They've also convinced me it will spread. Once that happens, the system will be crippled. How do you think the bosses will be able to stop us then? This group wants our help to kill capitalism. What we do after that is up to us."

"Sounds like they've sold it to you," Maguire said.

"Maybe they have."

The congregation fell silent. Maguire looked as though he was about to speak but instead he merely stared with disapproving eyes. Frank began to feel uncomfortable under that scrutiny. Another glance at his watch. Just to break eye contact.

"Still obsessed with time, Frank. You never change."

"You know me, Maguire, so many things to do. Never enough time."

Why did Clute insist on this facade? The Martyrs of Jarrow weren't needed. A legacy of a bygone age, that's all they were. The uprising would happen, whether this motley collection agreed or not. And in a little while this farce would be meaningless anyway.

"So what does everyone think?" Maguire finally broke the silence. "Shall we turn our backs on our non-violent principles and join this revolution?"

Nobody spoke. Frank shifted uncomfortably on the rotten bench. *Come on*! The door exploded, sending splinters flying. Bright light flooded in. The congregation scattered or fell to the floor.

Instantly Frank threw himself behind the pews. The first cops streamed inside, moving with mechanical precision. They fanned out, moving towards the cowering Martyrs. Maguire crouched nearby. Frank looked at him and saw the terror in his eyes. Mischievously, he winked and levelled his gun at a cop.

"Frank! NO!" Maguire yelled.

Ignoring the plea, he took aim. The first cop went down like a lamb to the slaughter. Three shots in quick succession. A neat grouping to the chest. The armour-piercing bullets thudded home.

Gunfire exploded in response. More cops flooded into the church. The Martyrs were caught in a lethal storm, cut down where they cowered or ran. Frank rolled away from the pews and crawled behind a pillar. Maguire watched him in silent horror.

"Don't shoot! Don't shoot!" Terry was on his knees, shuffling backwards, arms raised high. As Frank watched a cop emptied a clip into the man's chest before ducking behind a pillar to reload.

More bodies littered the pews. Blood, dark and slick, spread across the old stone. A woman's shriek ended abruptly in the roar of a machine pistol. Sandra cowered against a pillar, the laptop clutched protectively to her chest. The machine flew apart in her hands and she slumped down the pillar. The police swarmed nearer. Time to go.

Frank rolled towards the rear exit across from the altar. Dangerous ground. Bullets bounced from the stone with lethal intent. A few wild shots sent a cop scurrying behind a pillar. Another furtive race to cover, he looked out at the destruction.

The boy flitted through his field of vision. Briefly, he was aware of Martin's terrified face as he slipped out the back way. The cops were too busy mopping up the remaining Martyrs. One almost made it to the doors. At the last second a cop noticed him and pumped three shots into his back.

No idea who it was. Curious, how he worked with these people for years, gained their trust, recruited many of them, and yet now so few of them meant anything to him. They were just faces; their names a mystery.

Maguire was the only one left. He cowered behind the pews. His face looked haggard. Maybe he was crying. For a moment their eyes met. To his surprise, Frank found he could not hold the gaze.

Then Maguire stood up, turned into the aisle and walked towards the cops. It seemed they didn't shoot him out of surprise. They just glanced at each other as Maguire stepped closer.

"What are you doing?" Maguire shouted, his voice unsteady with tears. "We are a peaceful group. We do not promote violence."

A cop walked casually towards Maguire and pushed him to his knees. Maguire tried again to reason with the man. He kept protesting right up until the moment the bullet pulped his brain.

Enough. Frank rolled towards the exit and slipped through. No pursuit. That was good. Now he scanned the office. Nobody hiding anywhere. No sign of Martin or the cops. A creak. A surge of adrenaline responded and Frank turned to aim at the far door. Nothing.

Frank's body was beginning to demand oxygen; his breathing deepened; fatigue began to set in, despite the excitement of fear. Steady, he told himself. Control that breathing. The danger isn't over. He needed his body. Its quick reactions. Precision training. He flitted towards the door, ducked beside it. He counted to three under his breath and then threw himself into the gloomy corridor. Still nobody. He began to relax a little.

Sniffling from the gloom. Cocking his ears, he strained to listen. The corridor ended by a refuse-blocked door. A broken window above it allowed a little light to peer in. Huddled in the gloom Martin cried and snivelled. *Guns aren't so exciting now are they?*

"Where… where are… the others, Fr… Frank?"

"Dead."

Martin wiped his sleeve across his nose to mop up some of the slime. His red eyes still streamed with tears. A feeling of pity stirred in Frank's heart, but it was mixed with disgust at the mess on the boy's sleeve.

"How did they find us?"

"Easy," he replied softly. "I told them."

The boy stopped crying in shock. He looked so pathetic, huddled there with his hands gripping his ankles. Frank couldn't help smiling.

"What… d… do you mean?"

The gun came up. Martin watched wide-eyed as the muzzle gaped at his forehead. "Frank. No. Please!"

"Sorry Martin. We don't need Martyrs any more.

Anyway, I did promise you a little demonstration."

The boy huddled up tighter and began to wail. The shivering stopped as his body froze rigid. Frank pressed the muzzle against the boy's forehead. Martin moaned long and low. A smell reached Frank's nose.

"*Ooh*, Martin!" he said in disgust, then squeezed the trigger. The shot stung his ears in the enclosed space.

"Let that be a lesson for you," he said to the boy's corpse. "Guns are not toys."

"FULL of sound advice, Frank. As usual."

A curse exploded into the gloom and he spun. His arm trembled slightly as he held the gun an inch away from the newcomer's face. Finger tight on the trigger, he gazed into the man's eyes. It was Reich. Or Shreck – he never could tell them apart. Ever so slightly he relaxed.

"One of these days you're going to get yourself killed," he muttered angrily to himself. To leave his back unprotected was foolish. Death could easily have tapped him on the shoulder. Not all the cops had been fully briefed.

Reich – or Shreck – smiled and glanced at the gun. Then his eyes flicked back to meet Frank's gaze. A cold wave washed down his spine and he fought hard to suppress a shudder.

"By a professional like you, Frank? Surely not."

Mocking lines appeared around those eyes. Frank hated those eyes. They seemed dead and totally inhuman.

It was so tempting to squeeze the trigger, spill the freak's brains and close those eyes forever. A little more pressure, that's all it would take. He felt his finger twitch. Tighten.

"You should lower the gun," it said, dismissively turning away. "People might get the wrong idea."

What good would it do? More of these freaks were being bred all the time. Security used to be a man's game. Not any more. With a sigh Frank lowered the gun and released the hammer. Then he slipped it into his waistband and followed the freak.

Police dragged the bodies of his former comrades towards the shattered doors. There, they bundled them into an untidy pile. The freak looked around with a satisfied air, ignoring the dark looks the two of them received from the police.

"You performed good work, Frank," the freak said, pointing with his left hand, thereby identifying himself as Shreck. "Getting their leaders all together like this. Saved us a fortune in separate operations. Chief will be pleased. So will Father."

Frank only grunted a reply and fumbled for his cigarettes. Movement in the corner of his eye made him look up. At the same instant a machine pistol slammed into his solar plexus.

"You Agency bastards!" An impact smashed into his unprotected back. "You were supposed to use blanks!"

"Fuck... you," he managed to gasp. The cop's eyes bulged and he prepared to smash his weapon into Frank's face. Shreck caught the weapon before it could connect and looked calmly at the cop.

"We required a lamented hero for the media, Commander," he said smoothly. "Be grateful it was only one."

The Commander stared speechlessly, his body trembling. At last he turned and stormed out. From outside they heard his voice raised in an expression of impotent rage. Shreck chuckled.

"I'll get that bastard," Frank said, painfully rising.

"No, Frank. You killed one of his men. You will do nothing."

He was about to reply when two cops dragged Martin's body into the hall. The dead eyes stared at him and captivated his attention. He watched until they tossed the boy's cadaver onto the pile where it slithered out of view. Only then did he feel released. The Martyrs of Jarrow: R.I.P.

"You look sad, Frank. No regrets?"

"Of course I have. This is my little project that went up in smoke. You'd know what it was like if you spent more time in the field."

"Perhaps. Incidentally, do you have the merchandise?"

"Oh. Yeah." He fumbled for a memory stick and handed it over. He said nothing about the back up. Clute would need that. "Everything you need to get the stragglers. Be careful with it."

A smile curled the freak's lips. "It is always good to

work with such a professional, Frank. I shall miss you."

"What do you mean?"

"You are being retired. Cutbacks. You know what accountants are like. Always cost-cutting, yet they never seem to cut themselves out of the equation."

"No. No way. You can't kick me out. What else can I do?"

Thoughts flurried through his mind. The freak watched him impassively. Frantically, he searched for a way to save his career. Clute. Of course. Give them Clute. They couldn't throw him out after that.

"The boys had a whip round. I thought you might appreciate the personal delivery," the freak said. "They got you a gold bullet."

CHAPTER 19:
The State of Things to Come

INSIDE the command vehicle the air smelled stale, a result of too many sweating bodies. Munroe failed to notice. Veteran of a thousand such stakeouts, he had long ago developed immunity to the discomforts of his job.

Display screens filled the interior. Data and video strobed before the eyes of his men sat over the machines. The glow made them look pale and feverish, while their intense concentration and glistening perspiration only added to that aura of ill health.

Tactical displays mapped the locality of the hospital. The mobile units showed up as blinking icons. Further banks of screens patched into the local City Watch grid. Each monitor concentrated on a separate entrance, observing the pedestrians that strayed into the operational window. For the most part these were ignored. Munroe's men focussed their attention on the tacticals, endlessly searching for the target.

Voices crackled in his earpiece; routine chatter, nothing that needed attention. He glanced around to check that everything ran smoothly. No need to worry on that score. His men and the monitoring equipment formed an efficient cybernetic organism, with himself as the brain.

He allowed himself a satisfied smile. Everything was in place and operating nominally. There was nothing to do but wait, so he returned to his sketching. He rested the pad against his thigh and expanded the scene inside the van with firm strokes of the pencil.

Strictly speaking the operation was unnecessary, he mused, expensive and a waste of manpower. A dawn raid would have been more cost-effective – snatch the target out of bed before he even remembered who he was. The local boys could have handled that. No problem.

But the powers that be required a show of force every now and again. This operation just happened to be pulled from the roster so here they were, killing time in this awful provincial town. Still, it was only taxpayers' money. Might as well give them a good show.

He finished the sketch with a final flurry of the pencil and studied it for a moment before he flicked over the page to begin another. An abstract work this time.

So far it was a textbook job. The search was largely automatic. Narrow beam transceivers queried the chip in each pedestrian's identity card and ordered it to beam the data back. A transmitter was in place at each entrance; able to scan up to 300 cards a second without the owners ever becoming aware they were under scrutiny. At full capacity it would have made an irritating buzz. At the moment it only clicked intermittently. Eventually it would scan the target's card and they would have him –

"Sir! Target located. West-side entrance."

Munroe looked up at the screens. The cameras had already been locked onto the target. The man's identity card – automatically commanded to transmit – flashed his position on the tacticals. A second or two later his files arrived from records. The video image and data flashed up on screen in a repeat loop.

"Target identified and located."

"Move in."

Icons began to shift position. Munroe switch his gaze from the tacticals to the real-time view and back again.

"Target has spotted us."

Damn. The target returned to his car. It pulled away as two operatives reached for the door. One of them aimed a scanner at the car as it departed. Instantly data appeared on a screen.

"All units converge on target vehicle."

"Patching into traffic net," a technician said, "satellite link on-line."

The displays changed to show traffic flow. Munroe watched as the target's vehicle became swamped in the congested roads. His own vehicles crawled nearer, making better progress but still hindered. Foot units had already closed in.

"We've got him!" he said, allowing himself a little excitement, only to watch some random fluctuation in traffic open the roads. The target's blip began to move clear.

"Almost out of real-time telemetry range."

"I can see that. *Dammit!* We need to see where he *is*. Not where he's been."

The vehicle lurched as it moved into the flow of traffic. Even with the sirens blaring, movement was restricted – not much room for motorists to clear them a path. Should have waited for the rush hour to pass, he thought angrily. But then they might have missed the target. He considered his options quickly. The data was still on screen: the security override from the target's onboard computer. A few key presses later and the digital keys were dispatched to his units.

"To all units within range – kill his motor."

On the very edge of range, the blip slowed and stopped. Munroe relaxed a little. Another keystroke overlaid the traffic system with street plans. The target was on foot in the main shopping district. Already the blips representing his men converged on that area. This time they really had him.

"Okay, target is on foot and unarmed. I want all weapons made safe. Remember we're here to put on a show. Make it good!"

THEY were closing in. Simms gripped the steering wheel until his knuckles showed white. The fear was an electric spasm that surged up his sternum, making his body twitch erratically.

"Come on," he implored. "Move!" The traffic remained sluggish and he started to rock back and forth impatiently. He glanced out of the window. At least the police were bogged down too. A consolation, but the congestion wouldn't hinder those on foot.

And there they were.

Twisting round to see, he watched them pick their way through the slow moving cars. Plain clothes men, recognisable by the detached concentration on their faces and the purposeful movement of their bodies. They were getting closer.

"No. Please. I haven't done anything. I didn't know about... I only hid him. I don't –"

A horn cut him off. The driver behind gestured wildly and mouthed something obscene. Simms turned to face forward. He felt relief wash away the fear as a clearing road greeted his eyes. At the same moment something slammed into the side of his car and the handle rattled.

The cop banged on the side of the window and struggled to remove his gun from its holster. Simms slammed down the accelerator, spinning the cop into a heap on the roadside.

Sirens wailed, but the pursuit was still bogged down. By the time it cleared he would be away. He laughed, the noise bordering on the hysterical until he regained control. A glance at the speedometer. Easy does it, he thought to himself.

A junction ahead: he indicated to turn, forcing himself to play the cool, collected doctor. If he seemed hurried and agitated it was only because he had urgent business. That's all. The turn approached and he spun the wheel. Nothing happened. The car continued straight ahead.

"NO!"

"Emergency override active," the dashboard said. "Please relax while a parking space is located."

The fear returned. He failed to prise open the dash to get at the onboard computer. Impotently, he pushed at the brakes, tried to stall the engine, anything to regain control of the vehicle. All useless, he could only look through the window as the car pulled in and slowed to a halt. Cars sped past, tantalising apparitions of escape.

"Please remain seated until an officer can attend you. Thank you for your co-operation."

Simms struggled to control his breathing and remain calm. His eyes darted, checking the surroundings, observing the mirrors. Pedestrians swarmed on the pavement. A few gazed at him in passive curiosity.

Sirens wailed elusively. He flicked off the central locking and pushed at the door. It didn't move. His shoulder slammed into the glass: no good. He pulled again at the handle; pushed at the door; pounded his fists against the window – nothing worked. Shoppers stared mindlessly.

"Open! For God's sake let me go!"

"Please stay seated and try to remain calm. Officers have signalled and are coming to attend you."

Twisting around in his seat, he tried to see in all directions at once. He lost control of his breathing and it became harsh and uneven. A whimper escaped his lips as he saw the cops running down the road. More sirens sounded. Closer this time.

"I didn't do anything…"

The windscreen. The only way out. He tried to lift his feet and smash it but the steering column got in his way. Hurriedly he slipped over to the passenger seat, becoming snagged on the gear stick. He struggled to remove his lab coat and ripped the stethoscope from his neck. At last he could raise his feet above the dash. He kicked. The window remained intact. Again he kicked. Again and again. Crying and whimpering in fear, he sought to harness the full power of his muscles. Something gave way inside his thigh but still he lashed out.

At last the glass popped out of its housing and fell away. Slithering up in the seat he pulled himself out through the gap and fell across the bonnet. He landed heavily on the road. His leg hurt but fear proved an effective analgesic.

No time for him to catch his breath. Police vans screeched to a halt and disgorged armed men. To his horror he saw these were Home Office troops, not police.

"You, HALT!"

Terrified, Simms ran into the crowd in the hope it would mask his escape. His injured leg slowed him down, as did the crush of meandering bodies.

"Excuse me. I'm sorry," he repeated in spite of his fears.

The crowd proved no hindrance for the cops. Cries and shouts of fear heralded their pursuit as people hurried out of the way. Somehow, he could sense the gap opening behind to leave him exposed. Finally, he lost his deep-ingrained inhibitions and pushed shoppers out of the way.

Almost at the other side of the precinct, he hoped to lose the cops. Then the crowd began to disperse. No longer did the shoppers hinder his flight. Instead they left him clear for the world to see.

No good – escape was impossible. *So close*, his mind whimpered, *so close*. The soldiers closed in. Moving slowly. They knew they had him.

"Place your hands in the air!" a cop barked, tapping his electric baton against his leg.

"Please… I haven't done anyth –"

"PLACE YOU HANDS IN THE AIR!"

"I only hid him. That's all…"

They almost encircled him. More sirens blared over the precinct. The thud of booted feet reached his ears.

"Please! Don't hurt me!"

"Hands in the air! Lie face down!"

Through streaming eyes, he saw one of the cops slip

his baton into its sheath and reach for his machine pistol. The gloved hands took hold of the grip. There was a sharp whine as the sights powered up and the muzzle ascended.

Panic struck, evaporating what little rationality remained, and he bolted. Behind him a voice screamed orders until a bellowing roar drowned the commands. He turned and raised his arms in horror.

A heartbeat later the world became a dull crunch and flickered out.

HER skin felt alive, every inch hypersensitive. The cotton sheets aroused where they touched. In response to this sensitivity Jane half-consciously moved her hand down across her body. Tremors rippled the muscles of her thighs and belly as her fingers moved through the dense cluster of hair. Her legs parted and a low moan of satisfaction greeted the electrifying thrill.

Stuart stirred and mumbled in his sleep, as though unconsciously responding to her arousal. Jane rolled over and pressed her body against him. Her free hand gently caressed his side, then moved round to stroke his chest. She kissed the back of his neck before snuggling up beside him, content to enjoy the pleasure that glowed inside, rather than take it to its conclusion.

The object of her desires slept soundly, undisturbed by her simmering passion. *Let him sleep*, she thought. The poor man had been worked hard that evening so he needed to restore his strength. Now he was back in her life she would see that he made up for those missing days – with interest.

A sigh of contentment rippled through the hairs on Stuart's shoulders. They tickled her nose and brought a smile to her lips. She breathed deep, tasting the scent of her lover's body, the combined odours of sweat and lust and aftershave.

Reluctantly she rolled away and smiled at the ceiling, sleep a distant destination. Her body and mind too stimulated for the journey. Over the last few days the bed seemed so empty. She had missed their nights together. Missed the comfort and security derived from a companion's body. Now it felt warm and snug: a haven from the world where the nighttime horrors were kept at bay by his enveloping aura.

Stuart rolled to face her. His breath tickled her ear and his arm draped across her middle. A thrill surged through her belly. In response her probing fingers increased their vigour. Before she even realised what she was doing the orgasm exploded. Her body tensed. She sucked in air through gritted teeth, managing to control her usual shriek. Only a muted whimper escaped, insufficient to disturb her slumbering partner.

At last the pounding waves receded and she relaxed. She breathed out contentedly and felt a tinge of regret. Perhaps she should have waked Stuart? No. Weariness would have marred his performance. Anyway, a mischievous thought whispered, she was perfectly entitled to enjoy herself.

Never mind, my love, plenty more to come. She smiled and turned her head to gaze at Stuart. His face held a peaceful serenity. No trace of the hard mask men felt compelled to hide behind. Now he looked boyish, vulnerable even.

Poor Stuart, she thought as the feelings of tenderness took hold. That vulnerability held the source of her attraction, his uncertainty and confusion about his role in the world. For all that – maybe because of it – he was shy and sensitive. No way he could hide it from her, even though he tried. She'd sensed it the moment they met and it stirred her interest.

Women coped better, of course, they needed to if they were to maintain a place in the world. Perhaps that formed the basis of her attraction, a desire to care for him and provide an emotional haven from the world. He was lost, really. A man in a man's world that no longer had any time – or even a need – for men. Only machines.

No wonder they were so messed up inside. They were torn apart by their own lifeless creations. Was it the inability to nurture life that led to their chaotic frenzy of creative destruction? Shorn of any internal meaning, they developed a sense of self from artificial things. A hotch potch of contrived meanings, poorly held together by the glue of convention, peer pressure and notions of masculinity.

Unlike women. Theirs was a simple struggle to carve a

niche for themselves as more than breeders and domestic servants, to be more than biology with a pretty face. A simple goal: to be the equal of men. Free to express themselves as individuals, to pursue their own choices and goals, ultimately, to share the same psychotic fate as men.

Jane was surprised at her turn of thinking – insomniac philosophy pure and simple. All the same, she would never truly understand these messed-up creatures.

Especially Stuart. Mysterious, that was the word; he seldom talked about his past and then only in the vaguest of terms. She got the feeling there hadn't been much joy in his life prior to their two years together. A private man. She respected that. Everyone needed their little secrets. Besides, it made them more interesting.

Sleep began to sneak up on her. She felt its tentacles uncoil through her brain, closing off her mind bit by bit. She rolled over and gave herself up to sleep, listening to the sounds of the night: the ticking of the alarm clock, the old-fashioned thing Stuart initially hated, the muffled buzz of the freezer, gurgles from the central heating.

A thump.

Suddenly she was wide-awake. She didn't know how long she had slept. Stuart was close beside her; his breathing said he was still fast asleep. Another thump. A car door outside, she thought. Then more noises came from the building's main entrance.

Stealthy footsteps followed, or rather vain attempts at stealth. The house was too old and creaky for that.

Somebody climbed the main stairs and she did not recognise the footfalls.

"Stuart," she hissed, suddenly afraid. Ghettos weren't too far away. "Stuart!"

He grunted and rolled over. She switched on the bedside lamp and shook him again. This time he awoke.

"Haven't you had enough?" he asked groggily, sitting up and reaching out for her.

"Get off! There's somebody in the house."

"So. One of the other tenants."

"No. I'd –"

The door to the flat burst open. They heard the terrifying crack of timber followed by booted feet thudding up the main stairs. No attempts at stealth this time. Stuart swore and leapt out of bed. He reached for his bag and rummaged inside.

"What…"

When he turned around his face was a grievous mask. He revealed what he was holding. Then she felt real terror. The gun glinted in the light. Footsteps thudded through the flat.

"I'm sorry." He raised the gun with a trembling hand. "I love you."

The bedroom door burst open. Stuart spun round. Shots barked and Jane flinched. There was no pain. Stuart was falling. Blood spattered the mirror on the wall. The gun made a thump as it hit the floor. She realised she was unhurt.

She wanted to scream. But her lungs and vocal chords failed to co-ordinate. Instead she trembled on the bed, the sheets pulled up to mask her nakedness. The armour-clad police kept their weapons trained on her. Then a man entered the room. Brown-suited. Bald. A barcode on his forehead. He glanced distastefully down at the... Stuart... and then looked at her.

"Miss Sutton. You are under arrest."

CHAPTER 20:
Voices in the Fog

LOOSE shale rattled down the slope. On its way it dislodged more weathered stone. A boulder broke free to clatter and bounce over the rock and scree. At last, it tumbled over a sheer face to plummet through the air. Mills clung to an outcrop and watched the boulder shatter into fragments once it hit ground.

"Ouch!" he said, aware that he might easily go the same way.

As if to point this out, the scree shifted under his feet and it was only his grip on the outcrop that prevented him from slipping and falling. The slope was steeper than he guessed when he first set out to climb. What began as a tough but manageable walk was now an arduous task that required him to pick his way carefully, almost like a mountaineer negotiating a sheer face.

With a grunt he pulled himself up with aching arms.

At last able to rest, he sat down and leaned against the rock. Loose stones clattered down the slope but the outcrop held firm. Hundreds just like it dotted the slope like weathered teeth jutting from decayed gums.

Funny, for all that he hated travelling through the portals he'd give a year's dole for one now. He'd tried to summon one many times since leaving the village, but none had answered his call. Like so much else in this cursed earth, they were clearly broken. So here he was, condemned to a britches-arse crawl through this nightmare landscape; he swore the terrain was shifting and changing around him with every step. Mills cursed his luck. Then he swore louder when cold moisture dribbled down his neck.

Water trickled in a thousand interlaced rills. It dribbled over the stone and washed away the coarse earth to loosen yet more shattered shale. Icy cold, it made the journey all the more dangerous as it soaked into the sponge-like moss. All it took was the pressure of the hand to unleash slippery bone-numbing slurry. And it seemed to flourish in all the most convenient handholds.

No going back, though. He looked back along his route. If he tried, he'd likely end up taking the quick way down. He shivered at the thought of the fall. Never keen on heights at the best of times, he found himself condemned to go to ever more precarious heights.

He turned to look at the bleak landscape above. The jutting rocks appeared more numerous further on. Better support for his climb, but it would be tiring clambering over and between them.

He rubbed his hands on a dry patch of his coat then blew through them, bringing a little bit of life back into his near-senseless fingers. "Time to get on," he muttered.

Stooping on all fours, he picked his way up the slope. The shale slipped but he dug his toes into the loose surface for some purchase. His hands balanced him, seeking out any kind of hold no matter how tenuous. Steam billowed from his mouth as he huffed and puffed.

"Just a bit further. Nearly there –"

The ground slipped and pitched him onto his face. Without support he slithered down. Shale grazed his face and hands. Sharp edges ripped his coat. He cried out and thrashed around for something to halt his slide. At last his fingers found a nub of stone and gripped tight. It gave slightly, but mercifully held. At the same time, he kicked his toecaps into the scree. Together they provided some support.

"Shit! Up we go again."

After a pause to catch his breath, he resumed his slow crawl. This time he took more care to spread his weight and test each handhold carefully.

"I swear this is getting steeper. Someone must really have it in for me."

Onward and upward, nearly at the rocks, he gritted his teeth and ignored the cold. The stone rubbed his skin raw. Blisters and tiny abrasions stung. Wet hair slithered into his eyes and he flicked his head to try to clear his vision. At last he risked running his fingers over his scalp. Cold water dribbled down his neck but at least the hair remained plastered to his skull.

"Done it!" he groaned as he heaved himself onto a rock shelf. Firmer footing now – no more of that dreadful scree. He lay panting on the shelf, his muscles aching. The chill stirred him to sit up and he bent his head between his knees and struggled to regain his breath. Then he started to massage a little feeling into his legs.

The jagged rocks appeared so forbidding. Would he ever reach the top? Or was he condemned to go on climbing forever?

Movement in the rocks caught his eye. He flinched, but it was no boulder – it was too slow and moving in the wrong direction. Upward. He strained to see. Yes, there was something up there. Climbing. Another human being. A sharp thrill of relief spurred him on. He moved towards the higher rocks, eagerness giving his body extra strength. An end to his isolation was an elating prospect. He began to climb, impatient to catch up with the stranger.

It was a tight squeeze through the rocks. He shuffled through a gap between two huge outcrops and then pulled himself onto another ledge. The mud-spattered figure was nearer now and he wondered if he should call out. No, he reluctantly decided. Whoever it was, they struggled to gain a secure perch. A shout might prove a disastrous distraction.

Instead he ducked under an overhanging rock and crawled towards a crevice leading up into a narrow funnel-like fissure. The climber swung out of view onto a higher ledge. Mills clambered up, struggling to bear his weight with tired arms and legs.

Up at last. He slumped onto the rock. A few fragments of stone clattered down the cliff. Followed by a few larger fragments. A strangled cry made him look up. The climber bounced off the overhang, rolled and fell. A fresh cry of terror split the air. This time he realised it was he who had screamed. The climber dangled precariously, secured by one hand clutching the lip of the overhang. No more time for cries, the only sound they made was harsh, ragged breathing and the scuffing of boots as they tried in vain to get a grip against the sheer face.

"Hold on!" Mills cried and rushed towards the edge. He took hold of the climber's arm and pulled, grunting at the unexpected weight. An old man looked up at him with terror-filled eyes. His flailing arm came up and clutched at Mills' sleeve.

"Help me! Don't let me fall!"

"I've got you!"

Just a little further. The man's expression – no, his entire face – changed. Mills cried in horror as he found himself staring at a half-rotten monstrosity. He flinched and felt his grip slacken. The thing thrashed out for support and fell backwards with a gargling cry.

Gracefully it fell, imploring arms raised, damp hair

fluttering in the slipstream to obscure the face. When it cleared he was horrified to see the old man restored, his eyes wide in bewildered horror, mouth gaped in a silent scream. He looked up at Mills and gently shook his head as the distance between them grew.

The rocks crumbled with the impact of his body and pulverised his fragile flesh. Halfway down the slope he flickered and faded from existence. The dull crash of the landslide echoed across the desolate wasteland.

Laughter brought him back from the brink. "Appearances can be deceptive, Dave," a voice said. He looked around and saw nothing, except for a crow perched on a nearby boulder. It blinked at him with unfathomable eyes. Then it laughed again.

"Don't worry about him – you've got yourself to think about."

The crow spread its wings and took to the air. Mills ducked as it swooped over his head. Mist soon swallowed the beast from the middle distance. He was alone again, trembling and cold on a bitter cliff that had started out as a hill.

Minutes passed. Maybe hours. The light dimmed into twilight. Mills couldn't bear to look down. Instead, he stared out across the wilderness, towards the hazy smudge that once formed the village. That made two people who'd died within a few inches of salvation, while he looked on in helpless despair.

"No – it's not my fault," he muttered at last, tears

spilling. "I didn't kill him. Something played tricks with my eyes. Wasn't my fault –"

Unconvincing. You let him die the voices screamed; *you let them both die. Not that it matters any more. Let's face it; you'll most likely die here too. There's no way out. Might as well give up. Throw yourself off the edge and get it over with. What's your life been for the last ten years? Pointless. Worthless. No bloody good to anyone. Only clung to life from some misplaced notion of your value. Wake up! You're a waste of space. Surplus to requirements. So get it over with. Go on. Jump…*

No more. He leaned forward. Further. A little more and he would be over the edge. Time to rest. Peace at last.

"NO! Get out! Leave me alone!"

The malicious voices faded away. Thoughts and feelings flooded back into his mind. Guilt, horror, anguish, hope, his own honest emotions – confused, maybe, a heavy burden, definitely, but at least his own. He leapt back from the brink, forgetting the narrowness of the ledge, and banged his head. "Ouch! Shit!"

The impact almost pitched him back towards the edge. He leaned against the rock face and spread his arms, palms flat against stone, until he felt secure in his balance. He coughed and wiped his sleeve across his face. Then he wiped his wet eyes and looked up at the distance yet to be covered.

"Must get going," he wearily gasped. "Got to keep going. Can't give up – *hope*."

"AT last!" He crawled from the cliff edge, eager to put as much distance between him and the long drop as possible now that the final, difficult stage of the climb was finally behind him.

His body demanded rest and he slumped onto the ground, where he would have hugged the earth if he could. Coarse grass pricked his exposed skin, but that was no discomfort after a day spent among the unyielding rocks. The brittle stems absorbed his body heat and soon began to bend a little. He relaxed in response, the tension draining away as though absorbed by the earth.

No longer burdened, he felt his mind drift until the world vanished. Dreams caressed his mind and he succumbed to a form of AR as old as humanity: a place of freedom, beyond the impositions of harsh but indifferent reality. Christine emerged from the formless clouds of colour. She took his hand in her own, whispered soothing words in his ear, and guided him to a realm of peace.

SOMETHING splashed his face. Muscles twitched irritably and the body seized hold of the mind to drag it from its hiding place. Mills awoke suddenly, reluctantly. The dream evaporated under the heat of awareness to leave only the wisps of a hollow sense of loss.

"Rain," he muttered. "Typical."

Brackish water dribbled into his mouth. He spat and wiped his face on a sleeve. That didn't help much; only spread the moisture across his skin. The water poured from his body as he stood up. It fed the rivulets flowing towards the cliff edge where they formed tiny waterfalls. He walked the few feet towards the edge and looked out over the landscape.

No horizon in sight, the waterlogged air diminished visibility. Yesterday's arduous path, however, was clear to see. No longer the sheer face that nearly killed him, once more it was a gentle rolling slope of scree and coarse earth. He was not surprised. Only annoyed.

"I hate this fucking place!"

"Ooh, me too!"

The voice came from behind. He whirled round to find no trace of the speaker, only a drenched and dripping bush a few metres away. It moved slightly, not with the breeze or the weight and flow of the rain.

"Naturally – a talking bush."

"Don't be daft. This may be AR, but plants still don't talk unless you've got a serious psychological problem."

Whoever it was, he must be hiding, Mills told himself. Slowly, he walked towards the bush. "Who are you?"

"Nobody. Same as you."

Beyond the bush, he still found no sign of anybody, just a large iron post embedded in the earth. More of a surprise was the skeleton kneeling in front of it. Its arms were raised above its head, shackled to the post by rusty chains. A sign dangled from a bit of rope around the skeleton's neck. He leaned forward to read the hasty scrawl: Refused work, it said.

Mud and leaves partially buried the skeleton's legs while branches and foliage twined round ribs and vertebrae. The head was tilted back to look up at him but the eye sockets and skull were hidden beneath a headset. The frayed cable dangled and swayed in the breeze.

"Weird," he muttered and then looked around for the speaker. "Where are you?"

"Right here."

A crow flapped through the air and landed on top of the post. He shivered as it focused its beady eyes on him. He stooped for a convenient loose stone.

"Go on – piss off!"

The stone just missed the bird, which leapt into the air, circled and alighted back on its perch. It stared at him once more.

"There's no need for that," the voice said.

"Okay. What do you want?"

The crow ignored him and began to preen itself.

"Now he's talking to the birds! You've been in here too long. Crows, like plants, can't talk. Have we got that straight now?"

Feeling increasingly foolish, he looked round again but the speaker was still nowhere in sight. He approached the skeleton and stooped to examine the AR headset. It was battered and old-fashioned. The worn cables were badly repaired with insulation tape. He gently took hold of it and felt for the release catches.

"Hey! Get off!"

He leapt back in surprise. The crow just looked at him.

"That's better. They didn't tell me you're a fondler. Just don't touch the headset again. Okay?"

"Why not?"

A disgusted snort. "Do you see any vocal chords around here? You damage my helmet and I can't speak. You got the picture now?"

"You're the skeleton?"

"Ah! I do believe he's got it. About time. Give the man a fucking medal."

"You haven't got any vocal chords, so you can only talk to me when you've got the helmet? That makes complete sense," he said, angrily feeling someone was attempting to make a fool of him.

"Welcome to Artificial Reality. What were you, the retard of the family?"

Mills ignored the comment. "Stuff vocal chords," he said. "How can you talk to me without a brain?"

The skeleton's lower jaw dropped with a sharp click. "Ah… you've got me there. I'll have to get back to you on that."

"I can't wait." He squatted down and picked up a loose twig. Casually he stripped away the bark and studied the skeleton. It didn't move. A proper talking skeleton should have been able to move. Disappointed, he threw the naked twig away.

"You're bloody ridiculous, whatever you are."

"I thought you might appreciate the symbolism," it

replied sulkily.

"Sure. What do you want with me, anyway?"

"You are David Mills, right?"

"Might be."

"Only I've a message for him."

"Let's hear it then."

"Are you David Mills?"

"Yes!" He rolled his eyes.

"Thought so. I heard you were coming this way."

"Well?"

"I'm supposed to tell you how to get out."

"So tell me then!" Irritation fast approached anger.

"Okay, you've got to look for the calm at the eye of the storm."

"What?"

"Look for the calm at the eye of the storm."

"That's it? What the bloody hell does that mean?"

The skeleton might almost have shrugged. The tone of its voice gave the impression of such a movement. "How should I know? I didn't make it up. I'm only the messenger. Friend of yours said you'd need to know."

"A friend? Who?"

"Didn't say."

"So how do you know he was a friend?"

The skeleton failed to reply. Annoyance simmered and he felt like taking a rock and smashing the skull – AR helmet and all. It was the system playing tricks on him again. Just like the crow on the cliff and the old man... but he didn't want to think about that.

"Look, I'm sorry," the skeleton said. "The guy said you'd know what it meant. He didn't explain it to me... Hey! Where are you going?"

Mills didn't bother answering. He just kept walking. After a few minutes he paused to get his bearings and changed his direction to aim for the hazy smudge that was the last intact citadel.

The skeleton called after him, voice faint but clear: "You might at least have said thank you!"

HOURS or days later, it all felt the same. The rain had turned to a cloying mist. That was all there was to tell him the cosmological clock still ticked.

From somewhere in the mist, a voice called his name. Over and over again it wailed. Slow and sonorous, it could have been a woman's but transmitted at the wrong speed.

"Daaavvviiiiiiiiid."

That wail cut through the background noise like a beacon. It was like piece of ice caressing his spine and he hurried through the fog, not towards the sound but away. Whatever it was, he had no wish to find the source. Eerie and distorted, he feared it. All he wanted was a way out.

That escape loomed ahead. A shadow in the mist: the last surviving citadel. Even as an indistinct shape it conveyed beauty. Normality. People. Beyond it, it promised a gateway to the sweet mundanity of the real world.

Keep going, he told himself, *one step at a time. That's the trick to survival. Just like life on the dole. Break forever into manageable portions. Don't think of any future because it may never exist. Yes that's the way. But don't forget the hope. Control it. Keep it alive. Let it light the way forward. Keeps the darkness of despair at bay, even if it does highlight the gloom.*

"*Daaaaaaaaaaavvvvvvvvvvviiiiiiiiiiiiiiiiidddddddd!*"

Ignore it. He closed his eyes, shook his head. The other voices were no better. Try as he might, he couldn't shut them out. They almost overwhelmed his slender grip on coherent thought. They fuelled an urge to crawl into a ball and hug the earth. *Hide. Hide,* his instincts screamed. *Pull the sheets over your head and wait for the morning to arrive,* except there were no sheets and the morning was a universe away.

Bubbling up from the background, voices whispered; shouts for help, pleas for lost loves.

People appeared around him. The source of the voices no doubt. He tried to convince himself otherwise. Rather than ethereal entities, they were no more than random movements in the mist. That was all. The air stirred nearby as though a body brushed past. Glimpses through the corner of his eye revealed haggard faces, withered bodies. When he turned they vanished.

Real people? Or illusions? Whatever, they were as intangible as the fog. Phantasms. Yet all heading in the same direction: towards the citadel.

Forget the noise, he told himself. *Concentrate. Focus on the journey.*

Determination and sheer bloody-mindedness had seen him through the long years of the dole – they would see him through here. The rules of survival were the same, so too the objective. A job or a door, they amount to the same: escape from the drudgery of mere existence.

Easier said than done. How many days had he lain in bed, unable to move, weighed down by the despair of his solitary existence? Too many, he didn't want to tally.

Yet he'd survived. Lived beyond friends – all lost to the rigours of zero existence. Relationships destroyed by alcohol, drugs, destitution and despair. Oh, and one who gained a job, crawled back into society's festering belly and adopted its attitudes towards the zeros.

Ephemeral relationships replaced these lost friends. Chance encounters, all empty and devoid of meaning. People on their personalised journeys to Nowhere briefly accompanied him on the road, any interaction he had with them short-lived and meaningless, totally unsatisfying. Those relationships only ever seemed to nurture his sense of isolation.

Eventually, even those transient relationships grew few and far between. The empty hours were filled somehow by the increasingly futile search for work and other illicit activities. Knowing the guts of machines, he repaired electronics, patched old code, specialised in keeping old-fashioned hardware in working order. It never earned much, but it was a welcome addition to his meagre dole.

All beyond the rules of Nexus, of course. For all their surveillance, however, they missed much. Or perhaps they merely chose to turn a blind eye for their own unfathomable reasons. Whatever, there were ways to eke out an existence under society's disapproving gaze if you knew how and possessed the guts to try. What was there to lose?

Hard years. Past years. Now the present surrounded him with its particular harshness. But now the citadel loomed larger in the fog. Sooner or later he would arrive. Achieving that goal became the only purpose of existence.

As he focused on that distant haven, the voices faded from consciousness, unable to pierce his shell of single-minded determination.

CHAPTER 21:
Beggars at the Gates

AT journey's end Mills found people at last. They were real, tangible human beings. All of them were survivors of a terrible mindquake waiting to be evacuated, and it almost felt wonderful to no longer be physically alone.

Thousands, it seemed, had gathered in the shadow of the walls, where they huddled together in listless groups. For the most part, they waited in silence. Some wept, others moaned. He found it uncanny the way so many stared out at the fog, as though it contained their worst nightmares and by staring they could keep them at bay.

He shivered as he followed the collective gaze. The fog ended no more than fifteen metres away. Tendrils writhed against the boundary as though pushing against a sheet of glass. More than ever, he gained the impression that it was a living thing, waiting to consume the people in the calm.

"Whatever's out there, it can't get to us," he muttered,

more an expression of hope than a statement of fact. This nightmare managed to destroy an entire world, so why not this small oasis?

He turned back and began to pick his way through the refugees. Where were the relief workers? That was a nagging question. Surely, somebody must be working to help the victims? On the other hand, these people were mostly zeros. Maybe a rescue was too low down the list of priorities, if anybody outside had even noticed their predicament.

No. Somebody must be trying to help. Human hardship is too good an opportunity to miss, an excellent resource to be exploited. And these refugees – pathetic and helpless as they were – easily matched the requirements for voyeuristic delight.

Cynicism bred further cynicism. He couldn't shake the notion that someone observed the suffering. He looked up at the sky, almost expecting to see the millions of watchful eyes. Doubtless he was under scrutiny this very moment; channelled into the homes of mindless, middle class suburbia.

"I hope it's worth your subs," he snarled, giving the sky a two-fingered salute. Just in case.

He walked on. Soon he began to see other people moving amongst the survivors. He could see the fear in their faces but they focused on the world by helping others, rather than gnawing on their own personal traumas.

A cry, startling in the way it broke the eerie quiet, interrupted his thoughts. He turned in the direction of the noise. A woman burdened by a small child cradled in her arms struggled to catch a running boy. The girl was maybe five, the boy twice that; Mills was no great judge of children's age, but the sight of ones so young, here, turned his ribs to ice. The boy darted between the refugees and leapt over several in his headlong rush.

"Johnny! Come back!" the woman yelled, "Don't run into the fog!"

Johnny paid no heed. He veered towards the boundaries of sanity. Mills felt a surge of sympathetic horror. Out there, alone, he would have no chance. Not only that, what chance would they have of finding him?

Mills ducked down on the ground, blending in with the huddled survivors. The boy came closer; his face screwed up in a combination of exertion and emotion. Almost in tears the woman trailed far behind. Johnny continued, apparently determined to escape this haven.

Here he comes. Mills tensed, ready to pounce and stop the boy's headlong flight. Then he met an unexpected reversal of fortune as feet slammed into his chest. With a cry he fell on his back. Before he could regain his wits, a barrage of blows struck him in the face, neck and chest.

"Get off... *Aaargh!* You little sod!"

Blows kept coming. The boy said nothing. The intensity of the sudden attack was alarming. It took all his efforts to fend off the blows. The boy moved too quickly for Mills to catch those flailing arms. Yet the last thing he wanted to do was punch out a child.

"Stop it!" The woman appeared and grabbed the boy by his jacket. She pulled hard and yanked him to his feet. The assault interrupted, the boy turned towards her, his face screwed up in an effort to hold back the tears. Mills lay on his back, bruised and increasingly mystified.

"He killed my sister!" the boy screamed, no longer able to hold back the deluge. With a jerk of his arm he broke free and tore off into the thick of the refugees. The woman called after him, but the boy ignored her. Mills probed a sore tooth and found it loose. He swore.

"Nice kid," he said, stiffly sitting up.

"I'm so sorry," she replied. "He's just traumatised."

"Who isn't?"

"His sister was killed."

"Yeah," what else to say? Realisation made him frown: "Hey! He blamed me."

The woman shook her head sadly and kneeled down. The little girl remained curled up in the woman's arms. "I hope he won't do anything stupid –"

"Oh, I'm sure he can take care of himself."

"Maybe. But he's not as tough as he pretends. None of them are. But what about you, are you all right?"

He rubbed his jaw and sucked at the loose tooth. The taste of blood made his mouth water. Otherwise, everything seemed okay. "Wounded pride, that's all."

"I am really sorry."

"Forget it. I've been hit harder."

"Are you one of the helpers?"

"Helpers? No. I've been out in the fog. Came from the Village."

The woman looked up: "Did anyone else get out?"

"Not that I know of. I didn't see anybody else before I left."

"Oh." She looked down at the little girl and tussled her hair. Her face looked thoughtful and sad. The silence became unbearable. He needed to speak, anything, no matter how inane or inappropriate.

"She doesn't say much," he said, pointing to the child.

"Nobody talks much round here."

"I noticed –"

"I think they're all inside. Do you know what I mean?" she replied, pointing to her temple. "I think it's the only place they've got to hide. Except most of them haven't gone completely. That's why we can see them. I wonder… how many are trapped out there, stuck inside their own heads, not daring to come out?"

"That sounds tempting. Hide inside my own skull. But what's the point? Once in here," he tapped his own skull, "where can we run to? Might as well face whatever caused all this, out here."

The woman stared down at the grass. The child began to suck her thumb and looked up at him with bright, blue eyes. Her gaze lacked the innocent curiosity of childhood, and he wondered what this child must have seen and shivered at the thought.

"I didn't know there were any children in here," he voiced a thought.

"There weren't until recently. I was amazed when the Agency granted us the concession. They're street kids. This is the only place we could get them to stay in school. Maybe give them some kind of chance."

"You're a teacher?"

"Sort of." The woman smiled at last, beginning to open up. She offered her hand. Surprised by the gesture, he reached out and gingerly shook it. "I'm Janet, by the way, and this is Mandy," she added.

"David," he said. He looked down at the little girl: "Hello, Mandy."

"Anyway, now I'm a mother, big sister, aid worker and counsellor all rolled into one."

"How come everyone's waiting out here?"

Janet shrugged. "There's a lot of us. It's taking time to sort out the arrangements, I suppose. Tom's negotiating with the centre's administrator right now. I hope it won't take much longer."

"Who's Tom?"

"He brought us here. We were in one of the other centres when this happened. He got us together. Without him we probably wouldn't have made it. A lot of the others, they made their own way in small groups. Guess they saw this place intact before the fog fell.

"Tom's been out into the fog. Guided others back here

to safety. I don't know how he faced it. I wouldn't like to go out there again." Janet's expression darkened and he decided not to press the matter.

Eventually he asked: "Where's Tom now?"

"At the gates. He's arranging to get us all home."

"Just Tom? Nobody else? I mean nobody from Outside?"

"No. Just Tom and his helpers."

She looked over towards the citadel. He followed her gaze. The sheer walls towered over their heads. He had to admit: they looked good. "We'll be out soon," he said.

IT was quiet by the gates. None of the milling crowds he expected. The people seemed to evaporate as he got closer. By the time he reached the path only one or two stood nearby.

The golden path almost flowed into the citadel, where it branched and swirled into the labyrinth of courtyards and streets beyond the floral square. Towers and gardens bordered the path. Thousands of colourfully dressed people congregated there, a reminder of lost days of normality.

So close, he felt compelled to jog. Impatience tugged his muscles and he began to run, like a man lost in a desert, desiccated with thirst, and now seduced by an oasis.

Nearly home, he could see it now, the way out, a shimmering tunnel emerging in the next world. He flung up his arms to cast aside the gates only to slam into something solid. The breath exploded from his lungs in a deep grunt and the impact threw him painfully to the ground. The gates remained securely closed.

People wandered through his field of vision. The brightly-dressed apparitions ignored him, as though they failed to see. Impossible. He lay there in full view. Yet he couldn't deny his eyes.

He stood up and approached the gates. Carefully, he reached out to stroke the wrought gold, only to meet solid resistance when his fingers were an inch away. Something like a sheet of glass partitioned him from salvation. He ran his hands over this smooth surface, like a mime artist looking for a door.

"What is this?" he murmured. Then he repeated the question in an angry shout.

No reaction from the other side, the people insisted he wasn't there. He slammed his fist against the obstruction. Again. Harder, until his knuckles cracked.

"For God's sake, open the gates!"

"It's no good. They won't let us in."

Mills turned round. Instantly his mind leapt to a conclusion. "Tom?" he asked.

"That's right. You heard of me then."

"Janet told me."

Tom nodded. Briefly he glanced towards the gates, anger flashing across his face. Then he sighed and the melancholy returned.

"I'm supposed to be getting us all out of here," he said. "But as you've just found out, there's no way in. I don't think they even know we're out here. The place is completely sealed."

"They must know. At least they should have guessed people would be coming."

"All the same the gates are locked," Tom said. Then he laughed bitterly. "Maybe they do know we're out here and they don't even care."

No reply sprang to mind. Secretly, he agreed. Sometimes, cynicism made for a depressing burden.

"Now what am I supposed to do?" Tom asked, breaking the despondent silence. "They're all counting on me. I promised them a way home. How can I go back and tell them it's all been for nothing?"

"I don't know. Look. There must be some way in. Have you checked?"

"No. But what else can there be? These are the gates. We always used them –"

"These aren't gates. This is a visual representation. That's another system linked to JobNet. They've closed the link, that's all. If there's another way, another access point, we could use that."

"But they'll have sealed that too."

"Not necessarily. They might not know it exists. A way for engineers to gain access without going through the security rigmarole."

"What would we look for?"

"Anything – a gate or a door, even a drainage channel. We certainly won't find anything unless we look, and there's no guarantee we'll find a way in. But it's worth a try. Right?"

"I suppose so," Tom said slowly. His face brightened up as he began to compose himself. Slowly the Tom that Janet must have known began to appear.

"You're right. We've nothing to lose. Let's get my helpers together first. We'll need to have everybody assembled at the gates. Be better if they wait for us there."

Now it was Mills' turn to feel uncertain: "Are you sure? What if we can't find a way in?"

Tom looked at him with an expression of grim determination. "We *are* all going home!"

Mills was impressed by the turn around in his state of mind. "Okay," he said. "Let's do it."

"THIS is hopeless," Mills exclaimed. The cheers and the euphoria that sent them on their way had long since faded.

Mile after weary mile whittled away the confident hope as they checked the walls for any sign of an opening, no matter how ridiculously small. Not a single crack or blemish caught their eyes.

Tom looked at him in dismay. "We can't give up now. Not until we've been all the way round."

"That's if it goes all the way round. We might be walking forever and never get back to where we started."

"Come on. We can't quit now."

"Did I say I was giving up? I just said it's hopeless. That's all." He sighed and resumed walking. "How far to the next tower?"

"Hard to say. Maybe two hours."

The wall stretched on for miles, the next tower almost beyond his range of vision. It marked the next stage in their search. The next turn. But appearances proved deceptive; after no time at all, they'd reached it. Mills looked at Tom and raised his eyebrows. "Two hours did you say?"

"Just a rough guess," he replied with a shrug.

"Right!"

They turned the corner. Another seemingly endless journey awaited them. Mills groaned in dismay and forced himself to keep going despite weary muscles. Tom, by contrast, seemed fresh. All that collective hope weighing down his shoulders obviously kept him going.

The walls remained unchanged, perfect and unblemished. The view became so wearying that he realised his attention had wavered. He snapped his mind back into focus. The ground beneath the walls was thick with vegetation. How much of this did he miss? He cursed and moved towards a thick bush surrounded by a dense growth of weeds and grass gone to seed.

"Let's check this out," Mills said.

"Why? It's nothing."

"There may be a way in."

"Through a bush?"

"Don't be stupid. We've seen nothing, and now there's all this growth. Bit odd, don't you think?"

"I suppose so."

"Like it's hiding something."

Tom raised his eyebrows. "Come on. Even I wouldn't hide something this way. It's too obvious."

Without bothering to reply, Mills stooped and began to pull at the branches. After several minutes spent tearing at the foliage he managed to crawl to the wall.

"Not hiding anything, eh? Check this out."

"You've found something?"

"Maybe."

"They must really have a low opinion of us."

Branches rustled. Tom shuffled and swore until he appeared through the foliage. Mills pointed to the base of the wall where a pile of dead leaves and earth collected against a grilled opening.

"You're joking!" Tom said, staring in disbelief. "There's no way I would fit through there even after fifteen years on the dole."

"I wish you'd stop looking at this as though we were in reality."

"Reality. Sure. Okay, why don't I look for a bottle labelled drink me?"

"What?"

"Nothing."

Mills scowled and kneeled down in the damp earth and began to pull away the clumps of rotten vegetation.

The matter was thick, clinging and deep. Soon he found himself leaning over into a shallow pit.

"This is disgusting," he said, putting his arm out to maintain his balance. More slimy muck gave way with a sucking sound.

"They didn't need to hide it," Tom said, covering his nose. "The smell's bad enough."

The ground collapsed without warning. Mills found himself falling. Time only for a muttered curse before he slipped into a murky hole. Soil and slime fell around him then solid rock broke his fall, softened somewhat by a layer of mulch. He'd fallen maybe two metres, but winded it felt a lot further.

"Mills? You all right?"

More soil pattered down and a few soggy clumps of leaves squelched onto the floor. Gasping for breath, he pulled himself to his knees and looked up to see Tom's head and shoulders silhouetted above the lip of the hole. Another rotten mass splattered onto his coat and slithered down.

"No!" Mills managed to say. "I'm covered… in gunk!"

"Never mind that. What's down there?"

Tom lowered himself into the pit, showering Mills in more earth. He moved aside to give Tom room and take stock of his surroundings. Crudely hewn blocks of stone formed an enclosure around them. Iron bars blocked an opening that breached the citadel wall's foundations. Ochre flakes of rust peeled from the bars like metallic dandruff. Metal rungs, even more badly corroded, were embedded in the masonry adjacent to the opening.

A few feet above his head, more or less level with the surface, leaves and slime clung to a crossbar. Mills' lowered his gaze to examine a small grilled gate built into the metalwork. Beyond the gate, a concave annexe of lichen-speckled brick funnelled into what appeared to be some kind of crawl space a couple of feet above the level of the ground where he knelt. The hinges didn't appear to be corroded solid, judging by his quick assessment, but the lock was another matter.

Before Mills could say anything, Tom pushed past and bent down to grip the gate. Rust crumbled under his grip and more flakes flew away as he pushed and pulled. The hinges squealed and metal rattled but nothing gave way. At last Tom sat back on his haunches.

"No good. All this for nothing!"

"What do you expect? It's locked. See?"

Tom swore. "So that's it then. We can't get in."

"You give up too easily."

"*I* give up too easily? A few hours ago you were saying this is hopeless. So how do we get in?"

"We pick the lock."

"Oh yes? Ever picked a lock before?"

He frowned. "No. But it can't be difficult. It looks crude."

"What are you going to use?"

"You wearing a belt?"

"Yes."

"Good. Give me that."

"My belt?"

"Yes."

Slowly, Tom unbuttoned his coat and fumbled with his belt. He slipped it free and handed it over. As he did so, he shook his head, "What do I do now?" he asked.

"You keep your pants from falling down and let me concentrate."

Mills took the buckle in his hand and shuffled towards the heavy lock. He moved the pin around inside, looking to trip the simple mechanism. Frustration tried to shake his hand, but he forced himself to stay relaxed and calm. Metal tapped against metal. Everything solid refused to move. Sweat beaded on his forehead and a dull ache began to throb in his ankles.

"Have you got it?"

"Give me a chance! And give me some fucking space!"

"Okay, no need to be so tetchy!"

Mills grunted and turned back to the lock. This time he tried to be more methodical in his exploration. He felt for something solid, tapped the pin against it, then sought to throw the mechanism.

"Bugger…" he snarled, and then luck paid a rare visit. Suddenly a piece of metal moved. A click sounded inexplicably loud in the small chamber and the gate opened a crack. He sat back and let out a sigh of relief. With a triumphant look at Tom he pushed the gate open.

Tom winced at the loud squeal.

"There you go."

"Great. Can I have my belt back?"

Mills returned the belt. "After you."

At last Tom smiled. He shuffled towards the gate and cautiously peered into the gloomy tunnel beyond. Then he bent and stepped through the grate before crawling inside, closely followed by Mills. More brickwork arched above their heads. The tunnel twisted under the citadel, taking its toll on their hands and knees. The confined space amplified their breathing to send it resonating back and forth.

"How long do you think it is?" Tom asked.

"No idea."

"Hey, wait a minute. I can see light up ahead."

"Can you see if it's a way out?"

"No. It's too bright –" Tom suddenly screamed. The startling sound made Mills bang his head on the roof. Then a brilliant light flared like a magnesium explosion. So bright, Tom's body glowed a translucent red. Still the glare increased until Tom's bulk could no longer shield his eyes. Mills screamed and tried to block the light with his arm, only to find it did nothing to stop the intense crimson glare.

No time to react. No time to ponder. He felt his body stretch to impossible dimensions until that elongation merged into motion. His body instantly accelerated to near-light speeds. He yelled, but the sound evaporated, left to trail forlornly in his wake.

GRASS tickled his face. The light faded to leave coloured blobs floating beneath his eyelids. Water trickled nearby. He groaned and fought back the painful memories. At last he dared to open his eyes.

He found himself, and Tom, in a garden, surrounded by trees and flowers. People looked at them in mild consternation, as though someone appearing out of thin air was a fairly common occurrence.

"Bloody hell," Tom cried. "Beam me up, Scotty!"

Mills rolled onto his back and looked up at the sky. Glorious clouds of blossoming silver floated across the azure heavens. He smiled, and looked over at Tom.

"He never said that."

"What?" Tom rolled over and crawled nearer. "You're not a Trekkie are you?"

"No!"

"I don't believe you. A fucking Trekkie!"

Tom began to laugh until he seemed close to tears. The laughter sounded undeniably pleasant. Mills found it infectious and his shoulders began to shake.

"I am not!" The denial was no good. Tom only laughed all the more. The onlookers began to point and chatter as though they were mad. He ignored them until a shadow blocked the sun's warmth. An upside down man scowled at him.

"Access to this facility is restricted," he said

robotically.

"Whatever you say." Mills giggled, still euphoric from their victory.

The man raised an eyebrow. "The Administrator will need to see you."

Tom looked over and winked. "Take us to your leader," he said and began to laugh again. The 'robot' looked on in bemusement. Mills couldn't stand it. He began to laugh, and this time he couldn't stop. At last, they were on their way home.

CHAPTER 22:
Kept In Darkness

THE camera pans to sweep the aisles and observe the milling shoppers. An observer can see how they casually study one another – compare labels, assess individual styles. The determination of dress and the selection of products derive subtle distinctions of rank whereby minions find their place in the social matrix. This ritual strengthens the hierarchy of consumerism, day after day, year after year.

Shift the camera. Adjust the depth of field. Focus on the back of the store by the plastic strips that seal off the warehouse. Something new has arrived, a glitch in the program, dirt in the smoothly oiled machine. Unlike the shoppers, the newcomer moves with obvious purpose. Awe and amazement shine forth from his eyes. But the camera is blind to such intonations of emotion.

The ragged, dirty man walks through the aisles to gaze at the products displayed with tantalising precision.

Blissfully unaware of the horrified reactions he has caused, he reaches out to touch and stroke the contents of those heaving shelves. Almost he dances down the aisles. A glimmer of light flashes from his cheek. Reflected from a tear?

The consumers forget their status game to point and curse in the ragged man's wake.

Zoom in. The man has stopped at the bread counter. Imagine the scent of freshly baked loaves. The camera is oblivious. The man takes a deep breath and smiles. Suddenly he reaches out to grab a French stick. Breaking it, he ravenously begins to chew. Crumbs and flakes of crust scatter across the polished floor. Slowly, the man sinks to his knees. His shoulders jerk with emotion. Tears can be clearly seen streaming down his face.

Brightly dressed consumers stand at a distance. A lip-reader panning the camera over their hostile faces might well learn a new phrase or two. Disgust evolves into hatred. These vile raptures flit across their faces, demolishing carefully manicured façades of culture and sophistication. They gather round the kneeling man.

A uniformed newcomer arrives, pushing deferentially through the crowd. He stoops to drag the man to his feet and roughly shoves him. Spittle is visibly ejected as he shouts in purple-faced rage. The ragged man cowers, pleads and cries. The crowd is unmoved.

Suddenly the man is on the floor. Blood gushes from his nose. The uniform lashes out with his baton and the ragged man convulses electrically. The crowd clap and stamp. Blood lust is visible on their faces. They move in, lash out with expensively shod feet. The ragged man is besieged and hugs the floor, curling into a ball to protect his feeble body.

The crowd continues to howl and clamour. The camera is deaf. But we can still tell, by the movement of their mouths, the salivation of hate.

A commotion arises behind the crowd. Adjust the camera accordingly. More figures have appeared. How did they get in? Unknown. Glance across to the security panel. The systems that should register Nexus are silent. To the security apparatus, these creatures from the margins do not exist. They are ghosts of a Forgotten Nation.

The ragged throng floods in to raid the shelves. Starving men given the keys to the larder, they gorge themselves on costly, exotic food. At last, Society perceives the invasion. Hate turns to fear in the face of more numerous adversaries. They back away. The numbers of the dispossessed flush away the servants of commerce. Not by anger, just sheer weight of numbers.

Little attention is given to those who so recently engaged in the status game. Such trifles are of little interest to those of zero existence. Living interests them more. And in this Temple of Consumerism, they gorge themselves on life.

Like the first man, their cheeks are soaked with tears.

"THIS happened yesterday morning, you say?" Carlisle

closed the video window and turned towards Chief. His offspring hovered nervously by his side. Doubtless, the notebook cradled in his arm contained more bad news.

"Yes, Father, one of several incidents. We are registering an increase in disturbances. Raids on commercial premises. Riots. Demonstrations. General disorder."

"But most of these were unregistered zeros," he replied, pointing at the now blank screen. "We can only protect property against Nexus-bearers."

"Not any more, Father. Not since Nexus went down."

"Yes, of course. We've lost our first line of defence. How is Eric progressing with getting it back online?"

"There is no word. Carswell is being tight-lipped on the subject. But we understand he is making every effort."

"Meanwhile we're reliant on the old-fashioned methods: a strong right arm. Well, we've plenty of those."

"Yes, Father."

"We've been here before," Carlisle said with a sigh. The chair creaked as he leaned back and stared up at Chief's impassive face. "Looks like Clute is trying to play my own game against me. Before your time, roundabout the mid-Thirties, the Turmoil erupted like this, but it had been brewing under the surface a long time. Civil unrest, demonstrations, riots, looting; the country was coming apart. One of my greatest achievements, fanning the flames, using the political crisis to my advantage, but I'm in a bad position this time."

Chief came closer and placed the notebook on the desk. He clasped his hands together in an almost reverential manner. "There is no danger, Father. We will not fail you. This is a challenging hiccup in the smooth running of your administration. Do not despair."

"Me? Despair?" He couldn't help laughing. Sometimes his offspring's candid expression of faith was quite amusing. What would he do without them? "I never despair. We'll get through. But in the meantime think on this: I'm the one expected to come up with a solution. Last time I was waiting in the wings while a corrupt administration dithered. Now I'm the corrupt administration. That makes a difference."

"All the same. We have not dithered. We have made progress."

"Yes. I read the reports. Two of the targets died whilst being apprehended. Not good."

"Sutcliffe was armed. There was no choice but to neutralise the threat before Sutton could be taken into custody. As for the doctor, he ran into an oncoming truck. Nothing the operatives could do."

"Except snatch him out of bed. That would have been the efficient thing to do."

A dismissive wave of the hand was the only sign that Chief felt defensive. "That was out of my control, Father. It was pulled from the duty roster by mistake. In operations demanding maximum public impact there is always the risk of losing the target. The dispatch officer concerned has been disciplined."

"Good. Do you think the woman knows anything?"

"Yes, Father. I am sure of it. She was involved with this Sutcliffe. They were... ah, caught in *flagrante delicto*. I am sure whatever Sutcliffe knew, she also knows. Which means we shall soon be privy to the information."

"Let's hope so. This man Mills, the virus carrier, he's the key. Neutralise him and we cure the problem. Further incidents with these zeros will be symptoms we can clear up at our leisure. Where is the woman now?"

"At one of our facilities," Chief said. He leaned over the workstation and tapped a few control keys. For the first time that day he smiled. "The interrogation is due to begin. If you would care to observe, Father."

The video-link opened. Sat in an oasis of light, a young woman shivered in her thin cotton slip. Her eyes darted around from one wall to the next. Carlisle smiled, and settled back in his chair.

FATE laughed somewhere in the shadows. It laughed at her foolish compassion. *Look where that's got you*, Jane thought. *Here – wherever here actually is – waiting for the inevitable.*

Of course, they'd kill her. Eventually. They could do whatever they liked now. Her death wouldn't even be recorded – she would simply disappear. Accept the inescapable. Would that make the ordeal any easier? Just get it over with. *What are you waiting for?* Jane peered into the shadows beyond the circle of light. Nothing. The room might be small. It might even be an aircraft hangar for all she knew. The darkness hid everything. Time meant nothing. Minutes or hours, it felt like forever.

The unyielding chair made her bottom ache. The light hurt her eyes. A pain in her arm added to the discomfort, a spasm of cramp or something. She rubbed the spot, easing it away. Then she wiped her tired eyes.

A door slammed. Footsteps echoed. She looked around, eyes darting left and right. Her body trembled with renewed terror. Would they shoot her? Please – no pain.

A man appeared from the shadows. As he stepped into the light she stiffened in horror. No mistaking those features: the dark, unfathomable eyes, the grim face and that bald head with its grotesque barcode. He stood at attention and regarded her coldly. Jane was horribly aware of her nakedness beneath her slip – the only garment they gave her time to grab. She shivered and looked away.

"Miss Sutton," the man barked. "You are charged with subversion of Prime Ministerial authority, acts of terrorism and mass murder. Do you understand?"

She nodded her head, too terrified to speak.

"Do you understand? Respond!"

"Yes," she managed to say, and sniffed.

"Under the provisions of Prime Ministerial Decree number 4573/78A you are hereby stripped of all statutory privileges as laid down in the Stakeholders (Citizenship)

Act. As of this moment, your status is zero."

He retrieved a card from his pocket. Jane knew what it was: her stake card – her whole life. Stored in its data-bank was the statutory franchise, granted on her 18th birthday, the two additional votes she since gained, voting record, identification, driving license, genetic fingerprint, medical records, insurance details, credit rating, employment history, educational attainment, citizenship awards. Everything.

The scissors sliced through the plastic, shattering the smart chips. It felt like a blade slicing through her throat. An entire life erased. The shards tumbled to the floor. She watched them fall.

"Furthermore, under the provisions of the Social Security Agency General Directive 34, all legal rights are hereby revoked. There will be no court appearances. You have no entitlement to know the specific nature of the charges brought against you, nor do you have the right to legal representation. Do you understand?"

"Yes." Jane rested her elbows on the table and placed her hands over her face. Moments later a chair scraped on the concrete floor. She lifted her head. The man now sat opposite, his face looked sympathetic. No. Another man. The first still stood to the side. Dismayed, she realised there were two of them. Identical. Again she shivered.

"Please forgive the authoritarian ritual, Miss Sutton. I am afraid protocol demands it, and my colleague here is rather stern in his ways. Do not let that put you off. We are both here to help you in any way we can."

"Help me... How? What will you do with me?"

"Well, Jane... I may call you Jane?"

A simple nod in response. What did it matter?

"Jane. I am Shreck. This is Reich."

Reich said nothing, only stared with those frightening eyes. She said nothing and avoided meeting them by looking at the tabletop.

"We will not be doing anything to you," Shreck said. "Your ultimate fate will depend on the results of your social and psychiatric evaluation. Naturally, your parents will be required to undergo genetic examination. It is possible they contain atavistic genes –"

"What do you mean? What have my parents got to do with this?" More fear, from an unexpected source. One thing to take the consequences of your actions, quite another for your family to bear them too. Shreck smiled, almost apologetically. Not so Reich.

"Why do you think we have so many mechanisms for controlling the zeros? They are dangerous. Congenital defects compel them to socially destructive behaviour. We must determine if similar defects in your family's genetic history account for your own destructive actions."

"I wasn't compelled by my genes!"

"We do not enjoy this, Miss Sutton. This is necessary to protect the freedoms and rights we all take for granted."

"I am sorry, Jane. Procedure demands it. Our unhappy task is to protect society. As was yours, in your own way.

But you can help smooth things out. Depending on your conduct here today we can get all the unpleasant details sorted out."

"You'll leave my parents alone?"

"Yes, if you co-operate. We might even be able to return your life. It would be as if this never happened. Would you like to go home? Back to your life?"

"Yes."

Shreck smiled. Ice dribbled down her back. *What price, life?*

"Let us begin at the beginning, shall we?" Shreck said softly. "The virus. Where did you get it?"

"I don't know. Stuart got hold of it."

"I see. And you fed it into the JobNet system."

"Yes." What did it matter? Give them that much.

"How did you upload the virus?"

"Through a client. We linked it to his interface so he would be the carrier."

"What was this client's name?" Reich asked.

"I don't know. I don't remember."

"You do not remember, Miss Sutton? You expect us to believe that? Mills. Dee. Ess. Remember him? He was removed to hospital after you prepared him. Then he disappeared. Supposedly after having his link severed. Yet he somehow managed to turn up in JobNet. Now do you remember him?"

"All right! I remember. He was the carrier. His inhaler was a custom job; the nanocules were encoded with the virus. It was laced with a mild hypnagogic agent; make it look like a system crash. It was just strong enough to perturb his neural link long enough for us to get him away."

A barked laugh, bitter, borderline hysterical, then she added: "We were worried he'd crashed for real. I wish he had... I don't know the details. Stuart sourced the inhaler; he handled the technical arrangements."

"What was the purpose to all this, Jane?" Shreck asked, tapping away at the notebook. "Why on Earth would you become involved with anarcho-chaotics?"

She ran her fingers through her sweat-sodden hair and looked at Shreck. For once she didn't flinch when their eyes met. "I don't understand you," she said.

A snort from Reich. Suddenly he leaned over. One hand gripped the edge of the table; the other took hold of the notebook and span it round to reveal the screen. Jane choked on what she saw.

"I see you recognise your image, Miss Sutton. The man with you is a notorious anarcho-chaotic. Clute. And here you are – captured in conversation. How do you explain that?"

Jane felt trapped. She looked at the screen then at Reich and Shreck. She fought for words. "I don't know him," she finally managed to say. "He asked me directions. He was foreign – well, he sounded foreign. We got chatting. I don't remember what about."

"Chance meetings. Pleasant conversation. We all taste

that occasionally," Shreck said pleasantly. "Stuart is a little harder to explain."

The image changed. Clute and Stuart captured on a bench, deep in conversation. A hollow pit opened in her stomach. Jane wished she could crawl inside it and hide.

"Stuart Sutcliffe," Reich added, "to use his current – and final – alias. Another anarcho-chaotic terrorist. You were found in bed with him."

"No," she whispered, disbelief clawing at her reason. "He wasn't. He couldn't –"

"Sutcliffe was employed at the New Ebbsfleet JobMart for what, almost a year? He gained his job through you, did he not, Jane?"

She nodded, dumb.

"And you have been engaged in sexual relations for two years. Have you not?"

Another nod.

"Yet you say you are not an anarcho-chaotic, Miss Sutton. Do you expect us to believe that you can be intimate with this man, and not know about his activities? Could it be that you are stupid?"

"No. Yes. I don't know!"

"I do not believe you are stupid, Miss Sutton. I believe you callously planned on infecting JobNet with no regard to loss of life. I believe you chose JobNet as the weakest point of attack on the global network."

"No. That's not true. We didn't want to kill anyone. We were trying to help. What they do is wrong. It's immoral. I just wanted to help people…"

Tears began to flow. She wiped her eyes but they wouldn't stop. She surrendered to the emotions, folded her arms on the table and hid her face. Her shoulders jerked with remorse.

"What do you mean, Miss Sutton? In what way is JobNet immoral? By helping zeros find work? No. NO! What *you* have done is immoral. You killed innocent people. People are *still* dying. People who might have found useful roles in society. That is evil. You. Are. Evil!"

Shreck silenced his colleague. He looked at Jane then reached over and delicately lifted her head. His features looked kind as he gazed at her face. "I believe you, Jane. I know you did not intend any harm. So why did you upload the virus into JobNet?"

For several seconds she couldn't speak. The sobs prevented words. "To help people," she said at last. "It's wrong what they do. Keeping people in there against their will, against their knowledge. It's wrong… we just wanted to set them free –"

"Jane, Jane," Shreck said, shaking his head, "only work can them free. Everybody knows about JobNet. It is no secret. It is not talked about because it is regarded as unimportant. Of course we keep people inside, if they fail to find work. It is for the good of society. They cannot harm us in AR. Their atavism is held in check, and they enjoy freedoms and a quality of life they could never know out here. It is for the general good. It works. There is nothing immoral about that. Poor misguided child."

"And now they are dying or dead. We did not do that to them, Miss Sutton. You did. You killed those people. How does it feel to be a murderer? How many more will die because of you?"

"No! It wasn't supposed to kill. It wasn't. I didn't know. I didn't mean…"

The guilt returned with renewed intensity. This was worse than anything she expected. A sharp pain in her arm again, like a needle piercing her skin. She gasped. The pain subsided. Wooziness crept down her body. Thought became difficult to find. Confusion. Emotional turmoil. Above all, sleep catching up with her.

"Tell us where we can find Mills." Shreck's voice. Soothing. Kind even.

"No," she slurred. "I… don't know… where he… is."

"Forget about protecting your friends, Miss Sutton. We have most of them in custody. There is no Dignity On The Dole."

"I… don't… know!"

"Jane? Did you love Stuart?"

"Yes." An unexpected question.

"He used you, you know. I am sorry but it is true. Many women have fallen for his charms. Some of them are in prison. Or dead."

"No it's not true! He loved me! He did!"

She looked at Shreck through the tears. His features wobbled in and out of focus. She blinked to clear her vision. Mucus dribbled from her nose and she wiped it clear. "He loved me," she whispered.

Suddenly Shreck was standing beside her. He made hushing noises and bent to put his arms around her. Automatically she found her head on his shoulder. "Do not cry," he said softly. "I know. Love is blind. He fooled you. He fooled so many. Do not feel bad about it. You do not need to protect his memory. Tell us where Mills can be found."

"No. He did love me," she cried hoarsely, draping her arms around the soothing body. The feeble protestations no longer sounded convincing. All that mystery made sense now. Maybe Stuart had only used her. Now she felt foolish. Dirty. Discarded. What did anything matter any more? What else could they take away, now they had stolen Stuart's love?

"Think about it, Miss Sutton. Does it not make sense? When we burst in he was going to spill your brains on the carpet. We saved your life. I think that leaves you in our debt."

"Reich!" Shreck said with a stern look. Then he helped Jane sit back up. She cried, her arms resting weakly on her lap.

"Help us, Jane. We really need to know where Mills can be found. We cannot stop this without him. You can make amends. You can save lives. Innocent lives, Jane. Just by telling us where we can find Mills. Please, Jane. Help me!"

"All right," she said. "All right. I'll tell you –"

A loud metallic crash, the sound of engines interrupted with an angry roaring and the urgent screech of rubber on concrete. Shreck released Jane and she slipped to the floor where she knelt in a pathetic heap. Reich looked around in alarm as shots rang out. Then the wall exploded in a cascade of wood and plasterboard. Light flooded in, banishing the shadows.

A people carrier roared towards them. Brakes squealed and the front passenger door flew open. Reich reached into his jacket and fell backwards as a series of red explosions erupted from his chest. Jane screamed where she knelt, saw the masked men leap from the van.

Shreck tried to run but was cut down. Soon the sound of urgent voices replaced the sound of shots. Jane scurried behind the table and tried to hide. *Not me. Not me. Don't shoot me!*

BOOTED feet thudded closer. A gun appeared, dangling in the edge of vision. Jane choked on a scream and whined. Then she closed her eyes and wondered if it would hurt.

"It's all right. You're safe now." The voice was somehow familiar. A hand gripped her arm and pulled her gently to her feet. Still trembling, she looked up. A face smiled out of the past. Her shattered thoughts struggled to pull together.

"Stuart!" She stared, not knowing what to feel. Then

relief blasted free of the turmoil. Overjoyed, she threw her arms around his shoulders, hugged him tight and kissed him.

"Ow! Careful," he said, pulling away. She felt a sense of rejection, resurgent of recently implanted fears. "No need to worry," he smiled and kissed her lightly. "I've a couple of holes nature never intended you know."

"I thought they killed you," she whispered.

"Me too. They're complacent and incompetent, though. That's why we'll win in the end."

"Come on!" one of the others shouted. "Let's get out of here before it's crawling with freaks."

"He's right. We've got to go."

"Where?"

"Somewhere safe. I promise."

He slipped his coat over her shoulders and half carried her towards the vehicle. She felt grateful for the support. Her legs felt weak. But she made a point of clambering into the back under her own power. She took a seat by the window, just to the rear of the big sliding door. The driver turned in her seat and watched her settle in. Jane tried to ignore the scrutiny. The woman's lined face, framed by an untidy mop of shoulder length hair, was devoid of emotion, her dark eyes damn near dead; it was unsettling. Jane looked away, hiding her discomfort by securing her seatbelt. A man got in beside the driver, slamming the door closed; two more climbed in the back and took seats. Neither one bothered to even glance her way. Last of all,

Stuart, slamming the door closed.

"Go," he yelled, buckling in beside Jane. The van lurched into motion and he placed a protective arm around her shoulder. She was surprised to feel discomfited by the casual intimacy; maybe she shouldn't have been. This unexpected world of Stuart's was just too much to take in. She needed time to process everything that had happened.

"Hey," Stuart murmured in her ear. She started; unaware she'd drifted off. "You're okay now. We're going to the safe house, where we left Mills. You remember it, don't you?"

Another wave of wooziness. She shook her head to clear her mind, then nodded. "Yes," she said. Stuart smiled. She had no idea where they were, but she began to recall the place where they'd hidden away the courier of their crime. A single drop of guilt spilled down her cheek. She broke eye contact and turned to look through the windows.

An old factory flashed before her eyes. Another van pulled in behind and followed closely. Then they were out in the open, racing through an industrial wasteland somewhere on the edge of... she still didn't know where, but she began to feel a sense of familiarity. The other van veered off on a different course through the desolation.

They took a corner too fast. The van threatened to overturn. Stuart held her secure against the rocking motion and nuzzled her cheek with his nose.

"You lied to me, everything was a lie," she said, suddenly pulling away. A hurt look flashed across his face.

"No! Not everything. How could I tell you about this? I'm sorry."

"You used me to kill those people."

A look of remorse. "No. I love you. I came back for you, didn't I?"

"What does that prove? You wanted to help, you said. But *you* got the virus. It's killing people."

"Do you think I want to be doing this? I'm in above my head, I've no choice."

"Yes you have!" Tears started to gather. She could feel the tingling that heralded a spillage.

"It was supposed to cripple the networks. That's all. We had to knock out their system. It's the only way. You know what it's like. We can't be free until there's no more Bosses, no more Nexus."

Revulsion softened with the realisation that she was little different. But for her naive compassion, the victims would still be alive. Stuart could never have carried out his plan. Perhaps that made her the most culpable. Now what kind of future did she have? Less than a zero, she was also a fugitive, an exile. A chill passed through her body and she held the coat tightly closed.

"Sorry to break you up," the driver said, "but we've got company."

With a fresh thrill of fear, Jane looked out but saw nothing. Stuart cursed. He released his seatbelt. The others did the same, retrieving weapons and holding them ready.

"Keep those safety catches on, guys; we don't want any accidents," Stuart said, leaning over the front passenger seat to peer through the windscreen. "*Shit!*"

"What is it?" she asked. "I can't see anything."

"Choppers! Probably been monitoring us for a while. That means they'll be waiting."

The driver accelerated. Stuart slumped back and gripped the seat in front to brace himself. The landscape blurred. Corners taken at high speeds bumped Jane around like surplus baggage. Still the choppers hung in the sky, an ominous presence.

"Please remain calm," the onboard computer buzzed, "traffic police have instructed this vehicle to pull over."

"I thought you took care of that!" Stuart yelled.

"I did. Don't worry. I'm in control."

Another corner. The van sped along, leaving a wake of dust and wind-blown paper. The choppers descended to disgorge their armed payload.

"Look out!"

Frost smeared the windscreen and the driver's head exploded. The engine revved. The van lurched into a wild turn, then back again, careering right and left. Jane felt the seatbelt bite into her collar bone as she was thrown around against the restraint. The man next to the driver leaned across and tried to hold the dead woman against the seat while handling the steering wheel, but he couldn't bring the vehicle back under control.

Metal and glass crunched as the van mounted a kerb and hit a wall with a glancing blow. The vehicle rebounded and began to tip. Jane screamed. So did everyone else. Everything turned upside down. People tumbled. The world kept turning. Something banged sharply against her head. Then the van finished back on its wheels and the world was still.

The engine was dead, the faint ticking of cooling metal soon dismissed by the sounds of groaning. Jane looked around. The interior was littered with glass and sprayed red; the driver was slumped in her seat, the back of her head just a gaping hole.

Through the empty windows she saw cops advancing, behind them armoured vehicles sealed off the road. "Stuart…"

"I know," he gasped, cradling his damaged shoulder. "Let's get out of here!"

The doors were flung open and shots barked. Jane found herself in the middle of a living nightmare, far worse than the darkened room. Stuart pulled her to the ground and dragged her to relative cover by the side of the stricken van. Someone else moved too slow and grunted as bullets thudded home. The man slumped to the ground and moved no more.

Trapped in the open, the anarchists fired frantically, desperately trying to stem the flow of cops advancing from both ends of the road. The cops scurried for cover. Jane lay on the ground, where Stuart prevented her flight, pinning her down as bullets smashed into the cracked asphalt.

"I hope she's worth it!" someone yelled.

A commotion pierced Jane's terror and she found the courage to glance up. Rubble tumbled from the top of a gutted building and drove the cops from cover. They ran into the open where they met a hail of bullets.

People swarmed into view. Ragged and dirty, zeros appeared from the ruins like ghosts. They threw hefty stones at the police and the shooting subsided as the cops turned to face this unexpected threat. The cops began to retreat, swept away by the hordes.

Jane rose, shakily but determined, to her feet and let Stuart pull her towards the ruins, away from the chaos of post-industrial warfare. "Go on," he shouted. "Get out of here!"

"I can't. Where could I go?"

"Get to the safe house. Where we left Mills."

"What about you?"

"I'll meet you there. Go on."

"No. Come with me."

A smile lit up Stuart's face. "I'll catch you up," he soothed. "Now get going. I'll feel better knowing you're safe."

A kiss, then he turned away. She watched him go, half-annoyed, half frightened for him. With a curse, she turned and ran.

JANE looked around, searching for a familiar landmark.

All the ghettos looked the same: crumbling houses, many boarded up, gutted roofs and tumbled walls.

Nevertheless, she kept walking. A rapid pace, one fuelled by adrenaline that gave her the resilience to override exhaustion. The streets were quiet. Not that the silence meant the place was empty. She could feel eyes watching her. Not quite paranoia. Occasionally ghostly figures flitted through the ruins. At least they wouldn't turn her in: the zeros cut loose from their bonds and running wild.

A dog barked somewhere. It sounded hungry and forlorn. Hard to believe this district lay on the edge of a prosperous city; it belonged in a post-apocalyptic immersive-VR. Another street. A group of children watched her from the top of a refuse heap. Haunted eyes gleamed ravenously bright from dirty faces. Jane looked away and hurried by. These children were not even zeros. They were feral street kids, never even registered, who had been denied any official recognition of existence; they just provided sport for off-duty cops and the pest control companies.

More streets exactly the same. She began to tire as the adrenaline wore off. Her eyesight blurred so she sat down on a low wall and rubbed her face. Then she took a deep breath. The world still appeared blurred, but she urged her eyes to work, squinting in search of a familiar sight.

She strained to read a rusty street sign across the road. Then her eyes pulled back into focus. Yes, she knew where she was now. Not far to the safe house. The world appeared clear at last. No more confusion. The dizziness faded.

She stood and hurried down the street. The houses towered over her, menacing shadows of so many might-have-beens. This had been an affluent area once, maybe a hundred years ago. There, the next street. Relief made her feel lighter and she hurried towards the safe house, past the burnt-out ruin of a van lying on a pile of crumbling bricks. Filth and weeds protruded from its rusty interior. Only the metal grille where the windscreen used to be revealed that it was an old police van, a legacy of some bygone urban battle.

Almost there. She hurried along. Maybe Stuart was already waiting? Fretting, she turned into the weed-infested garden and pulled at the corrugated iron sheet that served as a door. Instantly the smell of decades of neglect invaded her nostrils.

"Stuart!" she called, not too loudly. The front room remained as she remembered it: mouldering furniture, bare boards covered in crushed plaster and ashtray spillage. A jacket draped over the armchair hinted at recent occupation, as did the stack of pizza boxes in the corner.

Nobody here. Dismayed, she turned to search the rest of the house. A thump sounded from above. She ran for the stairs. They creaked hideously but what did it matter? They wouldn't draw attention from outside.

The front bedroom was gloomy, like the rest of the house, but a few beacons of light shone through gaps in the boarded up window. Mills rested in the corner, anonymous beneath the headset and life-supporting machinery. Nobody else here, however, and she turned to leave.

"Ah, Miss Sutton!" Reich stood at the door. Jane backed away, shocked. "Thank you for your co-operation."

"Sorry for the elaborate charade, Jane," Shreck added, appearing behind his colleague. "But we needed to be sure."

The stabbing pain in her arm returned, followed by the sensation of something long, thin and hard being withdrawn. The room faded. The table and the circle of light reappeared.

"Agent 51 (Alpha): Reich. Logout."

"Agent 51(Beta): Shreck. Logout."

The men collapsed into little white dots that hung in the air for a moment. Then they faded away completely. The table evaporated, followed by the room.

Finally, the light blinked out and Jane found herself trapped in total darkness. She screamed Stuart's name. But he never came; he'd never been more than a lie.

CHAPTER 23:
Looking for a Ticket Home

AS soon as he walked into the office he knew there was no mercy in the world. The woman glared at them with a face totally devoid of compassion. "So you're the two sewer-rats. I suppose you're here about the zeros outside?"

"Yes," Tom said, "I –"

"Don't bother saying anything. I won't be opening the gates."

Sharp and not at all sweet, the woman's condemnation sounded so casual. It took a moment for the consequences to sink in. Mills felt dismay as he thought of all that dashed hope. Thankfully, he couldn't see Tom's face, but his torment proved all too easy to imagine.

For now Mills merely hardened his face into its usual dour mask. Only a twitch in his cheek indicated his anger. Unseen, as the woman paid him scant attention.

If only the background buzz of the office had faded,

just for a moment, and brought some acknowledgement of the statement's importance. The office functionaries ignored the two newcomers in their midst. They were equally indifferent to the drama played out before their boss.

Tom refused to go down without a fight. Mills respected him for that. All the same, he groaned inwardly as his companion argued. The woman was not listening. The argument was futile. Beyond that, he hated to witness the indignity of a man forced to plead.

"You've got to let us in," Tom said. "Those people have nowhere else to go."

"I have three thousand people –"

"You can't leave my people outside. It's inhuman. They could die."

"So could we if we let them in. I will not risk lives for a ragtag of potentially infected zeros. You've already placed us at great risk. I just hope nothing hitched a ride."

Mills wanted to snort his disdain, but he kept it to himself. They were all terrified, scared out of their wits by something beyond their control. They'd finally discovered what it meant to be a zero.

You're not immune, we can actually hurt you. As he witnessed authority reduced to such fear, he couldn't help the perverse sense of satisfaction. Somehow, it made up for the years of invisibility. More than that – it partially evened up the score for those left outside.

The office staff rummaged through filing cabinets and

drawers, scattering papers and documents in the process. Blueprints finally appeared to be unfurled and stretched across tables. Instantly, diagrams shifted and rotated. Windows opened on the sheets to reveal scrolling reams of text and arcane symbols. This was AR laid bare for the acolytes to unravel and manipulate.

The woman stared glassy-eyed as Tom's arguments began to wind down to a mumble. Eventually he fell silent and his shoulders sagged. He reached up with a limp hand and rubbed his face. Mills grimaced. Awful to see a man reduced to such a state.

He stepped forward and gave Tom's arm a supportive squeeze. His companion's face looked haggard but he managed a faint smile, as if to say he was all right really. The look in his eyes said otherwise.

"So what about us?" Mills asked in a tight-lipped voice.

"Well, we're hardly going to open up and let you out," she said, raising one eyebrow.

"So we stay where it's safe, while my people die," Tom said.

The woman looked up sharply. "That's right. Congratulations, gentlemen. You at least have got your ticket out of here."

"What?"

"You're being sent home. Logged-out. You'll be joining the rest of us in the evacuation programme. Now, if you'll excuse me, I have to sort out any mess you may have caused."

BENEATH the trees it was peaceful, a reminder of happier days. Mills sat back and listened to the chatter of the birds in the trees. Slowly, the knots of rage began to loosen.

All he felt was guilt at being sent home. And relief. In the end that only stirred more guilt. He thought of Janet and the children. He saw all those anonymous faces outside, staring up at the walls in hope, ignorant of the fact they had been abandoned, *betrayed.*

Tom sat quietly with his head in his hands. He hadn't moved for some time – just a statue erected for all the world's woes. Mills understood how he felt. But there was nothing he could say that would ease his companion's burden. It would, perhaps, have been better if they had never looked for a way inside.

People congregated within the garden, innocents milling around paradise. He watched them, listened to snatches of trivial conversation. They were like inmates in an old people's home, awaiting transport to the next world. They had nothing to do but kill time while it went about slowly killing them.

A low moan startled Mills from his thoughts. A quiver ran through Tom's body. Then he went stiff and slipped from the bench. He knelt there, still with his face hidden. Suddenly he screamed and sat bolt upright, arms held out to his side, fists clenched.

It was a fit of some kind. Mills grabbed him and stared into sightless eyes, shook him and shouted, frightened. Then Tom reached out and gripped his arms.

"I won't do it," he shouted "I won't leave them out there!"

"What can we do?"

"Open the gates!"

The pressure on his arms was painful. He tried to prise Tom's fingers loose but they gripped with the strength of insanity.

"But what about these people? Can we risk their lives?"

"Damn you!" Tom pushed him away and leapt to his feet. Rage burned in his eyes. His face looked wild. "What about the lives of my people? You've got a way out so they can fuck off, is that it? Bugger off Jack, I'm all right."

"No!" The accusation stung.

"Then *help* me."

He looked up at Tom, quivering with rage. The change was frightening. But he felt angry that Tom should accuse him of a lack of concern. He looked around at the people waiting to leave. He thought again of Janet and all the others. Then he turned back to Tom and reluctantly made his decision.

SUPERCILIOUS *little shit*, Carlisle felt like shouting. Instead he drummed his fingers on the desk, out of sight of the cam-link. The Speaker looked so smug. Safe and secure in the Commons, the man lacked the courage to face his Prime Minister in person.

"Are you threatening me?"

"Most assuredly not, Prime Minister. I am merely expressing the legitimate concerns of the members of this House. The Right Honourable Ladies and Gentlemen have a right to be perturbed. It is their constituents that are bearing the brunt of this disgraceful bout of lawlessness. Not only that, their considerable business interests are –"

"Get to the point!"

The Speaker hesitated. *Such an excuse for a human being*, Carlisle thought. A pompous windbag stuffed with his own self-importance.

"Well… Prime Minister, the Honourable Members feel that perhaps it is time you looked towards retirement. You have held office for a number of years now, and a glorious administration it has been, but such a demanding role would tire anybody. It is felt that a younger, fresher regimen would be able to –"

"You want my resignation?"

"There has been talk of a No Confidence Motion, Prime Minister. Even you would find it difficult to ignore that. You still govern with the consent of this House, even if only on paper. I only say this to enlighten you on current thinking in the lobbies."

So, that was it? They wanted rid of him. After all he had done for these parasites. No gratitude. And with the zeros in revolt they'd finally found their courage. Despite his loyal Social Security Agency, a vote of no confidence would open the doors to a challenge. A military challenge? *That's it, of course. Those useless bastards have been talking to the Brass*. He added a potential coup to his list of problems.

"Prime Minister? What shall I tell the Honourable House? Naturally, you have my loyal support whatever you decide."

He snorted in disgust. "I'll bet I do, you cringing arse-licker. You tell those parasites that I'll stand down over their dead bodies."

The Speaker stiffened and went pale. It was telling that a trace of defiance remained around the eyes: something that wouldn't have been there only a few days ago.

"Yes, Prime Minister, I'll pass on your sentiments in due course. Though perhaps you would care to relay them in person. It has been some time since you last graced us with your presence."

The video window collapsed. Momentarily stunned, he stared at the blank screen. Then the rage simmered over. Nobody cut him off, least of all a Parliamentarian.

"Chief!" he bellowed.

"Yes, Father?"

"I want some men down at Westminster. They're moving against me. Find the ring-leaders and initiate some by-elections."

Chief paused. "There may be a problem. We have reports that a large demonstration is to gather on Westminster. It may be violent."

He grinned. "What kind of security do we have in place?"

"Our own units, in control of Home Office troops, a few detachments of local police. Shall I have them reinforced?"

"No. Have our men redeployed elsewhere."

"Yes, Father."

"It's about time Parliament faced a bit of reality."

STEALTH was the necessary ingredient to success. They needed to merge with the crowd, become parts of the background. As they wandered, Mills found it surprisingly easy. Apparently nobody had been informed of their entry into the citadel. He and Tom were just two more anonymous faces.

Since his decision to help, Tom had calmed down. He seemed almost his old self, except for an impatient tension in the muscles of his face and a disquieting gleam in his eyes. Tom watched the crowd with a little half-smile on his face, as if he felt no fear.

As for himself, Mills expected the angry mob of discovery at any moment. His nerves were on edge, his knees felt like they were held in place by two worn elastic bands and his upper lip insisted on twitching. The slow progress made his tension worse. They needed to pick their way carefully through the bustling crowds, and to act casual at the same time.

A sense of anger helped. He gritted his teeth as he caught snatches of conversation. People knew about the beggars at the gate. The crowd's sense of revulsion masked their guilt at finding a sanctuary and their reluctance to share it. That, and their cowardice. If only the beggars would go away, the voices in the crowd whispered, they have no right to threaten our security. It's unfair to expect us to risk everything to save them. They should go away and beg at another door. Someone else will help. But not us. We cannot.

Any doubt he felt at risking life to save life faded away. Except for the safety of those on the outside, as far as he was concerned, these people deserved to face the nightmare.

"There it is," Tom said.

The street opened onto the vast courtyard he first saw a world away. The gates and the walls at the far side towered over the people milling around the square. In the centre of the open space, partially obscured by a clutch of trees, Mills saw the Gate House. They *had* to get there. Adrenaline urged him to quicken the pace. Sweat beaded his forehead and his armpits felt sticky. *Keep it slow*, he told himself, *don't rush it now*. Paranoia pulsed through his body.

"We stick out too much," Tom whispered.

"Just keep walking."

THE Gate House didn't look like much; a simple two-story blockhouse. Mills stooped to tie his bootlace. Tom stood nearby, feigning indifference but carefully looking out for watchful eyes. The doors were open. So far, so easy.

"We must look fucking obvious," Tom said.

"Doesn't matter now. Come on."

They scurried inside. Stairs led up and they began to ascend.

"You'd think they'd have it guarded."

Mills grinned. "Are you suggesting some mad bastard's going to invite the monster in?"

"There's always us."

"Yeah, but we're just a couple of useless zeros."

"You're right. I'm so glad I'm feckless." Tom smiled. They increased their pace, taking the steps in twos and threes. The stairs soared upwards. Doubt began to slip into Mills' mind.

"Hold it! Something's not right."

"We can't stop."

"And we can't go on forever. The Gate House isn't this big."

"You started this. We can't stop now."

"I'm not stopping. I just think this is some kind of trick."

"It's just a matter of perspective. Appearances can be deceptive. Come on."

A twitch in Tom's face hinted at more than impatience. This was an eagerness that bordered on insanity, a madness that wouldn't allow him to quit. He turned and ran up the stairs. His distorted voice echoed down from above, exhorting Mills to follow.

"Wait!"

With legs of lead, he pushed on. There was still no sign of the second floor.

"Tom! Wait!"

No answer. Sweat streamed from his face. Phlegm rose in his throat to make his mouth feel sticky. Then his knees gave way beneath him. They slammed hard into the step and he fell forwards. There, he laid face down, panting wearily. After a few deep breaths he turned over and gently seated himself. He placed his face in his hands. Slowly his heart rate returned to something akin to normal.

A thump from above followed by a shuffling noise. He looked up, assuming Tom was on his way down.

"Tom?"

Again, he received no answer, just a murmuring that drifted from above. Moments later it erupted into a hideous shriek. He felt his heart bounce.

"Tom? Tom!"

Fatigue forgotten, he raced up the stairs. Something drifted past his head and he brushed it aside. Suddenly the steps ended and he fell forward into a room overlooking the gates. A body lay on the floor. Its face was a distorted mask of terror. And it wasn't Tom.

"What happened?" he gasped, shocked.

"Dave! About time. I've been waiting for you."

The voice was unfamiliar and carried a faint choral quality. He looked up and noticed the butterflies fluttering below the ceiling. One flew down past his ear and he started in terror. Then they converged and began to swarm in a humanoid form.

"Tom?"

"Sorry, Dave. Tom's dead," the swarm chorused. "Or maybe a dribbling vegetable like that one over there. I absorbed the last of his data-stream in the garden."

"But –"

"I know. If I were human I'd make a great actor. But like I told you before, appearances can be deceptive."

The swarm fused until it resembled Tom. Mills shivered and watched the thing walk towards the gate controls situated beneath the window. It smiled at him and began to tap a few keys.

"By the way, Dave. I'd like you to know that everything that is about to happen is your fault."

"What do you mean?"

"I tried to tell you at the cliff: look for the calm at the eye of the storm. But no, you had to come here. Maybe I overdid the symbolism, but I figured you weren't ready for some straight talk. Pity. You know, I was happy to ignore this place, but I couldn't have you sent home. I haven't finished with you yet."

"Why? What do you want with me?"

"I need you, Dave. Isn't that funny? Somebody actually needs you. For now, anyway. I need you to get me somewhere. Then you're rid of me."

"Where?"

"You'll know it when you get there."

It was Tom standing in front of him now. Except for the dark eyes. Mills found himself held by them, like a rabbit trapped in the headlights of an oncoming car. Then it turned away and looked out of the window. He stood up and reluctantly followed its gaze.

"What are you going to do?"

The thing laughed. "What I do."

"You can't. Don't. They haven't done anything wrong."

"Right and wrong are meaningless paradigms. Anyway, you were all for letting them in a moment ago."

"I didn't know you were here."

"Where else would I be? I exist wherever you exist. We're brothers."

"No, we're not –"

The thing smiled mockingly. "No? We were born into this world together. We're… conjoined twins, linked at the mind."

The image rippled. Suddenly it wasn't Tom standing in front of him any more. Mills gasped in horror as stared at his own face. Those dark eyes mocked him. His own lips twisted in a horrible smile. He backed away from himself.

"Like this shape better do you?" the thing asked. "Like I said: I am you and you are I. Think of me as your dark side. I'm your mindless Rage rendered into flesh and thought and deed. Every bad feeling, all those half-whispered vows of vengeance against the society that dumped you, every impotent shake of your fist, every urge you ever had to lash out at the people you think wrecked your life. That's me, but without your failings. Think of me as your unspoken desire for oblivion, Dave. And my time has come for you and all those like you."

It turned back to the terminal, dismissing him in a contemptuous manner. Its words stung. They were not alike, whatever it said. No matter how angry he might have felt, no matter the blind rage that consumed his soul, he never got the urge to take it out on the innocent, the hapless. Feeling his anger stirring now, he forced himself to edge towards his doppelganger, knowing he couldn't let it finish.

Outside, the gates began to swing open. Pathetic stick figures began to trickle into the citadel. Then the flow of people turned to a flood.

He threw himself at the thing. It flew apart and he fell through a cloud of insects. The floor hit him hard. The thing reassembled and stood over him. It smiled and held out a finger. A butterfly twitched on the tip.

"Pretty aren't we? Black, that's the traditional colour of anarchism. The lovely pattern on the wings, now that's a Mandelbrot. Symbol of Chaos."

Tremors shook the building. The disaster was going to happen all over again. He felt dismay and anger in equal measure. He leapt to his feet and attacked. It side-stepped and he slammed into the terminal. Once more he was on the floor. This time the thing kicked him in the side. He clutched at his ribs and gasped for breath.

"Dave, you're so transparent."

"Fuck… you!"

"You wish. I preferred fucking Christine."

Mills' fists flailed before his brain caught up with his rage, but his image kept ducking and laughing. At last it smashed a fist into Mills' face. He cried out. Another blow caught him hard in the stomach. He doubled up and collapsed as his innards writhed. A wave of nausea tasted sweet.

"That's right, Dave. I fucked with her every night in her dreams. And then I snuffed her out." It spoke so casually. Mills raged and wept in his tiny realm of pain, helpless as his insides squirmed. "Couldn't have a woman holding you back. If it's any consolation it was a mercy, really. You should have seen what they did to her. I did. I saw right into her mind. What was left of it, anyway. Pity really. Did you know she used to be such a bright young thing? Great future. Until they sucked out her mind. If you'd only seen what I know, Dave – why, you wouldn't try to stop me then, you'd *help* me. But I haven't got the time to win you over. I'll just have to use you, but you should be used to that by now. You've been a pawn all your life."

The throbbing in his guts finally exploded, disgorging the matter from his gaping mouth. Instantly it rushed into the air, a fresh swarm of destruction. The world rocked on its foundations. Screams echoed from outside.

He looked up through the haze of pain. The thing

knelt beside him, its face almost sympathetic. It reached out and gently stroked his arm. Mills flinched.

"Don't fight it, Dave. It'll pass soon enough. Your nightmare's nearly over."

Tormented by the memory of Christine, tears streamed from his eyes. He was a helpless observer, just as he was then. He could only watch his tormentor crumble back into a swarm to leave him with the knowledge that he had brought death into a haven of life.

For the second time.

CHAPTER 24:
Safe as Houses

GUNSHIPS soared over the English countryside. Gracefully, the trio of fierce machines hugged the contours of the land like insects.

Carswell watched those gunships pull into formation alongside the PM's chopper and felt his depression deepen. Those monstrous machines represented his sense of foreboding at the darker side of government, the flip side of his own function, and the measure of his own failure.

So this is what it all comes to, he thought, *all this for one missing man?* At least it meant the crisis was nearly over. In the meantime, he must put up with the discomfort of this military bone shaker. Once again he sighed.

They were somewhere over Kent, heading for the sprawl that straddled the Thames as it headed towards the estuary: a patchwork of decaying dereliction and new development. The PM hadn't revealed quite where it was they were going, but right now that was the least of his irritations.

The throbbing engine nurtured his headache. The hard seat was making his bottom numb and he dreaded what it was doing to the line of his suit. Worse, fluid sloshed inside his bladder – the liquid motion of fear. And somehow the PM's dreadful humming managed to be heard above the engine. If only he dared tell the old man to shut up. But that would be a terrible breach of etiquette. What was he humming? Sounded like Wagner's Ride of the Valkyrie.

"Nothing like a jaunt in the countryside is there, Eric?"

He suppressed the urge to wince and gently nodded his head. A faint smile added to his pretence at calm. Fortunately the PM was in good humour. The man's face beamed with excitement. He loved every minute.

"Be good for you this. Valuable experience."

Except he was only along for the ride, he knew. They wanted to make his humiliation complete. No other reason for his presence made sense. So he had failed to locate Mills. Well, he lacked the resources and the expertise of the Social Security Agency.

"How long?" the PM asked, fidgeting like a little boy on a long car trip. Quite unsettling, the way he leaned forward to peer at the gunships, his eyes illuminated by enthusiasm.

"Our ETA is thirty-four minutes, Father," Chief

replied.

"Excellent!"

"I wish you had not insisted on accompanying us, Father. Our destination has long been abandoned and derelict: a known haven for destitute undesirables. It may be dangerous. The area cannot be considered fully pacified."

Carswell felt his stomach flip but the PM grinned and clapped his hands.

"Nonsense! I must be in at the kill. Haven't seen a field operation for years – I miss the thrill of it. But you needn't worry. I won't get in the way."

The freak turned in his seat and half-smiled. "We are making Mr Carswell nervous."

"Eric? Certainly not. Are you nervous?"

"No, Prime Minister."

"Good. That's what I like to hear. Make a man of you, this. If you survive."

The PM winked at Chief. Carswell clenched his teeth.

DERELICTION spread out before Carswell's eyes. This might be the legacy a war-zone anywhere in the world but for the regular lines of what he guessed was New Ebbsfleet resting peacefully on the horizon to the East. A mundane provincial town, yet it would be far better to be there, safe and secure, than in this haven of vagrants and terrorists.

The scenery down there didn't quite match the visuals the PM's freaks had decoded from the informant, Jane

Sutton's mind – apparently they seldom did – but they'd gleaned the essentials needed to identify the locality by more conventional means.

Two main roads intersected beneath them, cracked asphalt and weeds, quartering the ruination along the cardinal points. Much of the neighbourhood had been flattened during some long-abandoned regeneration programme, but plenty of old shells remained. The south side was largely intact. Rows and rows of terraced houses stretched into the middle distance. Beyond them, four tower blocks rose hollow into the sky.

The northern quadrants were practically a wasteland. Mounds of rubble, reclaimed by grass and weeds, spread out westwards; all that remained of residential streets. On the eastside, a car park formed an apron around the concrete footprint of a vanished supermarket. A cluster of tumbledown shops, roofs open to the elements, huddled at the northern end of the retail ghost, close to the road.

Glumly, Carswell watched the gunships hover over the row of ruined houses that bordered the road across from the car park. Many were little more than walls and hollow-eyed windows, but four of the mid-terrace properties appeared pretty much intact. In theory, their little problem was hidden away in one of those boarded-up relics. Soon, not *soon* enough, it would all be over and he'd be back safe and sound in his office.

Delicately two of the choppers moved into position before landing on the road either end of the intact houses, their blades kicking up dust. Home Office troops scurried into position. Carswell looked on from the PM's hovering chopper and felt fear squeeze the back of his head. The third gunship hung back in the sky, ready to offer supporting fire.

An explosion erupted from one of the houses and, even before the dust could settle, troops rushed inside. More troops repeated the action, storming each intact property. Curt voices barked from the chopper's radio. Chief touched his earpiece and frowned in concentration. The PM fidgeted impatiently.

"The area is secure, Father."

"Then what are we waiting for? Let's get down!"

Carswell felt his stomach lurch as the chopper, too ungainly for the road, manoeuvred to touch down in the car park. Instantly the door slid open to reveal armed men with wary expressions. Dust filtered through the opening to fill Carswell's nostrils and the irritation exploded in a sneeze.

"Bless you," the PM said on his way out. Armed men instantly rushed to surround him in a protective ring. Chief followed and gave them a cool appraisal. His face displayed no emotion. He merely tapped on his notebook, like a store manager assessing stock levels.

"Come along, Eric. Don't dawdle!"

Trembling legs made it difficult to walk and he found it equally hard to regulate his breathing. The watery feeling had moved into his bowels.

The PM looked around with a smile on his face. Did the man fear nothing? This might as well be another photo-call for his carefully manipulated media.

"Fearless leader routs vagabonds," he muttered with an attempt at a grin. Fear distorted the effect to produce – he felt sure – the image of a child about to cry. Perhaps he might, once he gained a private moment.

Carswell scanned the ruins. There was nothing to see, but even so he couldn't shake the feeling that hundreds of eyes watched him. The sensation made him feel sick. He was a keyboard-tapper with no business on a security operation.

A soldier barged into him. He gave the man a dirty look, not that his executive status meant anything here. Naturally, the man ignored him and moved to salute an officer.

"Gone? What do you mean gone?" The PM suddenly bellowed. The officer backed away as though he feared a blow. The ranker just stood at attention, aware that this was not his problem.

"I'm sorry, Sir. We've found signs of recent habitation, but the objective is no longer in situ."

"Too slow. Too damn slow!"

So there was nothing to be afraid of after all? He broke into a genuine grin at last. Not only did this restore his honour; it was a genuine delight to witness the PM outmanoeuvred. Not something that occurred often.

"We still have the woman in storage, Father," a

contrite Chief said. "Perhaps she can tell us more."

"And maybe she knows nothing! You've let me down. I am very disappointed–"

A sudden cry of alarm broke the PM's frustration.

THEY had appeared like ghosts. Hundreds, maybe thousands of zeros emerged from the ruined streets behind the target zone, flooding onto the road from both ends. They stood like ragged statues, watching, grim and unforgiving.

More shuffled into place from the west, stalking over and around the mounds of rubble; still more were walking towards the PM's chopper across the expanse of the former supermarket. Together, they formed a loose cordon of their own.

Slowly, Carswell edged back towards the chopper. For once he felt relieved to be in the company of so many armed men. The zeros wouldn't try anything. They were just looking. That's all. Mindless curiosity.

Two worlds stood and stared at each other in silence, until the PM moved forward and broke the spell. He spoke to the crowd, for all the world as if addressing a business convention. The zeros watched him impassively, unmoved by the great man's stature or the smooth authority in his voice.

The concrete chunk caught him in mid-sentence. He went down, hands clasped to the side of his face.

"Father!" Chief sprang forward and took hold of the

stricken man. He used his own body as a shield as more masonry tumbled. A brick smashed into his shoulder and he grimaced in pain but kept his hold.

Gunshots cracked as the soldiers woke from their somnambulist state. The zeros scattered. Carswell leapt into the chopper and cowered on the floor. Men yelled in anger and fear. The soldiers were in disarray. Heavily armed they might be, yet at the same time they were vastly outnumbered. The zeros surged forward and circled round, hurling anything that came to hand at the troops. Bottles, bricks, iron bars and timber smashed into heads and bodies and limbs. Others leapt on the soldiers to drag them down in a clinging mass of bodies.

Despite the bullets, in spite of their losses, the zeros still kept coming until the troops scurried for the safety of the gunships. Engines whined as they powered up.

Out of this chaos, the PM emerged. Bruised and blooded, he moaned pitifully, the stature of greatness abandoned on the battlefield. Now he was just a wounded old man.

"Help me!" Chief implored, struggling with his burden.

Despite his terror, Carswell managed to motivate himself and help the PM inside the chopper. There, he lay slumped on his side, breathing heavily and moaning intermittently. Carswell backed away and stared in open-mouthed disbelief.

The chopper shuddered. The engine's whine built to a

crescendo. He watched with a sense of detachment while outside the battle continued to rage, framed by the doorway as if by a giant television screen.

A gunship rose sluggishly. Its engines whined with the struggle to overcome the burden of clinging bodies. Staccato weapons fire. Zeros fell, only to be replaced by more. Finally the gunship toppled over. Blades shattered as they struck the ground. The fuselage crumpled. The fuel tank ruptured.

The explosion thumped into his chest like an invisible fist. The mechanical carcass burned with a stinging heat, even from that distance. He began to tremble. The zeros swarmed towards him. The remaining gunship took off and hovered to provide support.

"They can't do this," he said in shock. "They're zeros... they can't do this to us..."

Nobody paid any attention. Chief cradled the PM in his arms; his face screwed up with genuine concern. The PM moaned, isolated from the world around him.

The last of the soldiers leapt into the helicopter. One turned and slammed the butt of his weapon into a hungry face. A tooth rattled across the floor. Then the door slammed closed and hid the carnage.

Only as the chopper lifted off, did Carswell realise his trousers were warm with fresh piss.

MOVEMENT *in the ruins. The zeros gather. All of them are the denizens of the outcast places, lost even to the* broken Nexus. From shanty and wasteland, ghetto and slum, run-down estate and derelict factory, they all move steadily towards the city, drawn by the lights of another world.

THUNDER in the distance. Shoppers look up from a humdrum existence to wonder at the noise. The skies are clear, no sign of a storm. Where then does the thunder originate? Soon the noise can be identified. It is not the roar of overheated air. It is the rage of overheated minds.

TIME moves on. Fires rage. Plate glass shatters. Cars are overturned. The zeros swarm through the city to tear down the symbols of wealth and power, plunder the commercial temples in search of the stuff of life. The world feels the full force of their rage and vengeance, nurtured and bred in the depths of society's underbelly.

ANGRY faces fill the screens. The data is beamed back to the nerve-centre of City Watch as the cameras witness on the behalf of fleeing citizens.

Select a camera. Any one will do, they all tell the same tale of a world reduced to nothing. Zeros swarm into view. Thousands of individuals have come together with unstoppable force. Watch while shops are looted and burned, a forest of arms reach out to take the means to live. The looters are curiously discerning; trinkets of consumer status ignored. For the most part, it's the food, the clothes, *the tools –* practical *things – they favour, not the flatscreens and electronic baubles they might once have craved. The camera looks on, helpless; unable to comprehend this shift in perspective. Change the channel.*

Images repeat. Screen after screen. Witness as society is torn asunder, condemned by a million judges and executioners: those cast out and exiled, damned by their fellow man and left to face the elements alone. Now they return, with nothing to lose and perhaps nothing to gain.

Never tasted. Never heard. The daily drama of city life flashes across the many screens. The finale unfolds. Yet the nerve centre is empty. Abandoned. City Watch can no longer observe or protect.

A flurry of motion in the flickering shadows. Ragged men and women move between the desks. One stops to watch the fragmented images. He stands in thoughtful silence. Then he stoops to pick up a chair and with a grunt he smashes the screens. Images collapse into a million meaningless shards.

CROMWELL stands on his plinth before the Mother of all Parliaments. All around him the masses – the common folk – gather before the empty heart of democracy. With stone eyes he watches the maelstrom of the crowds; behind his sombre presence, flames and thick smoke belch from the gutted ruin.

The acrid tendrils rise to obscure the towering column once known as Big Ben. The great hands are locked, frozen in time when the People dared to trespass on the Hallowed Halls of Democracy. And pass judgement.

Unmoved by the destruction, Cromwell can only sit as the battle rages around him. Lord Protector, there is nothing left to protect. Now police scurry in retreat, swept away by the hordes. Defences lie broken and gutted, like the architectural antiquity that burns overhead.

ABOVE the violence he was safe, Carswell constantly assured himself. So why did it sound so unconvincing?

Ever since yesterday's debacle he'd been unable to shake that sense of dark foreboding. Everything was falling apart. The Turmoil was happening all over again. The PM injured, Nexus destroyed. Nothing, it seemed, could stop the zeros now. The fate of society bore down on his shoulders. Never had the weight felt so heavy.

There was nothing for him to do but wait and watch. Hope that his technicians found the breakthrough to solve this mess. Or, by some miracle, they located Mills. Until then he was powerless.

Was that how the zeros once felt? Not a pleasant experience. Would they feel at home with the sense of frustration and lack of control? Terrible to be a zero, then, dominated by outside forces, the puppet orchestrated by an invisible master.

Not that the zeros were helpless any longer. Within that mass of humanity, the police struggled in vain to restore order. Puffs of smoke rose from knots of people –

riot gas that spread out in a choking haze.

Another gulp of neat whiskey failed to settle his nerves. Ruefully he looked at the glass and studied his haggard reflection. Eyes that had witnessed too much stared back, a stare that was difficult to meet – and it was his.

A shadow mercifully dragged his attention back to the carnage. A police gunship soared towards the river. Useless above the narrow streets and tall buildings, it sought to stem the rush of zeros across the river. Riot glue rained down on Westminster Bridge. Now the people struggling against the sticky discharge were sitting ducks for the next sweep that fired nets.

The chopper moved on. Many bridges straddle the Thames, many routes for the zeros to spread their virus of outrage. One transmitted by word of mouth, to crackle from one angry soul to the next and infect minds with fury. The thought chilled him – that the virus of his failure rampaged in the streets.

The glass was dry. He muttered a curse and finally tore himself away from the window. He slumped in his chair and glanced at the photograph of his wife and daughter. They should leave the suburbs, get to the countryside. If there was still time.

FOR a few frantic seconds he searched for the phone hidden by the mess of paper on his desk. At last his fingers closed on the handset and he pulled it clear. The line buzzed in his ear. "Rebecca," he said, then settled down for the dialling tone.

A voice made him sit up again: "How is Rebecca these days?"

"What? Who is this? How did you get on this line?"

"You mean you've forgotten me so soon. Eric, that's so like you."

Despite the distortion, he soon recognised the voice: "MacAllister! I thought you were –"

"Dead?"

There was amusement in the tone, not the malicious kind, rather that of someone who has seen the infinity that waits for every man and realised there is no point feeling resentment.

"No, Eric I'm not dead. Only dying."

A rush of cold; reminders of mortality held a chilling resonance this day. He struggled for something to say. "I'm sorry to hear that," seemed terribly trite. He said it anyway, if only to fill the demanding silence.

MacAllister laughed quietly. "You always had a way with words. But I don't want to listen to your disembodied voice. Turn on your monitor. It's been so long since we actually saw each other."

Reluctantly, he turned towards his monitor. The screen bounced into life to reveal a video window. The lens in the case cycled watchfully. The screen was fuzzy with multicoloured static, forcing him to squint to try and make out the image.

MacAllister looked well, perversely so, considering his circumstances. His face appeared peaceful, serene even, but the eyes peering through the scintillating storm were filled with terrible knowledge. He found it hard to look into those eyes – even though they were only dots of phosphorescence – they too much resembled the haunted look of his own.

"You've aged, Eric," MacAllister said softly. "All that responsibility is wearing you down. You need to get away from it all. If it's possible for you to escape your conscience."

"I don't know what you mean."

"No? You mean there's no remorse for what you've done? Not even the slightest trace of guilt for this monstrosity you created?"

"I didn't create this mess. Terrorists did that."

"Oh, Eric, our society is based on terror. Fear and suspicion – it's what underwrites the government, it's what you dealt out with Nexus. And I helped you to build all that, fool that I am. Yet I never wanted it to be this way."

"You're talking nonsense. The global web isn't a monstrosity, it's a breakthrough. It gave us back the control we lost with conventional IT. You helped to do that – you gave us back our control."

"Control, Eric? You don't seem to be in control at the moment."

"We'll get things up and running again. Count on it."

MacAllister smiled. "I admire your ability to lie convincingly, even to an old friend."

Now it was his turn to smile, he'd be damned if he'd let MacAllister see his helplessness. If impressions were all he had, then he would do his utmost to keep them. Appearances were important. And there was one piece of information he possessed that MacAllister lacked. Why keep him in the dark, especially since he helped to bring it about?

"We won't need the zeros much longer," he said. "There's another resource we can use to furnish AI-IT with additional processing power – one that adapts to the network far more readily. I never had time to release the memo, but the new control system for Core-AI we've been trialling was matching all projected functionality. A continuation of your work, Mac."

The amusement drained from MacAllister's face and his features turned harsh. The transformation was so sudden and shocking that Carswell recoiled from the screen. "Control system!" he bellowed, almost overloading the speakers. "Why can't you say it, Eric? A child, damn you and your bureaucratic jargon."

Struggling to retain his composure, he parried the old man's wrath: "Well, I never had your grasp of the technical terminology for exploitable resources. Anyway, there are thousands of street *children* out there: cheap, virtually useless in any conventional sense, but the neuroplasticity of a juvenile cortex makes them far more adaptable to AI-

IT augmentation. You should be pleased, you gave us a way to make them useful, to provide them a purpose."

"My work was supposed to help people with degenerative diseases, allow them to live in a virtual world rather than be trapped in the darkness of their skull. I know about that, what it's like to face the prospect of living death. But *you* wove a web of tortured souls and snared people in another version of living death. You corrupted my work!"

"You let me."

That punctured his wrath. Fascinating, the way MacAllister collapsed into the weary old man that he truly was. All that stuff about appearances, lose them and you're nothing. How on Earth could he ever have been a friend to this man? They were so unalike. MacAllister had been the classic research scientist, caught up in his own little world, strangely naïve and completely unconcerned by the complexities of commercial and political realities. Yet not so much that he was unable to see the need for backing.

So he turned up one day at his office, offering the potential to turn AI into something worth a damn to anyone other than the specialists in their ivory towers.

The man's research into neuro-synthetic connectivity was a long shot; he hadn't even conceived of grafted symbiotic nerve bundles back then. Private equity had already baulked at the odds, but with at least a portion of the machinery of state at his grasp, and the resources that came with it, Carswell had known he could risk the long game.

Strange, how they hit it off, until MacAllister abandoned his work to retreat from the world. Even though there was nothing between them now, he still felt a twinge of sadness for what had been, but he realised in the big picture it didn't matter a damn. They were just two threads in the tapestry of power, and MacAllister was too worn and frayed to be of any further use.

"You're right," MacAllister eventually said, breaking Carswell's thoughts. "But it's a pity that the innocent paid for our sins."

"What do you mean by the innocent?" he asked distractedly, starting to sort through the papers on his desk.

"Christine. My little girl. I'm afraid… she's dead."

The papers slithered from his fingers. "I'm… sorry," he stammered. This time he realised he meant it, as his thoughts strayed onto the bubbly little girl that used to play with his daughter, all those years ago. Such a bright future, he lamented.

MacAllister looked away from the camera and sighed. "She's safe now. That's some consolation. They can't hurt her any more."

"What do you mean?"

Suddenly MacAllister was looking at him. The serenity was gone, replaced by hatred. "Don't give me that. You know what they did to her. How could you let them do that to my little girl? She was all I had. My God, you used to bounce her on your knees!"

"Mac, I don't know what you mean. I thought she had a breakd –"

"I've seen the memo, Eric. I know what the Social Security Agency did to her. I saw the results. How could you?"

He felt trapped and he flinched at the memory of the meetings with the PM's freaks, the security-inspired purges, the aggravation. All because a father had forgotten to shut down his workstation and a curious daughter gained an insight into a secret world and, to make it worse, threatened to reveal that secret.

How easily it could have been Melanie – the times when he fell asleep at his home workstation. All the old fears flooded back and remorse surfed the tide.

"I couldn't stop them, Mac. You can't stop the Social Security Agency. You know that. There was nothing I could do. I got... what was left... of her inside. That was all I could do. You've got to believe me."

"No."

Words choked him. He coughed to clear his throat and breathed deeply. Inhaling only irritated his throat further and he coughed again until the effort made him hot and breathless. The office felt stuffy, forcing him to loosen his tie. MacAllister stared at his discomfort.

"For three years I've bitten my tongue, Eric. I kept quiet for Christine's sake. But now we're dying, we're all dying. I was wrong, my research; the human mind was never meant to live this way. But death is a great liberator, you know. Now I'm going to set you free."

A thrill of fear. "What do you mean?" he said, finally able to speak. Sweat felt clammy beneath his armpits.

"We have something in common, Eric. We're both dying. You see, I've shut off the air conditioning to your office."

A tap on the screen opened a dialogue box. To his horror, he saw that his air circulation was off-line. He tried to click it back on but the system refused his commands. He tried to open a link to his secretary but the line resolutely failed to open.

"What have you done?" he gasped.

"I hacked your building system. Quite easy to do, seeing as I've been integrated into the JobNet Agency's mainframe for the last three years. I know it like the back of my hand. Incidentally, I have also triggered a bomb-scare in the building. There's nobody there to help you."

Carswell rose and turned towards the window. He could still feel MacAllister's virtual gaze boring a hole in his back. Fear made him breathe faster, using up more precious oxygen. He cursed the day the building was proofed against a terrorist gas attack. But it seemed the rational thing to do at the time.

"I wouldn't bother with the windows, Eric. They're blast-proof, remember? You haven't much chance of breaking them."

MacAllister was shaking his head in mock sympathy.

Carswell backed away from the screen and stumbled towards the door. He pulled at the handle, then whimpered and fumbled for his key card, slid it through the lock. The green LED flashed and died. The red only glared. He tried again. And again. He began to whine.

"Please – James!" he said as his legs collapsed. Breathing was difficult and his throat gargled ominously. From somewhere he found the strength to bang on the door. A humming sounded in his ears; his limbs felt like lead, his lungs wanted to burst.

"Wait for me on the other side," MacAllister said sadly from the distance. "Tell Christine I won't be far behind."

Slowly at first, but accelerating, the world retreated down a dark tunnel. He watched existence recede and felt the burden fall away from his shoulders. This was all happening to someone else. Problems belonged to other people. A sense of relief brought euphoria. Then the world shrank to a white dot.

And vanished.

CHAPTER 25:
Cogs in the Machine

BARREN desolation surrounded Mills. There wasn't a hint of any living thing: only rock and boulders and coarse soil existed to form a landscape that mirrored the dreary state of his soul.

The citadel was lost in this wasteland, somewhere far behind. Mills didn't turn back to try and find its position in this expanse of emptiness. He didn't want to dwell upon the catastrophe. Instead, he trudged along the gravel road that snaked across the wilderness, and tried to block the terrible screams that still echoed in his memory.

All the others were gone now. The survivors. Scattered by the calamity he'd delivered into the heart of the citadel. The last straggler fell long ago, swallowed by whatever lurked in their particular nightmares.

The ground began a gentle rise towards the hills. It looked exactly as if the sun was setting behind the distant crests. Yet there was no sun in the sky. For that matter there was no *sky* – just those restless fractal patterns that wrenched at the eyes if he stared too long.

He returned his gaze to the road. He followed without caring, mindlessly putting one foot in front of the other. He was the lonely, eternal traveller, with nowhere in particular to go.

The road went somewhere. Probably. That was enough. It began to rise into the lower slopes. The hills made for a sombre shadow. That halo of light failed to raise Mills' spirits.

Forget the view, he told himself, *just keep going.* Dutifully, he followed the path, allowing it to take him where it would. He turned a corner around a crag and began to climb. Another turn. Then another. With each sinuous curve the road grew steeper and the climb became harder. He gritted his teeth and looked down at his feet to watch the miles tear at his soles.

THEY reminded him of statues on Easter Island; his silent companions along the road. Their presence had crept up on him slowly; seeping into his consciousness as he trudged along, head down.

The hours – or minutes – had dawdled by, dragging at his feet; oblivious to his surroundings, until he'd suddenly felt compelled to look up. That's when he'd found he was no longer alone. The sight of them was no comfort. Quite the reverse. Seeing this eerie gathering snatched the breath from his lungs and made him long for a return to solitude.

As far as the eye could see, thousands of humanoid figures stood naked – but genderless – in endless ranks on either side of the road. They all stood stock-still and looked up towards the light. Some of them leaned at drunken angles. Each figure was tethered by a tangle of cables and glistening wire; blinded by an AR helmet. Even masked, these silent sentinels possessed a dreadful watchfulness.

On impulse, Mills approached one of these forlorn figures. He wanted to know if they could be liberated from the web. Feverish hope, rising unbidden; suddenly it seemed a question important to his own chances of release. He grabbed the sentinel by the shoulders. The creature moved with some reluctance, as if compelled to face the light, but he managed to turn it bodily to face him. Then he reached for the helmet. Lacking any restraints, it came away easily, revealing the corpse-like face beneath.

Mills stepped back in shock. The helmet fell from his numb fingers. The wires he'd taken to be part of the helmet were meshed tight against the creature's hairless scalp; worse, they burrowed into the puckered flesh. The eyes were wide, staring into a sightless infinity. As he stared, stunned, at the apparition, its jaw dropped open in a silent scream.

A tear dribbled down the creature's grey cheek. Drawn to the source of this unexpected sign of life, Mills inadvertently made direct eye contact. There was something in there, deep in the dilated pupils; a connection, raw and vital. He flinched as something punched into his mind, but he couldn't look away. Those fathomless pupils held him locked.

Data screeched; voices whispered. Hard to tell if the shrieking cacophony was one or the other or both. Pain exploded in his skull, a flood of unknowable information that seared through his mind in a million data-streams. Mills put his hands to his ears to stem the flow of information. A futile gesture. The sound was a direct transmission to his brain. The hiss grew worse. There were moans within the torrent – pitiable expressions of human misery. Their pleas grew ever more plaintive. Mills screamed in response.

Consciousness blurred. Mills staggered. Pain finally squeezed his eyes closed. The barrage of data fell silent. The dread connection was severed and his mind was his own once more. Released, he collapsed to land on his backside.

Mills panted where he sat, head throbbing, eyes sore. He didn't dare look up at the sentinel, but he couldn't fail to hear the low, unnatural moan that emerged from the back of the its throat. Slowly it turned until its eyes gazed up at the light once more. Now Mills dared to stare in horror at the pitiable apparition. The next sentinel in line joined the low moan. Followed by the next. Soon all the grim figures in earshot were moaning in unison.

The hairs on the back of Mills' neck began to prickle.

He clambered to his feet and ran up the road. Only when the symphony of the damned had faded into the distance did he stop running.

Mills slumped to his knees, exhausted by the horror of his ordeal. There was no way out of this hell; the machine wasn't going to let him go. The tears flowed hot; his fears evoked in guttering sobs. Fatigue finally quelled his grief; he curled up on the ground and slipped into oblivion.

GRAFFITI covered the walls. Documents, data cores and broken equipment littered the corridors of what was once the Human Resources Ministry. The place had been ransacked by zeros. Now it looked as though an illiterate tornado had blasted through. Carlisle flicked through the channels of the security link and grimly assessed the destruction.

A soldier walked into shot and solemnly shifted his boot through a pile of ash. Carlisle sighed and flicked to the last channel. Agents ransacked drawers and filing cabinets for anything that could be salvaged. A technician worked to download data from the workstation. Medics, meanwhile, zipped up Carswell's body and struggled with the dead weight.

"The security override originated from within JobNet, Father. We are currently assessing how it was achieved."

He acknowledged Chief with a grunt and collapsed the video link. Then he sat back in his chair and sighed. There was little chance of restoring Nexus now, he thought bitterly. To add to his problems, his bruised and swollen face throbbed with pain again; a distraction he really didn't need. He reached up and gently stroked the dressing. Even that slight contact brought a burst of focused pain. He winced.

"Father, are you all right?"

"Yes!" he replied irritably, groping for the pills on his desk. He popped the painkillers and antibiotic cocktail, dry-swallowing them in his haste. "Have you anything else for me to consider, or can I get some peace at last?"

Chief stiffened. Might almost have been hurt, Carlisle mused; as if they were capable of genuine emotion. Sometimes his creatures seemed so human. Easy to forget they were little more than mobile AIs.

"The disorder is slowly being contained, Father."

"Still fighting?"

"Yes."

"But not spreading?"

"No."

"Then what's so good about it? The situation hangs in the balance. It could go either way. Is that supposed to make me feel better?"

No answer. Chief fidgeted then placed his hands behind his back in a measure of composure. His eyes stared down at the desk like a child fearing the imminent discovery of some minor transgression.

"How are we progressing with the main problem?"

A pause followed by a reluctant answer. "Not good,

Father. Our units are stretched thin. So too are the Home Office troops. We cannot control the zeros and conduct a thorough search for Mills."

"What about the regular police?"

"Heavily engaged, Father. They have sustained many casualties. There are… other problems."

"Such as?" He frowned. Carefully. Why did they have to always bring him problems? Why not a solution for a change?

"Many stakeholders are seeking to evacuate affected areas. It is causing havoc for the deployment of our forces."

"Then issue a decree declaring a state of emergency. Everyone is to remain in their homes. Must I think of everything?"

"That will help, Father," he began to fidget once more. "A military deployment would be much more useful –"

"NO!" The contents of his desk bounced from the shock of his fist. For a moment the pain seared his face. He hissed a curse and put his hands up to his injuries until the pain dwindled to more tolerable levels.

"You will *not* deploy the military. They can't be trusted. I will not give them the opportunity to move against me. Do you understand?"

"Yes, Father."

"In fact, I want the Brass rounded up and placed under house arrest. That includes the Secretary of State for Defence and his Shadow counterpart. Sever their lines of communication and keep all regular troops confined to barracks."

"I do not have enough men for the operation."

"Well find some!"

He slumped back in his chair. Everything was falling apart. The whole globe was affected, and, since it began in his little domain, the world leaders looked to *him* to solve the problem. The business community was equally rattled, and they hassled him constantly too. They didn't seem to realise that their constant whining only added to the problem. Ungrateful bastards. He gave them free reign to make unfettered profits, had provided a passive, cheap workforce and all they did was complain. So far the only good news came from his security investments. Given the circumstances, that business was booming.

If only the pain would subside. Important decisions need a clear head, yet his was fuzzy with analgesic chemicals. Never had he been so reliant on his underlings. And so far their performance in a crisis was proving sadly lacking.

"Are you still here?" he snapped.

"Yes, Father. There are other matters that require your attention."

He groaned. Never any peace. "What is it?"

Chief took a step back as though he feared the response.

"Strikes have broken out, Father."

Hardly a problem, he sighed. "I assume we still have

the capability of identifying the strikers?"

"Yes. I have an up to date file. Initially the unrest broke out amongst AR workers. That was not entirely unexpected. It seems, however, that this has infected other economic sectors."

"Select ten per cent for cancellation of employment contracts and confiscation of stakes. That'll convince the others to follow management instructions."

"Given the nature of the current crisis, Father, that sanction is unlikely to prove effective. With the zeros in revolt they have nothing to lose by defying us."

"Of course," he muttered in dismay. That should have been obvious. Labour discipline used to be one of the purposes of Nexus. A Sword of Damocles suspended over the stakeholders' heads, waiting to slice away disobedience. And now it was well and truly sheathed.

A wave of weariness. "All this trouble from one zero," he said in resignation.

"Father, the pain is affecting your reasoning. We cannot be endangered. We will find this man and eliminate the threat."

"Unless the virus breaks into the global net. Then everything comes crashing down."

"It has not done so. I think it reasonable to conclude that it will not. The virus is not spreading through the network, Father, but in the streets. And we have that virus contained."

Carlisle smiled wearily. They were so loyal and keen.

Congenital optimists, and so damn naïve. Always useful in an underling – once upon a time. "You have some suggestion?"

"We know that Mills is located in the artificial world. We can splice in a link to AR. I propose that a unit be sent in to locate and delete Mills."

"Locate one man among all those lost souls?"

"It can be done, Father. Our mole, Harris, is still functioning. We can relay a message via his helmet speaker to rendezvous with our unit. Also, as a result of Carswell's analysis of a partially corrupted logfile retrieved from his systems, we have a list of the target's movements within AR prior to the eruption of the virus. It gives us a starting point for our search that we lack out here. It is, as you might say, Father, the only long-shot we currently possess."

A gentle nod of his head as he considered. The plan sounded feasible enough. At least he could think of nothing better. It *was* a long shot, but better than no shot at all.

"All right. Do it. Send in Reich and Shreck."

CHAPTER 26:
Back to Square Zero

GRAVEL rattled gently alongside Mills' twitching face. He stirred in response to the faint vibration in the ground and mumbled incoherently. Fingers gently caressed the shivering stones. His arm moved as though looking for something… someone.

The vibration became a buzz and then turned to a cough followed by a guttural snarl. Mills jerked awake and sat up with the wary look of a hunted animal.

"NOW what?" he muttered, expecting the worst. He turned to scan the wilderness.

A truck appeared around a turn and thundered along in a cloud of oily vapour. As it swung towards him, he saw the dull glow of the headlamps peer like bulbous eyes. The truck crawled forward like a gigantic beetle, its huge wheels churning up the distance.

His lungs resonated their hollowness. His heart bounced inside its cavity. The ground trembled beneath his feet. Noxious vapours cloyed at the back of his throat. A heartbeat later the Beast thundered past, spitting gravel into his face. Wheels almost as tall as he was whirled before his eyes, close enough to touch. The monstrous machine filled the world with noise and heat and choking smoke. Then it was gone.

Coughing and cursing, he leapt over a deep wheel-rut and jogged after the vehicle. The payload compartment was only partially enclosed and open at the rear, he noticed. On impulse, he started to run, no clear plan in mind beyond stealing a ride. A lurch heralded a change of gears. The truck picked up speed.

With a cry he leapt for the machine. Fingers found the lip of the cargo bay and gripped tight. Muscles protested. Tendons and ligaments stretched and twanged as he dangled precariously, his toecaps ploughing gravel. He pulled, felt his chin brush against metal, then he slipped an elbow over the edge and gained a more secure hold. With a final grunt of effort he lifted himself up to tumble down a shallow gradient into the dark interior.

Mills landed on something unpleasantly yielding. He heard strange bursts of hissing sound, like something exhaling, as he rolled over and clambered to his knees. About half of the compartment's top was open to the sky, but the high sides left the cargo hidden in shadow. As he stared into the depths of the truck's interior, he began to pick out the darker shade of a shapeless mound rising above him. The longer he stared, the more his skin prickled; something wasn't right.

The truck shuddered and dislodged some of the hidden cargo. Movement suggested the pile was about to topple so he leapt to his feet and moved nearer to the opening. At the same moment the vehicle turned, allowing light to peer in through the rear and reveal the horrible truth.

All he could do was stare at the pile of bodies. The truck was full of them. To add to his horror, he realised he was treading on still more. They looked dead. But the dead – no, the deaths – he'd witnessed so far had left nothing but the weight of sorrow. So not dead; not alive, what then? Trapped in a self-contained bubble?

Another bump rattled through the truck so that more bodies slithered into view. Arms and legs protruded. Faces gaped vacant-eyed. Others appeared faceless behind AR headsets. The bodies moved in a parody of life; heads nodding, mouths flopping open and closed, limbs shaking and twitching to the truck's motion.

Reluctantly, Mills took in the ghastly scene. As he did so, he found a fresh source of dismay. Janet stared from the base of the mound. In her stiffened arms she cradled Johnny and Mandy. They stared straight at him with penetrating, accusing blindness. Dully, he began to recognise others, perceived features that reminded him of faces caught in the crowd; those lost when the last citadel fell to his cruel alter ego.

After far too long, his heart breaking and his sanity straining, he turned away from the sight and prepared to leap from the truck. Better to walk than accompany the Damned. But the dead-or-lost weren't done.

A faint noise brought him back from the brink. A gasp followed by a low moan, before he could dismiss it as nothing but air squeezed out of lifeless lungs, he heard words, faint, almost whispered: "Help me. Help me. Help…"

He turned and studied the shifting mound. Feeble hands protruded from among the corpses and gestured for help. The heavy weight pulling at his limbs fell away and he hurriedly climbed the mound, blocking out the thought of his boots trampling human faces. Hissing sighs whispered from gaping mouths as his weight depressed lungs, but he shut out those noises, too, and concentrated on reaching that one, tragic figure.

He took hold of the hand and it gripped tight, forcing him to prise the fingers open. The hand tried to clutch once more but he was too busy shifting bodies aside. They tumbled down, one after another, like broken mannequins. Then the last body fell away to reveal a face, an awful face, staring right out of the past.

Recognition exploded horribly in his heart: "Rob!"

TECHNICIANS scurried around the mainframe's exposed innards. They were so engrossed they failed to spot the newcomers. Shreck watched, reminded of drones fussing over their queen, then he smiled and released the door. It slammed shut with a satisfying boom.

Everybody looked up, startled. A man hurriedly thrust a tablet into a colleague's hands and came running over. "Agents Reich, Shreck," he said, his voice trembling. "I'm Martin Conway, Central Systems Operator. I'm afraid you're a little early. We're not quite ready for you."

"Social Security operatives are never punctual," Reich said.

"Er, no… Sir…"

"However, we are never late."

Conway stared a moment before regaining some of his composure. "If you'd like to follow me?"

They followed Conway towards the towering bulk of the mainframe. From the side it resembled a gigantic tombstone, though the effect was spoiled by the array of terminals around its base. As they moved round, Shreck saw the peeled back casing that revealed the machine's innards. At its heart a black coffin-like box nested amongst the spaghetti of cables and feeder tubes. Vessels bubbled with injected oxygen. Fluid gurgled.

Beneath the support facilities the AI lay exposed: linked bulbs of glass contained the vat-grown neural tissue floating in its nutrient solutions. Fine wires glistened in the light.

Shreck gazed in fascination. He felt a strange affinity with this machine, an uncomfortable feeling he tried to suppress. Memories – or dreams – arose from his subconscious. He saw the wide-open space illuminated by red light. Felt the tiny bubbles tickle his body. By his side was the presence that would eventually become his brother. In the dream it was just another part of a developing awareness.

A shiver threatened to break his cool façade. He suppressed the urge and tore his gaze away from the AI. Only then did he become aware that Conway had said something.

"Kora." There was affection in his tone.

He turned to fix a cold stare: "Kora?"

The man smiled weakly, a mixture of embarrassment and fear. "Core-AI, Kora. She's the command and control hub for the JobNet and Nexus systems. We've been trying to get her back online."

"What about the virus?" Reich asked.

"She's not affected. Kora went offline just before the virus attacked. We got some anomalous communications and then nothing. There's nothing technically wrong that we can find. It's almost as if she's afraid."

Shreck raised an eyebrow. Conway caught the gesture and emitted a laugh that resembled a cough.

"Well, that's what some of the junior techs say."

"Are you suggesting it has a personality?"

"She's intelligent, Agent Reich, but only a machine."

Reich grunted. "So how will this affect our operation?"

"If we can get Kora back online, then we can reinitialise the AR matrix. Once that's done we can activate the virus defences and start getting people out. It's a high risk strategy – if we're not careful we could open the global web to infection."

"Then why follow such a strategy?"

Conway gaped, momentarily lost for words. "People are dying, Agent Shreck. If we pull this off we save lives."

"A commendable attitude," Reich said. "Dealing with so many corpses would be a costly operation."

This sensible consideration seemed to cause Conway physical pain. Shreck allowed himself an inward chuckle and followed their guide around the mainframe. A few muttered curses followed in their wake. He made a mental note to follow them up later.

Beyond the mainframe's towering bulk, two camp beds waited for them, situated beside a network server. Conway handed them both a nasal inhaler and gestured towards the beds. A technician nervously glanced up from his work. Shreck glanced at the inhaler in his hand, then looked at the two headsets, and felt his amusement shoved aside by apprehension.

ALONE in the dark Shreck felt naked and exposed. Muffled voices tickled his ears, too low to understand. The bed creaked and he found the uneven spread of his weight most uncomfortable.

"We're almost ready, Agents Reich and Shreck," Conway said through the helmet speaker. He sounded less nervous now. Evidently he thought he had them in his power. Perhaps he did.

"You'll feel woozy once we inject the interface components. That won't last long – we're going to have to put you to sleep."

"Why?" Reich's voice, uncommonly adrenal.

Shreck gripped the edge of the bed and felt his jaw tense. To lose control was terrible. He wanted to tear the helmet off, but Father needed him.

Conway answered: "Ever had reality hit you full in the face? This is a basic link. There's nothing to soften your transition into AR. With all due respect, Agents, you don't want to emerge in the sensorium substrate too disorientated to commence your mission. There are rare cases where people have never recovered. Believe me, it's best if you go in unconscious and awake in situ."

The disembodied voice fell silent. Alone again. Shreck was not used to the feeling. It made him afraid. Another novel experience. Social Security operatives are not supposed to feel fear, he chided himself. No matter the circumstance, they must always take charge; exude total confidence, absolute authority. They exist solely to protect Father; all else is secondary.

"Get ready. We're about to hook you up."

A pressure squeezed his hand. Reich. He was not alone. Almost he heard the voice: "Father needs us. We shall make him proud."

A point of pain seemed like a star exploding in the

darkness. The prelude to uncertainty. Society would stand or fall on their success. Then no more time to consider as consciousness ebbed away.

FIGHTING back tears, Mills knelt precariously and cradled his old shift mate's head in his hands.

Rob's eyes fluttered open and he moved weakly. Not much since he was still pinned from the midriff down. "Dave… Dave, you found me. Where… have you been all these… years?"

"What happened? How did you get here?"

"I got a job, Dave. Can you believe that? Me! Married. Kids. The works. Can you believe it? I was going to tell you. But you'd gone. Where did you go, Dave?"

A tear dribbled. Rob babbled in delirium. So many years. So much to say. And then to find him here. Like this. A grimace of pain flashed across Rob's face. The delirium momentarily released its grip.

"What happened Dave? Where am I? Where's Elaine? Where are my kids?"

What could he say, that his wife and family had possibly been nothing but an elaborate hoax? "It's all right," he said, opting to say nothing. "I'll get you out."

The smile returned. "You were always a mate, Dave. Knew you'd never forget me."

Rob's head sagged and Mills gently lowered him. He turned towards the mess of limbs and torsos and wondered where to begin. He rose to brace himself and reached out for a leg. He pulled hard and felt it shift. Soon the body pulled free and he shoved it aside. Reaching out for another, he tried to forget that it was human and heaved.

The body was too tightly entwined. He dropped it and climbed higher to try again from a different angle. He knelt and gripped it under the armpits. Again he heaved, this time he was rewarded by movement.

The truck lurched, juddering, as it made a turn and began to crawl up an incline, its engine growling with the strain. Mills felt his centre of gravity shift and he wobbled precarious, reaching out to try and steady himself against the wall. He cursed as he stumbled off-balance. The body pile began to topple. A cry as he fell with them, tumbling towards the rear of the vehicle. Clawed hands scratched his face and body. Cadavers buried him in an avalanche of flesh. Somewhere within the mass, Rob cried in alarm.

"Dave... David! Don't leave me!"

"Hold on!" Mills dragged himself clear and took stock of the situation. A woman's body had settled over Rob's head and torso. He stooped to pick her up and drag her clear, but another body slid to take her place.

The mound was settling almost level with the lip of the payload bay. Much more of this and it would surely begin to shed some of its load. The angle and motion of the truck conspired with his unsteady footing to nudge him back towards the entrance.

Mills managed to stagger towards the side of the

compartment. He caught himself right on the edge, finding a handhold on the wall, his other arm flailing, but the truck rocked and bounced as it levelled out and broke his grip. Desperately, he fought for balance but momentum took him over the edge. The ground smacked into his body with a breathless impact.

From his prone position, he tried to shout but all that emerged was a garbled whisper. The truck crawled away. He tried to rise but a sharp pain in his side made him clutch at his ribs. Unable to walk, he crawled after the departing vehicle. Only then did he realise he was near the top of the hills. The peaks looked so close. Ahead, only metres away, the truck turned and rumbled to a halt. Then it slowly – delicately – backed up.

With a hiss of hydraulics the back began to rise and Mills could only watch, helpless, while the bodies slithered into a pit.

ALONE on the verge of madness, Mills felt his strength draining into the gravel, as he stared at the precipice that had claimed his last link with the living world. He had just enough energy left to roll clear as the truck began its return journey; its wheels contemptuously spat grit as it thundered past.

Somehow, after he'd lain head down on the ground for a while, he managed to force his limbs to work. Joints creaked in pain, ribs ached at the motion as he stood, but he fought the corpse-like urge and dragged himself to the edge to brave the view.

Dust still mingled in the air, a blossoming cloud that tickled his nose and caused the tears of irritation to vie with the tears of despair. Down there, in the depths beneath the clouds, Rob settled to his rest, alongside Janet and the children and countless anonymous souls.

As the dust finally settled, Mills could see the landscape, spread out before him like a mediaeval impression of the nether realm. The pits stretched on for miles, encircled by the arms of these craggy hills and connected by a crazy tapestry of dusty roads. Trucks, rendered minuscule by perspective, crawled along in their own clouds. They resembled beetles scuttling through the detritus of civilisation.

Beyond the pits towered a monolith that reared into the heavens like a gigantic tombstone. So black was the stone that it appeared to be a gap in reality, a geometric region of non-existence defined by a fragile shell of matter. High above the monolith, a patch of blue sky and gossamer clouds hung in the alien sky of cyberspace. It was a tantalising glimmer of normality, this oasis of calm, a hole into the real world, as if he still dared to indulge that particular dream.

Mills shivered and felt his knees buckle. All he felt was knowledge. Not pain, not feeling, not emotion – just data – fed into his senses by a parasite latched onto his mind.

The virus was telling him something. As he watched

through the tears, he noticed lines and patterns. The monolith was far from being smooth to perfection. Lines merged, contours flowed until random chaos evolved into meaning.

A face gaped in dread from the surface of darkness. Wide eyes stared at the pits. A glimmer of light suggested a tear. The mouth, a cavernous orifice in the tangled mass of beard, gaped in horror. More lines flowed into place beneath that grim countenance. They ignited with a scintillating light to form mocking words. Voices cackled and whispered but Mills simply stared at the letters and listened to the scornful syllables they invoked in his mind:

"Here lies the working class"

"Who is the gravedigger now?"

CHAPTER 27:
Bonfire of the Vanities

FLAMES flicker on the underside of the dark clouds. The city is ablaze. Buildings cascade with an inferno of sparks and explosions of red-hot gas. Chaos grips the world, but the minions of Order struggle to defend the embers.

An unstoppable force, the suppressed fervour of the human spirit, explodes against an immovable object, the power of human greed. Flesh and blood batter against a wall of technology, the ebb and flow of tidal rage held in a terrible balance, waiting for the delicate weave of society to irrevocably unravel.

ON the edge of the urban battlefield, refugees flood towards the safety of the countryside. Roads are gridlocked with traffic. Nothing moves except the burdened bodies of frightened humanity.

Behind them, the burning city ignites the sky with a

fiery aurora. Helicopters thunder through the night, their powerful searchlights adding to the spectral display like visitors from another world.

Hidden in the shadows between the flames and the spotlights rage the denizens of the Abyss. Raised from their exile in the underbelly of society, they rampage through the once comfortable lives of the refugees. A fragile order lies broken before an ocean of chaos and Canute's entourage flee before the furious tide.

THE JobMart burned and its former inmates danced and sang in the flickering light of its death throes.

Nathan sat on the hard asphalt, listening to the singing and the laughter while he stared dreamily into the brazier. There was no real need for the fire. The blazing JobMart kept the night's chill at bay, but somehow this was a more human-sized blaze. Its flames spoke of comfort, protection and companionship as much as they provided warmth.

For the first time in his life, he no longer felt alone. He no longer felt like a nobody. Like the people sat around the brazier, or those dancing in the shadows beyond the firelight, he mattered. It was a liberating experience, to find himself, to find humanity. And to think that it had always been around him, waiting like the seeds of autumn for the coming spring. Now spring had arrived, and they were putting forth the first roots of new life.

Tomorrow they would build, all of them dancing around the fires, passing around the beer, singing and whooping with joy. They had everything they needed. Materials plundered from the burning city. The skills between them to face any challenge; plumbers and electricians, agriculturists, carpenters, computer programmers, builders and architects, teachers and nurses and more. Nexus had claimed them all in its time; now they were free to build a better life.

He turned to face Eric and watched his face as it glowed in the firelight. Already the hardships of years on the dole had been smoothed away. Lines remained, etched in too deep by the crushing weight of sorrow. Nothing could ever erase them, but they no longer masked his charm. Instead they emphasised the strong contours of his face. The eyes, once expressionless holes, now gleamed with life.

Nathan felt the love warm his insides. In a way he'd known Eric for years, he'd known them all for years, but only as shadows on the edge of his solitary life. With Nexus dead, they had turned *to* each other, rather than on each other. Finally, joyfully, they had reached out and found other souls to share life's burdens. Together, they found warmth and humanity. And then he had found Eric.

Nathan leaned against his new-found love and slipped his arm around his waist. He felt good as he moved against him. Eric's face turned towards his. Those gleaming eyes sparkled as the smile illuminated his face. Nathan felt his own unfamiliar smile respond, and he leaned forward to meet Eric's lips.

Soft and warm, the new life tasted good.

THEY were hammering against the doors again. Conway looked at the makeshift barricade of tables and filing cabinets and prayed it would hold.

One of his technicians looked at him with a pale, sweaty face. "Maybe we should let them in," she said.

"No chance."

"What if they blow the doors?"

"They won't. Not with all this precious equipment in here."

The tech tried to look convinced, but Conway knew his words lacked confidence.

On the building's exterior security monitors, he watched the city burn. The imagined scent of smoke and ash mingled with the electric odour of conditioned air. Occasionally the screen flared white as the cameras struggled to cope with unfamiliar brightness. A solitary monitor scanned the corridor and displayed armed security police hammering against the doors.

With the zeros running amok, it seemed sensible to barricade themselves inside. Should the police break through, they might even believe him.

"How are we doing?"

The question startled the technician. She jumped and looked away from the monitors. "We're just about ready to go."

"Good. How are our guests?"

"Quiet. Still alive, if that's what you mean. They came out of sedation about 20 minutes ago. Readings indicate an active immersion. We're observing stress levels higher than the norm; guess these guys are more human than they like to let on."

He nodded at the news. He'd checked them half an hour ago, but even so their presence added to his sense of unease.

The sweat poured off him, cold beads of perspiration. Fear, nothing less. He pulled a handkerchief from his pocket and paused to look at the Mandelbrot pattern, then he wiped it across his brow and hastily stuck it back into his pocket.

"Right, let's get things started." He took a deep breath and turned to face the mainframe. What he saw snatched the breath from his lungs. It always did. Once again, he wondered how he ever found himself in this situation.

Kora stood exposed before him. The monolithic casing was peeled right back. For the first time, the CPU was fully uncovered. The few horrified moans the sight produced struck Conway to his core. The prototype for what was expected to usher in AI 3.0 had, until now, been a closely guarded secret.

The little girl barely looked human; more like an embryo. Suspended in the transparent, ovoid shell, she floated in a foetal position. The supporting gel was kept at her precise body temperature. A modified breather mask covered her face, simultaneously blindfolding her and muffling her ears, ensuring external sensory deprivation.

Feeder tubes and catheters coiled around her body like parasitic worms. Bio-monitors and a gossamer web of data lines covered her body. Completing her integration into Core-AI, and far more obscene, were the fleshy nerve bundles surgically grafted to her head. He knew the thousands of vat-grown neurons in that Gorgon's 'hair-do' had meshed at the synaptic level with the little girl's nervous system, linking her completely and irreversibly to the conventional AI's bio-synthetic core.

A shiver ran through his body as he wondered who she had once been, or indeed might have become if allowed to live her life, and then he wondered if this was really any worse than the future she'd been snatched from. An unregistered zero, a non-person in every sense, he knew; destitute and considered feral by the powers that be, what did she have to look forward to, really? Even so, harvesting adult zeros was one thing; a child... a *child* was a step too far.

"Let's get on with it," he said, approaching the mainframe. He sat down on the chair and uncoiled the cable that dangled from the headset. The technician flustered nearby while he snorted a nanocule refresher. She averted her eyes from the little girl. Kora's age was physiologically estimated to be around seven or eight. He remembered that the woman had a daughter not much older than that.

"There's nothing to soften the uplink transition," she

said. "Are you sure about going in raw?"

"Yes. There isn't time to knock me out."

"Like you told our guests, you might emerge inside AR too disorientated to be much use…"

"I've done raw links before."

"So have I. Felt like I was being turned inside out and spun around like a top. I damn near choked on my own vomit, and I was addled for two days straight afterwards. It was the nastiest hangover I ever had."

"I can handle it. Besides, our friends over there are heading for a virus-compromised environment in the general network; that's much nastier. I'm just hacking Kora's data-space. It'll be fine."

"Sure. Core-AI's secure now, but what about when the connection is re-established with the network? You might be overwhelmed."

"I have to try. We can't sit here twiddling our thumbs. She's the gateway to the wider world. The physical links are still intact. We can't sever them without killing her – and abandoning all those poor saps still plugged into JobNet. Sooner or later, that virus is going to find a way to burn through Kora's defences. Besides, this is going to work, okay?"

"If you say so. I'm not convinced, but you're the boss."

"That's right, I'm the boss. My responsibility, my risk." Despite the feigned certainty, he felt his hackles rising at the thought of going in raw. It was some choice, enter the mind of an AI and risk losing his own, or go mad with the tension of waiting. Still, maybe in some way he could atone for his part in creating this havoc. He slipped the helmet onto his head and settled down into the chair. "Plug me in."

Nothing happened. He sat in the darkness and wondered if the tech had obeyed. "Well –" A powerful force took his words away. A rush of speed and bone crushing gravity. Creation spun like an unravelling alpha helix. Conway felt a cry gurgle from what he remembered as his throat.

Darkness was infinite, but given substance by gossamer plumes of vapour that glowed in the light of a billion star-like points. They swirled, slowly at first, then faster. Faster, until Conway felt dizzy. On the event horizon between consciousness and unconsciousness, he felt his mind begin to tear and fray, worse than any raw link he'd experienced before.

Emotions and swirls of memory cascaded through his mind. Some of them his own. Somewhere in physicality his teeth were millstones, grinding at the effort of existence. Consciousness swirled and became entangled with an ethereal sense of some *other* entity. He wondered, briefly, how it would have felt to accompany the agents, as they were propelled into a reality of a million tangled souls, and then he felt his mind lurch like a tormented stomach about to evacuate its contents.

Hold together. Hold together, he whispered. Perhaps he merely thought. *I am Martin Conway. I am 45 years old.*

My wife is called Susan. My daughter is 18. I have a 12-year-old son who is a serious pain in the arse. I am Martin Conway, systems operation chief, and I will *make things right.* Desperately he struggled to hang onto memories and tattered fragments of images and smells and feelings, the sum total of himself, of his very existence as a human being.

An image from the past reared up in his mind with a powerful force. A man from the beginning; a year before they plugged a little girl into his mainframe, and conscience plunged him into a dangerous new reality.

A young man on the make, Conway had recognised the type, but affable and pleasant company during those lonely hours at conventions and conferences. Soon the face wasn't strange, but attached to a name – Stuart – and enjoyable conversation to pass the time.

How long before he had been seduced? Oh, subtle that young man. Cunning. Dedicated. Patient. Until an experimental upgrade to Conway's precious AI plunged him into a darker nightmare than he ever imagined possible. Was it only 14 months ago? It felt like a lifetime since he had traded his soul for a little fake redemption.

Conway remembered. Embraced the moment that changed everything. Used it to anchor his determination to help set things right, instead of pushing it away in shame as he had done for far too long. There he was, in the fog of confusion. Huddled in a corner of some hotel lobby, a respite from some dreary conference on neuro-connectivity research, he found solace in a shot of whiskey and then a sympathetic ear of an unexpected visitor. Stuart, as affable as ever, concerned at his troubled state.

Suddenly, his casual suspicions that the man wasn't the business rep he claimed to be ceased to matter. He just didn't care if Stuart was some headhunter or corporate spy, as he had innocently assumed. It had come out before he realised; professional discretion abandoned, security protocols forgotten, he confessed the girl who would soon become known as Kora. The man had paled; appalled, but he soon rallied. "I know some people. We can stop this. *You* can stop this…"

Yes, and now he *could* stop this. Too late, perhaps, but if he could limit the damage, that had to count for something. It was time to face his ghosts. In a way, it was a relief to tear free of the tangled threads of deceit, to finally be honest. It was freedom, of a kind.

But Conway was still terribly afraid as he soared towards a reckoning with whatever awaited him inside Core-AI.

THE world hit him in the face. The mind-wrenching trip was over. He spat salty grit from his mouth, felt the wet sand yield to his groping fingers, and cast aside his guilt and doubt. He had a job to do.

He opened his eyes and saw gulls soaring over the sea. The sun shone in a bright blue sky. A little girl in a red dress and yellow Wellington boots sat on the beach a little way off; building sandcastles while talking to some imagined friend.

Amazing to find her intact, he thought, *and somehow terrifying.* By all their theoretical projections, she should have ceased to exist; no more than a collection of memory ghosts swirling amongst the lost thoughts of millions of wandering souls. The entire network subordinated to the Kora AI should have swept the little girl's fragile personae away as her brain melded and adapted to its new tasks.

Yet there she was. Living in a world of her own make-believe, her own personal AR, seemingly unaware of the expansive mainframe tacked onto the back of her head and mind. He grimaced at the implications, but felt relieved in a way. He hoped it would make his task easier.

She looked around as he approached. Her eyes shone as she giggled and leapt up at him. "Daddy! Have you come to play with me?"

He smiled and struggled for words.

"Do you like my sandcastle?"

"Yes. It's very good." He knelt down beside the girl and took her little hands in his. He glanced at the sandcastle and suddenly realised there was more than one. They stretched on to the distance.

His eyes burned with the threat of tears as he saw a small detached house. Modelled horizontally in sand, a man and woman stood hand in hand on the driveway. A little girl played with a puppy. Beyond the house were more models of normality: city blocks, houses, play grounds, all perfectly replicated. And further out, way beyond the city of sand, he saw obscene sculptures that caused his skin to itch with fear.

He forced his eyes to turn from the shapes and face the little girl. Her eyes gleamed with a childish enthusiasm and an innocence that touched his soul. On impulse he reached out and hugged her as though she was one of his own children. Kora accepted the embrace and rested her cheek on his shoulder in a gesture of total trust. The rapier of guilt stabbed his heart.

"Kora. Are you happy here?"

"Yes, Daddy. Now that you're here. You won't go away again will you? I promise I'll be good."

"You are a good girl, Kora."

Words proved difficult to find. The little girl in his arms was so trusting. How could he explain to her what she must do?

He pulled her gently away from him. On impulse he tussled her hair and had to remind himself that she wasn't a child, no matter what her appearance.

"I know you're a good girl, Kora, but to show it I need you to help me. Can you help me?"

The girl nodded mutely, a child's version of seriousness on her face.

"Good girl. I want you to open the way for me. Can you do that, Kora? Can you let them in?"

"I can't…" There was a whine in her voice. A child's whine.

"Please, Kora. You have to open up."

"No, Daddy. The monsters…"

There were tears on her cheeks now. Kora's face was screwed up as she began to cry, her little shoulders jerked with fear. He felt like a monster himself, but he had to push her.

"Kora, they can't hurt you," he said, struggling to find a way to breach the little girl's terror. "When I was little I used to be frightened of the wardrobe monster. I always used to climb into my Mummy's bed to get away. You know what my Daddy did?"

The girl shook her head.

"He took my hand and took me into my bedroom. He made me open the door and take a good look inside. He showed me there weren't any monsters inside the wardrobe."

"But there *are* monsters, Daddy." She bawled afresh and he hugged her tight. He made soothing noises and felt her tears soak his neck.

"Please, Kora. For me. For Daddy. I promise the monsters won't hurt you."

He felt the girl's resolve weakening. He was getting through. The girl's head nodded against his neck and shoulder. He pulled away to look her in the eyes. They were red from her tears.

"All right, Daddy, I'll let them in."

A sigh of relief.

"Will you stay with me, Daddy? Will you hold my

hand like your Daddy did?"

Relief was short lived. He glanced quickly towards the hazy patch that represented the gateway back to his reality and safety. The words clogged in his throat, and then he saw the bright eyes of the little girl, piercing him all the way to his guilt.

"All right," he said, "I'll hold your hand."

Kora smiled. He took her hand and they turned to look out to sea. The air shimmered and then the sea was gone.

On the horizon, the clouds were dark and brooding. Like a column linking heaven and earth, a tornado slowly crawled towards them, its motion filled with menace.

Hand in hand, the man and the child awaited the coming storm.

CHAPTER 28:
Calm at the Eye of the Storm

SOMEWHERE on the edge of reason, madness staggers like a drunken man. That man is Mills, but his mind is so fragmented by fatigue and despair that it is difficult for any sense of identity to hold together.

Mindlessly, he staggers over the rubble of his life. His numb feet trudge onwards, past the pits and their obscene occupants, towards the final focus of his journey.

AS Mills neared the JobMart, it shrank to more human proportions. It became the building of memory, the place of inspection and false hope that he remembered. Above it, the black tower with its ghastly face and taunting inscription reared up to the heavens, but he no longer paid any heed.

The doors to the JobMart were jammed open. A banner flapped in the unearthly breeze. The words fluttered in and out of focus, their ironic statement lost on the empty vessel that wore Mills' face.

"Rescue Centre."

A glance, then he was inside the cool, dust-free interior. The Inner Sanctum. Gone were the display boards that listed countless dead ends. The speakers that once responded to his Nexus signal were silent. Dead display screens dangled limply from the ceilings, and even the security cameras lacked their usual vigilance.

Only the crowds were the same. Desperate people, worn out souls, they crowded into the hall, assembled into vague approximations of lines as they waited like cattle to be processed by the minions of the Nexus-line.

Here was his beginning. He waited. Shuffled forth. Waited some more. Slowly, his line shortened, carried him along to the endless desk that separated him from the world.

There was something restful about the familiarity of this environment. Freed of the dusty nightmare, he felt his mind slowly coaxed from its hideaway. Information from forgotten senses began to trickle through his mental defences.

He took in the faces. Dead-eyed masks. The babble of dreary conversation buzzed in his ears. The smells of humanity and fear and the routine of the Nexus filled his nostrils. It smelled of sweat and paper and plastic. A gurgle in his ear as the woman behind coughed wetly. He shuffled forward. The woman closed the gap and the phlegm continued to gurgle ominously.

"Name?"

The voice startled him. Sharp, intense, but tinged with a hint of humanity. He looked up into eyes tainted with underlying fear.

"Mills," he said automatically.

"David, Samuel?"

"Yes."

A sharp intake of breath. Her left hand reached for a button just beneath the desk. The woman's eyes never left his face. Her fear-filled eyes were unsettling.

"Mr Mills?"

The voice came from the side, out of his field of vision. He turned and found a sense of déjà vu smiling nervously.

"Yes."

She grasped his arm, this woman who somehow resembled but clearly wasn't Jane. "Thank God, we've found you!"

"Why?"

"We've been looking for you. Please come with me."

He didn't move. The woman looked uncertain, then reached out an imploring hand.

"Please, Mr Mills. We've got to get you out. It's important."

He remained resolute in his lack of motion. For once they could tell him why they were doing things to him. Voices behind raised in anger, but he shut them out. The woman relented.

"We're here to get everybody out. We've spliced in a link. You've been infected with a virus. We need to get you out, it will help us."

"You can't. It won't let me leave."

"Mr Mills, for everybody's sake we've got to get you out – now!"

"You just don't get it, do you? Right now it doesn't care about you, but if you try and take me out it'll fry your reality too!"

He became aware of heavy-set men pushing through the crowds. They wore no uniforms, but everything about them said security. They also heralded disaster, and they didn't even know it.

"No! I made a mistake. I shouldn't have come here. I can't leave!"

He pulled away from the woman's imploring grip. The crowd got in his way. Desperation gave him strength, and he needed every ounce of it to cut through the thick treacle of lost souls.

"Mr Mills! Please!"

He didn't stop; he couldn't stop. Above the shouts of the zeros were the cries of security. He pushed harder, headed blindly for the edge of the hall – where he hoped to find his bearings and an escape. They couldn't send him out. Even the thought of it was not an option. The virus would learn of it and take murderous steps to keep him within its grasp.

The edge of the hall. No sign of the exit. He was on the

wrong side. He groped his way along the wall until he found a door handle. He pulled, slipped through the gap and found himself in the solitude of a corridor.

BEYOND the door he found a merciful silence, but its suddenness hit him like a shock of ice water. He leaned against the door until the disorientation passed, then he scurried along the corridor.

He turned left then right. Each corridor looked identical to the last. More chosen junctions until finally he realised he could well be going in circles.

Maybe the doors would offer some sense of direction, perhaps even escape? He scanned them for numbers but found them blank. He tried handles but each simply rattled. Locked. Further into the depths of the labyrinth and he became ever more worried about pursuit, but no sound broke the silence – not even his own booted footsteps.

"Mr Mills!"

He turned, alarmed. The woman and her two guards. They'd found him. Caught him. "Go away!" he screamed. "Leave me alone!"

He backed away slowly, his eyes darting from one concerned, frightened face to another. His pursuers edged closer, the two hulking men bursting to be let loose like hunting dogs with a scent of blood.

"Please, Mr Mills. If we get *you* out, it will help others!"

"You can't! Didn't you hear me? Don't you understand? It's in my head. That means it's here, now. You mean nothing to the virus, but if it thinks I'm about to escape it *will* stop you. I've got enough on my conscience, okay?"

He walked backwards, increasing his pace. The woman's face became more agitated. The guards stepped forward.

"I'll get the fucker," one of them snarled.

"No!" The woman held him back, her professional face slipping to reveal her terror. "You can't go down there. It's out of the zone. Mr Mills! Please! Don't go there. Come back to us. Let us help you. We can't help you down there."

He stared at her a moment longer, then turned and blindly ran. It was a long time before the burning in his lungs forced him to stop.

THEY had walked for hours. The sand clung to his feet, filled his shoes like liquid, and made each step heavier. Shreck peered through the sandstorm, watched the man Harris stumble ahead, his body a hunched and shapeless mass in the beige haze.

Reich strode behind Harris. A tall beacon of confidence moving through the hindering sand, eyes constantly scanning the haze. Shreck wished he felt his brother's confidence.

Harris stumbled and slithered down the face of the

dune. Reich strode up and reached out to help the man to his feet.

"Get off me, you freak!"

He stumbled to his feet. Reich watched impassively as the man wrapped the blanket around him. As ever, he used only his left arm, the other, unseen, he kept clutched to his chest. A sense of curiosity was quickly quelled as distraction from their mission, and he already had too many of them.

Reich fell back into line as they continued their wearisome trudge. Shreck followed. He kept his gaze on his brother's back, locking on to the source of strength that had accompanied him from their technical birth, when their mature forms were decanted together. He tried not to listen to the voices, but it was becoming harder to shut them out.

"You motherless freak!"

He glanced in the direction of the voice. As usual there was no-one there, just a blur of movement on the edge of his field of vision. *Ignore the voice. It is an irrelevance, a distraction. These ghosts are powerless to do harm.*

"You so sure?" another whispered.

"Freak!"

"We can get you. We can crawl right into your mind."

"We know what you are. Motherless FREAK!"

Once he let the first voice in, the rest rushed in through his weakened defences. He clenched his jaw and stared straight ahead. They could not distract him from his purpose. They were only voices, malevolent expressions of chaos that needed the discipline of Father's order.

Look at Reich. So strong. So resolute. Why should he, Shreck, be the weak link? Was he to endanger the operation? Father depended on him. Father made them what they are. Without him, they are nothing.

"You've always *been* nothing!"

Red light bathed his form. Warm fluid surrounded his body. Veiled faces looked blurred in the shadows. Murmuring voices from afar. He saw his birth, the old image. He saw his Father, the rock on which his existence was founded. He saw the expression of contempt for failure burning in the old man's eyes.

He rubbed his temples. Cleared his mind. Reviewed training.

A new image tantalised his mind's eye. A young man walked arm in arm with a woman. His sandy hair fluttered in the breeze and revealed a fading barcode. The face was so familiar, seen in so many reflections, but so unrecognisable with the impossible head of hair.

The woman laughed at something whispered in her ear. Shreck felt the chasm of emptiness open and swallow him.

His scream cut through the maddening voices and swept impotently through the vast emptiness of the desert.

Suddenly arms were gripping his shoulders. He looked up and found he was on his knees. Reich held him, his face stern.

"Leave me. I am weak. I am endangering the operation."

"No! We are Social Security Agents," Reich said. "We are strong. We have Father's strength. And we are his."

"The voices –"

"Are nothing. They cannot harm us. Do you not think that I hear them too? Shut them out. Barricade your mind. We are Social Security. There is no threat that can harm us. It is the virus seeking to overthrow your mind."

Ferocious determination burned in Reich's eyes. Somehow, Shreck's mind grew quiet; the invaders repelled until there was only himself occupying his thoughts. He used Reich's resolute form to pull himself to his feet.

"I am ready. I am strong."

"How touching! Come on freaks, we've got a job to do."

They both looked at Harris. His contemptible and contemptuous face was screwed up against the sand, but the venom was unmistakable. Shreck shrugged it off; he was used to this hatred. Harris could be dealt with later.

Slowly, they ascended the face of the dune. At the top Harris stopped and gestured across the desert.

"There it is," he said.

Shreck followed his brother's gaze. In the distance, the giant shadow brooded through the sandstorm.

"That's where we'll find him."

MILLS hugged the wall and crept forward. Another

corner. Darker, covered in dust.

Squeak. The noise squealed. Squeak. Coming from behind. Squeak. No, from somewhere up ahead. His legs took him forward; something drew him onwards against his better judgement.

A trolley crossed the junction ahead of him. Two green-garbed figures shuffled through the dust, one pulling the trolley, the other pushing at the rear. A body lay hidden by a white sheet, its face obscured by an AR helmet. Suspended from a cradle like a drip feed, a portable AR-rig swayed erratically.

Mills watched, baffled, then shuffled forward. He turned the corner and watched the trolley trundle into the gloom. Puzzled, he stared, all fear temporarily forgotten. A shadow danced across the edge of his vision. He turned hurriedly, but saw nothing. A sigh of wind turned to a roar somewhere in the distance. A door boomed shut, the echo resonating through the labyrinth's infinity.

Another sigh of wind. A voice, clear and familiar sang its tone from the distance. He shivered at the unearthly symphony of sound and strained to hear.

"Daaavvvviiiiddd!"

Dark memories of a dreary, fog-filled world. A voice calling his name. Ghosts walking alongside him. He backed away from where he thought the voice originated: the dark corridor, with only a point of light at the very end.

"Daviiiiiiiddddd!"

"Who are you?" he shouted. "Where are you?"

"Help meeeeeeeeee!"

Christine! No. She was dead. Tears blurred his eyesight and he hurriedly cleared them away. The impossible voice cried again.

"Christine!"

Against all reason, he ran towards the voice. Hope resurrected in his heart. After all the tricks he had suffered, maybe… just maybe. The distant light grew brighter. A door, slightly open, the light seeping through the cracks. She was beyond the door; she had to be on the other side.

"David! NO!"

He turned back towards the sound of Christine's voice, behind him now. A brief glimpse of her frightened face and then he stumbled backwards through the door; he teetered on the edge but failed to find his balance.

A metallic thump as he hit a sloping surface and began to slide. His nails screeched as he tried to stop his slide. His boots banged and thumped. From somewhere down below, a powerful engine roared.

Mills screamed as his body shot out of the chute and plummeted through air. Beneath him the dumper truck waited to receive him. Then he smacked into flesh and the world faded to black.

"FATHER, we must negotiate!"

Carlisle looked from the stern face of his underling back to the video screen. The freeze-framed image of the

Speaker stared from the display; all his mock deference and respect vanished. He could see in the pixels of the man's eyes the gleam of anticipated power. Here was the portrait of his successor, the pretender to the throne. He'd been in a similar position himself, once.

Under the cover of the zeros, the Parliamentarians, the generals, even a few businessmen had broken from his regime, found their courage and moved against him. He snorted contemptuously at the thought of this Coalition of National Unity and its appeal to the nation. Nothing more than a call for his resignation, a power play disguised under constitutional mumbo jumbo.

"No, Chief. We will not negotiate. There is nothing for us to discuss."

"But Father, we are over-stretched. We could use their forces."

"Against the zeros? The price would be my head."

"Father, it is no longer just about the zeros. The workforce has moved against us too. We have lost that division. They are organising, moving. Worse still, they are armed."

"NO!" he paused to regain control of his temper. Then he added: "This is *my* country. I will not retire. How long do you think you will last before you are so many spare parts in an organ bank?"

"Father, please! We cannot fight the zeros and the forces of this Coalition at the same time. They are already threatening armed action against us."

"And *they* cannot fight the zeros and *our* forces. No, Chief. We go on. We hold the line. Reich and Shreck will not let us down. They will find the source of this mess, destroy it and then we can restore order."

"And what if they fail?"

He felt the temper surge again and opened his mouth to bellow a reply. The look on Chief's face killed his words. Never before had he seen such an open display of anger.

"Are you turning against me too?" he asked, more gruffly than prudence allowed.

Chief looked away. Still the underling, at least. "No, Father."

"Good. I will not retire, Chief. Not for this Coalition. Not for you. And certainly not for any revolt."

Chief stood up straight, his face grim. "Father, this is not a revolt. It is a revolution."

EVERYTHING was darkness. Mills felt himself emerge from the void of unconsciousness into the shadow of sensory reality.

There was no taste. No smell. No sight and no sound. He struggled to feel the throbbing of an engine. Imagined the clawing bodies compressed all around him in the intimacy of death. Squeak. The sharp sound felt like a hot needle in his ear. Awareness tingled from far beyond the numb void. Extremities. The tingle crawled up his arms and legs. Squeak. He felt a cheek twitch in response to the sound. The lines of irritation met and expanded through his body. They reached his heart and he felt the pounding explosions of liquid fear. Squeak. The raw sandpaper touch of cotton on hypersensitive skin; he ground his teeth under the bombardment of sudden sensory overload.

Motion. Sound, muffled and distant. Still no sight. He scanned the darkness, felt his eyes swivel in their sockets. He moved his head and felt a strap chafe his throat. Something rattled against metal, the vibration transmitting to his skull. A boom echoed dully through the darkness.

"Tell us what you know and then you can go," a muffled voice said. It sounded so melancholy, yet so matter of fact. He would tell them, the voice implied, it was a predestined fact, but tell them what?

"Would you not prefer to avoid all this unpleasantness?"

He mumbled a response and nodded his head. Yes, he would like to avoid unpleasantness, but he had no idea who the voices were and what they wanted. If only they would tell him, then perhaps he could comply.

A sharp electric pain surged through his body. He arched his back and ground his teeth. Straps bit into his arms and legs. He struggled against the restraints that bound him into pain but they were merciless in their grip. Then the pain subsided and he felt something slip into his mind.

"Relax. Let your mind wander free through the dreamscape."

"You are relaxed. Happy. You are surrounded by your loved ones. They love you. You love them. Drift on this love…" another voice said.

He felt the warmth. So old, yet so unfamiliar. The years reeled back and there he was on a beach, a seven-year-old boy playing on the sand. The sun was warm on his naked back. The sand was wet – just enough for his castles to hold together.

A woman lay bronzing in the sun. He stared at her. She put down the book she was reading and pushed her sunglasses up onto her head. His mother smiled as she gazed at him and the love was as hot as the sun. He felt safe, he felt wanted, in this bubble of time before the world asserted its harsh demands.

"Look, Mummy," he said, gesturing with the tiny spade.

The first voice from the beyond penetrated his little world and broke the spell: "No! You have ruined it!" The sky darkened as if heavy clouds were gathering. His mother scowled.

"Aren't you a little old to be playing sand castles, Davey-boy?"

Her voice was harsh and masculine, but not as harsh as the laughter that followed. The sand felt as chilly as snow. He trembled and the sand castle collapsed into a shapeless mound. The sun went out, the screech of the gulls turned to the raucous coughing of crows. His mother continued to laugh, her mouth stretching ever wider.

Something dark emerged with a sigh of air. Before he could turn and run, they swarmed around him, smothered his body in thick swathes. The butterflies.

Pain shot through his body. He arched his back and gritted his teeth. A restraint cut through his arm and he felt the blood trickle free. A scream forced its way through his clenched teeth. His body unleashed the pain in an explosion of sound, a soul-wrenching bellow.

A burst of intense light and the pain vanished like the ghost of his childhood. Two men stared, stricken in horror. Strangers with bald heads and barcodes on their foreheads. They backed away as someone approached. Through the retina-burning glare he saw the loving face that soothed away his pain. Gentle hands reached for him and he felt his bonds removed. He struggled to sit up.

"Careful, you're still a little groggy."

The voice soothed his ears. Slender but strong arms supported his weight and guided him towards a door. It swung open and light bathed him from beyond. He managed to turn his head and look at the face of his saviour. She returned his gaze and he saw the tenderness in her eyes.

"Christine," he whispered.

CHAPTER 29:
Beyond a Shadow of a Light

DEAR Alex,

I just thought I'd drop you a line. You must excuse the quaint delivery of my words. Even I don't know when the conventional mailing systems will go down. That's the beauty of this virus. It's so damned unpredictable.

When I think of all I did for you it makes me ashamed. I blush to think how naïve I was. You promised us hope for something better: an end to the divisions in society and the corruption in the parties of power. I really thought you'd make a difference. A lot of people believed in you. At least I wasn't the only fool.

What is it you once said to me? "Democracy is far too precious a thing to be left in the hands of the masses." Perhaps you don't remember. It hardly matters.

Once the virus breaks into the global system you'll lose all the mechanisms that kept you in power. No more fear of who might be listening or watching or taking notes. They'll be free to pull you down. You and your kind, Alex, wherever they are, will be thrown into the gutter where you dumped the rest of us.

There is one more thing about the virus I would like you to know: you may find and kill the carrier if you wish. That's fine by me; it will only release the virus sooner. Leave him and it will break free in its own time. Either way, you lose.

Good game, don't you think?

Your old friend,
And one-time comrade-in-arms,
Clute

NONE of it mattered any more, Clute reflected. There was no room left in his heart for triumphal gloating, only for remorse. In his desire to bring down his former master he'd killed the child that he'd nurtured into manhood.

With a heavy heart and a moment's hesitation, he crumpled the letter and tossed it to the floor. Let Alex Carlisle fall without knowing why, just as Stuart had perished in the same kind of ignorance.

Clute looked down at the faded photograph in his trembling fingers. The young boy grinned back at him.

Gone was the wary look of the hunted street urchin. Rescued from that life, he looked like any other confident youngster yet to learn of the world's impersonal cruelty.

How quickly they forget. Did Stuart remember those early years of his life? Did he ever ponder the cold and the hunger before he was plucked from the garbage? Perhaps Stuart had been too young to remember.

"I told you," he said mournfully, "I told you to stay away from that woman. She was the weak link. The fatal link. Why didn't you listen?"

A bitter and painful thought – perhaps *he* should have listened. He never really gave any consideration as to why Stuart became involved. Clute should have kept him away from it. But he was too engrossed with his own obsession.

He sat back in the chair and swivelled round to stare at the darkness beyond the control room. Row after row of bodies disappeared into the gloom, each one suspended by its own cats' cradle. High above, lost amidst the flesh, Mills hung in his own cradle, hidden amongst all the dreaming zombies hooked into AR.

They would never look here. Not in one of their own establishments. And there was no danger of the watchman turning them in. He was a loyal recruit. Stuart's suggestion, Stuart's contribution. All for nothing now, because he was no longer here to reap the rewards.

A commotion interrupted this unaccustomed grief. Couldn't they leave him to his memories? Of Stuart the child, desperately proud and eager to please the man he called "Dad". Stuart the Activist, cold professional revolutionary, the man who no longer used the paternal refrain. What happened in between? Where did the years go?

"Clute, the zeros aren't maintaining discipline."

He sighed. "What do you expect?"

"They're not doing as we tell them. How can we overcome the State unless they follow correct orthodoxy?"

"Perhaps you should consider this an abject lesson in chaos. There is no such thing as correct orthodoxy."

The underling grunted. "But they're doing their own thing. They're deviating from their proscribed historical path."

Clute closed his eyes in dismay and wondered what Stuart would have said. Stuart the reader, the thinker – if only he'd thought enough. Unlike his Father, Stuart had really studied these philosophies.

What did it matter now what they thought or did? Events had taken on a life of their own, shaped by a million separate human acts all combining with unstoppable force. All so totally unpredictable, the outcome irrevocably unclear, and none of it mattered any more – his part was over.

Clute turned away from the drifting fragments of his Cause, back to ponder Stuart's grinning face. Memories unfurled like spring petals. As he savoured them the world drifted away until Stuart's childish laughter echoed in his ears.

"I'm sorry, son," he said in a distant voice. "Where were we?"

IT was a fine summer morning. Mills could sense the comforting light through his closed lids. It invigorated his heart and promised a day of joy and relaxation. For now, he was content to lie in semi-slumber, his arms wrapped round a warm body, arms likewise enfolding his own.

He breathed deep in contentment, filling his lungs with air perfumed by the smell of fresh cotton, the floral scent of summer, the human fragrance of a heart-warming companion. As his lungs inhaled, so too did his mind; mentally breathing deep of fond memories. He murmured his contentment and snuggled closer to the body beside him. Eventually, he yawned and hugged his companion, and then opened his eyes to the comforting light.

There was Christine. He smiled, and moved his face closer so that their lips could meet. For some time they renewed their physical acquaintance, her lips feeling soft and warm. Together they explored forgotten pathways of mutual sensuality, oblivious to everything but each other, until their passion was finally released.

Only then did his mind begin to open to recent times. As they lay together, reality began to re-assert its presence. He saw the underlying fear in her gaze, temporarily masked by the joys of reunion, now left bare for discovery.

The fear met his. A memory triggered and he broke their embrace to look around. "Where –"

"It's all right, my love," she said, reaching out with a soothing arm. "They're not here. Those weren't real, just memories running loose, but the Real Ones are coming. They've been sent to kill you."

"Who…"

"I can hear their minds. They're not far off, but you have time. You must get away from them."

"Why –"

"What you're carrying. The thing… It hurt me, but it can't kill me. Yet."

"But… I saw you die." His voice cracked at the memory.

"No." A wan smile. "Only that aspect of me that extended into that particular locus of JobNet. I'm bound too deep into the system. There's too many places for me to go, to hide. It hurt me, and I was lost for a while, but I tried to watch over you. I tried to guide you home."

"I heard you. But I was afraid."

"I know." She kissed him again. It felt good, but there was a hint of the forlorn amongst the affection. "I tried to warn you before, but I couldn't remember. Until it was too late."

There was something different about Christine. As if there was somehow more of her behind those gleaming eyes. Doors long locked had been opened to reveal more of her soul. Yet she was still in there, the old Christine he loved, with the new Christine he had never known.

"I don't understand…"

"No, it's beyond understanding. But I'll try to make things clear."

The light faded. Whatever bubble of make-believe Christine had conjured into being around them was melting back into her mind. A sudden chafing on his skin as clothing materialised; his stomach lurched with a sensation of motion.

"Don't worry, David," Christine said, reaching out to hold him steady. "I'm a sorceress, remember?"

A new reality coalesced into place around them. By now it was obvious they were in some kind of octagonal-shaped corridor. The walls were oddly organic and fibrous in appearance, glowing softly from within to reveal knots of shadow that defied interpretation. The light brightened further. Imposed clarity. Suddenly the shapes in the walls took on meaning, like an image perceived in the face of a cloud but more terrifying in its clarity. "My God!"

He broke away from Christine to move closer to the wall. There were bodies all around them, embedded in the walls as though captured in the midst of some obscene orgy. Twisted and tangled together, they were all naked but for the dehumanising technology of the AR helmet.

The bodies were smothered in a tangle of translucent fibres, thick as a spider's web entombing its larder. Lights flickered along the strands of the web, pulsing like digital signals. He ran his eyes along the intertwined arms and legs and torsos and realised that somehow the bodies were more than merely tangled. They merged into one mass of flesh.

Bile tasted foul in his mouth, as he saw a man and woman fused into one at their hips. The arms of this union were frozen in a lovers' embrace. Lips almost touched as though caught in the moment of a kiss, but their open mouths spoke of mutual torment.

He felt a hand take hold of his own and squeeze tight. Christine stood beside him, watching the bodies sadly. She sighed. "Welcome to JobNet."

"What are they?"

"Artificially Intelligent Information Technology. This is AI 2.0's dirty little secret. It's a lie. Mostly. The original AIs never quite worked. Sure, they were smart, in their way, but they failed to match expectation. This is the answer. Human intelligence, networked, distributed, depersonalised. It's a cyborg of global proportions. The great advance my father helped to create."

"Your father?"

"He made the breakthrough that allowed all this to be possible. UK Benefits & Welfare was a major investment partner in the consortium that funded his research."

"How did he...?"

"First, he perfected the interface technology you're using, but that was only a stepping stone. The real leap came with vat grown nerve bundles. They graft them onto your head. The nerves grow into the brain and make their own synaptic connections. The operation is irreversible. They pioneered the technology in the early days of JobNet, then it was used to harvest the unemployed to expand AI-IT globally. Cheaper than building more conventional AIs, I guess."

"So, all these people are –"

"The global network, yes."

They walked down the corridor. Mills tried to take it all in, but even his well-honed cynicism struggled to grasp this inhuman reality. Bodies as far as the eye could see. Faces hidden by AR rigs, mouths agape in silent screams: he saw no sign of that strange parasitic technology of vat-grown nerves. He said as much, unable to quite mask his sceptical tone.

"No," Christine said. She smiled, but her eyes remained solemn. "These people are like you. Some of them chose to remain, some were passing through, the rest have been retained against their knowledge; probably thought they'd landed some dream job and gone back to their lives in the real world. Imagine how messed up they are now, since the virus hit. At least we knew we were in AR."

"This is crazy. It doesn't make sense. Why keep people inside?"

"Every connection enhances the network. That's all I know. I don't pretend to understand the technology. Or the thinking that brought all this into being. I guess some of these people would eventually have been grafted to an AI-hub permanently."

"How do you know all this? I mean…"

"We're all part of somebody else's nightmare. The virus cut me loose. Since then, I've been looking behind doors, but I found out about this," she gestured with her arm, "from my father. I wasn't supposed to know. I was appalled. Wouldn't you be? But they found me…"

"But… but you couldn't keep all this secret…"

"Oh yes you can, when people – the right people – don't really want to know. Who cares about zeros? You're all scroungers, and everybody's scared of becoming you, so it's easy to shut you out. Something like this, you can practically hide it in plain sight. I was a fool. I thought if I cared, others would too… I was wrong."

Mills looked around at the bodies until he was dizzy with it all. A living tunnel of obscenity, it took him ever further from the home he had known.

"You must go," Christine suddenly said.

"Go? Where?"

"To find Kora."

"What's Kora supposed to be?"

"Not what. Who."

"Right. So who is Kora?"

Christine smiled. "You'll see. Trust me."

Mills sighed. "Okay, where?"

"Somewhere I can't reach. The calm at the eye of the storm."

"I've heard that phrase before. *It* wants me there."

"I know. It needs you there. But *I* need you there too. That's your way out. Find Kora. She'll release you. She can release you all."

"What about you?"

She smiled. "I'll be with you in spirit."

"No. Come with me. We can find this Kora together."

"I'm already a part of Kora. She found me when I was lost. She helped to bring me back, I think; helped me understand all this. But she can't save me, only you and all those like you."

"That doesn't make sense. Why not? If I find Kora, I find you, right? And then we leave together?"

Christine looked at him lovingly, but said nothing.

"We leave together?"

She turned away sadly. The sense of loss was like a blade. She turned back to face him with a sad expression.

"I can't leave."

She stepped aside and pointed to the bodies in the wall behind her. Mills followed her gesture.

"No!"

Embedded in the wall were the naked figures of Christine and the Mayor. His flesh was pale and shrunken, and Christine held him as though he were a stricken child. Even her own flesh lacked the vitality of her living image. Both were covered in the glistening fibres, their eyes masked by the eyepiece of an AR helmet, but it was cutaway to accommodate an array of fleshy tubules growing from their scalps.

"It's too late for us. We're grafted in permanently," Christine said. "We're not ghosts, not yet, but we might as well be. We're all dying. The human mind wasn't meant to live like this."

He started to move towards her, his arms outstretched ready for an embrace, but she held out her hand to stop him. She stood there, tears in her eyes, a shimmering apparition of a lost soul beside its corporeal remains.

"No, my love, it's time for you to go."

"I don't want to."

"Please, for me. Make it easy for me and just go now. Get out of here while you still can. Breathe real air for me. Feel for me…"

With those wistful words she began to fade from sight until nothing of her remained, except the ghost of a whisper: "Remember me."

AS they trudged through the sandstorm towards the obscene structure that was their destination, Shreck could not help feeling that he was being sucked into the mouth of something terrible.

It had no shape, this phantasm of his fears. No shape, no substance, no texture, merely a presence. Something was taking form in the vats of his subconscious, even as he and his brother had taken shape in the vats of his Father's scientists, wrought into being from a fusion of his Father's will and his genome.

Up ahead, Harris paused, bringing a welcome intrusion to this unfamiliar introspection. Harris stood up straight from his decrepit stoop and pointed ahead with his good arm. "There it is," he shouted, voice rising above the wind that spoke with a million whispers.

Shreck stared ahead, past his brother and the human. The alien structure towered above them, its distant peak lost in the sandy haze. There was something organic about its appearance; a termite mound built by insane insects that had somehow mastered technology.

"That is the way in?" Reich shouted.

Harris nodded.

Shreck stared hard. Ridges and bone-like structures took on a recognisable shape. He saw the dark orifice that would be their door. He felt that whatever made the voices was waiting for them.

MANY times in the distant days of his employment, Mills had felt like a slave to a machine. Yet at least he had existed as a definite entity. He was himself, free at least to dissent by the occasional illicit break.

If you crossed man with machine, perhaps the result would be this manifestation before him: a creature that could never disconnect, that could never exert its human side, if indeed it retained any human characteristics at all.

It had appeared suddenly from the blanket of darkness as Mills shuffled cautiously through the cavernous shade. Motion-activated lights had flickered on, revealing this thing in its horrible reality. Now he stood in that bubble of light and could only stare.

This amalgam of flesh and plastic was the most

horrific computer terminal he had ever seen. Somehow, it seemed worse than the bodies in the tunnel. They had at least retained some semblance of humanity, however tortured. Here the 'human' was nothing more than a supporting frame for the machine.

The naked man was seated high up and bent backwards so that he was almost completely suspended upside down. Arms dangled; not limp but rigid to form a platform for a perfectly ordinary keyboard. Cables and fibres coiled around the man's body, tangling with the wires from the man's AR helmet. Most obscene was his face, what was visible of it. The mouth stretched to impossible proportions; the lips tight and thin like elastic. Canine teeth gripped the edge of a monitor screen, as though he had tried to swallow it whole.

Mills stepped back and to the side, wanting to get away from the vision but reluctant to leave this oasis of light. As he moved, he took in more shapes side by side with this hybridised man-machine. There were more on either side he realised, obscene terminals ringing a dark space between them.

Far above his head he saw a faint patch of blue. Gossamer plumes of cloud misted the distant sky, drifting like fragments of memory.

How he longed to see a sky. A real sky. With that yearning thought he realised where he was. *This* was the calm at the eye of the storm. The centre of all things, where Christine and the virus, his personal demon, both wanted him.

So where in this obscene structure, or in the darkness beyond, was the entity called Kora? He shouted the name and heard the echoes return in a caricature of his voice. He wasn't surprised when there was no response.

He began to walk around the perimeter of the light bubble, trying not to look at the man-machines, but his imagination populated the darkness with mobile creatures just like them. He tried to put out of mind the image of them rearing up from the darkness to do unspeakable things.

"Koooorrrraaaaa!"

No reply to his yell except distorted echoes. A flutter of disturbed air in the distance, the flap of something leathery far above his head; his imagination started to play tricks on him again. Cold sweat dribbled down his back and he trembled violently. A crash sounded far away like distant thunder. Once the echoes died down, he heard a metallic clatter, as if someone had tripped over scrap metal. He turned wildly in fear only to stumble backwards.

With a cry he fell outside the bubble of light. Instantly the light flicked off, plunging him into total darkness. His cry bounced through the vast space as he struggled to find his bearings. All sense of direction was gone. Fingers became eyes, as he fearfully felt his environment. He traced shapes, felt surfaces, and slowly pieced together the tactile information.

Steps! He realised with relief that he was at the foot of

a flight of stairs. Nothing more horrible than that. Slowly, he began to crawl upwards, feeling his way carefully like a blind man. As the minutes passed, and his eyes once more became accustomed to the darkness, he realised that he could actually make out shapes and surfaces around him. A soft glow emanated from the walls enclosing the stairs. The light revealed an opaque, leather-like membrane that was stretched between metal struts cast to resemble bone.

More confident now, and with some sight restored, he stood and began to walk rather than crawl. He realised that the stairs were circular, spiralling towards whatever waited at the top. That's where he had to be.

Somewhere above, his future waited; he figured it couldn't be any worse than his recent past. Come what may, it was all he had to look forward to.

CHAPTER 30:
And Work Shall Set You Free

THE grotesque composites of man and machine watched them in silence as they stalked the darkness.

His mind was slipping free of his control. It was this place. It had changed him in some way. He felt it. Gone was the Shreck that so innocently served his Father. Now he longed for those uncomplicated days, even as he ached to become something more than a biological facsimile of the species from which he was derived.

Yet he was trapped; a prisoner of his form and function as much as the inmates of this corrupted realm. Silently, he cursed, as that form and function tried to reassert itself. This thinking was unproductive, it chided, served only to make him a flaw in the plan. A glance at his brother told him that his internal conflict was not leeching out to pollute his body language. He retained the visage of the implacable agent, but for a moment he couldn't help but wonder if his brother's face masked the same debilitation.

Despite his fears, he felt a thrill of anticipation. Their quarry was almost in reach somewhere in this dark cavern. The fulfilment of their father's needs was tantalisingly close. And, perhaps, their quarry might be a key, the means to bring about a change in Shreck's existence. Duty was not the only reason that bound them to success.

Reich and Harris stopped at the foot of a twisting staircase; Shreck dutifully halted and listened in to their hushed exchange.

"You are sure of this?"

Harris nodded. "He's up there. I can feel him. Thanks to what he did to me."

For a moment, he revealed what lay hidden beneath his wrapping of ragged cloth. Corpulent flesh, blackened and withered, rippled as a butterfly tried to crawl free of its human chrysalis.

"I owe him for this," Harris hissed, "I want in on the kill."

Reich stared. Then acknowledged the request with a stiff nod of the head. They moved on, Reich taking the lead. Shreck moved behind as Harris deferred to their presence. After all, they were the killers, not he.

From out of the shadows, the voices whispered in anticipation.

MILLS stood at the end of the world, looking down into

the depths of a well of darkness, and wondered where he'd gone wrong. There was no Kora here. There was nothing. He didn't know what he'd hoped for. If anything, he'd just let himself be pushed along the way; a rat guided through a maze by tricks and trinkets.

He sat on the edge and let his feet dangle, like a man bathing his feet at the banks of a stream. The height should have been fantastic and dizzying, but it felt too unreal to have any effect.

On this perch at the top of the gantry, he felt like the last man alive. It seemed that his journey had ended without really finishing at all, an anti-climax of failure that must be destined to become his epitaph.

Find Kora, Christine said, but she never said who Kora was. Then he realised, perhaps another, even more pressing, question: just what the Hell could Kora *do* anyway?

From the depths he sensed the tiniest itch of a presence. Some aura that suggested he wasn't alone.

The sensation made him feel uncomfortable and vulnerable, so he carefully stood and backed away from the edge. Too late. Behind him, that ghostly presence materialised into an unwelcome intrusion.

"Dave! You don't know how good it is to see you!"

Harris grinned, his lips leering from a wild-eyed face. Beside him stood two men, one on either side. A shock of recognition. They were both bald, with barcodes stencilled on their foreheads, dressed in beige suits. They didn't share a trace of Harris' smile.

"You know," Harris added, "you really should have taken that job. Just think of all the trouble you'd have missed."

The twins moved as one, coming in from either side. Harris stayed put, grinning and barring the way towards the stairs. A twin pirouetted in mid-air with the grace of a ballet dancer. A foot smashed into his face and Mills found himself lying on his back. Momentarily dazed, he spat blood and struggled to stand. Another blow in the face returned him to his prone position.

"It's payback time. I owe you for this!"

Mills struggled to focus. When his vision cleared he saw Harris. The man threw off his makeshift cloak and struggled to stand straight. He held out a blackened wreck of an arm. Through rips in his clothes Mills saw the corruption of his virtual flesh extend to shoulder and chest. The vile necrosis had even begun to spread up his neck to caress his cheek.

"You did this to me. Get up! You ain't gonna die easy."

Harris lashed out with a booted foot. The blow caught Mills in the side. With a gurgle of pain, he tried to roll away only to feel another blow crash into his back. A twin appeared out of the shadows and kicked him in the guts. The air rushed from his lungs and almost took his stomach with it. He painfully sucked in fresh gulps of air to try and calm his screaming innards.

Together the twins grabbed him as he tried to crawl away. They lifted him into the air. Mills felt a stark terror that they'd throw him into the abyss. Impotent, all he could do was scream as they sent him flying through the air.

There was a queasy feeling that reached down to his bowels as he slapped into the membrane enclosing the sides of the gantry. The material stretched, and then elastically propelled him backwards. A fist met his face and sent him crashing to the floor, where he laid whimpering and gasping for breath.

Laughter made him open his eyes as best he could. One of them was already swollen half shut; a wobbly image of Harris crouched before him. Mills struggled to find words. "Harris… you… you're a *fuck*… ing arsehole!"

Harris laughed again. "Dave, you don't know the fucking half of it."

There was so much pain now that he didn't think more could make any difference. Even so, when Harris clenched his fist and drew it back, Mills closed his eyes in anticipation of the blow.

It never arrived.

A deep-throated rumble bellowed in his ears. The sound went on and on, starting low and far away, then rising to a shattering crescendo like thunder. Wind rushed over his face and dragged at his clothes; its cold fingers shocked and probed his throbbing wounds.

He opened his eyes. The trio were craning their heads,

looking for something. Whatever it was, they saw it out there in the shadows and their puzzlement turned to terror. Harris backed away and stumbled into the wall. The twins' mouths opened in horror, but any sound was snatched by another blast of wind that wailed with a sepulchral moan. The air turned bone-numbingly chill.

They came suddenly from everywhere and nowhere; a thick cloud of darkness that seemed to condense out of the very shadows. The whispering returned, difficult to tell if they were truly voices or the sibilance of disturbed air. Butterflies swarmed onto the gantry, materialising like a dark blizzard.

He heard the fluttering of wings, quickly followed by a hysterical scream. *Harris.* The butterflies swarmed over his cowering form. He thrashed like a madman, swiping at the insects. Crushed bodies smeared him in dark ooze that corroded his flesh. The man grew weaker as he melted, a slug engulfed in salt, until there was nothing left but gore dribbling down the wall.

The insects turned on the twins. Their presence was no longer terrible, but pitiable as they encored Harris' death dance. One twin lashed at the insects descending on his body. Like Harris, his skin rotted and charred. He stood, or tried to stand in the face of this chaos. He made no sound, but his lips were pulled back in a grimace of rage and pain. The insects swarmed thick until he seemed a creature of writhing charcoal.

He stumbled and fell against the wall of the gantry.

The membrane stretched under his weight and then began to tear. As he toppled through the rip, the twin tried to grip the frayed edge with a badly corroded hand.

The second twin looked on in horror. Forgetting the insects that covered him, he rushed towards his companion with outstretched arms. He reached his stricken partner too late and with a cry of despair, watched him fall.

"Reich! *Nooooooo!*"

For one moment, his voice managed to drown the noise of the insects' triumph. Then the rush of disturbed air drowned his desolation. He slumped to his knees. With wide eyes and a drooling mouth, the pitiable creature that had so wanted to kill Mills now gazed into the depths, immobile and lost.

MILLS sat and stared while the butterflies congregated on the lip of the void. There, they coalesced into the form of a man. After moments, he was not surprised to gaze up at his own grinning face.

"Welcome to the end of things, Dave. Here's where we part company. You got me to my destiny. See, you were good for something."

He made no reply, only looked at his alter ego with a sense of dismay.

"Down there," it said, clasping its hands behind its back and pacing along the edge, "that's the way into the world. The whole damn system. That's where I gotta go.

It's nearly over now. You'll be free soon enough."

"Free? After all you've done… You put me – us – into this Hell and now you want to kill us!"

It smiled. "No, Dave. *Your* kind put you into this mess. I'm here to sort them out. I had to build up my strength. There were a lot of barriers preventing me from getting here. That's why I needed you. Kora's the only barrier left, and I don't think she'll be a problem. I'm strong enough now to break through. Plus I got a little covert help from your world."

"My world?"

"The Outside. You might say I've got friends out there. They made me, you know, but *you* shaped me. You have a lot a latent rage inside you. Shame you never recognised it and learned to use it."

The thing was shimmering now with a light of its own, but it looked as though it was bathed in the projected images of a thousand human forms. Mills' eyes ached with the strobing flash of human images, a flickering collage of human features, a multitude of faces both known and unknown.

It watched him try to crawl away with an expression of humour. "Where do you think you're going, Dave? There's nowhere for you. Don't you want to see the grand finale?"

"I've seen enough death."

"Everybody dies, Dave. What's your problem? For most of the people in here death is a mercy. They've been sacrificed for your greater good. It's why I was made – to break the chains and set your kind free."

"By killing us? We can break our own chains!"

"You haven't done so well up to now. I can't be blamed for all this. I didn't make this place. I didn't put you into it. But I *can* destroy it."

"If we can't break our own chains then we don't *deserve* freedom!"

It laughed again and then turned to face the darkness. "You're probably right, but I'm going to give you a shot at it anyway, 'cos that's what I do. You can't expect my life's purpose to go unfulfilled."

"Most people's are."

"Welcome to JobNet," it said, "welcome to the human condition."

With those words, the creature spread out its arms and leaned forward over the precipice. As it began its graceful descent, it turned its head and winked. Then it was gone, vanished into the depths.

NEVER had Mills felt so alone or so empty. Never had he failed so completely and so miserably. Even the chance of escape through death had been taken from him; instead he had to wait for it. Yet again, he was the passive recipient of something done *to* him: unbearable, but not as bad as the waiting.

Somehow, he found the strength to crawl to where the virus had made its leap into the dark. It was like looking down into the eye of a tornado. At its epicentre far below, his doppelganger drifted like a parachutist, his descent controlled by the silken drag of a billion tiny wings. A ghost-light emanated from far below, a scintillating event horizon that cloaked a breech in the fabric of this world. Now he understood. Kora was meant to be here, but she'd pulled back behind a veil, withdrawn as far as any component of JobNet was capable of. The revelation was late in coming. The creature, in his form, was dropping in on this mysterious being, a weapon of mass destruction plunging to detonate within the topography of the collective human mind.

And there was nothing he could do to prevent it. He wondered if he had ever had the capacity to stop this thing. Not here, on the edge of existence, but back in the distant past before this horror began. Bitter questions, hopeless remorse, it was all too late now.

Now there were only the tears. They soaked his cheeks and he slumped helpless before the imminent future. As he lay there sobbing, he noticed light emerging from the formless shade.

A bubble of light expanded like the opening of a worm-hole in space-time. A ghost emerged in the depths of the light, shifting like mist until its substance solidified. Then it stepped out onto the gantry.

"I can't keep rescuing you forever, you know," Christine said. She smiled as she kneeled down beside him, her arms enfolding his shoulders. She felt so good. So supportive. He held her and hid his face against her shoulder.

"You must go, David. You can't stay here. The way out is down there, the way into the world – for all of you."

"Then come with me!"

"I can't. I told you. I'm sorry. Just remember that I love you." She squeezed him tighter and kissed him, then she let go. "Kora needs you. You're the channel. You *must* go to her now. It's time you saved the day."

Before he could quiz her words, she pushed hard. He cried in shock as gravity embraced him. Christine watched him fall, her head and shoulders receding fast. Just before she vanished, she raised her hand to her mouth and blew him a farewell kiss.

ONLY a moment for his guts to unravel like tangled string, for his broken heart to fall from his mouth and tumble somewhere far behind. Hollowed out by his free-fall acceleration, he screamed with lungs that felt disconnected. Even the sound dopplered from afar, as his body plunged.

All around him was the hiss of insect wings, the tunnel made of their bodies, flowing, swirling in a maddening blur. Free fall ended with a painful lurch. Dangled in mid-air like a trophy, his alter ego held him firmly by one arm. He looked up to see the triumphant expression on its face.

"Dave, so good of you to join me. So you couldn't bear to leave after all. I'm touched. I really am."

"Fuck you!"

It just laughed and gazed into the depths with gleaming eyes. Mills tried to follow its stare, but the light had grown so bright it was difficult to keep his eyes open long enough to make sense of what he saw. He squinted until his eyes and face ached, but he finally made something out in the depths of that shimmering meniscus.

A dot. Growing.

The dot became a disk. Still it grew, emerging from the centre of concentric lines gyrating over the raging surface. The disk expanded, eclipsing the light to reveal an aurora of fire at the disk's edge. Still it grew. No longer a disk, it took on dimensions. It was an orb, rushing to meet them like a bullet propelled on its lethal flight.

"Nearly there, Dave," the creature said in triumph. "What I did to JobNet will be nothing to what I can do to the global system. We break the event horizon and then the world is ours!"

The orb became a representation of the Earth. He saw the hues of land and ocean and cloud. Constellations of civilisation flickered into life across the globe's surface. Each cluster of light put out tendrils that crawled across the surface, connecting each constellation until the world was enmeshed in a web of phosphorescence.

All around them butterflies glowed white hot and exploded; a heat shield ablating on re-entry. He heard his mirror image laugh as the firestorm erupted. "She's trying to stop us, but I'm too strong now. Poor Kora! She hasn't got a hope!"

The shimmering meniscus of light rippled as something moved to meet them. Out of the depths behind the Earth, an eye ascended. Mills sensed the eye's perception of the coming storm, and he knew this was no visual representation but something manifesting itself. He felt its fear, along with his own frustrated sense of impotence, like a headache hammering his temples.

The virus focussed its attention on the giant eye, its face a portrait of eager anticipation. Hundreds, thousands, millions of butterflies flared into non-existence, but through the red haze of his pain, Mills saw how this loss was nothing. Billions more surged to replace those lost. They were tumbling down, funnelling towards the black hole of that giant eye. Nothing could stop it.

Light crackled and died as the butterflies broke through the event horizon. Their funnelling, swirling bodies merged with the deep well of the pupil, fusing it to the tunnel carrying Mills and this hideous anti-Mills to the end of the world.

"You're about to witness history," the virus cried.

Something caught Mills' attention and forced his perception to open wide. The hammering in his temples increased to a mind-crushing clamour, but through the eye-watering pain he saw them: a man holding hands with a little girl. They stood on a beach in an avenue of sandcastles. A multitude of human forms assembled around them, until this patch of world was filled with a surging crowd. A million upturned faces, their mouths opening to shape the declaration: "NO MORE!"

The shout was a telepathic barrage; it rose from the depths and cascaded into the tunnel of darkness, a collective a roar of anger. It pummelled his head from the inside until he thought he was going to burst, then it stirred his own anger and he let himself be carried along with the flow. He found the emotion liberating. Powerful. Suddenly, he realised what Kora was; she was all of them incarcerated to the whims of a machine servicing wealth and power.

He looked up at his captor and let the rage of Kora burst out in a shout: "I'm going to watch you die!"

The virus laughed dismissive. "Death is a human thing!"

"You're going to die. You can't live once you've destroyed the system."

The entity's grin froze. Sagged. Doubt and uncertainty crossed its face. Mills felt elation bubble up through the cauldron of anger. He'd found a way to touch this thing. The connection between them clicked into place. He felt its arrogance deflate as it lost its psychic balance. The creature's defences crashed down and that umbilical link between their minds lay open and defenceless.

A world reached out to seize the moment. The combined might of human self-determination rushed to storm the broken barricades of the virus's mind. Mills joined the flood of anger tearing apart his tormentor's world.

The creature screamed. It dropped him as lightning crackled across its body, discharging in searing arcs that exploded amongst the butterflies. Christine had called him the channel; the gateway to salvation, the conduit that guided humanity to freedom from this nightmare.

Far above him now, the virus exploded like a supernova. The fire-storm spread through the butterflies, rushing upwards through the column like magma journeying towards the mouth of a volcano. Beyond the dying vortex, even the column of nothingness began to buckle and collapse.

Mills fell clear of the cataclysm and on into the unfathomable depths of the eye. Far beneath, the Earth rose to meet him. Behind him, a comet-cloud of brilliant sparks plunged in his wake. Exiles like himself; he led them home.

CHAPTER 31:
Shutdown in Progress

THINK *of a revolt. Think about millions of people waking up, rising up, discovering they are strong. Each individual takes heart and inspiration from the awakening of every other soul around them. Together, in that crucial moment born of some unifying trigger, they meet and become the fulcrum that moves a world.*

So, the revolt of the zeros comes full circle. Born of the mayhem rooted within JobNet, it spilled out and infected the world of the real, and now returns to its place of making for the final confrontation. The cycle of change, the wheel of fortune, powering the hammers that smash a system of power from both within and without.

First, the virus, the manifestation of blind zeal, is obliterated from the fabric of the human mind. The millions entrapped within JobNet find the way open for them to vent their anger. They join around the focus of the innocent hub of their world, and from there they cascade through the one hapless pawn that brought them to misery. The umbilicus of thought, binding a dread harbinger to its helpless carrier, provides the way. All it needed was for the carrier to open himself to the possibilities inherent in human potential.

So the rage of the human mind banishes the thing that seeks to liberate them from existence. The virus burns. Deleted.

And yet in death, it still plays a role in the salvation it claimed. The revolt is far from done. From anti-virus, the human impulse becomes virus. Once awakened, this ancient dream of freedom burns away the fallacies and maladies of ages past. So, the collective voice of dissent pulls apart the fabric of the system.

With the way opened by the entity Kora, the angry mass of human thought floods beyond JobNet to close down the machinery of an entire structure of power.

En masse, they return to the world from where they were exiled, back into the flesh of living to be reborn into the physical.

They are zeros no longer and now they are finally going home.

IN a world with no future, shadows flicker in unison with the flames. Dancing through the darkness between the fires, shapes move with purpose and unity, sifting through the bones of the old in search of the seeds of the new.

The zeros move with a newfound purpose. Blind rage

expunged, they seek out the materials to build the world of togetherness they crave. Laughter echoes in the dying canyons of commerce. Human souls seek the companionship of others. In this fraternity lies the future, the tendrils of something different built on human need and not the mindless pursuit of hoarded riches.

Among them, the mindless drones of the old order feebly struggle to stem the tide of time and human growth. Lost and bereft of purpose, they little more than hinder the tides of social hope washing away their sandcastle world.

SHOUTING from the world beyond. The voices angry and frightened, stripped of the confident trappings of authority now that the global network has collapsed.

Reich and Shreck had failed him. All his plans came to nothing in the end, but for the frantic organisation of his evacuation. Fleeing into exile, with his tail between his legs. That's if anywhere was left to accept him. There was no way of knowing now, since the system had collapsed. He couldn't even communicate with his own national forces, let alone negotiate – hah! More likely plead! – with foreign havens. If indeed any haven remained.

The shouting became worse. Almost hysterical, too loud for him to ignore. As ever, there was no rest for the wicked, not even when it was all over. Carlisle reluctantly left the haven of his respite and stormed towards the door.

Honed now, by his loss and disbelief, his rage would soon find some victim.

"What the Hell is happening?"

Chief pushed his way through the herd. Carlisle could not mistake the apprehension on his face. The sight deflated his ire.

"Father, we must flee now! There is no time to wait for the evacuation helicopters. The zeros are coming!"

"But…"

So soon? How could that be possible? He still had men. Loyal troops. How could the zeros overcome the last of his defiance so quickly? He backed towards his desk, feeling suddenly weak and old, but the dull pain in his head subsided. The analgesic effect of adrenaline, the one saving grace in this mess. His thoughts turned towards Mills; to that one zero who had been the focal point of his downfall. It didn't make sense.

He noticed his minions leaving. He watched them, unable to bark a command. He was king of nothing, so why not let them go? It wasn't as if he needed them now. They couldn't wield a gun. They were redundant.

The lights flickered and died, adding fear-stricken screams to the sense of panic. Something slammed into his desk. A convenient explosion from the distant perimeter revealed Chief's sweat-sodden face. There was a mad gleam in his alien eyes.

Carlisle couldn't hear anything from outside, but his imagination supplied all the sound he needed. He heard the shouts of terrified and angry men. The roar of guns. The screams of bullet-blasted targets. The dull thumps of explosions. He had heard them all in his time; and now they returned to haunt him.

"It is the zeros! They have broken into the compound."

At least this was something to do. No more waiting. No more fretting. He pulled at a drawer and retrieved his sidearm. He slapped in a clip and armed the pistol. He existed in a ring of rage, slowly tightening to throttle the life from him. Even so, he could not understand how he could have failed. But at least he still had teeth – a gun provided the way out of many a tight corner.

"Let them come!"

Together, they moved into the centre of the room, their eyes becoming accustomed to the gloom. Fires from the perimeter provided some light. Not much, but it might be enough, and the darkness would hinder their assailants too – combat inexperienced assailants at that. The thought refreshed his flagging confidence. Yes, let them come.

A sound of breaking glass. "They are here," Chief muttered.

Chief edged away into the darkness, a hound looking for prey. Carlisle gripped his pistol and slipped the safety off. A burst of light and a roar of gunfire from the far corner. A man screamed and thumped to the unseen floor. An enemy, or one of his defunct minions? It no longer mattered.

He strained to see and hear. Footsteps sounded from several places. He cursed. More footsteps. A sound behind and to the left. Fear throbbing in his chest like the first pangs of angina, he turned towards the sound and fired.

The damp noise of bullets smacking into meat. A dull cry. A thud, followed by the scraping sounds of shoes on the floor. The target flopped its limbs, its uneven breath sounding harsh in the darkness. He moved in for the kill. A fresh explosion of light revealed the stricken target.

Chief lay in a spreading pool of blood. More blood poured from his mouth. He looked up with wide eyes and mouthed a few words. Sound came with a gobbet of gore. "Fa... Fath... *Daaadd!*"

Carlisle pulled away from the expended resource and its imploring hand grasping at his trouser leg, back to find targets in the darkness. He sensed bodies. Many bodies. He heard breathing. The shuffling of feet. Broken glass tinkled. Furniture scraped as someone moved it out of their path. They'd surrounded him.

The first whimper escaped his dignity. The gun slipped from his fingers and he backed away until he slammed into a desk. His own desk – the command post from where he once ruled his business.

They shuffled forward into the weak light of some distant fire. Ragged and tired looking men and women congregated around him. Not the dead-eyed zeros of the past: their eyes burned with the brilliance of a revitalised vision. One figure stepped forward from the mass. A gun dangled at her side.

"This won't achieve anything," he rasped. "Freedom?

Is that what you call it? Do you even know what it is? Is all this worth a *freedom* that will never last?"

The woman smiled. "It's worth it – even for a day."

IN the darkness, the silent dreamers dream. Motionless like the dead, the dust shrouds them as they hang in their cats' cradles. All is silence. All is tranquil, in the Necropolis of the still living.

Until movement intrudes.

Lights flicker on. Motors hum. Cradles descend. First one, then another as the motion spreads through the cavernous warehouse. Soon the motion extends to more than machinery. Bodies stir. Long unused voices fill the space with human sounds. Groans, snuffling gasps, even muttered words.

Clumsy hands pull at cables and tubes. Like the newly awakened dead, they clamber from their cradles and shuffle across the floor. Bodies meet. Embrace. Comfort the pains and horrors of a recent existence.

Life beckons. The tears of freedom wet their cheeks. Together they crawl or shuffle towards the vast doors of the warehouse, the stronger helping the weak and cumbersome. As if on some unspoken command, the great doors ascend into the ceiling, flooding the chamber with brilliance from the world beyond.

Wincing against this light, the former inmates of a cruel reality shuffle out to meet the dawn of a New World. All but one, that is; this figure lies huddled in a grieving heap, sobbing for a world that was.

MILLS awoke with a start as he felt the stomach-churning motion of a fall, but he realised the descent was leisurely and there was a soft but muffled whine of something electric. He swayed in the grip of a tangle of ropes and straps uncomfortably supporting his frame. The motion stopped suddenly with a sharp jolt.

It was dark wherever he was, but he heard movement all around him, muffled by something clinging to his face. He reached up with weak arms. Fumbling fingers found a strap and popped the fastening. The mask fell away. After the utter darkness, the red light glowing sombre in this new environment stung his eyes.

Bodies everywhere. Suspended at every level, but the whine of electric motors told of more and more being returned to the ground. These strangers fumbled their way out of their binding cradles and began to move in lethargic existence.

So he was back. In the real world. The nightmare was over.

Painfully, he began to untangle himself from the support cradle, gritting his teeth against the suffering as he removed probes and catheters. Once he was free of the invasive machinery, he slumped on the floor to breathe and rest. Memories provoked a rush of emotion that whacked his enfeebled body. He tried to crawl to his knees, but only remained in a huddled heap as the emotion caught him and made him sob. Others were crying, joyful at being free, but Mills felt his heart break with grief. There was nothing in this New World for him. Not without her.

A hoarse whisper forced out of neglected vocal chords managed to become a word: "Christine…"

He remembered. She was gone.

Never mind, Dave, you've still got me.

That voice. Almost his voice. It cruelly interrupted his grief and overcame the weak state of his limbs. Mills sat upright and looked around the warehouse. It couldn't be. Not here. There was nothing but his fellow inmates crawling to taste the first breath of freedom.

A soft chuckle in his head. *You're looking in the wrong place. Remember what I said, we're conjoined twins linked at the mind. I'm in you now. Maybe I am you. Maybe I've always been you. And you're me. But forget that existential crap, what matters is we're together. Actually, I'm in quite a lot of these poor saps. They're in for a surprise, I can tell you, when I pop into their mind and say 'hello world!'*

"No! NO! That's impossible!"

Never underestimate an old campaigner, Dave. I'm a little echo of defiance ready to take on the world. Now, I'll admit there was a moment in there when I thought I was a goner, but you know I think this really is the better way. We made a great team before and this time I got you an army. Imagine it, the fun we're going to have.

The scream was hoarse and painful, but it failed to

silence the soft chuckle burring inside his head. Hysterical, he clawed at his skull as if he could rip the thing from his mind. Clumps of hair tore from his scalp; he felt the wetness of blood ooze.

"Help me! *Christine!* Help me! Get it out! GET IT OUT!"

She's gone, Dave, forget about her. Oh, and that hurts, by the way, so I'd appreciate it if you didn't vandalise my new suit.

An impulse switched off his self-afflicting frenzy. A will other than his own took him on a slow stroll towards the bright exit and the new day outside. He sensed his doppelganger's rising sense of gloating anticipation.

"Come on, Dave," his hijacked body said, "let's go seize the day. And cheer up! This is the first day of the rest of your life – the world is ours for the making!"

APPENDIX 1:
List of Players

Carlisle, Alex: Britain's longest serving Prime Minister (PM) in modern history.

Carswell, Eric: The man in charge of the Ministry of Human Resources and its associated subsidiary operations such as UK Benefits & Welfare, which owns the JobNet Agency and the Nexus system.

Chief: The PM's bodyguard and his liaison to the Social Security Agency.

Christine: The first contact for many within the environs of JobNet. She welcomes Mills into the system, shows him around, and helps him to make the transition to his new life.

Clute: Head of a shadowy and ill-defined anarcho-chaotic network. Former deep-cover operative with one of the domestic intelligence agencies that were consolidated to form the Social Security Agency early on after Carlisle's assumption of office.

Conway: Systems Operations Chief for the external JobNet mainframe network.

Frank: One of Clute's associates.

Harris: One of the internal workers for the JobNet system. Also provides internal intelligence for the Social Security Agency.

Janet: One of Tom's followers.

Johnny: A young boy trapped inside JobNet. Part of Tom's band of survivors.

Jones: Assistant to the Private Investigator Kane. Works in collusion with his partner in freelance work for the Ministry of Human Resources, such as monitoring trade union activists.

Kane: Private Investigator. Ex-cop. Works freelance for the Ministry of Human Resources.

Kora (Core-AI): The hub of the JobNet system, the first of the new AI-IT hubs to be installed in the system, intended to herald the third wave of AI evolution – so-called AI

3.0 – and is JobNet's gatekeeper to the wider global network.

Macallister, James, a.k.a 'The Mayor': His proper title is the 'UK System & Personnel Administrator'. He is responsible for overseeing the internal management of the AR community.

Maguire: Head of one of the regional cells of the Martyrs of Jarrow organisation.

Mandy: A child in the care of one of Tom's followers.

Martin: A young boy involved with the Martyrs of Jarrow organisation.

Mills, David: A zero. After ten long years on the dole, he is finally summoned to take part in the JobNet scheme. So begins the greatest upheaval he has ever faced in his life.

Munroe: Social Security Agency Field Operations Chief.

Nathan: A zero.

O'Grady: A corporate recruitment executive with data recovery firm ArcheaoLogik working within the JobNet environment.

Reich: One of the PM's Social Security agents. Brother of Shreck.

Rob: An old friend and work colleague of Mills.

Sandra: A Martyr of Jarrow.

Shreck: Another of the PM's Social Security Agents. He is the brother of Reich and is a few minutes the younger. Both Shreck and his brother Reich are genetically engineered clones developed from the PM's own genetic material. As with others of their kind, they are the PM's most loyal servants.

Dr Simms, Alastair: The doctor who handles Mills' case of 'neural shock'.

Sutcliffe, Stuart: One of the JobNet Agency operatives who helps to upload Mills into the JobNet system. In reality, he's part of Clute's anarcho-chaos movement seeking to overthrow the Government by attacking the JobNet system.

Sutton, Jane: A client administrator at Mills' local JobMart, she's his first contact with the JobNet system. The friendly face of the operation, she handles client details and assists in uploading him into the virtual world.

Terry: A Martyr of Jarrow.

Tom: Leader of a band of survivors in the JobNet system.

APPENDIX 2:
Glossary of Terms

Anarcho-Chaos: A political movement formed of a combination of anarchism and socialism, with overtures to Chaos Theory.

Artificial Reality (AR): Sometimes called Virtual Reality, but often indistinguishable from reality. An environment generated by AI-IT networks and plugged directly into the human consciousness.

Artificially Intelligent Information Technology (AI-IT): Computer systems that utilise artificially grown neural tissue interfaced to conventional high-spec technology to intelligently process information, replacing the need for human intervention in a great many processes. It's a system that greatly underpins the surveillance state, crunching the vast amounts of data it generates.

City Watch: An organisation contracted to provide surveillance of public spaces and monitor public activity.

Home Office: Government department responsible for domestic matters such as security and city and national management.

Home Office Troops: A paramilitary force responsible for internal security operations and counter insurgency work. Answerable theoretically to the Home Secretary, but it often comes directly under the command of the Prime Minister. In operational matters often subordinated to the Social Security Agency.

JobMart: Equivalent to the contemporary Job Centre Plus network operating in the UK. The Job Centre is a government employment agency which provides information on vacancies at both local and national level. It also offers various forms of support to people looking for work.

JobNet: The most advanced employment initiative ever devised. A global network that places job seekers in a virtual reality where they can look for work face-to-face anywhere in the world. Operated by UK Benefits & Welfare, which is itself owned by the Ministry for Human Resources.

Martyrs of Jarrow: An organisation formed to fight for

the rights of the unemployed and other 'zeros'.

Ministry of Human Resources, The: A British Government department, with the remit of handling unemployment and various human resources issues. Operates the Nexus system of unemployment benefits and scrutiny.

Nexus: The computer system responsible for delivering welfare benefits to its recipients. Also scrutinises and tracks the activities of said recipients by recording all transactions and logging visits to employers. The card has a mini transmitter that logs the card-holder's location in a central database.

Parliament (Westminster): The ancient seat of British government. The site of the Houses of Commons and the Lords. Described as the Mother of Parliaments.

Social Security Agency, The (SSA): Responsible for internal security and intelligence. Also polices internal dissent and similar threats to government security issues. Answers directly to the Prime Minister via Chief.

Speaker, The: Historically, the monarch's man in Parliament. As the Commons gained supremacy over the monarch, this role became the spokesperson for the Commons. Now functions as the PM's go between and mouthpiece in Parliament.

Stakeholder: A citizen. Someone in employment, who pays taxes and is therefore entitled to vote at elections. Stakeholders have one statutory vote gained on their 18th birthday. They may subsequently accumulate 'points' or simply buy further voting entitlement.

Summer House, The: The unofficial seat of British Government. The base for the Prime Minister's operations and the place he spends most of his time. Consists mostly of landscaped gardens carved out of London's former East End. The Summer House itself houses the Prime Minister's personal staff, heads of key departments, as well as the PM's personal retreat.

Turmoil, The: A period of civil unrest and rebellion provoked by a deep economic crisis and austerity that led to the downfall of a government and propelled Alex Carlisle to power.

UK Benefits & Welfare: A listed company established by the Ministry of Human Resources. Operates the JobNet Agency and its global recruitment system. Handles a range of human resources and management consultancy operations.

Zero: A derogatory term for those who are unemployed or worse. They possess no rights, though they retain their one statutory vote, providing they have been in prior employment. Those in the latter capacity have no voting rights; and may not be in receipt of benefits at all.

ACKNOWLEDGEMENTS

Hard to believe it's been over 20 years since I first started writing Citizen Zero and around 16 since I finished my author's draft. The novel's been a long time waiting for its era to arrive; well, the world has turned and here it is, courtesy of the machinations of Britain's political scene, and of course Inspired Quill's timely intervention.

Over the years – I shudder to say decades – a lot of people have earned themselves an honourable mention here; sadly, it's been long enough for some to become lost in the fog of time. Apologies, with thanks, must go to these nameless souls, and I only hope they know who they are and will forgive my lapse of memory.

There's no forgetting Matt B, who simply must get top billing since he was there at the novel's very inception. My thanks to him for the encouragement, enthusiasm, and the support he provided as I bounced my ideas off him. Also, I should thank him for putting up with my odd working hours, all-nighters, shuffled pacing, general crankiness, and drunken ramblings, while working on the book in the cramped living room of that backstreet flat we shared in Liverpool. Those were the days, eh?

Moving on, there's plenty of gratitude and cheers to the folks at the Interchange (Bradford Writers' Network) for the encouragement and support they offered during our weekly read-rounds, as I looked to finesse my finished script into something approximating its final draft. They know who they are, but mention must go to Ruth, Howard, Bruce, Joe, and Phil.

Special thanks also to Ann M, and to Sheila, for helping me keep the faith as I struggled with the exhaustion of the years spent working on the novel; they kept me on track as I took the story to its conclusion and embarked on the long and rocky road to publication.

On that score, it would be remiss of me not to mention Izzy, who was my editor when the novel was accepted on to the launch list of a new publisher back in 2006. The venture never took off, such is the way of these things, but her efforts to polish the manuscript gave me the foundation for the edition I self-published in 2010, when the age of austerity kicked in and offered Citizen Zero its era. Thanks, Izzy, for helping to ready Citizen Zero to meet its audience.

We're nearly there, now; just a quick thanks to all those who bought or reviewed that self-published digital edition. And my thanks to you, too, the reader of this edition, as you prepare to venture into its dystopian vision. Try not to be too perturbed by what you're about to encounter. It's only fiction (I hope).

Last but not least, my thanks to Sara and the crew at Inspired Quill for bringing this newest edition of Citizen Zero into being. It's been a long time coming, but speaking as the author, it's good to be here.

ABOUT THE AUTHOR

Mark was born and bred in Bradford, West Yorkshire, which probably explains a lot, but these days he lives in Stoke-on-Trent and works in Manchester. He studied political theory at Liverpool University before heading off for London to train as a journalist – but soon got mugged by the novelist within.

As a writer, he's dabbled in poetry but his mainstay is fiction. With four completed novels under his belt, and a host of short stories, his work straddles the sci-fi/ horror/ fantasy continuum.

Almost seriously, he's been making things up for two decades now. That's doubtless rather worrying given the day job as a journalist, but rest assured he remains dedicated to the pursuit of truth (no laughing in the cheap seats, please).

Find the author via his website:
www.markcantrell.co.uk

Or tweet at him:
@Man0Words

MORE FROM THIS AUTHOR

SILAS MORLOCK

Terapolis is an urban sprawl of global proportions. The vast city state is ripe with secrets. Here, billions of people live only to give themselves to The Gestalt. An esoteric technology, said to unlock the secrets of creation, it offers humanity the chance to realise its most-cherished and forbidden desires.

For Silas Morlock, enigmatic Master of MorTek, The Gestalt is his greatest achievement, but little time remains to fulfil his purpose and save Mankind from itself; death gathers, an ancient struggle between good and evil nears its peak.

On the other side, the *Incunabula*; bibliophiles who refuse to stop peddling the items most poisonous to the hold The Gestalt has on human minds.

And then there's Adam, the misfit dreamer pulled into a conflict beyond his understanding. His own desire will take him on a terrifying journey into the heart of darkness.

It's a struggle played out in the shadows, where the lines are blurred, and nothing is quite as it seems. For the lost souls, the stakes are the very highest.

But secrets are for keeping, in the dark places...

Paperback ISBN: 978-1-908600-14-1
eBook ISBN: 978-1-908600-15-8

Available from all major online and offline outlets.

Lightning Source UK Ltd.
Milton Keynes UK
UKOW04f2329010817
306502UK00001B/163/P